CROSSING ZION

Rock on!
Peace

The pure in heart will avoid the struggles, detour the tar pits, blind their eyes to the sirens. The problem is that in avoiding the paths that contain the tar, you may never reach any destination; in avoiding temptation, you may remain pure, but irrelevant. Life is tar pits and sirens.

-Donald A. Norman

KEITH MARK JOHNSON

CROSSING ZION

Shipwreck Publishing © 3/13/2004
All rights reserved.

A WORD ABOUT CROSSING ZION

I had dinner with a 50 year old real estate agent in Absaroke, Montana a few years ago. He was from San Diego, but loved the south central Montana lifestyle and conservative politics. We chatted until the conversation turned to religion. Before we had gotten very deep into the discussion he grabbed his half glass of almost expensive cabernet sauvignon, looked me directly in the eye and proclaimed that he didn't think he had ever committed a sin in his entire life. It became difficult for me to know where to go with our discussion after this statement. And now when I think back about that evening, I realize, he is the only person I have ever met who probably won't get 'Crossing Zion.'

Two years later I met Keith Johnson in a junior high portable. I had the pleasure of watching 'Crossing Zion' develop out of Keith's generosity and love for his daughters, his women, and his friends. I felt the magic of discovering how similar my life had been to his. I realized we are all on our own individual journey's across our fear filled Zion's. Johnson's gift to me and every flawed human being, is the lesson that it is our broken-ness that saves us. That we can survive and prosper by allowing ourselves to be less than perfect. That all the trophies, certificates, degrees, or summits cannot satisfy the need to be intimate with another human being, or replace the laughter that comes when two friends get together to share their lives with each other. And that to be intimate we must first learn how to give, accept, and forgive.

Crossing Zion' is a guidebook for living. It is an affirmation we are not alone. It is a recipe for recovery and health. It is an expression of love and a source of light we can use to enrich ourselves and everyone we touch around us.

Thank you, Keith
-Jeff Peters

Keith, thank you for being so honest and open in your book. It was liberating for me to read your words and in your pain see myself. Unfortunately we are all led to believe that feeling pain and self-loathing is wrong and we are weak if we can't break free from that. So we all spend our days with our game faces on, hiding our true selves in the darkest corners of our minds. It takes far more courage to accept who we are and bare our demons to the world. I hope that I may some day emulate your strength.

-Patience d'Arcy

WARNING

The contents of *Crossing Zion* address the joys and perils of dangerous adult activities, namely climbing, step-parenting, divorce, and extra-marital affairs. In no way, shape, or form, does the author recommend said activities as a life choice. All are potentially lethal, with extra-marital affairs being particular damaging to one's health. While all events in this text are true, certain names, dates, and birth defects have been changed to protect the innocent.

Who can give law to lovers? Love is a greater law to istelf.

-BOETHIUS 480-524 AD

Overture
Allegro

THE SHIPWRECK

And this is the simple truth; that to live is to feel oneself lost. He who accepts it has already begun to find himself, to be on firm ground. Instinctively, as do the shipwrecked, he will look around for something to which to cling, and that tragic, ruthless glance, absolutely sincere because it is a question of his salvation, will cause him to bring order into the chaos of his life. These are the only genuine ideas, the ideas of the shipwrecked. All the rest is rhetoric, posturing, farce.

-SOREN KIERKEGAARD

In the Silent Spring of '92 I didn't own **The Book of Truths**. *I did own the fact that my second marriage was in ruins and, as a result of the consequent emotional exhaustion, I'd bailed on a ten year teaching career. I also understood that save for my two young daughters I no longer trusted anything I'd ever believed in. Shortly thereafter, I discovered that the ground moved when I walked and that only when climbing on cliffs could I achieve a hint of serenity. By summer, I was coherent enough to appreciate how everything I thought I knew would have to be tossed, that I couldn't pretend to like me anymore, and that I would have to start my life completely over. And as that dark summer wore on, I knew with every breath I took that I had become exactly what I was always afraid of... and there was no way I wanted to own 'that' book of truths. Thus, desperate for answers, I piled every piece of climbing gear I owned into my tiny Ford Fesitva and drove away from the Valley of Tears to the I-90 on ramp. And there I sat. Frozen with the question: which way God?*

-From the **Shipwreck** *Journals*

ANGELINA ARMONI

There is a point in life where you crawl to the edge, leaving behind every sign, rule, methodology, norm, and meaning you ever knew. You stare down at death and know that you must somehow find the strength to turn around and face your life. To go any further will be the end. And with that final bomb of reality blasting through the bullshit, you turn and face the truth. You learn that in your darkest hour, there is no one there to help you. There is no one there to advise you. There is no one there to pray for you. There is no one there. It is just you and whatever force you believe has led you here.

You do not want to smile in these situations. You do not want to experience sensual fulfillment. You do not want the ten easy steps to success or a ladder to materialistic solidity. You want your mother. You want her to come and take away the bad things. You want her to hold your head. But your mom isn't here. And cry as much as you want, the edge lets you know you're going to die if you do not change the direction of your life; right here, right now. And it is at that moment, teetering in the wind, with one foot dangling and one foot pointing south, you will find out what it means to be a human being.

*-From **The Shipwreck** Journals*

∧∧∧∧∧∧∧∧∧∧∧∧∧∧∧∧∧∧∧∧∧∧∧∧∧∧

[AUGUST 2001: THUNDER CREEK TO ELDORARDO TRAVERSE]

Langdon Towne and I sat on a chunk of warm, white granite, staring out at an advancing bank of fog as it rose up Thunder Creek valley. We had moved fast all day, gaining over 6,000 vertical feet before leaving bug territory and reaching the glacier's edge. After preparing camp, we'd scrambled up the eastern shoulder of Primus Peak to gain a classic view of Mounts Logan, Buckner and Goode changing shades of pink and purple in the backwash of the sunset. Feeling we'd finally earned our moment, we rested. Langdon spoke first.

"I wouldn't be anywhere else."

"Me neither," I replied softly.

"Well... that isn't entirely true. If I could be anywhere, I'd be in bed with Lyla Pascerella." Towne wasn't joking.

"She was the one, huh?"

"Yep. My god, I loved her body. And damn she liked my body. It was pure magic. Unbelievable! And I'll never have it again."

"How can you be sure?"

"Nope. Never again. I blew it. You only get something like that once. If you blow it, you blow it. And I swear to God, you would blow it too. *Job* would have caved in on this one."

1

"Ya know, Langdon, things might work out. I mean n*ever* is a pretty strong word."

"Yeah, right... Here, lean over so I can knock on wood a couple of times."

We chuckled lightly as a warm breeze swept over the ridge. Towne's ability to constantly grab life's snags, blast them apart with humor and thereby turn them into something usable was one of his many gifts to me. In fact, once while driving to a clinic to have a sore checked out, he had shared a truth that I learned to use every waking second of every sleepless night. This is what he told me as I stood at the clinic counter, explaining to the receptionist why I was going to pay in cash:

"You've got to develop the art of turning negatives into positives or you'll lose your fucking mind."

Later, as I checked my nose in the rear view mirror, his voice rolled on in its confident way. *"You know, who ever said you can't make chicken salad out of chicken shit has never been starvin. You know what I'm sayin?"*

I did.

As the light of late summer in the North Cascades faded slowly away, I decided to share the dark secret I'd been packing like an anvil on my soul for the last ten months. Being careful to avoid character annihilation, I explained as delicately as I could that a "friend of mine" was embroiled in a steaming love affair and that his lover, though a virtual princess of saintly virtue, was somewhat encumbered by a husband and two young children.

Towne, who had a knack for spanking middle class mores, turning stuffy heads and pissing off puritans, burst into a twitter of mirth. He then started pounding a beat on his knee and spit a verse of hip-hop. This is what he rapped:

"When love leaves a house
And it starts to burn
There will be no rest
And no where to turn."

I recognized this as a line from **The Book of Truths**. I nodded my head in rhythm but had that look crawling across my face where somebody tells you something that you don't quite get and then you smile like you got it while they keep smiling back waiting for you to answer the punch line, but you can't, so you keep smiling and they keep smiling and seconds become minutes…

Sensing my awkwardness, Langdon stopped drumming, scratched himself, coughed politely and then looked me square in the eye.

"How old's your friend?" he asked.

"She's thirty-four. The guy is older: like forty something."

"And she loves those kids?"

"Uh huh."

Towne paused for effect, before emitting one single word: "Trainwreck."

I looked away, visibly shaken.

"Want my advice, kid?"

I did.

"Your friend needs to go off and find herself while she can still spell joy."

With the last pink glow of the sunset fading to gray, we walked back down to our camp. Ten hours of marching straight up a mountain side has a way of unwinding even the tightest kinks in one's chords, and, thus, with a surplus of endorphins still warming my veins, I decided it was time to crack the door and reveal a truth or two of my own. I told Langdon that my life felt like a wild book with a frantic story line with every page a new chapter; starting and stopping: now I'm this; now I'm that; now I'm here; now I'm there-- doors constantly opening and closing before I can adjust my senses to the smell of the room.

"Sounds perfect to me. Sounds like you've found out why you're here."

"But I'm not sure I can keep this up. It's like I'm going to run out of love to give."

"That's not possible," he said with an all knowing grin. "Love is infinite."

∧∧∧∧∧∧∧∧∧∧∧∧∧∧∧∧∧∧∧∧∧

The next morning we hiked around the northeast side of Austera Peak and found a rock outcropping on its southern flank where we dumped our packs and lounged like lizards in the sun. Langdon unwrapped a Powerbar, took a huge bite and started laughing as he looked out west to the awesome hanging icefalls of the Mcallister Glacier. He sighed heavily a couple of times before he spoke.

"I still miss her. Can still feel her when I breathe. I close my eyes and she is right there. It's unreal how a woman gets in your blood and recycle through your heart every four hours for the rest of your life."

"You know you've never told me what really happened."

"You're too young. You might take it wrong, get the wrong idea of what this was about."

"I don't think so."

"Too risky. You might go out and do the same thing."

"I already have."

"Hmmm. You have a point. OK, my son. Get out your pad and make yourself comfortable because there is no short version to this one. She was too good for that."

At that, Langdon took a sip of water and cleared his throat. He pulled down his baseball cap to keep the sun off his nose and began his tale.

"You know her name wasn't Lyla Pascerella don't you? It was much prettier than that, but I have to protect her, so I'll stick with Lyla though her real name fit her more to a T."

"OK."

Langdon paused, drew in a deep breath and let it out with the melancholy patience that true-love demanded. "I'll call her Angelina Armoni, but that's not her name either."

"Jesus, Dude, why don't you just call her by her real name? I'm not telling anyone."

"Karma. Can't screw up the Karma. All right. Let me get this one straight. I need to sift for a second." He looked out at the expanse before us, took a another bite of Powerbar and a sip of water. "OK, I have it now. First, I have to give you the *Basic Rules of the Human Condition*:

1. *If you live, you will suffer.*
2. *If you risk, you will lose your ass.*
3. *If you find any joy, you will become addicted to that joy and soon learn the meaning of Truth #1.*

Now the story. It comes in parts. The first one I'll call *The Curse*."

"I think I've heard this one. This is about Irene right?"

"Yeah. But there's a new twist. You want me to tell it?"

"Of course."

"OK. So, anyway... Irene comes to me in dreams every night. Full color."

"Sweet."

"I mean this has been going on for years. Especially if any new females start to enter the situation. Then it's complete action. And, of course, I always go back to her."

"How long you been going through this?

"Thirteen years."

"Whoa. And how long does she stick around?"

"You mean after I dump the new gal who I kind of had it for?"

"Yeah."

"Hmmm. Maybe a week. As soon as she knows she's got me."

"Whoa! Why?"

"You ever been truly, completely, madly in love?"

"Yep."

"Then you know the answer. OK. So get this. Angelina comes down one night and neither of us can resist, so we go to bed."

"Awesome."

"God, yes, she's killer. But anyway, part of me is thinking, OK this will be the *real* test."

"Test?"

"Yeah. True test of *The Curse*. If we make love and then I want out of there or think of Irene right in the middle of it, then I'll know I'm still not over her and that will be that. I'll give up. I mean if Angelina Armoni can't break the curse, then there's no point in even trying anymore. I'm doomed.

Completely fucked. Ya know what I'm sayin?"

I did.

"Well, guess what? She was perfect, and I sure as hell didn't want her to leave. Ever."

I screamed, "Yeah!" and threw my hand up to give *Langdon Towne**** a high five.

"Anyway, later that night I have this dream, and, sure enough, Irene comes to me."

"No way!"

"In color. Standing over my bed. Wanting me bad. Classic irresistible stuff that I fall for every time."

"Awesome!"

"But get this. So I'm lying there, watching her show and I just look up and say, "You need to leave now, Irene." Her face drops. She suddenly looks tired. She doesn't know what to do. So I tell her one more time to 'go away' and the dream ends. It's finally over. Angelina broke *The Curse*."

"That's unreal."

"Yeah. And I've never been so miserable in all my life."

---

*Langdon Towne was the name Kenneth Roberts gave to the young, central character of his epic tale, <u>Northwest Passage</u>. The likable, well meaning Langdon, a budding art student, deeply in love with the wrong woman, and a friend to characters of all shades, was real to a fault. Like so many of us imperfect people with dreams and passions, Towne was befallen by a series of timely circumstances that quickly had him fleeing for his life. To save himself, he wound up enlisting in a hard-core branch of the military, Roger's Rangers, and was soon running off to fight in a war against the French and St. Francis Indians where he would learn more than he ever bargained for about the true meaning of hell on earth. Robert's ability to capture the intensity of the suffering and heroism while showing how the tables can turn so quickly on one's life, is a tale for the ages.

The coincidence of my favorite inspirational author also being my favorite character in my favorite novel was not missed, and I mentioned this to all who had and hadn't read both works. When Towne and I became close during the summer of 2001, I pointed out that I'd thought his name being that of my fictional hero was a miracle of coincidence. His reply was typical of his dark-cloaked humor, "Dude, Denial ain't just the name of a river. Ya know what I'm saying?"

I did.

THE HOURGLASS

TRUTH #17:

*If the universe ever gives you what you wished for; you will soon be
miserable. The famous know this, as do the wealthy, the gurus, and the men
who would be kings. All have wished for a change and all have tasted the
poison of their desires fulfilled.*

-From **The Book of Truths** by Langdon Towne

∧∧∧∧∧∧∧∧∧∧∧∧∧∧∧∧∧∧∧

[1985-92: THE VALLEY OF TEARS]

The subject of the day was fights in a marriage and my climbing partner,
Tim, suggested that the ugly kind of fights, the unresolved type that burn,
smolder, and leave you feeling sick, were like golden sand leaking out of an
hourglass. He went on to say that if the skirmishes continued, it didn't take
long before even the lift of an eyebrow would send irreplaceable grains of
love down the hole. Soon, the two of you were staring in desperation at a
gilded, empty, glass, knowing the only way to refill it was to turn your entire
world upside down.

The topic then changed to love affairs, and I took the metaphoric lead,
explaining how "falling in love" was such a beautiful disease. I went on to
say that I knew of no legal substance like it. That when it grabbed your heart,
there was no stopping the pull. It was like you'd never seen flowers before,
never heard songs on the radio before, never felt like floating around doing
the mundane with such a sense of joy and purpose before. I told him how the
act of falling in love with Zoë had produced omni-potent feelings of worth so
strong, so spiritually uplifting, I was certain they were from God. Tim found
this amusing. I told him how I had read where smell was now considered one
of the strongest determiners of compatibility and that Zoë loved the smell of
me, that she would ask for my sweaty t-shirts to wear at night, that she would
put her face in my neck and breathe in and out, and that the smell of her skin
made my blood run wild, that her neck smelled of salt and wheat after she
went for a run- and that I knew she was the one. I went on to say that I had no
doubt she and I would find the strength to pull our sled of baggage up any
mountain, no matter how wicked the angle or storm. He looked away as I
went on explaining in detail how, "Just looking in Zoë's eyes," had altered
my being. How lying next to her, this Aphrodite in the flesh, had brought
meaning to my existence, and how I knew I would give my life for the honor
of defending her. She was my purpose. She gave me worth. I was the soul-
mate of Zoë; my soon to be wife #2.

It was Tim's philosophical lead again. He grabbed the symbolic sharp end and layed out his plan for success in marriage and life. He said it came down to commitment. Tim, usually more analytical than lyrical, went on to explain, almost poetically, what he meant. He said that to understand its importance, one had to imagine being out in the middle of the ocean, trying to stay afloat with no clue which way to swim. He went on to say goals are the island, the speck of land in the distance that one must swim for--no matter what--in order to stay alive. Despite storms, sharks, and anything that might get blown your way, you must swim for that island. Keep your focus and you will reach it. That is commitment. Then he looked at me. "No commitment, you drown."

In the rainy summer of '92 there *was* no island to swim to. Six years of committed battling with my soon-to-be-ex-wife-#2 had drained every last speck from our hourglass. After suffering through another Christmas of pretend togetherness, the two of us had stomped off to a cliff and tossed the fragile work of art into the abyss. What remained of sacred vows now laid scattered in the rocks and bushes and dirt. And yet, even in that state, I still found myself wanting to hike back down there, get on my knees and try to find pieces to put us back together.

I'd tried to hang in there until her middle son's birthday party, but shortly after a nerve-shattering spring-break, I gave up, moved out of our five-bedroom house and then watched in impotent horror as my personal cell of solitary confinement filled with the jeers and taunts of a cruel and absurd universe.

In June, a couple-friend of mine came to my rescue and asked me to housesit for them while they traveled abroad. It was a perfect arrangement as their home was minutes from a sport-climbing area, and a beautiful place to hang with my two daughters whenever they were allowed to visit. I had thought a couple months of- *no work and all play*- would do me good... that my nerves would quit sparking... that I would find something about me that seemed adequate. But by late summer, I was still fighting with the wife, still climbing like shit, and still packing around a *Cosmic* kick me sign.

To pilfer any one of a thousand moonshine songs, I was about to wind up one of those second time around guys, "Who lost it all:" Lost the second wife, lost the second job, lost my daughters in the first divorce, lost the dog in the second, lost the second house too, did manage to drag the dog behind the truck, owed money on the vet bill, owed money on the psychologist bill. It was all gone and nothing I knew or stood for really mattered anymore.

Over the last few "lost" years, were it not for the ritualistic Wednesday night visits to my daughters and the every other weekend duty of picking them up and dropping them off at their mom's house so they could be raised by her boyfriend, I would have probably found a way to drag myself behind a truck.

As the end of that dark, rent-free summer approached, I tried to slow down and listen for answers.

For the umpteenth time I read passages of Kierkegaard, trying to find solace in the concept of shipwrecks being the path to truth. The prose of wise men had usually helped in pointing out the absurdity of trying to take life too seriously. But, this day was different. My tools of quick fix wellness were no longer working. Maybe it was the late summer rain mirroring back what my future looked like. Maybe it was because my elbow, knees, and back were killing me. Maybe life without my kids, my wife, or somebody to walk up to and look at and touch and smell without any weirdness just seemed pointless right now. Maybe it was the reality of basically feeling alone, alienated and scared all the time. Maybe it was the cold clarity that there was no comfort here, no comfort anywhere, and no way out of me.

Kierkegaard talked about a place in men that is a virtual sea of grief. In my recent years, I had navigated and charted the exact location of that terrible black-hole. It churns in a spot below the chest, above the stomach, and behind the solar plexus. It is the cavity that contains the soul, the heart, the library of feelings that make or break a man; and for so many of us, it is a place of darkness, emptiness, and sorrow. Scrape away at most men and there is disappointment and sadness lurking in that shadowy place. Talk to any man who has fallen out of touch with his purpose, his place, his reason for being and ask him what the hole has done with his worth. We try to escape this gaping darkness with distraction, obsession and addiction. But the hole will be there, waiting in us like a funnel of the damned to suck dry our serenity. The only way out, the only way to gain sanity is to break down and surrender to the reality of grief. Yes, there is horrendous sadness and it can only be released through tears. You must acknowledge that dreams and expectations have not been met, that no matter how hard you tried, it was never enough, that love has somehow slipped away despite desperate efforts to find and contain it, that every turn in the road threw something your way that you were not prepared to handle and therefore, failed and failed and failed, and it was that song that you went to bed with, that voice that you heard in the morning calling you to rise, beaten and weary, sitting with a haggard frowning face staring back from the mirror with frightened eyes that needed to be strong, yet there was nothing left: no strength, no hope, no sense that anything would change. And with this shell you walked out the bathroom door and into the world each and every goddamn day.

I held still and felt the agony rise up. And I wept.

I wept for the loss of my children, for the loss of my lover, for the failure to help my sister, for the numbing bewilderment I felt around my parents, for the countless botched attempts to find a meaningful purpose with which I could earn my daily bread, for the reality of being a pawn on a chess board, for the dread of raped nerve endings and a wrecked appetite, for knowing that time was running out on my chances of finding a companion who could be my Donna Reed and be there at my side during my worst moments to look at me and laugh with me and convince me, this stumbling, bumbling screw up who never got out of Bedford Falls, that "Yes, Clarence, it really is a wonderful life."

THE GUILT

TRUTH # 67

Life is easier than you think. All that is necessary is to accept the impossible, do without the indispensable, and bear the intolerable.

- From the **Book of Truths** by Langdon Towne

∧∧∧∧∧∧∧∧∧∧∧∧∧∧∧

[AUGUST 2001: NORTH CASCADES NATIONAL PARK]

Langdon and I hiked around the dark side of Austera Peak, weaving our way through crevasses and up low angled snow slopes until we found a spiny ridge overlooking the rugged Macallister Glacier. The walk had loosened Towne up, but I still wasn't sure I could dive in with both feet. We sat in silence, with him occasionally glancing at my face.

Again, he spoke first. "Guilt," he said. "When did you first feel guilt?"

"That's kind of hard to say."

"No, it isn't. Just hold still for a minute. It's right there, like a bright blue flash in your memory vault."

"Uh.."

"Just close your eyes, relax and float down stream. It is believing. The shower works for me. Just standing there, letting the water run off my head. Everything comes into view. Try it sometime. You hold still, and it will come."

"So what was yours?" I asked.

"My first taste of guilt?"

"Yeah."

"The first time I came."

"Whoa!"

"Yeah. I remember it like it was yesterday. I was up in the attic with my much older, dope loving, prison bound cousin."

"God, does everybody have a cousin like that?"

"I certainly hope so. Anyway, he taught me a thing or two about how to have fun with my weenie. The next thing I knew I was overwhelmed with this feeling of euphoric delight. It was awesome. That must have lasted a whole five seconds or so. Suddenly I saw little blue flashes and sparks. And it was at that exact moment, lying on my back with my thing in the air that a new feeling entered my guts for the very first time. I felt this hole open up in my belly. It was horrible, seedy and empty. It felt exactly like shame looks.

And there it was. Guilt. I was ashamed to be me. From that moment on, I didn't want to look my parents in the eye."

"Jesus! How old were you?"

"Five."

"Oh my God!!"

"Those were the exact words I said a couple of times before I shot those blanks. Of course, I no more than got them out then I found myself muttering the *other* phrase I've been saying ever since."

"What phrase was that?"

"Oh shit."

THE LOSER

I came off the mountain a ruined man with a book in his hand. It was my book. I had just written it while lying in the rocks waiting for my heart to stop. It didn't. So unclear as to how one is supposed to know when the heart is officially done beating, thereby eradicating one's need to endure further suffering, I kept writing until a Confessional had been orchestrated on the green pages of a 6 x 9 Steno Note Pad. It was a Confessional for my children, my sister, my parents and anyone who might have loved me. Like any man about to meet his maker, I apologized for my blunders and inadequacies, while hopefully shedding some grace on my many shortcomings. I didn't ask for forgiveness. I'd screwed up too badly to have a go at that. I just kept writing until my pen stopped moving. Then I waited. When my pen started moving again, I wrote some more. What came out was the blind truth. It went like this until I knew I was done and ready to hike back to my car and head for my favorite hideaway: The City of Rocks, Idaho.

-From **The Shipwreck Journals**

^^^^^^^^^^^^^^^^^^^^^^^^

[JULY 2001: SEATTLE, WASHINGTON]

"You are a loser!"

Those were the last blasting words used by my lover's husband before he stormed off to tear her apart limb from limb. He had found the love letters and pictures the night before. It was the eve of their daughter's 6th birthday and as he slammed his Jeep Laredo door shut, twelve six year olds were on their way to his home for a celebration they would never forget.

I had stood there, head bowed, taking it with the humility the situation called for. The behavior of his wife and I over the last two months had reached treacherous levels of passion with neither of us being able to cut the mad chord of love and watch the other sail away to reason.

After a couple of days of denial, I got her last phone call, which came at 3:00 AM after she had downed a half-bottle of brandy (she doesn't drink) to work up the nerve to stay alive for another twelve hours of verbal and physical abuse. I tried to talk her up to the bed, tried to keep her talking. She did not want to live anymore. She was in love with me and did not want to live with him anymore. But "the winner" was threatening her with taking away their two kids while ruining me in any way he could. It was terrifying.

I told her over and over that I loved her, that he couldn't take the kids, that none of his threats would hold up in court, that she needed legal counsel and a place to stay and get clear of the abuse, that she wasn't a lying piece of shit but the most wonderful, spirited, and beautiful person I'd ever known. I told her to keep fighting, to never give up.

In the morning, I lost my fight and will to go on. I packed the car and drove aimlessly to my parent's, then to my daughter's place in Walla Walla, then through most of north east Oregon, before hiking all the way from my car to a phone booth to call my mom and say I wanted to come home. I was scared to be alone. I drove six hours back to her house and collapsed in a heap.

I spent two days, frightened and grieving before calling home to check my messages. Asiki, a Sudanese refugee student/athlete who was living with me before heading off to college, answered and informed me that Ann had called on Thursday to warn me that her husband was on his way down to find me; again. After seven days, this latest shock wave made it very clear that she had not had a break from the abuse.

And I, the spiritual warrior, sat at my mom's, powerless. I could think of nothing but the endless stream of wicked details he would uncover to enhance his nightmarish rage. I got up the next day and drove off to the mountains.

The theme shifted to the should haves: should have stayed away, should have called it off back in June after I had left to get over her, should have taken back all my pictures and letters from her, should have gone away, gotten busy and waited it out.

After hiking for hours to gain a ridge, I set up camp and slept in fits with the theme: "I HAVE RUINED ALL THEIR LIVES!!!!" playing like an evil disco beat through my ears. I kept waking up to a phone ringing. I lay in my tent as fear took complete control of me.

In the morning I finally got up and walked to a rock. I was as low as I could ever remember, no way out, no hope. I had lost her. He might kill me. He might kill her. Her kids would be in therapy for a lifetime.

I wanted to move but couldn't. I had to hold still. Had to feel this. And as I sat there during the longest silence of my life, eye to eye with God, one word came floating up and out through the black hole: "Love." I picked up my steno pad and wrote the words down as a torrent of truth poured forth.

The Loser

I am a loser. I have lost my whole life. Every step since I can remember has been filled with loss and pain. The darkness and doubt manifested into a phobia and by the age of eleven it controlled my worth. To compensate for my inadequacy, I learned to climb mountains and crags and took on huge responsibilities. I was controlling, sought the attention of beautiful women, and revealed my soul to no one. I was utterly alone.

It was not until I was thirty and fell in love that I learned this did not have to be so. This could have healed me had our love not been a forbidden voyage. My first wife and I divorced with her getting complete control of the kids while the promise of the second marriage quickly eroded under torrents of guilt and self-loathing. So began ten years of digging for answers. There were no easy stretches. Through it all I loved her, loved my kids-- but it wasn't enough. My kids lost their innocence. And I lost the love of my life.

And through it all there was this child in me, a sweet vibrant boy whose world went dark too early, who screamed in fear to the night, who trembled at the dawn not knowing how to take another step, who wanted to be loved, adored, cherished and held. But love had deceived him, disappointed him, crushed him, crucified him and left him alone and questioning for over thirty years. He was still a freak, still a loser.

Something clicked inside me like a spark; the tiniest imaginable flick of light. It was a click in this, my darkest moment, that said: "Get up. Do not give up now. Do not quit now."

This is the Truth
I have ruined my life before
Lost my faith before
Lost all my dreams before
Been wished dead before
Had no control over the fate of loved ones before
Had my world stolen before
Have dealt with death before
Have dealt with grief before
Always I come back, God
I will deal with this

I was able to walk, though slowly, and I thought of what I must do to stay alive in the next two weeks, for it was now a question of my survival. I thought of how I would have to go home and surround myself with friends and the athletes I coached in order to be safe. I thought of how many friends I'd made since I came awake in my thirties. How all my friends had been through loss; how the only friends I could stand were the ones who had lost, who were humbled and non-judgmental of others who had failed or suffered.

I was a loser, suffering all the consequences of a risk strewn life and a knack for navigating into troubled waters.
I was a loser, with friends and family who would support me to hell and back.
I was a loser, and I was not alone.

[AUGUST 2001: THE CITY OF ROCKS]

Kristan looked up from the *Shipwreck Journals* and exclaimed: "Oh my God! This is wonderful!!"

"What?! I doubt anyone besides you would call it wonderful…No one's going to want to read this stuff."

"Are you joking? Sixty per cent of marriages end in divorce. Over thirty per cent of married people wind up having affairs. This stuff is *gold*. Trust me."

I did. Kristan was perfect. A divorced Mormon searching for truth, she had shown up at *The City of Rocks* in the middle of the night after getting my telephone message of distress. I needed a friend, and Kristan was the exact friend I needed.

She and I were at opposite ends of love's spectrum. Where her cup was running over with a double shot of hope, I was stranded in the great empty where all I had counted on to keep me afloat was gone; where the only thing left to hold in the morning was a trickle of coffee dripping through the cone, and the sound of that trickle was what I was clinging to. For in that cup was all the comfort I would be allowed. And in a strangely magnificent way, it was all I needed.

Kristan didn't share my love for that morning cup of coffee. No coffee, no cursing, no foolish sex. But like any Mormon worth her whities, she was curious about the wild side and I felt it my responsibility to educate her. She was beautiful, safe, good to her core, kind to all, and willing to never place judgement on my twisted descents. She even tolerated my references to Langdon Towne.

"I don't *want* to like him," she'd tell me with a sheepish grin. "I mean, I know I shouldn't, but I can't help but want to keep reading that *Book of Truths*."

Kristan knew where the edge was. Good Mormons don't divorce. And she had. And unlike me, she couldn't lie.

"Jesus, you've got balls, Kristan. You must have really rocked the boat with that divorce. When did you know it was over?"

"On my honeymoon."

"Ouch."

"But, it took a long time before I could do it. I waited to see if it would change, if I could somehow fall in love with him. But it didn't happen. It was so sad. He was such a nice guy. I was sick the whole time I was married to him."

"Yeah. When one is pretending, the whole body revolts."

"...and the sad part is, I think most people are pretending."

THE BOOK OF TRUTHS

TRUTH #13:

If you ever have five minutes of peace and/or happiness, give thanks.
Yes, get on your knees and pray your ass off to whatever God you think is
watching because you know the shits about to hit the fan and the bowels of
hell will soon unleash their fucking cannons on your soul. *

-*From the* **Book of Truths** *by Langdon Towne*

∧∧∧∧∧∧∧∧∧∧∧∧∧∧∧∧∧∧∧∧∧∧∧∧∧

[August 2001: North Cascades National Park]

The weather had remained uncharacteristically perfect, allowing the hike
from Primus to Eldorado Peak to seem like a vacation rather than the micro-
epic I had assumed it would be. We sat down on an exposed hunk of rock,
near a crevasse, and marveled at the view.

"Ya' know I'm not the praying kind, but, I have to say, I got down on my
knees last year and prayed for someone to love. I was so sick of being alone."

"And which God did you pray to?" Langdon grunted, trying to scratch an
itch right behind his shoulder blade.

"The one that's all about love, of course."

"Good choice...Hey, can you help me here?"

I grabbed my collapsible ski pole and scratched the illusive itch as he
directed traffic up, down, left and right.

"Anyway, I got down on my knees and said, 'God, could you please bring
love to my life? I am weary of being alone and always going back to my ex-
wife #2 when I am like this. And could you make her vibrant, and loving and
kind, and athletic and beautiful? And could she like my kids and make a
good mother to them? A soul mate would be good, God, if that sort of thing

---

*Towne's prolific use of the F-word and other swear words has been a source of contention with
publishers, as his books have been bannd from public schools as well as several countries where he
has been called a 'devil.' Towne contends that "repression kills expression" and that "he is only
speaking the truth." When I once asked him about the amount of cussing in his work, he started to
laugh and put it like this: "I know. I know. But I learned a dirty verse in the 4th grade that made me
laugh so hard, it changed my life. That year I learned every cuss word ever spoken. God, I loved the
4th grade!" When asked what the verse was that had changed his life he laughed, cleared his throat,
then sang:

    "Jesus Christ Almighty
    A bug flew up my nightie
    Bit my tit and made me shit
    Jesus Christ almighty"

actually exists…and I tried to think of anything else, but that was all that came out. I thought it had to be enough."

"Was it?"

"Well, yes and no. I got exactly what I wanted, except for one tiny detail, that little box at the top of the list that you are suppose to check off thereby nullifying the rest of the order."

"The married or single box, eh?"

"Yep."

"I'll bet she liked you."

"Yep. She loved me. And I loved her. So I let her go. Some things don't make sense."

"Life ain't fair: *Truth #1.*"

"That's for sure!...and what's *Truth #2?*"

"When in doubt, follow the route, or if that doesn't work, refer to *Truth #1.*"

"Ya know, I don't mean to come off like a puss, but I spent the last ten years of my life trying to do good for others and ..."

"I know you have. It's what you have to do to overcome a sense of failure."

"I know. I know. And after I came back from that trip to Zion, I gave myself as unselfishly as I could, tried to repair as much damage as I could, tried to shed light for anyone who might have lost their way."

"That's why you're here."

"Yeah. It led me to myself. And it led me to her. After all that, you'd think I could have done the right thing. Instead, I feel like I ruined her life."

"Yep, you did."

"Thanks."

"And my guess is: it's probably the best thing that ever happened to her."

At that Langdon began to pound on his leg as he burst into song... a *Supertramp* classic from back in the day:

***"So your life's become a catastrophe, well it has to be, for you to grow, boy**.*"

Towne flipped the short ski pole into the air as he smiled, "And that, my friend,…"

The tool came twirling down with his fingers snatching it by the narrow tip as if he had intended to catch it backwards.

"…is *Truth #3.*"

∧∧∧∧∧∧∧∧∧∧∧∧∧∧∧

Langdon Towne could definitely pee in public. In fact, he was one of those "bigger than life" personas who could walk up on a stage and belt out a show tune to a pack of eighth graders. Langdon rocked in ways I could only dream of.

Towne, the author, was becoming well known and revered in an ever-widening circle of climbers and celestial travelers. Some went so far as to consider him a modern day sage or quasi-guru. His sole claim to literary credibility were two small books he had self-published and sold out of the back of his car, climbing shops, and 'one-with-his-bun' book stores such as *Elliot Bay*. The work that had turned heads was a one-flight read called *The Book of Truths*. Were you lucky enough to find a copy and flip open the book, here is what you would find:

TRUTH # 1

Life isn't fair. If life were fair, the frogs wouldn't kill the bugs, the birds wouldn't kill the frogs, the farmers wouldn't kill the birds, and the pesticides wouldn't kill the farmer with the carcinogens he sprays on the apples you munch everyday to keep the doctor away.

∧∧∧∧∧∧∧∧∧∧∧∧∧∧∧∧∧∧∧∧∧∧

Which brings me to the bigger picture and the point of bringing Towne into this tale. In all fairness, *Crossing Zion* couldn't have been written without my singular relationship with Langdon. Towne was about truth, and coming clean, and being real, and saying what needed to be said rather than choking on one's correctness until pronounced pliably dead. Towne was about joining the living and casting off the weights of Christmas Past. He could not be labeled. He could not be pigeon holed. There was no box that fit him. There was no box that would hold him. As he often told me, "They all got handed boxes, and they all climbed in except me." He'd grin and then hold up his hands, "Look Mom, no box!"

Towne is real, and he isn't. He floats between worlds, between countries, prophecies, eulogies, epitaphs, customs, and beliefs. He is all things holy as he espouses blasphemy. He is character personified as he pinches your ass and tries to steal a kiss. He suffers. He rejoices. He carries all the baggage, harvests and failures of the ages. He is the disease and he is the cure. To hear him say it, he is nothing more than a true wretch, a human being: "One with all, and all with none." And for this simple truth: "No matter how clean your linen, or filthy your socks, we are all the same...," he exists.

Over the last year, we'd become close, sharing ideas, philosophies, and views of the world. Langdon's attitudes helped me make peace with life's ever-changing injustice. In return, I validated Towne and gave him one more reason to be.

Though I had never read a word of his work before that late summer trip to The City of Rocks, the name Langdon Towne was familiar to me as the hero of *Northwest Passage*. In fact, if I would've had a son, I would have named him Langdon. (Both my daughters have given thanks they were girls.)

Of course, I didn't get to have a son, but I did get to have a major meltdown. The year was '92, the wheels had come off my bus, and all I wanted was the truth. I wanted someone to tell me what it meant to be a human being. No one knew. Everyone's theories were so much smoke and jargon. I had been saved, counseled, twelve stepped, men's grouped, told to be nice, told to bitch, told to commit, told to run. Nothing made sense. I listened to the words of the great men of the ages and saw how they were ignored, crucified, ridiculed, and revered in death. None of them professed to having the answers to parenting, to divorcing, to honoring parents without being consumed, to loving while packing a spear hanging from the heart, to learning to chant verses of courage while grabbing one's ankles in the position necessary to work in the public domain. Not one of these great men spoke in a universal tone that matched the absurdity of real life. Not one. Every voice had holes. Every doctrine was flawed with the sweat of the walls from which it was written. I was still a teacher, a son, a brother, a father, a husband, a coach. But I was not a human being. I was utterly alone. I was a phobic, addicted to my ex-wife #2. And then came Towne and that ***Book of Truths***.*

TRUTH # 81:

You are human. To deal with your pain, you will distract. *You are composed of fragile chemicals, tissues, and impulses. Sometimes they work. Sometimes they don't. To deal with the reality that you are just a crossed wire away from wandering the halls of a mental ward, you must distract.*

TRUTH # 82:

Choose your distractions carefully. *Risk, love, sports, money, gambling, work, power, drugs, sex, and child-rearing; it's all the same. In the end you will wind up on your knees. Please know it is not your fault. Just remember to pick the distraction that has the least chance of emptying your bank account and leaving you stranded on a street corner with a sign in your hand.*

---

*Towne's first work had been rejected by a plethora of publishing houses. All rejections rang the same: "Captivating. Couldn't put it down. With that said- too short. Your use of quotations could pose copyright infringement. Can't publish something like this if author is unknown. Your writing, while engaging, is difficult to target. Adult themes? The market is saturated with self-help and memoirs. Consider smaller publisher. Pick up copy of 'Writer's Market.'

Towne's response had been to clean out the remains of his checking account and self publish *The Book of Truths*. He could only afford to print 427 copies. He sold the Truths out of his car and local climbing stores. In thirteen weeks they were gone. Only a steaming affair with a 5'9" chestnut mom kept him from riding this wave all the way to fame's teaming shore.

TRUTH # 83:

Distraction will lead to addiction. Please know it is not your fault. Distraction keeps the pain away. More distraction keeps the pain away longer. Even more distraction keeps the pain away even longer until distracting ten times more than you never thought you would keeps the pain away only half as long before. Soon, every breath not spent distracting will feel like you've got a shotgun in your mouth with a toe on the trigger.

TRUTH #84:

Addiction will lead to God. Addiction eventually sucks every last ounce of hope away, until all you're left with is your wretched soul, shipwrecked on a naked ridge, alone, terrified, staring death in the eye. At that point, you will be on your knees crying, "God, oh God, just give me another chance! I want to live! I want to live! And it is from this space, on your knees and shaken to your core, that you will be willing to listen, to learn, to heal, to hold, to love, to be, to endure, to gain, to appreciate-- all that you wasted. **

**Towne had a flair for the dramatic. He often mentioned that his greatest fear was that he would die alone. He said that his one true passion was falling tragically in love. When I once commented that though he often spoke of love, I never actually saw him in the vicinity of a woman and that friends were wondering, he laughed and pointed out that only married women were together enough to interest him and that "one can't exactly be seen in public with someone's wife, now can one?" When I took a risk and suggested to him that adultery was historically cited as a cardinal sin, he had away, coughed up a hair ball and then uttered, "Fuck that! I know the truth." He went on to tell a story of how he had discovered the truth during his years of isolated wanderings through the jungles, valleys, and deserts of solitude.

When I asked him what that truth might be, he had said to me in a low, scratchy voice that sounded prophetic, "Scorpios. Auburn haired, olive skinned, and about 5' 9". I'm addicted. Don't ask my why, but that combination is what I'm living for. I keep finding em. Or," he nodded and smiled as if to acknowledge the presence of a higher power, "they keep finding me. I've said no to every drug and addictive substance on God's green earth. But, and this *IS* the goddamn truth, I CAN'T say NO to an olive-skinned, auburn-haired, Scorpio."

When I got to know him better and was dabbling in my own brand of dark humor, I took the liberty to jokingly say, "Langdon. I don't think you are ever going to have to worry about dying alone."

At that, he looked up from his can of Slim-Fast and asked why.

"Because you are probably going to die with some jealous husbands hands around your throat!"

I had expected a laugh out of the ever sardonic waste land that was Langdon's twisted wit. Instead, he turned, looked at me with big, kicked-dog eyes and began to cry.

All he could say was, "I know. My God, I know."

FOUR BELLS

TRUTH #14

Our little lives get complicated. *It's a simple thing. Simple as a flower, and that's a complicated thing.*

-*From **The Book of Truths** by Langdon Towne*

∧∧∧∧∧∧∧∧∧∧∧∧∧∧∧∧∧∧∧∧

[1977-1982: CLIMBING, AVOIDANT PARURESIS AND A FIRST-BORN CHILD]

The third warning bell went off in '77 when my first wife and I came home from a romp up the former Mt. St. Helens, giddy with the joy of mountain conquest. We walked into my parents' house, as we always did back then, and my mom met me at the door with the news that one of my best-friends had jumped off the I-5 bridge and was found floating in the Montlake Cut. I felt a jab hit my gut and let the emotion fall about as far as my false rib before I took a breath, stopped it, looked at the floor, then at my mom, and then asked her what was for dinner. I had arrived as a man.

After the trauma of being raised in the 60's, I came out of the public school system a phobic, not trusting anyone or anything, and promptly marrying the first nice girl who slept with me at college.

Tim had gotten into climbing and was begging me to try it. My only taste of mountaineering had been blisters on the boring snowfields of Mt. Adams in '74. I thought it was a pointless use of energy, plus, there was no place to pee in private on those endless white slopes. Eventually, Tim managed to coerce me into climbing the Tooth by its 4th class North Side, and, though the experience was heinous, I found myself dreaming of more. Both of us went to the library and devoured every book we could find on the subject. *The Golden Age of Mountaineering,* where men pushed the envelope of courage and fear on the flanks of north faces, filled my nights with tales that captured my heart in a way that could only be compared to the thrill of watching the *Beatles* sing *She Loves You* on Ed Sullivan when I was nine.

In '76 I still had heroes. I watched Dr. Chris Chandler summit Everest on a TV bi-centennial special, and I knew I wanted his life. Suddenly I understood why I was here. I wanted to stand at the top of the world.

Climbing in the late 70's was awesome. Every mountain excursion was an exhausting, tendon-shredding, out-of-body adventure. Each weekend Tim and I completed a new, painful chapter in Alpinism 101, learning lessons with tenfold the impact of a month in college.

My first wife learned to climb with Tim and me. I needed her; she was the only person on earth who understood my overpowering need to hide the fact that I couldn't piss in public. Though I didn't know it, I had a severe phobia, an unexplainable acquired psychological condition I can now look at from the comfort of my forties and correctly call *Avoidant Paruresis*. But back then I simply thought I was crazy and that my inability to urinate around another living soul was the cruel stone I had to roll up hill for the rest of my days. The trick was to carry on a pretense of being normal while making up reasons to duck out of sight to take a leak. From the age of eleven on, I had to come up with a never ending cycle of little white lies and lame excuses to ensure I could pee alone. Throughout my formative years, I chose not to date; the idea of trying to locate a private toilet while making small talk with a pretty girl was more than I wanted to deal with, so I didn't. I played music instead.

My wife was nice to me and tolerated my condition by pretending I didn't have it. That was perfect. As we got more into climbing, the awkwardness that my phobia presented often reared its head on the featureless terrain of glacial slogs as there was no place but the bottom of a crevasse to hide. At that point, pretending I didn't have a problem sometimes resulted in climbing eighteen hours with a bladder full. I thought that having my wife around would help me screen myself so I could go. I was wrong. The pain of not being able to relieve myself all day was never as bad as the embarrassment of hiding behind my wife to do what every man in the world could do in front of a firing squad.

From early adolescence on, I had become convinced I was one of God's banished children and developed that intense competitiveness of a kid with something to prove. Now in my twenties, I saw the rewards that mountain climbing could offer: with book deals, TV documentaries, and a sense of worth. I wanted to meet the best climbers and learn their secrets. And I did. I made friends with the likes of Jim Nelson and Steve Swenson. I would have made friends with Walter Bonatti and Dougal Haston and an army of Brit legends if they hadn't live on another continent or hadn't recently been killed. From Nelson and Swenson, I learned that going light meant going fast and fast meant safe. Those two always came back.

Thus, friendship transformed into hanging with climbers who could help me gain a rung up the ladder towards being included on a Himalayan expedition. Of course, I would want my wife to go. I knew that without my security blanket, I would be in trouble. I wanted her to get better at climbing and got pissed off because she couldn't keep up with me.

The first warning bell went off when after a few successful climbs my confidence went up and my eye went side ways, checking out other female prospects. Anything to gain an edge. I was turning into a machine, a stud figure who could eliminate unnecessary feelings and emotions save for the euphoria of a summit or the intense joy of hanging out with guys who had the same goals.

Climbing, the ultimate ride of denial, was now my way of getting as far as possible from anything resembling my trembling soul.

The reality of death in the mountains reared up right away when Dusan Jagersky and Al Givler, from whom I'd taken my one and only mountaineering course, fell off a peak in Alaska. After that I got to witness a favorite past time of other climbers: judging and criticizing the mistakes of others. I listened and I learned.

Chris Chandler was the second bell. As a young, perky acquaintance, visiting Chandler at work and at his home on Vashon Island, I saw that my hero lived in a tiny trailer, was divorced and living with a night-club singer, was paying a fortune in child support, and smoking weed 24/7 to keep his sanity.

When I asked him naïve questions like: "Well now that you've done Everest, there must be nothing left to do?" Chris would look at me as if I might be joking and then let me know that there were still a million challenges and Everest had been just one of them. I got to see another side of the climbing community brotherhood: behind Chandler's back, he, like any climber who earned the spot light, was the victim of jealous pot shots and attacks on his climbing abilities.

The only thing I saw slowing me down from Himalayan success was my phobia, which wasn't getting better and presented more challenges than any of the climbs I trashed myself on each week. I was a scared child of a man, trying to control everything I could because I couldn't control anything I wanted to. The worst part was the lie. On the outside I looked the part of mountain hero. I was the all-American kid, the scholar, the athlete, talented, bright, and beautiful. I was expected to shine, to excel, to make my family proud. On the inside was the Phobic: dark, tragic, and loathsome. It made no sense. It was pathetic. It took my youth and any sense of joy. And it would get worse. I lived in fear of losing my mind, of breaking apart like glass. Fear had become my main emotion. And fear steals everything. I was twenty-two and unable to talk to another living soul about who I was.

Which was why I had to climb. Scaring myself in the mountains helped me feel normal. Being gripped up on a cliff allowed me to deal with being twice as scared down on the ground. Climbing temporarily reclaimed for me a sense of control, dignity, and honor; that sense of worth would last the length of time it would take to head back home and awaken to another day of pretending everything was going to be OK.

Then I read about Rheinhold Messener's solo ascent of Nanga Parbat and the light to freedom clicked on full power. He had it down: One partner, or no partner. A girl friend in camp. Big mountains. Big fame. He was a visionary. Solo in the Himalaya. At last I would have a way to piss alone.

I too adopted a Spartan life style with every climb a training exercise for the next bigger climb. I was in love with beauty, whether it was women, sunsets, or mountains, and I knew that I would die in glory, descending a corniced ridge in a whiteout, just like my first hero Herman Buhl.

I went back to school and got a teaching degree in order to provide a life style conducive to having time off. Teaching would allow me to live anywhere in the country. I also spent free time writing and recording music-- a hobby inspired by the *Beatles*-- hoping that selling a hit song would provide the cash flow necessary to feed the climbing addiction.

Indeed, I had a plan; but my first wife was developing one of her own. She wanted to have a baby. No problem. We'd do that too. She could take care of the kid while I kept busy earning the pay check and climbing.

I began to wake up to the realities of being a father as I washed my hands with an iodine sponge in the sinks of Valley General Hospital, waiting for the C-section delivery of our first born. Standing there scrubbing down in slow motion, I actually thought to myself, "What if I don't like it? What if I want to put it back?"

I walked through the operating room doors, frightened of what I might do.

And then Kate popped out of her mother, and the doctor turned her bloody purple face towards mine, and my voice went up six octaves and came squealing out with notes I had never heard before:

"OH MY GOD!! SHE IS BEAUTIFUL!!"

An arrow flew across the room and buried itself in my heart. It was love at first sight, the first time that had ever happened to me.

The nurse handed her to me, wrapped in a blanket. She was screaming and wailing at the horror of being born. I propped the little purple, placenta-covered football in the crook of my arm and began to say her name, "Hi, hi Kate, hi," and her eyes looked at me, and her crying promptly stopped. "I love you, Kate. I love you."

I went home that night, buried my face in my pillow and wept, and bawled, and wailed.

There would be no Everest or K2. I knew it. I loved her. I could feel it. I would not want to leave her for months at a time. My God! She had pierced my armor and collapsed my walls with one look. I was ruined! She had me. I could not die. I would have to love her forever.

I shook until every fiber of me had turned to love, the 4th bell ringing 'til dawn.

WHAT GOES AROUND

TRUTH # 15

A man will sell his soul for promises of sexual favors. Please know it cannot be helped. The need to repopulate is the fundamental flaw of the species. Our loins control us, and there is nothing we can do about it. All that is good and evil can be summed up through either the expression or repression of this desire to recreate. Man will never harness it. Man will never control it. It controls man, and modern society has yet to figure out that simple truth. Therefore, we swim in a river of lies, denial, and scum. Eventually, saints and whores all sacrifice their health to please their God of choice.

*-From the **Book of Truths** by Langdon Towne*

∧∧∧∧∧∧∧∧∧∧∧∧∧

[1985-92: THE VALLEY OF TEARS]

Tim and I didn't climb together much during the 80's though I remained in Himalayan mode: head down, one foot in front of the other, ready to sit out storms, ready to out last wretched conditions, ready to push my entire being past the breaking point, ready to lay my life on the line for reasons too absurd and personal for anyone to understand. Problem was I wasn't climbing mountains anymore. I was raising Zoë's three teenage boys full time, my two daughters part time, dealing with my ex-wife #1's boyfriend controlling the house in which my girls were living, teaching a classroom of 4th graders fractions, and trying to keep some hope in a darkening second marriage that hadn't seen a break in the storms since the day I said "I do."

Everybody had a piece of wisdom to give me in '86. These were some of the *Truths* I was told by those who cared:

1. You reap what you sow.
2. The fuckin you get ain't worth the fuckin you get.
3. Play with fire you get burned.
4. What goes around comes around.
5. You get what you deserve. Get used to it.
6. I wish I'd never been born. (In reference to the pain my divorce caused a certain loved one.)
7. You've ruined everyone's chances of happiness.
8. Love brings up all things unlike itself in the name of healing.
9. Do you accept Jesus Christ as your personal savior?

Zoë and I had developed a rhythmic marital pattern that involved fighting during certain days of her menstrual cycle. My only defense against her bewildering mood swings was a lonely suitcase, packed and waiting to be wheeled out the door. Our fights were as regular as the drool of Pavlov's dog. Every season had its rhyme, its reason, and its drama to remember:

During the summer, she'd do her thing with her sons and I went rock climbing with my daughters.

During the fall, school started up, and I was too busy to care that Zoë was too busy to spend time with me.

During the winter, I would pack my bags and move out of our five-bedroom house after another Christmas of pretend togetherness.

During the spring, the cherry blossoms would bloom, and Zoë would too. We'd go to the ocean, she'd write my name in the sand, and I'd be hooked.

By that last Christmas, the years of constant brawling had drained every last gram of gold from our clock. I knew we'd reached the summit of dysfunctional madness when the holidays arrived about six months too soon. On Christmas Eve, as our five little children danced out in the living room to "Little Drummer Boy," she and I were in the bedroom, four letter wording each other with me eventually locking myself in the bathroom. Later, after one of the kids knocked on our bedroom door to ask if it was time to open presents, we made our way back out to the festive living room, red-eyed and ashen faced, trying to regain composure as acid pumped through our veins. Red and green boxes of joy were being distributed about the room, my little five-year-old daughter, smiling in a lacy dress as gifts were placed beside her. I took a breath and tried to absorb the beauty of the moment, when a sudden guilt-charged jolt hit my belly. Her pile was noticeably smaller than the other four kids. I did a quick gift count and realized that she had half the presents of her step-brothers and sister. My heart did a back flip down my stomach into my bowels, and I ran downstairs trying to breathe as I frantically rummaged through cupboards and closets, searching in vain for a toy, doll, or stuffed animal which I could wrap and put Santa's signature on. When I came back up empty handed and glanced at her innocent, patient eyes, I knew that she knew. She had been forgotten. Chaos reigned supreme. Happy fuckin holidays.

On Christmas Day, after dropping off my daughters at their mom's, I turned on the radio to the *Talking Heads* classic: *Once In A Lifetime*. I nearly beat my steering wheel to a pulp as I pounded my fists blue to the rhythm, screaming along to any of the words I knew:

"*And you may find yourself living in a shotgun shack,*
And you may find yourself in a beautiful house, with a beautiful wife,
And you may ask yourself,
Well, how did I get here?"

Now with our sets of kids gone, and a week of vacation left, the two of us joined up long enough to head over to Snoqualmie Falls and toss our precious hourglass into the abyss. Through the remainder of the vacation, we didn't talk, or try to patch things up, or make time for each other, or even eat our meals together.

"And you may tell yourself
This is not my beautiful house!
And you may tell yourself
This is not my beautiful wife!"

During the spring I stopped eating and eventually walked away from my teaching career, my future, and every dream I'd ever had.

During the summer, a close friend let me house sit for him. It was strange to watch as the dynamics of my free rent, climber's-dream existence shifted because, as soon as it was OK to climb everyday, it didn't seem as joyful or as important. After a long month of trying to keep up with an array of hyper-intense young climber types, I found myself wanting to hang out with "just my kids" as they were the only two people I knew who seemed perfectly content to drive with me to different areas and simply play in the rocks and dirt.

My descent reached a point where I no longer felt capable of forcing a smile, even around my little daughters. I handled it by tossing myself down a mine shaft of exhausting solo alpine excursions that thoroughly consumed my emotions and pumped just enough endorphins through my veins to grant me the grace to put on a fatherly act whenever it was Poppa's turn to play.

Through such Herculean efforts, I expected to appease the Gods and earn some serenity. I was wrong. It was Sisyphus who I was destined to emulate rolling a giant stone up hill for the sole purpose of watching it roll back down from here to eternity.

The gong started banging when the act of crawling into bed, after an exhausting multi-day alpine binge, produced nothing more cathartic than a couple less hours of insomnia. I was in trouble. Climbing was no longer working. Nothing was changing in me. Nothing. So I sat. And I trembled.

My heart wailed for any semblance of something solid to cling to. All I knew no longer made sense. I couldn't pretend anymore. I couldn't make up reasons to look on the bright side. I dreaded the weekly agony of trying to force a smile around my kids. So anxious was I that, before heading down to pick them up, I had to run up hills to the breaking point, trying to lace my veins with enough endorphins to bring a hint of hope to my cheeks. My daughters weren't fooled and learned to play quietly with whatever they could find floating in the back seat of my Ford Festiva.

THE SHIPWRECK

TRUTH # 165:

You are human, therefore you will seek what you do not have. *Call it Greener Grass. Call it plain old greed. Call it what you want. It is a basic human need. Just know that if the universe ever gives you what you wished for, you will soon know the true meaning of misery. The rich and famous know this. They have everything they ever wanted and happiness is still a silver spoon in someone else's pocket.*

*-From **The Book of Truths** by Langdon Towne*

^^^^^^^^^^^^^^^^^^^^^^

[AUGUST 2001: INSPIRATION GLACIER]

Langdon took another nibble of *Powerbar* and chewed it slowly, trying not to yank the gold-work off his teeth. He paused to sip some water, then began telling me the *Curse*.

"Angelina turned to me in a Fred Meyer and told me she wanted to marry me."

"Whoa. That had to hurt. But, wasn't she still married?"

"Details. Details. The married part wasn't the problem. The married with children part was."

"Oh."

"She was this close," Langdon held up two fingers. "She hadn't been in love with him for years. She had been alone for even longer. She was raising the kids by herself."

"Sounds par for the marital course to me."

"Yep. Man, people are stupid when it comes to love."

I concurred with a nod.

"I was going to wait for her. There was nothing else I *could* do. I told her you leave a marriage because the marriage ain't working, not because you met some guy who you want to devour a whole lot more than candy."

"That was some good advice."

"Learned through trial and error of course."

A wind swept over the ridge, turning the air instantly cold. Towne and I instinctively reached for our jackets and whipped them on. My little green steno-pad fell out of my coat and flopped on the rocks below my feet. I nestled down on my pack and stared off at the hanging icefalls, jagged ridges, and deep green valleys below the Inspiration Glacier.

A thought popped in my head. "Dude, is it possible that you can love more than one person at the same time?"

"You're joking right?"

I wasn't.

"You want to hear what I think?... I think it's abnormal that we're supposed to love just one person. And our whole life? Think about it for a second."

"But you've been married."

"Twice. And I would have married a third time if Angelina would have taken a left instead of a right. I still believe in marriage. Still believe in monogamy. It's just... well, it just doesn't work. Kind of like raising kids. We still do it even though all we manage to do is fuck it up. Ya know what I'm sayin?"

I did.

"So where was I?"

"You were in a Fred Meyer, getting proposed to."

"Oh yeah. So..."

Towne grabbed his water bottle and took a swig as he paused to sort the rest of his story. My mind raced off to my own movie, my own nightmare, my own *Shipwreck* which, while maybe a tad less dramatic than Towne's and certainly lacking his weathered non-chalance, had reduced my heart to a plate of glass, dangling from two sweat-drenched fingers, about a mile above eternity.

∧∧∧∧∧∧∧∧∧∧∧∧∧∧∧∧∧∧

The morning after meeting with Ann's husband I was preparing to drive Kate's boyfriend across the state for a surprise *embrace* in Walla Walla when Ann called. Sobbing, she informed me that she had to meet with me one last time.

"It's over, huh? He got to you?"

"Yes."

"And you can't see me anymore, right?"

Suddenly it occurred to me that through all the loving, we never had a "plan." It was just love with no intent, no hope of ever being together until her life had come around to some form of order. It could have taken years for all I knew. I didn't care. I could wait for her. Not anymore. Hope had died.

Ann and I met the morning after the *embrace* in Walla Walla. All the preparations for tragic events could not have prepared me for the sight of her grieving over the loss of me. We held each other and wailed. I tried to encourage her, to say the right things, to love her with all I had right up to the very end. She pulled at her hair and screamed she was going insane. I told her to cry, to get it out, that it took two weeks to adjust to any crisis, that

I would always love her... my voice sounded like I was reading a bad movie script. I knew that. I kept talking anyway. And then I had to drive away. One of us had to. She couldn't. So I did. The *Road Warrior* limping off into the wasteland.

It was the saddest parting of a life of sad partings. There was no way out, no happy ending, just fear and a barrel full of loathing pushed into her face.

I drove home, crawled into my apartment, saw Asiki standing in the hallway, laid my head on his shoulder, and started to cry. He patted me and rubbed my back as I sobbed hysterically.

"Asiki, oh God. Oh God! I had to leave her there. Oh God! Oh God!"

"It's OK man. It had to be. It had to end."

"I've killed her. Oh God. I've ruined her life. Oh God."

"No man. This was not just you. Everyone plays a part in this."

"Oh God, Asiki, I am a bad person. I am bad."

"These things happen. These things happen to so many people..."

He walked me back to my bedroom and while I knelt at the foot of my bed and ground my face into the mattress, he sat there, rubbing my back, and holding my hand as I lost everything.

Kris came in, sat down on the other side of me and rubbed my head and shoulders. There those two stayed for what seemed an eternity as all hope poured out of me. They were not frightened. They were not ashamed of me. Both of them had known pain, had known loss, and neither were about to let me go through this alone.

Asiki and Kris, holding the man who had fallen before them, both survivors of separate wars, different continents, but same issues. Adults out of control. Always the same. Hate overpowering love.

But they were love. And love was everything.

The next night, the phone rang at 3:00 AM. Ann had downed a half bottle of Brandy, written my name on her fridge and decided to call me despite the risk. She was terrified and laughing. I told her to get out of there.

She told me of his threats to take the children. I told her he couldn't. I told her to get legal counsel. She was so ill prepared for all this madness.

Why hadn't I talked to her of a plan of action? I had waited for her to make up her mind. I did not want to force the issue and then wind up to blame for a choice she had not wanted. That all seemed like so much horseshit now. But, that was my style-- to rely on my natural abilities and guess the rest. It worked for playing guitar, but for things like divorce and lawsuits, it was a bogus approach. Since I lived most of my life like a guitar solo, I too was ill prepared for the reality of angry people and lawyers. It scared me. I told her I was going to lay low for awhile and gave her a number where she could reach me if she needed to find me. I told her I loved her about fifteen more times and then she hung up.

Four days later she called to warn me that her husband had left the house and was going to try and find me, again. I wasn't home.

Asiki was at the apartment alone and after he listened to the message he got out a knife, grabbed a microphone stand and waited patiently for her husband to arrive. A product of the bloodshed of civil war, a little scrap with an angry white dude did not give him an ounce of concern.

He told me over the phone, "If he comes here, I will let him break in and then I will cut him, beat his ass and toss him off the balcony and then call 911. They'll lock his ass up." He wasn't joking.

Ann's frightened warning broke something in me and I could no longer keep dreadful visions of her being hurt from reducing me to a stricken mess. I packed the car and headed into the mountains to try and walk myself back to sanity. The garden had been trampled, leveled, and laid to waste. The fields were a sea of mud and blood. War had come to my heart and the ship that had carried me deep into the mountains, ran aground on a ridge and left me stranded, shipwrecked.

And the coward that I am and could never out-run, surrendered to reality. Fear once again controlled the universe. Love was a dream I had once held. Gasping for every breath, I sat on a rock as wave after wave of terror crashed into my ears... and images of her husband's hands, crushing her soft skin, erased all memories of beauty and worth. I waited for my heart to stop beating. And when it didn't stop, I picked up my pen and began to write:

I'm in trouble God
My heart has fallen for what I can never have
I'm in trouble God
I have hurt someone who I loved more than life
I did wrong God
I borrowed from the wealth of another
It has left me now
Abandoned and empty

I'm in trouble God
I saw love
Saw it and felt it
Unwrapped the rags to find it-- this beauty
I always thought I had it God, but never touched it
Never held it inside me
Never felt my skin smile
Never wished I could do so much so simply
So easy to move my hands
So easy to move my lips into a smile
A thought of her playing for me, smiling for me
The most beautiful sight I will ever see, never again

I sat on the ridge stripping away layer after layer of denial and rationalizing and diversion and deflection and focusing on the positive and trying to make sense of the reasons, the causes, the excuses, and there were none; there were no more lies to conceal.

Breath by breath the truth emerged through the clearing fog-- the smoke screen that had surrounded my life with deception and self-pity and thoughts of compensation and revenge and greatness; and the last swirl of mist cleared and there I was: fearful, trembling, and naked.

And I fell before this force that had led me here. And I prayed for help, but not for me, for her, for him, and their children. I begged God to turn the light of mercy on their home and bring truth and peace to the fire, to bring water to their lips, to put faith in their hearts.

And in that space of absolute surrender, I heard the truth:

Until I could walk in honest delight at simply having been given the breath.

Until I could rejoice at the touch of the sun on my skin and the sight of a flower.

Until I could yearn for nothing more than to know there was peace in the hearts of my children.

Until I could walk free of desire and self-serving needs.

Until then, I would walk alone, with only the spirit of the universe as my companion.

And until I made peace with that force, I would never dream in the color of love again.

DRAGGING DANCER

TRUTH #94

Give thanks for your misery and know that no matter how bad it truly is, it will soon be so much worse. Remember that Heaven only helps those who help themselves. Therefore, please avoid insulting auditory such as, "Dear God, I can't possibly handle one more f...ing thing." Wrong call. Self-pity is a rocket red glare to your higher power. Soon, you will be begging for yesterday, when all your troubles seemed so far away.

-From the Book of Truths by Langdon Towne

^^^^^^^^^^^^^^^^^^^^^^

[AUGUST 2001: DRIVING TO THE CITY OF ROCKS]

"Hey, Johnson." Jake Burley, a senior-to-be-super-jock, jumped over the seat and checked his hair in the rear view mirror. "When was the first time you went to *The City of Rocks*?"

"92."

"And you were getting over your ex-wife, huh?"

"Yep. My ex-wife #2."

"And now you're getting over Ann, right?"

"Yep."

"Dude, this is where you go when you've got nothing left, huh?"

"Hmmm... I suppose you're right." I stared ahead at the wasteland of southern Idaho. 'So many miles and so much time,' played through my mind.

"Does it work?" Alden Crag, the brains and glue of our cross country team was seated next to me.

"We'll see."

Alden had been silently reading with *The Cure's 'Disintegration'* weeping on my tape deck. At his feet were stacks of stories I'd written since I'd started making pilgrimages to *The City of Rocks*. It had been my intention to make sense of the reams of candid angst and come with up some kind of story line, a thread to connect the tales. I wasn't sure I could do it.

The boys had spent the first hours of the drive gobbling up the pages like candy. This surprised me as I figured no one under the age of thirty would get it. The reading was not intended for young fresh eyes. It was meant to be read by the jaded, the questioning, the cynical, the down-trodden, the displaced forty-year olds who had a belly full of emptiness to show for giving away their lives to causes they no longer understood.

"Hey, Johnson! I just found the story where you drug your dog behind the truck. Dude, I can't believe she didn't die!" Jake was laughing from the back seat.

"Hmmm. Dragging Dancer. Now, *that* was a bad day. Thank God black labs are tough."

"Hey, Johnson. Did you really try to slit her throat."

"Oh yeah."

"Oh man, oh man, Johnz! Tell us that story!"

"I thought you just read it?"

"Yeah, but it's way cooler when you tell it. C'mon Johnson," Jake whined.

And so, I began telling the tale of Dancer, the dog I drug behind a truck.

^^^^^^^^^^^^^^^^^^^^^^^

"Please hurry back and don't bring a puppy home," were the last words I uttered as Zoë raced off to her ex husband's house to help deliver her ex-dog's puppies. When she returned a day later she was carrying a black little fur ball.

^^^^^^^^^^^^^^^^^^^^^^^

"Wait!" Alden asked for clarification. "So let me get this straight. Zoë was married to someone else before she married you?"

"That's right," I replied to his inquisitive, single eyebrow, stare. "Zoë and I were both still married when we met. But, that's another story."

Alden pursed his lips, trying to make sense of a lifestyle diametrically opposed to the values of his wholesome, conventional, eagle-scouted, upbringing. "So...." I went on with my story of shame.

^^^^^^^^^^^^^^^^^^^^^^^^^

Zoë came through the door the next afternoon with a puppy. "I couldn't leave this one," she explained. "She was the runt of the litter. Sugar wouldn't give her a nipple. What could I do?" We named our new addition to the family, Dancer (after the first climb Zoë and I ever did at Smith Rock.) The puppy immediately grew ten sizes and managed to consume the little window of available space I had hoped Zoë would reserve for me. Just when her youngest son had stopped swinging from the breast, along came this grinning black lab to wag a tail in my face. Dancer spent her time between naps tearing up our house. When we put her outside she tore up the garden. Being a black lab, her favorite snacks were garbage and cat shit.

By spring, marriage number two was having its problems. At the end of the school year I suggested that we take the kids and Dancer on a family backpack to try and restore some sanity. Though I was utterly spent from teaching, fighting, step-parenting and attending twelve-step meetings, I felt that a good hike and some beautiful scenery would loosen the stranglehold on my nerve endings. Later that evening, after a fight with Zoë about something I can't remember, I got on my knees and asked God to help us: to please let our dysfunctional family have a touch of luck. I knew it was a stretch. A fundamentalist, 'born again' friend of mine had once pointed out that God hated adulterers, which explained why my life was constantly going in the shitter. I asked this friend if God ever forgave people for their sins and he let me know that if I accepted Jesus Christ as my personal savior I still had a chance. As he spoke I wondered about the millions and millions of Bhuddist, Hindi, and Muslim adulterers. Were we all going to hell? I didn't ask.

Despite my doubts, I kept praying. And it worked. I awoke to perfect weather. I raced off to the store to get provisions for the two-day excursion that nobody besides me really wanted to go on. Loaded up with treats, I raced back, organized back packing gear for six, loaded up the car and waited for the boys to arise. Zoë let me know that she would drive separately. I would take Dancer and my girls in our little pick up truck; she'd take the boys in her Subaru wagon. Around noon, we secured Dancer in the back of the truck with a leash of climbing webbing, and headed off to the Teanaway. The two hour drive to the trailhead seemed extra long as I was mulling over life's strange turns while trying to make 'nice' conversation with my kids.

At last we reached the start of the thirteen-mile bumpy, dusty dirt road that leads to the trailhead for Ingalls Lake. I stopped and asked the boys if they would like to pile in the truck with the girls and Dancer to avoid eating dust for the next half-hour. They just gave me a look and rolled the window back up. Thus, with no takers on that offer, we drove on. The weather was awesome and I began to feel somewhat hopeful that this might be a good idea after all, and that just maybe this would be the trip to bring things back around. I thought about how so many of our problems really began with me and how if I could get some rest and quit acting neurotic half the time, maybe things would....

"Dad, where's the dog?!" Kate's voice had a twinge of panic.

"What?" I looked in the rear view mirror then looked over my shoulder.

"Dad, where's Dancer?" Kate was now on her knees, turned around looking in the back.

I looked again. No dog. SLAM!!!!

I got out as the hairs on my body began to stand up. It was one of those horrific frozen moments where time slowed down and seconds became minutes. As I walked back, staring at the dog leash, with no sign of the dog, the girls jumped out and raced around behind me. I gritted my teeth and approached Dancer as the world began to swirl into a nightmare-like space. I leaned down, looked behind the wheel and saw smoke coming off her smoldering skin. The only hair left was on her head and tail. Upon closer examination I could see holes worn through her coat, with tendons and bone exposed. She was looking at me, still alive, but for how many more minutes? The girls began to shriek wildly. I knew what I had to do.

The boys and Zoë came around and everyone began wailing in brutal anguish. The din just added to the surreal feel. I unhooked Dancer's leash and calmly asked my stepson if he had a knife. He gave it to me.

Zoë asked me what I was going to do and I told her I was going to cut Dancer's throat to put her out of her misery. She began crying harder, "Isn't there anything we can do? Can't we save her?"

I knew there wasn't. The kids' screams intensified. Zoë corralled the little ones while I picked up Dancer and carried her to a flat spot... took the knife out and held it to her throat. She still had fur on her head and neck and I drug the blade against it trying to reach an artery. It did nothing. My head fell for a second. I looked around for a large rock thinking I would have to bang her head. Jet engine white noise pounded through my skull. Just then, Dancer lifted her head slightly, looked at me, and then licked my fingers with her soft warm tongue. I dropped the knife. Her tail wagged softly. "Jesus Christ! Oh God, oh Jesus!!...."

"Keith I have to try and save her!" Zoë bawled behind me. "Where is the closest vet? Cle Elum... Ellensburg?"

"I have no idea, probably Cle Elum." I carried the dog back to her Subaru. She and her middle son sped off in a cloud of dust.

I stood with my little kids, their cheeks stained with tears and dust. I had ruined everything. The coffin had taken its final nail. There would be no tomorrow for this family.

We drove slowly to Cle Elum. I couldn't look the vet in the eye as she told me that Zoë had taken the dog to a better facility in Ellensburg.

What do you say to young children when you've just drug their favorite pet five miles up a gravel road? What do you say to your wife who already can't stand you most of the time? Zoë had a hundred reasons not to make love with me, and now this. I knew we'd never have sex again.

We pulled into the Ellensburg vet and walked to the surgical lab. There on a table stood what was left of our dog. A doctor was stitching and suturing, cleaning and gauzing, Dancer's hideous wounds. My eyes started to well up with tears and I looked at my wife weakly, hoping she wasn't going to come at me with a set of scissors. She moved quickly toward me and threw her arms around my neck and sobbed. We held each other crying. The kids were crying. The nurse was crying. Everybody was handing out tissue. And it was all my fault. The vet said that Dancer would recover. He said that black labs had an incredible ability to endure most anything besides being flattened by moving automobiles.

Zoë asked me to make love that night. I couldn't believe it.

The rest of the summer was spent spraying Dancer's giant scabs with a special burn lotion and taking her for walks to help her deal with the depression of wearing a cone on her head all the time. When the walks didn't work, we went and got her a kitten. Krissy fell in love with it and named her Lipshin, which sounding a whole lot like Lipshits, we soon changed to Nubbin. Dancer loved her kitty and would spend entire days washing and cleaning her baby. When the tiny thing couldn't take another bath and tried to get away, Dancer would swoop down with her cone and pin the puss inside. After a shaky beginning, the two worked out their differences and became the best of friends. Nubbin would sleep with Dancer every night. During the day she would take a nap lying against Dancers belly. The two of them wrestled and played. Dancer would clean her face and ears. They were quite a pair.

As soon as the task of spraying Dancer required one set of hands, Zoë took off with her kids to visit her aunt, leaving me alone with the dog. After a few days of sitting home, I took the hairless dog on a road trip to Smith Rock, where I soon learned there were two kinds of people:

A: The ones that saw your scabby, clear-cut, cone-headed dog and went "Oh my GOD!!!! You poor thing. What happened? Isn't that sad?"

B: The ones that give you a wide, wide berth while walking a deep arc around you going, "Sweet mother of God!!"

It seemed about a 50/50 world to me.

∧∧∧∧∧∧∧∧∧∧∧∧∧∧∧∧∧

"Hey, Johnson," Jake was picking at something behind his ear, flexing his bicep as he spoke. "So why am I thinking I'm the kind of guy who would have walked up to ya and been like, 'Hey, Dude, what's up with your dog? It looks like Freddie Krueger!' "

"Hmmm. I think I'm one of those wide berth types. That's probably why all this happened to me. Anyway…."

∧∧∧∧∧∧∧∧∧∧∧∧∧∧∧∧∧∧∧∧∧∧∧∧∧

Incredibly, Dancer recovered completely that year. She wound up with tiny scars on both front elbows, but that was it. She could run again, play again, eat cat shit again, dig up roses and other expensive bushes again.

Dancer and Nubbin stayed best buddies until the morning Nubbin caught the front wheel of a fast moving car with her face and was killed out front of our house. It happened the night before the girls and I were leaving for Smith Rock for a five day climbing trip. The timing couldn't have been worse.

I drove the forty lonely minutes down to their mom's house, packed them in the car and then headed back to our house. I couldn't talk. I was terrified of what I had to say and kept forming sentences in my head. None of them were tactful enough or kind enough. Just before we got home I told them I had some terrible news. I told them Nubbin had been killed. I told them she had been hit by a car out front of the house. That was all I said.

There was a second or two of silent registration and then the two of them opened up the flood gates and started wailing and squirting tears all over the car. It was terrifying to see them so distraught, but I held the wheel steady and kept my focus straight ahead. Something inside told me to let them go. They bawled like this for a good five minutes and then they stopped. We put

Nubbin in a little shoebox and buried her in the back yard. The girls put flowers on the dirt mound. We walked back up to the truck and headed off to Smith. With their bellies now cleared of the pain, they were fine the rest of the trip.

Dancer, however, was never the same. None of Zoë's other pets: the turtle, the fish, the parrot, the ferret, were any fun. By this point I was rarely bringing my kids around that house and getting another kitty made little sense.

Last year, two years after our divorce, Zoë called me late one night to tell me Dancer had been hit and killed out front of her house on the same street that had claimed Nubbin. She was sobbing and asked me if I would come up and hold her. I sat in the dark not knowing what to do. She hadn't called me in over six months. She was engaged to marry. Afraid to open my heart up again, I told her I was sorry, but that I couldn't come up there. I told her it was best to keep the cord clearly cut.

But it wasn't cut. And I lay there, guilt ridden all night, knowing I should have gone up to hold her. How sad. I didn't understand the rules back then. You don't stop loving just because someone did you wrong.

∧∧∧∧∧∧∧∧∧∧∧∧∧∧∧∧∧∧

"Hey, Johnson. Ya know what I just thought of?" Jake had his face inches from my head.

"Let me guess…" The young Burley had a rare gift for turning every utterance into a sexual reference.

"No, seriously, Johns. You know how you said you don't stop loving , just cuz someone did you wrong?"

"Yeah?"

"So… I'm making out with this girl and she starts rubbin' up against me and I wind up blowing my load in my pants. And why did I tell her that I was just sweaty? Was that kinda wrong?"

"Dude," I shook my head in feigned disgust, "you are the most over-sexed virgin I've ever known."

Alden Crag picked up the *Shipwreck* to resume his reading. All he said was: "Oh my God."

We pulled off for gas and grub in La Grande, Oregon. The boys bounced out of the car, their energy matching the late afternoon light. They were not supposed to be here. This was not my idea. This summer's pilgrimage to *The City* was to be a lonely mission of healing. The previous year had been a bewildering, emotionally draining overload and I needed time to grieve and bring some sanity back to my life.

The day before, the phone had rung as I started packing. It was Jake, the track superstar who I coached and mentored. When he heard my plans to go off rock climbing for a week he started whining in that voice he used when he wanted to sound three, "Hey, Johnson, I wanna go!"

I had tried to explain to him that no one was invited on this trip-- that I needed time. I wasn't sure I could climb. I knew I couldn't smile. I was a walking corpse of grief.

"I'm not fun anymore, Jake."

"That's cool, neither am I."

"No, seriously. It's bad. I'm a drag to be around. I can't even smile."

"So?"

How could I explain to a strapping, blonde, bubbly Mormon kid with two loving parents that the ex-wife #2 who I had been passionately off and on again with for the last thirteen years was getting married in two days... and that it made me sick because she wasn't in love, and you don't get married in middle age if you're not in love... and that only two weeks ago we had gone for a long walk and she'd told me that she wished she was still married to me... and she'd held my hand and kissed me in a way that let me know how much she still loved me... and that for the first time in over a decade of yearning for her tragically, I had been able to tell her that I loved her, but wasn't *in love* with her anymore, but with Ann, who was married and would probably stay married and never see me again. And yet, with all that said, I told her I didn't want her marrying someone she wasn't passionate about.

That walk with Zoë had been wonderfully surreal because earlier that same day Ann had shown up at my apartment to tell me that she was still *so in love* with me-- that she thought about me every millisecond-- and that she couldn't see me anymore because she was choosing to stay in her marriage for the kids.

And I drove home that night after a last tender moment with Zoë thinking how strange, strange, strange. How wonderful and strange.

And a week later, when the phone hadn't rung with Ann's voice anymore... and Zoë called to tell me she was going through with the wedding plans-- and I went to work to find out that the newly hired *Captain Queeg* * principal who had taken over our loving high school to crush all joy, kick out a handful of thugs and raise a few test scores had made the business decision to unload my teaching career... I knew I'd reached the breaking point. It was time to go away. And how did I explain all that to Jesus let alone Jake Burley?

I started heading out the door with another load of camping gear when the phone rang again. I knew it was Jake.

"Yeah?"

"Hi Keith."

It was Ann. She wasn't supposed to call me. But she had to. One last time. She had mailed me a 'Dear John' letter and she knew it wasn't right. The sound of her voice changed my landscape. She told me she was going to make it. She told me she still loved me. She told me she was going to stay in her marriage and raise her kids. She cried softly. And then I said something to make her laugh. I always made her laugh. I told her I loved her and that she would find her way. We said goodbye. And the sky had changed. There was color again.

The phone rang again. I knew it was Ann. I picked up the receiver and told her, "I love you so much!"

"Thanks." It was another one of my track stars, Alden Crag, telling me it was all right with his parents if he went with Jake and me.

"But....I...."

"Jake said you're bummin and it would be best if he had someone to hang with so he didn't annoy you too much."

I told him I was going to *The City* to write, to grieve, to spend time alone, to come to terms with this latest avalanche of loss. I added that I was as low as I'd ever been, a complete disaster, and absolutely no fun whatsoever.

"Sounds fine to me." Alden's voice hadn't registered a single click on the emotional Richter scale.

I told him I'd probably stay at '*The City*' two weeks, that I wasn't coming home in time for the beginning of the cross country season and that I'd already talked to Coach Erickson and explained my need to lay low for awhile.

"No problem. Jake and I already talked about it. We'll take a bus home." Alden Crag was smart.

I hung up and a few minutes later the phone rang. It was Jake. He told me he thought it would be fun to ride a bus all the way from Idaho to Kent. "I can sing Mormon songs with all the people on the bus."

I explained once again that I wasn't in the mood to fuss with cooking or taking care of anyone's needs. I added that the last thing I needed was to feel guilty cuz' I was failing to make someone happy. He laughed and offered up a line that would be the year's turning point:

"Dang , Johns," he said in all seriousness. "All I need is a couple packages of hot-dogs, some cheesy wieners, and a can of lighter fluid and I'm good for a week."

I laughed at that one. I didn't want to. It was too early since being shattered to even think of laughing. I was still a ruined man. Nothing could make a shattered, ruined man laugh. I knew that. And Jake Burley: "*I go to bed late and get up early*" already had.

Yeah, the boys could go.

Footnote:
Captain Queeg was the half-comic, half-tragic petty tyrant who took over the battle-scarred Navy Destroyer: The U.S.S. Caine, in Herman Wouk's classic novel about World War II, <u>The Caine Mutiny.</u> For me, the parallels between the hyper-paranoid Queeg and our new leader were frightening.

Act One

CROSSING ZION

"The Rules Have Changed Today
I Have No Place To Stay
The Lord Has Flown Away...
My Tears, Have Come and Gone
Oh My Lord, I Have To Roam
I Have No Home! I Have No Home."

Time Has Come Today -*The Chambers Brothers*
'Best rock anthem ever from'a band of brothers who rocked!'

From: "Sing alongs for a Shipwreck"

The Natural

There's a scene in the movie **The Natural** where Glenn Close and Robert Redford get together to have a lemonade and after a bit of small talk she leans up close and friendly and asks her former beau what happened to him- why with all the promise, potential, and dreams of being the 'best' there ever was- he dropped off the face of the earth? And for a moment he opens up to her and begins to reveal his dark secret, his vulnerability. "My life didn't turn out like I wanted," he offers meekly. Whereupon she validates his pain and insecurities by getting up and leaving.

That scene may be as simple as the theme of this narrative. I'm not sure how many of us had our lives turn out like we wanted. And, honestly, how many of us would have chosen the particular route we've wandered if God would have come down from on high and asked us to reveal the blueprint of our dreams? How many would have chosen to have the kids when we did, taken the job we didn't want, put up with the control-freaks, the in-laws, stayed addicted to lovers, supported friends, loved our family, cleaned the cat box-- if we didn't have to? And what if you didn't have to? What if you packed your car and left and wandered off in the muck until you either died or found your way home?

-From **The Shipwreck** *Journals*

LEAVING BEDFORD FALLS

I'd gone into the 80's with the mindset of a wrecking ball. I had a ton of energy and the dynamite to match. I had no idea what I was doing, but I thought I'd figure it out after the dust had settled. My thirties were all about taking risks, blowing up my life, seeking pleasure, accumulating objects, and proving once and for all that I too could be a man of substance. I was hell bent on acquiring Hollywood's version of success: romance, adventure, that beautiful house, the beautiful wife, the large automobile, all the neon signs that I was somebody of significance. I puffed up, postured, scrambled up short cuts, sought out quick fixes, and ran up the 7 easy steps to the top- any cost, any price for a chance to make the fear go away. And when I walked into the UW Football Stadium and stared at 70,000 people, I knew, without a doubt, that I was still a nobody. And my cheers seemed hollow. And my joy lacked passion. I'd become a moving target for Mormons and Amway.

-From the **Shipwreck** *Journals*

^^^^^^^^^^^^^^^^^^^^^^^^^^

[AUGUST 1992: LEAVING THE VALLEY OF TEARS]

Despite the exhausting effort required to row my boat against the tide of emptiness, I found myself still trying to fill the primal need for belonging with the singular attention of a woman. And in that stormy spring of '92, when Zoë and I called it quits after destroying another Mother's Day and the fury of impotence quickly transformed into the wasteland of grief, I realized I had walked away from my one and only friend. I was not just losing my lover, my wife, my mistress, my partner, but the only person who I had allowed to know me, to see all sides of me, to hold me when I cried, to love me when I was ugly. She had cured my loneliness and the fear of losing that singular connection to love's force was the bond that kept me addicted. Without her, I was alone on my raft in the middle of the ocean with no direction, no compass, and no paddle.

Now, as the late August rain fell against the windshield of my little Fesitva, I stared at the patterns of drops, and wondered where the bottom was to despair. And what about the effects of my choices on my kids? They'd watched me tumble overboard, had seen my world unravel, had watched my confidence and laughter fade away.

Now, all the posturing that had once appeared so vital and had allowed me to sacrifice my connection to my kids, had been kicked into a fetal position.

Now, doubt and fear leaked into my voice, my eyes, and sighs. It is one thing to fall off a ship and tread water until you figure out which way to swim. It's quite another to do it while holding two little darlings in your arms.

I pulled over to the side of the road, a map of the entire Western States tossed on the floor board. My fingers were white on the wheel. I sat staring at the wipers beating their mantra: "Which way, God? Which way, God?" Where was the place that could lead me to the truth? Canada? Wyoming? The Rockies? Southern Utah? The Sierras? I trembled like the guy who upon being released from prison, walks down the dusty block to a pay phone and asks if he can be let back in.

I thought of Krissy, who at the age of three, had stood at a candy counter with me, unable to choose between a hundred different treats. Her little face look worried and her lip dropped and her eyes shut down and I felt her tiny fingers grow rigid in my hand. And my heart broke because what was supposed to be fun, wasn't fun. And if buying a treat wasn't going to work, then what the hell was I supposed to do with the rest of the day? I wanted to call her right now and comfort her, and tell her I knew exactly how it felt to be scared of making the wrong choice. But she was with her mom and I was here paying for a choice I'd made back when Pac Man, beer, and Nazareth were an engrossing escape from the rigors of collegiate mediocrity.

I headed east on I-90 figuring an epiphany would pop as soon as I got out of North Bend. Climbing through a driving rain on Snoqualmie Pass, my windshield wipers could barely keep up with the onslaught. I started thinking that warm and dry sounded good. Scratch all mountain ranges. Maybe I'd just crawl back in my "safe" rut and head down to *Smith Rock*, Oregon.

Over the last few years, at the suggestion of a colleague, Coach J. Peters, I'd gotten in the habit of heading off to climbing areas by myself. "Best thing in the world for ya, having time alone, solitude. It's the key to getting well," he'd recommended.

Coach J. told me often that 'he knew my pain' and on our many walks he'd tried to shed insight my way without directing my path. When I talked of my troubles with Zoë he let me know that women were to be cherished, adored, and worshipped for what they do to the shape of our universe, for the pleasures they bring just by smiling in our direction, for the thrill of walking in front of us in a pair of jeans, for the beauty of their butts when they squat to pee outdoors, for the way they can be thoughtful and caring and nurturing and loving to all creatures, for their soft lips and softer skin, for the children they offer to the world, for rubbing their elbow against yours in a movie theater, for leaning over at just the right time in just the right way, for looking in your direction and making something in your loins burst forth thereby reducing your age in half, for all the wonders of life's greatest mysteries that . could only be known through knowing them.

"But!" he pointed out with a laugh, "As wondrous as their worth may be, they can never know our secrets completely. They do not have the cure for the disease of failure."

He went on to say that for a man to be truly whole, he had to be validated by another man. It was primal and as real as the beards we shave, the sweat on the balls we scratch, the stench of the jokes we think are funny, and the contortions we'll put ourselves through for a little recognition. We adore our women, but we love our friend. The friend can put up with our mistakes, our weaknesses, our need to push and to seek the limits of the envelope, our need to flirt, to help a little kid throw a ball, to lose our way and need a road trip for recovery. A friend knows the look, knows when to stand next to his brother, and when to shield him from the arrows heading for his heart. And he knows when to walk away and let him stand tall.

I had looked in his eyes, and despite his sincerity and beauty, felt that familiar ping of my shield protecting me from the closeness of another man. I was still a freak and Coach J. wasn't. He couldn't know me. No one could.

Despite my obvious aloofness, Coach J. wouldn't give up on me. He once grabbed me in the hallway after listening to my latest round of self-recrimination. This is what he told me on that day my soul had turned to a wasteland:

"Johnson, there is one difference between human beings and other people."

I looked up at him as his eyes narrowed and his finger came within an inch of my nose. "Uh-huh?"

"The ability to forgive."

Then off he went, with the light following him down the hall.

∧∧∧∧∧∧∧∧∧∧∧∧∧

Smith Rock was a place with blue skies, plenty of room, and fabulous rock. It was also social enough that one could meet interesting people from all parts of the globe. That sense of connection had been a great source of growth and healing over the past six years. But, things were different now. I wasn't sure I wanted to run into anybody. I had to figure this one out on my own. Smith might be too fun for me.

I pulled off I-90 in Ellensburg, the central hub of all roads leading somewhere wonderful. But, which road was *the way*? I anxiously limped out of the car and did some dynamic stretches as a Winnebago with Idaho plates pulled up and an ancient couple stared at me from the comfort of their fortress.

The couple stepped out and smiled my direction. They were about seventy and wrinkled as pitted prunes. I had my map spread over my hood.

"You look like you're heading somewhere," the little shriveled lady said in a kind, squeaky voice.

"Yep, going climbing. Although, I'm not quite sure where. Lots of choices."

"Oh yes!" she said with heart felt enthusiasm. "Washington is a beautiful state! Just beautiful! So many wonderful places to visit."

"Yes it is."

Her husband walked up with a map, bow legged, and quiet. She was the talker.

"We have been vacationing in Washington every summer since we retired."

"Where you from?" I plopped a leg up on my hood, stretching out my hamstrings.

"Elba, Idaho."

"Huh? I know Idaho pretty well, but I don't know where Elba is."

"Oh, it is a small town south of Rupert and west of Malta."

"Hmmm. I've heard of Rupert. I taught in a two room schoolhouse in Howe, Idaho, my first year out of college."

"Oh. Then you've certainly visited *The City of Rocks*. We live just a half hour from the park."

"*The City of Rocks*?" I looked at the little lady and answered back quickly, "Well, I taught in Howe, Idaho back in 1980. I heard of *The City* back then but I never went there."

"Oh. *The City* is wonderful. Just wonderful! Now climbers come from all over the world. Such nice people too. Germans, Italians, French. It's a beautiful place! Just beautiful! You should visit."

The way she said *visit* was so sweet. "Would it be too hot there right now?"

"Oh no. September is lovely in *The City*. Just lovely!"

There it was: *The City of Rocks*.

I laughed at how a complete stranger suggesting something could throw my heart wide open to a new idea, while listening to the pleas and prodding of someone close to me did little more than make me want to do the opposite. Leona Quinn, a struggling divorcee with voluptuous everythings, had been trying to get me to go to *The City of Rocks* for over a year.

"Long routes on perfect granite!" she'd told me over and over. "The place is magic. The camping is amazing. The sky goes on forever. And so does the climbing. Every time I go there I find something inside myself that I thought I'd lost."

Of course, I never went.

Now, some warmth and a hint of confidence was all I really wanted. Warm air, nice rock, alone time, and the space to sort out thirteen closets full of ghosts.

BURLEY AND TOWNE

I headed out of Ellensburg, hell bent for Idaho. I thought of calling Leona to see if she'd want to join me. But I couldn't do it. She was too good looking to be safe. I'd wind up wanting to do it, and then, right after we did, I'd feel guilty and want her to go home. I knew that. I needed to be in love to make love. And I was still in love with Zoë. Leona knew this. And she loved me for that. But, she still would have done it. And I loved *her* for that. But not this time. Not this trip. I needed to be alone. So I didn't call Leona.

The miles went by with my head drifting in and out of moments won and lost. I wondered what Zoë was doing, wondered how my kids were, wondered if I'd made a mistake in not calling Leona. I pulled over for gas in Baker, Oregon, terrified that this trip might lead me nowhere, that I might spend the entire time frozen in sorrow. I wasn't sure about *The City of Rocks*. What if I didn't like it, then what? Knowing how scared I must have looked, I tried not to make eye contact with the gas station attendant as he scrubbed my windshield.

The temperature on the *Bank of Idaho* sign read 83 degrees when I got out of the Festiva in Burley. Perfect. I stocked up on provisions at Alvin's Grocery, then realizing I'd forgotten my spaghetti colander, walked into the adjacent Thriftstore to pick one up. Rummaging through the second hand cooking ware, I noticed a shiny new strainer, priced at 50 cents. Underneath it was a misplaced, yellowish book. On the cover was an etching of a climber, stripped to the waist, giving the finger from a seated belay position. Three words fell out of my mouth: "OH MY GOD!"

There it was: ***The Book of Truths***, by Langdon Towne.

"I don't believe it!! Leona is going to shit!" I screamed as a blonde family with eight little kids picked through the dusty silver ware and cups. My hands trembled. Above the word '*Truths*' some kind soul had stuck on a little pink sticker with the price: 25 cents! And not only that, it was *half off everything in the store day*!!!

"Thirteen cents for the *Book of Truths*?!! You have got to be freakin kidding me?!" I shouted to the litter of toddlers crowding around me.

I grabbed the colander and the book and danced up to the counter, the first joyful moment I'd felt since Zoë took a bubble bath with me back in June. I asked the clerk if I could borrow a phone and she pointed outside to the payphone across the street. I ran over and dialed up Leona. Her answering machine let me know that she was out of town for a few days and to leave my name, number, and the time that I called and she would get right back to me.

I walked out of the booth almost afraid to open the cover. How had I managed this? What channel had I fallen in to? Maybe it was that same force where someone points out something to you, say a certain kind of car, and the next thing you know, that car is all you see on the road. Maybe Leona's constant references to her 'guru,' *Langdon Towne,* had raised my consciousness.

"Only 427 copies were ever printed," she'd told me. Her copy had been stolen out her Corolla while parked at a trailhead. It had been the low point of her own year of despair. I remembered her lamenting, "You would think that after I had that poster and those bumper stickers made up, God wouldn't have let some prick steal the one thing I actually valued in this whole damn world!" Now, here it was! *The Book of Truths*! I stared at the yellowing bit of wonder, knowing I was holding something profound and rare. I picked it up and randomly opened to **Truth #139**. Here is what it said:

TRUTH #139:

Your curse is your blessing, your blessing is your curse. They are one and the same. You will never find peace without a curse to move through. You will never experience sorrow without a blessing to lose. You will strive for perfection and fail. You will fall into despair and find your beauty. You could hold still and hear the same answers that you would find if you were to walk the deserts, mountains and valleys of the world. But you cannot hold still. It is your blessing. It is your curse.

∧∧∧∧∧∧∧∧∧∧∧∧∧∧∧∧∧∧∧∧∧∧∧

"Thirteen Cents?!" I cried to the heavens. "Holy, Mother of Buddha! I'm sorry Leona, there is a God!"

I ran to my car holding the book and the colander feeling like I not only needed a shower, but a cleansing of my entire being. Towne's truths while perched on a warm rock ledge above the abyss would be just the ticket home. Alone time. Healing time. At last I was ready. It was time to face down my life. It was time to find the truth.

ERIC SLOAN

The road to the park gave me time to ponder how thankful I was I hadn't invited anyone along on this trip. Besides my loathing of having someone and their baggage glued to my hip all the time, traveling alone allowed me the flexibility to discover random miracles such as walking into the Thriftstore. As the pavement turned to dirt, and the Festiva began to rattle, I looked in the rear view mirror and caught the fear in my eyes looking back. Yes... even though I was still scared, I would rather be alone.

I pulled into the *City of Rocks Reserve* as the setting sun turned the whitish granite to gold. Bounding about on warm, gorgeous boulders, all doubt faded as to whether this was the place. When the sun dipped away, I thought about my kids and decided to drive down to the town of Almo to see if there was a pay phone. As I drove up to *Tracy's Store*, an old, gray, rusted-out, van pulled out.

"Oh my God, that's Eric Sloan's van!"

I waved out the window and whipped my car around. Eric was a kid from Alaska my daughters and I had met at Smith Rock in the spring. He was living out of his van and following the warm weather from one climbing area to the next. He had become a good climber and a great dumpster diver, able to eek out a couple weeks of eats off a $1.50 and somebody else's left-overs.

"Eric!!! When did you get here?"

Eric stuck his shaved head out the window, and smiled in a way that suggested he had been expecting me to show up any minute. "Dude, two weeks! It's been *sooo* nice! This place is awesome!"

"How are you?"

"I'm doing good, except I tore something in my shoulder the first week I got here."

"Ouch!"

He grinned, nodded, and said real slow in his twangy voice, "Crankin the crimpers."

My daughter, Kate was the one who first introduced me to Eric. Standing in the Smith Rock parking lot, waiting for the rest of us to come out of the canyon, she had started talking with a scruffy teenager who was sitting in his van, carefully preparing carrots and potatoes for his evening meal. He invited her in out of the chilly wind, and the two of them were a force by the time the rest of us came walking up. Eric had his MSR stove fired up on the pavement next to my car, his soup simmering away, with Kate giggling and talking a mile a minute.

I soon found out that Eric was a teenager from Anchorage, who, upon graduating from high school, had worked through a long summer, saved every penny he made, bought a Dodge Van, and then drove the Al-Can highway with the sole intent of earning his stripes as a fully committed climbing bum. Upon arriving in the lower 48, with winter on the way, he had headed south, winding up in the southern states of Arizona, New Mexico, and finally Texas. After wintering in Heuco Tanks he had started migrating north, trying to arrive at climbing areas, just as the season was in its prime.

The next day at Smith Rock, we hooked up with Eric and as we walked down to the dihedrals area, ducking under overhangs during rain and snow flurries, he told us of his year of growth. As he talked I realized the kid had rocketed into man hood thanks to the main ingredient that shapes the character of all human beings....suffering.

Pain and loss, if handled appropriately, are the great teacher. Suffering leads to self-examination and consequent humility. One learns to ask for help, to have faith in self, to accept one's plight, and to give thanks for anything that goes right on any given day. "Without hard work and suffering there could be no pleasure worth having," John Muir had said. No doubt, Eric was living Muir's truth, working his fingers to the bone on every rock climb he could hike up to.

Eric knew the meaning of *destitute*. He'd run out of money in Albuquerque and learned how to locate food banks to fend off starvation. His Dodge van had broken down in Texas, whereupon he'd learned what a "Temp" agency was and how it felt to stand in line with down and out men, waiting all day for a chance to work hard labor at minimum wage. Eric got to Heuco Tanks with money enough to camp for free and live off scraps and cast offs that campers and hikers tossed in the garbage. "Calories were calories," he had said.

My little family sat under the overhang of *Chain Reaction*, listening and learning from this scrawny kid who had wandered into our lives for no other reason than the fact that Kate was not afraid to talk to anyone.

One of the perks of taking my girls climbing every weekend had been that they got to hang with men who were out having fun. Sometimes it was a group, sometimes just another partner, but there was one constant in every encounter, all these guys were full of life and they all adored my girls. Thus, every other weekend, my kids would be filled with kindness and genuine love from the words and actions of an array of men. The girls were treated as unique individuals, validated as worthy, and listened to with patience and interest. This community of climbers, which I often grew tired of, was our one haven; our shelter from the storm.

The side effect was my daughters learned to trust men, to talk to strangers, to listen to the stories of all people, whether they looked shiny or not. They learned that the cover to each book, was just something to flip open, and that the real story lay inside, waiting to be told. They learned to listen, and that *every one* will talk to you and treat you with respect if you simply act sincere and utter… "Hi."

The girls learned that "Hi" was all it took to make a new friend, to become someone important, to develop a relationship that would add color to one's life. They learned that partners would come and partners would go, but love stayed constant if one stayed in the flow.

∧∧∧∧∧∧∧∧∧∧∧

"How *you* doing, Keith? How's Zoë and the kids?"

"That's why I'm here." I smiled and did my best imitation of Eric's inbred okie voice. "Healin the heartache." I went on to tell my tale of the last six months of trial by marriage.

When he'd seen me at Smith, Zoë had shown up with her son Peter. Despite the snow flurries and rain squalls that had swept through our campsite, we appeared to be a 'happy' family. By the third night, the relentless bone chilling wind had forced us to pack and head for a motel.

I remember feeling lucky as I paid for the last room available in the only Motel I'd spotted with a vacancy sign. As I handed over the cash, several large Native Americans with baseball caps and beers poured through the door, joyfully asking for room keys. They'd locked themselves out again. Turns out, we'd found a room during the annual 'Soft-Ball-Tournament' and were sharing the motel with a legion of hammered batters who seemed bound and determined to outdo the joy of last week's excess with a night of pounding on walls, pissing on sidewalks and locking themselves silly out of rooms with screams of "Budweiser!!!" reverberating out of windows til dawn.

That, of course, had been our last trip as a family. Now it was just my daughters and me. And my Festiva.

After my phone call to the girls, Eric had me follow him to his camping spot just outside of Almo. It was a circular pull-out area next to the Almo dump. Though lacking in wilderness charm, the sight was free.

That night the pristine desert sky shimmered and the temperatures plummeted. In my attempt to not over-cram my tiny Ford, I had left behind my bulky, ancient, -15 degree sleeping bag. Instead I'd brought my 'brand new,' ultra-light Minima synthetic bag rated to 40 degrees. When I pulled it out of its tiny virgin stuff sack, it looked like two sheets of pressed nylon. Hmmm...

Around 1:00 AM I awoke shivering and began trying to find more clothes to put on my head in an attempt to keep warm. Nothing helped. I turned on my headlamp to see if there was an article of clothing that I had missed and spotted two pair of underwear which I promptly slid over my head. Lying next to my sleeping pad was the *Book of Truths*. Since sleep wasn't an option, I opened the cover, and peered through a leg hole to see what Towne had to offer. I read Truth #4. Here is what it said.

TRUTH # 4:

You are not alone. Pull your head out, look around and join the human race. Quit being a self-absorbed prick trying to mask your insecurities by hiding behind the smokescreen of petty accomplishments. Did you design the flowers, the tamarack, or southern Utah? Did you come up with the idea of 'cumming' to reproduce? Well, then, shut up, take a deep breath, and quit saluting yourself. Instead, walk up to any stranger in any grocery store and ask them how their day is going. Chances are, if they think you're sincere, they will tick off a list of tribulations that will have you thanking your lucky charms you were born in your skin and not theirs. That is enlightenment.

^^^^^^^^^^^^^^^^^^^^^

I set the book down and closed up my sleeping bag hood. 'No wonder Leona loved this book!' I thought of one of our walks up the trail to Little Si, with me growing a touch jealous as she rattled off these *Truths* which she considered gospel. Ever competitive for undivided attention, I pointed out that some of Towne's visions were nothing more than *bastardized* versions of inspirational quotes I'd read somewhere else. I suggested that 'just maybe' her *Guru* was a bit of a pirate, plundering the philosophical riches of far greater minds than his own.

The conversation went silent, as if Leona were trying to see if my face was serious or not. Sensing my insecurities, she calmed me down by telling a story of how she'd been at an *Elliot Bay Book Store* reading where Towne had openly admitted to stealing quotes with a 'devil may care' attitude. She said that during the writing of the *Book of Truths* he had quickly run out of original thoughts and began pilfering, as he put it: "Words of wisdom from dead-people." When a hand went up and he was questioned about his ethics, Towne replied: "Fuck em if they can't take a joke. The fact that I didn't write it, doesn't diminish the importance that somebody once said it. Nobody has ever filed a lawsuit against writers of those illustrated sex-manuals who stole all their contorted positions from books written in India before Christ!" Leona said that comment had brought the house down.

SCREAM CHEESE

The next day the sun arose brilliantly and Eric, who had the five star routes dialed, took me on a tour of *City of Rocks* classics. Following Eric around like an old dog with a new bone, it was hard to remember that I'd left for this trip, gravely concerned that I might be too beat up to climb.

Just a week before, I'd taken a massive leader fall off an overhanging sport route after breaking *Cardinal Climbing Rule #1:* Don't Climb Angry. Blind from rage over Zoë cancelling a date, I'd climbed a route four letter grades harder than I had any business leading. Near the top, with forearms flaming, I'd boldly skipped a protection bolt in an attempt to show the universe that I was a man. Right before the anchor chains, my hands began to open up and my legs went into sewing machine spasms. I stared at the chains of safety, four vertical feet above me, knowing that if I grabbed them I was saved and that if I went any farther and fell, I'd most likely be dead. It was one of those phenomenal: 'And seconds became minutes'...moments.

Divine prudence intervened. I warned my belayer- 80 feet below me- that I was going to fall, then shoved off and flew into the void. The ensuing whip into the lower wall felt like the impact of a car wreck. Relieved to be alive, I inspected the damage, thinking I'd surely broken both my ankles. Upon being lowered to the ground, I realized they were still functional, but my lower back felt like every disc had been flattened and fused. I limped home in tears, once again questioning the virtue of anger.

But that was a week ago. Now, though it hurt to walk, I needed to walk. And though climbing still seemed self-serving, I need to climb. Climbing still did absolutely nothing to solve a single problem that any one on the planet would consider worth while. And yet, without the magic of the wand that had swept over me on those rocks with Eric, there was no point in going another step. There would be no resume to fill when I got home. There would be no job. There would be no me. Climbing today hadn't been about facing life and death. Just life. My life. I needed it back and those few hours, ascending and laughing with Eric, had reminded me why I was here. On the last climb, Eric ran the rope up a 5.8 ultra classic called Skyline. Had I led the route, it would have taken me an hour to place enough protection to feel safe. But Eric, seasoned from a year of running it out on monstrous nut busters, flew up the climb, relaxed and placing safety devices scantily. Inspired by his performance, I expected to dance up behind him. However, moves he had flown through, were giving me second thoughts and at one point-- when I reached the edge of a short blank slab with a roof above it and no obvious way around the crux-- I had shouted up,

"Hey, Eric, WHICH WAY?"

Down from the top came his okie-twang, "Summit or Plummet!"

I grimaced at the joke, my hands sweating in the chilly air.

"THANKS!" I shouted up. "This thing's hard!"

Eric shouted down, "IF IN DOUBT, FOLLOW THE ROUTE!"

That cracked me up. A *Towne-ism* from the mouth of a babe.I started laughing and noticed the rope running past a series of under-clings. I followed its path and flashed through an 'easy' sequence of juggy handholds with my feet smearing lightly across a bunch of nothing. Just past the roof I could finally see Eric's head fifty feet above, poking over the top.

Within minutes I had climbed up next to his tiny perch at the top of the *Incisor.* The moves had felt great once I'd relaxed and quit worrying about trying to keep up with the kid. As the sun dipped behind the western hills, we rigged up our rappel.

"Eric, I think the trick to life is like that series of moves down there; don't think too much."

"No doubt. Sometimes you just gotta go. It's like, when you're stretched out to your max, trying to make a desperate clip, yarding in a ton of rope, and there's that little sick moment... If you start thinking right then about how truly fucked you really are: dude, you're hosed."

We got off *Skyline*, alive with that energy so singular to high risk sports. It feels as if every cell of your body has been kicked into perfect balance; your vision clear; your focus crystalline. I started coiling up the ropes and Eric bounced over and said, "Hey, *Scream Cheese* is open, let's run up that before we go down to the dump."

I looked at him knowing what he was thinking. He wanted me to lead the route. (*Scream Cheese* is a bolted 5.9 classic, with a spooky run out between the 4th and 5th bolt. Hence the name: *SCREAM Cheese*.) Eric had been talking about me doing it since I showed up.

We arrived at the base of *Scream* and dumped out gear on a slab of pocketed granite. I walked up to a sloping ramp just below the first bolt and started flaking out the climbing rope. I kept taking huge breaths of air, trying to relax.

Eric piped up. "How you feeling bro?"

"Oh, pretty gripped. You know what I was just thinking about?"

"Nuclear war?"

"Not exactly. I was thinking I may never get over wanting to have sex with Zoë. I wonder if I'll ever meet someone powerful enough to blast her out of my soul?"

"Dude, you'll meet somebody when the time is right. You gotta close the door on that one before another love come through."

"I'm not sure about love anymore."

"Well... is it love you're after, or companionship?"

"Both."

"Cuz, you *have* companionship."

"Yeah, but a *companion* isn't someone you want to kiss in the morning."

"Well, I don't know about that." Eric started giggling, "You haven't even tried me yet."

The act of climbing bonds you temporarily to your rope mate in a way that is remarkably intimate. Good partners are kind to each other no matter what, and eventually, after being together countless times, can speak without talking; the voice of their movements telling each other everything that is essential to reach the summit.

I looked up at the roof below the 5th bolt, swallowed hard, tied the sharp end of the 10.5 rope into my harness and handed a loose coil to Eric. He shoved a bite into his belay device as I reached my arms shoulder high and lightly placed my fingers on gorgeous suit-case handle edges. The finish line loomed 90 feet above.

I took another huge breath, dipped one hand into my chalk bag, and shifted my focus to that "leader" mode... where nothing is allowed in the head but positive energy. There are no thoughts of failure, of falling, or missing a move. It is pure white focus.

The first two bolts were easy to reach, but the climbing above got steeper, and the holds became finger-tip width. Above the 4th bolt was a roof, (my nemesis as my recent injury would attest.) I climbed up under the overhang and tried to feel blindly above for handles on which to yank myself through. I felt nothing of the sort.

(Note: The trick with the *Cheese* is to pick the right sequence of holds. Blow that, and you've got a good chance of flying off the wall. At that point it's up to your belayer to clamp down on his device and save your life. Thus, the saying, 'my life is in your hands,' truly applies here. Consequently, the realm of belayed climbing is all about trust, a peculiar irony to the sport, as most climbers I've met have trust issues crowding their closet.)

I felt a slight hint of panic zap through me and then clicked it off. I could feel my forearms pumping up and tried to place my feet in a way that would take the torque off my arms. It was time to move or I wouldn't be able to grab anything. I stepped left on to an incut foothold and launched up, slapping my hand above me. I found a couple of tweakers and grabbed for all I was worth just as my right foot cut loose, sending my body in a barn door motion.

Eric yelled out encouragement from below, preparing himself to hold my fall. But I didn't fall. I don't know why or how, but my feet miraculously reconnected with the wall and my fingers held firm.

Shaking on my tiny holds, I hollered down, "Shit! That was close!"

"You off route?" He yelled up.

"Yeah, but if I can stick the next move, I can make the clip. Watch me close. Kay?"

I pulled myself up over the lip, and grabbed a set of tiny edges that felt like jugs.

"Nice!" Eric yelled up.

After leaning left and making two committing moves, I looked at the slab above me and realized all the decent holds- except a couple of sick looking blunts with sharp little points- were gone. They were all I had, so I stepped up on the last good foot hold and reached for two peanut shaped finger holds. I pinched them for all I was worth and carefully lifted a leg, my breath coming in spurts.

"Watch me!"

"I Gotcha, bro. Hey! You got this thing…. You look good!"

I pulled through the remaining part of the climb and reached the anchor chains in wild elation. Throwing my arms in the air and screaming at the sky, I was grateful for the chance to re-gain some honor. For a moment, I knew the warrior in me would never quit. As the Idaho sunset began to paint my face in deepening shades of pink, I understood why outcasts, misfits, and freaks were attracted to this sport. It's a circus for the damned, a playground for the children who missed the bus to Joy-Ville. It was the only place I dared to go when my ship started sinking. Where else in this world could one's heart be transformed in seconds from wreckage to a yacht?

WELCOME TO MY HOLE

That night, before retiring, I thanked Eric for talking me into leading again. I headed for my tent and arranged my clothing as best I could, trying to gain a few degrees of warmth. With my Minima sleeping bag hood pulled tight around my head, I lay in the darkness, cheering myself up with a kaleidoscope that was all about Zoë. I thought of a night, when after we separated for the third time and I swore upon the altar of God that I would never, ever- so help me God- be suckered in to her web again!….I wound up at her house because she had called and told me in that breathy voice of hers that she was sick and tired of petting her cat on a Friday night. When I got there she was dressed in a loose fitting scarlet robe, and kept leaning close to me, pouring cups of *Sleepy Time* tea. Later, after her teenage boys had gone off with friends for the evening, she asked me to come to bed and read with her. Zoë, was probably the most well-read person I'd ever known. Being gainfully involved in endless post grad classes and book clubs, there wasn't much under a hard cover that she hadn't devoured. She had an unquenchable thirst for knowledge, was infinitely curious, and could carry on a conversation with anyone from a street bum to a senator. "Bums are a lot more interesting," she had once quipped. These striking qualities of hers, so unlike the rigid shiny box I was hiding in, were what I had admired most and had wanted so desperately. And it was these exact same qualities that soon led to a constant source of friction as she was always leaving to attend lectures, book clubs and readings instead of staying home and crawling in to bed to pound my bones. I could never understand it. To me there was making love to her and then everything else. To Zoë, there was everything else, and then me.

But, on this one night, with the house empty, the door closed, the planets aligned, and the two of us getting along famously, she asked me if I was ready to read her some of the stories I'd been writing since we'd separated. I told her no. I explained to her that because she was so entangled with me she might be offended, or even worse, she'd have to sit there and say something nice even if she hated it. She smiled at my insecurity and then scrunched up to me, rubbed my shoulders, and put her mouth to my ear. My resolve destroyed, I headed out to my car and came back with a collection of shorts and poems I'd written during the previous year.

"Uhm, I started nervously, "I'm just going to read you a short one. OK?"

"OK!" She smiled and grabbed her knees-- all ears.

The Winner

Winners always have a reply that is a little too canned-- a look that is a little too calm.
Winners don't know where the dirt is-- don't know where the dark is.
Winners can't handle losing and will blame and destroy in the face of it.
Winners know that loss is the great enemy and grief is its whoring mistress.
Winners have rights and the world is fair and just to them.
Winners are to be feared-- they will not understand you when you cry.
Winners want heroes, though the heroes they admire are never real, since all true heroes have a dark side, a painful side, which led them to the light and greatness.
And these are the true heroes:
They are the single moms, raising children on hope and a dime.
They are the single dads, showing up each and every Wednesday and alternate weekend to give their child a slice of their life.
They are the humbled, stopping to help a lady fix a flat tire on the side of the road.
They are the ones who would hold your hand and let you cry if your world collapsed.

I didn't look up, but could hear Zoë staring at me. In a voice so gentle you could balance a feather on its notes, she asked if I would read another. So I did. I told her it was a little something I'd written about those dreaded weekends when the girls were with their mom and I was sitting in a strange room somewhere, waiting by the phone for *Zoë* to call me.

I write from the desert, for I am lost in that wasteland that is myself, my agony, my despair. I am too frightened to move, with so much needing to be done. Trapped by the pain, I can go neither forward nor back...just locked here where I have been for years and years. Each time I break out, I briefly see the light only to plunge back in again. I cannot eat, or sleep, and feel my body killing itself. For a month I do not rest. I rage through each day, am hunted down each night. Like a cornered beast, I move quickly to guard my exposed heart, strike back quickly to defend my vulnerability. Turmoil creates chaos, which leads to madness.

She called me last week, our anniversary and all, to tell me she still loves me. Of course, I tell her to come see me. And why not? What is left of my heart that is worth defending? I have watched the magic dry up as the last two weeks spiraled out of control. There is nothing left of me, but questions and pain. So she comes to hold me, then leaves. I sleep with the smell of her neck on my face.

My children, her children, the two of us, my parents, we are all hurting. I sit and ask God what to do, what is the lesson in all this? And the answer comes again: To heal myself, to become the person I have always wanted to be. But how? And life goes by, each day a miracle that I don't see, because I miss her and miss the feel of her hand more than anything on this earth. I travel with the weight of failure and despair pulling me down, down off my mountains to the gutter.

She kissed me last week. As if from God, the sun came out and messes created over the past weeks, were neatly packed up and dealt with. Her kiss unleashed the knots that were torturing my face and neck. My skin regained some suppleness, my eyes had a hint of focus. All this because of her, because she touched me and affirmed my worth. How pathetic to be dependent on her praise of me. How resentful I am that I need her. How lost I am without her voice.

Zoë sat in a hush for about thirty seconds and then said softly, "You know Keith Mark, whenever I've taken five minutes to slow down, whenever I've held still, I've trembled in dread of being faced with me, of being alone, of being empty, of having to listen to the tapes in my head of how I ruined my life, your life, your parent's life, your daughters' life, their mom's life, my boys' life; how there is nothing I can do to change what's happened, there is no going back, and I'll never, ever, be able to pick up the pieces and put it right."

She buried her face in my chest and let me hold her. Trying to be gentle, I

hummed the only lullaby I could remember:
"And when the bow breaks, the cradle will fall
And down will come baby, cradle and all."

I had wanted to see Zoë every night after that evening of love. She, however, found a church club to join and combined with her job, her three boys, two other clubs and a women's group, didn't have time for my silly needs. As a result, she didn't call me until I had totally given up and gotten her out of my system.

THE BERLIN WALL

On the morning of the third day, the etchings of another chilly, sleepless night were cut into my face. As I downed an extra cup of coffee, I realized I was running out of zip. I felt drained and anxious. Used to not sleeping since I gave birth to my first born child, I didn't mind the fact that I was averaging under three hours a night. It was the sickly anticipation of helpless shivering that started getting to me. I began mulling over in my mind the possibility of heading further south in search of warmer rock.

I sat with my cup of coffee, my yellow steno pad, and *The Book of Truths.* Eric came over and burst into an okie wail. "YO! Dude!! How did I know you'd be one of the people with that book?! The *Truths* was the talk of Camp Four in the valley. A couple guys said they'd even seen a copy."

I grinned. "How do you like the cover?"

I held it up for him. He smiled at the shot of Towne giving the finger and then opened the book. Here it what he read:

TRUTH #58:

If you ever catch yourself getting cocky or arrogant, look up in the sky and apologize. Yes, apologize your ass off and then drop to your knees,cuz you just fucked up big time, and the only way out will be to wade through whatever vat of Kim Chee God chooses to dump your way for being such an asshole.

∧∧∧∧∧∧∧∧∧∧∧∧∧∧∧∧

That night we built a fire out of wood scraps from the dump and were joined at our campsite by two East German climbers: Herman and Gus. The Berlin Wall had just come down and these former enemies of freedom were now fully enjoying their first tastes of America. That we could be sitting next to a field of cows in Idaho, discussing issues with a couple of 'communists,' seemed surreal. I thought about how I had spent my entire youth living with the specter of nuclear annihilation. It had always been there, very real, and very evil. I remember getting taught in grade school to duck and cover if the bomb went off. There was a plan for the ages.

We'd learned from our leaders that, Communism was bad, and the people who lived under it were bad, and that we were good and God liked us best, because even our money said: "In God we Trust." Of course, most of us weren't sure we trusted anybody, including God, and by the time the Vietnam War had wormed its way through the senior class of our high school, most of us sophomores had figured out that the only thing bad about the world was the adults running it. We didn't really care who those adults were, we just figured all of them were trying to kill us. And so it went until the wall came down and all those kids from the other side, who had felt just like us all along, poured over to the west and raised their fingers in peace.

And just like that, we all knew we weren't going to die of radiation poisoning. And for a brief moment, I remember feeling a tad less guilty that I'd brought children into this world.

Now, sitting next to Gus and Herman, as the fire of plywood and stumps crackled, I breathed in a sigh of praise for this incredible moment of proof that good had triumphed over evil.

Herman and Gus told stories of existence behind the wall, with its shortages, evil working conditions, pollution, apathy, depression and surrender. Gus talked about the fall-out of tyranny; how the twisted hand of Stalin had stolen any sense of peace and creativity, replacing it with bitterness and paranoia.

Staring into the flames, I couldn't help but think that on a smaller, very personal scale, the heinous conditions on the East Side of the wall were a metaphor for the disillusionment and disappointments of relationships, love and life. Who on this planet could truly look in the mirror and say they were free? Who was free of meaningless obligations, and self-inflicted tribulations, and stupid choices, and fears and neurosis that crippled passion and one's willingness to give and love and prosper? I had never met an adult yet who felt he had done all he could with his life. So often I had found myself staring at a clock of nothingness, unable to escape the weight of futility as anger and discouragement captured the best of intentions. So often I had stood in awe as the winds of absurdity tore through my sanctuary, sweeping my wits and reasoning over, down and across mine fields and barbed wire to a place where the sun couldn't penetrate the soot and ashes, where birds couldn't be heard through the blowing whistles and sirens, where a valiant heart that did not know where to go or where to turn, afraid that the safety net had vanished, that all roads led back to despair, that all hope of life ever being kind was lost-- had faded to cowardice under a steel gray sky. Love, had always been my war zone.

I looked up at Gus and Herman and blurted out, "I've been married my entire adult life, and I could count on one hand the weeks of happiness I've known."

I gave them a short summation of my first marriage and my cycle of sorrows with Zoë. I talked slowly, trying my best to explain our on again/off again tragedy. How we became the couple I swore I would never be, stomping out of restaurants, making up three weeks later, stuck on a roller coaster that would have put most tax paying Americans in a *White Room*, banging their heads off a padded wall.

Upon hearing my reference to the Cream classic, Herman perked up and grinned into the fire, "Vite Room, yah. Ees Goot."

Gus, who spoke better English, looked right at me and started singing the haunting chorus, sending shivers up my sciatic nerve.

"I'll vait, in dis place, vhere da sun never shines
Vait in dis place, vhere da shadows run from demselves."

I was stunned. "Dude! I grew up on Cream."

"So deed I." Gus grinned.

Gus, went on to say that he was on this trip to get over a tragic relationship, that he too was still not over his ex, that he couldn't find anyone or anything to replace her face. "Nudding compares," he'd said while gazing into the fire. As I listened to him paint a tale, strangely parallel to mine, the lesson broke through that no matter the origin, race, religion, color, age, amount of training, education, life style or income: love was love and heartbreak was heartbreak. Gus and I had that kinship of soul wreckage that connected us like lost brothers. He knew what I knew. He felt what I felt. We were a couple of veterans of love's war of wasted nerve endings.

Gus told us that to survive conditions in the Soviet Bloc, they'd done what all teenagers do: fallen in love with music and scored an education through the school of rock and roll. They were a breathing library of rock, from the Beatles to the Blues to Nirvana, they knew every album, song, and trivia headline. Rock and youth, the antidote for tyranny.

Suddenly Eric, who hadn't said a word in over an hour, piped in with: "Hey Keith, show these guys *The Book of Truths*."

At that I handed *The Book* to Gus, who took one look at the cover and said: "Eef you effer haff fife meenitts of hoppiness, git on your knees and pray!"

"What the ...?!!!"

We all lost it, slapping hands and staring at each other in disbelief.

"You are shitting me!" I screamed. "You can't even get a copy in this country. How the hell do you know this stuff?"

"Ya! Towne ees big in central Europe. Much guilt and much pain. Peoples luf Towne."

Eric and I just stared at each other.

Gus told us that just before the Berlin wall came down, a copy of *The Book of Truths* made its way east and with the black market being what it was, within a month there were thousands of copies in print at $19 American dollars a pop. Capitalism at it's finest.

Gus flipped through the book looking for his favorite page. He found it and let me read it to the crowd. It was Truth # 48. Here is what it said:

TRUTH # 48:

If you make love with a new flame and find yourself longing for the one that got away, make up an excuse and leave before she has a chance to finish her cigarette. This simple test will save years of confusion, guilt, and heartache. If at all possible, do the deed at her place, to expedite a safe and hasty retreat. Remember, it is not your fault and if you decide to stay, no amount of sedation is going to unravel that knot of misery.

^^^^^^^^^^^^^^^^^^^^^^^

While we giggled, Gus let me know that the test worked. I studied his young face and thought, 'God, oh God, the years we waste pining for what we could never handle even if we could have it.'

Before we retired for the night, the four of us did the climber thing of emphatically exchanging numbers we'd never find time to call. I crawled in my icy tent and tried to imagine the life of people who had been invaded and conquered and forced to live under oppression. How could those human beings not have fallen into despair? Despair. It seemed such a fitting image for the plight of man, people trapped in lives that were not their own, prisoners of systems, careers, duties, and titles, prisoners of relationships.

My mind drifted to the barbed wire and mines that exist for so many of us stuck in a marriage gone bad, metaphoric, but as real as the Berlin Wall. I opened up my steno pad and let my pen move across the page.

The Prison

You awake one night in a bed with someone who does not know you. You wouldn't be there except that person lying next to you signed a contract claiming your life, binding you to services rendered unto death.

Your life becomes a series of "going through the motions with a smile on your face," taking care of necessities, birthdays, holidays, bills, little thrills to let the world know you are a happy family, while you learn to find little places to escape: the shower, the bathroom, sitting in the car in parking lots, where your eyes go blank and the reality that you cannot get out grabs your throat and pulls you down, stealing the air from your lungs.

It isn't your significant's fault. It isn't yours. You were too young. The kids didn't help-- forced the two of you even farther apart with the constant demands and the 24/7 responsibility. Now the kids are all you have in common. That look they get when the two of you are together; that little glow of happiness is the only thread binding your heart to her.

Your glance becomes more desperate as you search for something to restore your sense of joy. You look for beauty and distraction while you hear your voice whine inside your core: "I'm getting old before my time."

Your wife wants comfort, so you walk into another room. The next day, feeling guilty, you buy her a present and agree to take a trip. This starts a new routine of buying and planning, perfect antidotes for the vacuum of emptiness, mopping up your soul. The "things" you buy bring little smiles and the trips you endure bring little more than a deeper tear in a pocket that is beyond mending.

You built your life, your character, your fiber on doing the right thing, on being strong, stoic in the face of adversity, on taking care of others, of being loyal, faithful, and able to take what is left after the meal is finished. You've read all the books, all the magazine covers at the check out line. You know that marriage is hard work, love is hard work, kids are hard work, life is hard work. Nobody is really happy. Love is an illusion, something that happens to somebody else, but not to anyone you know. You aren't sure if anyone loves anyone. It is all obligation and ownership, rights and correctness.

You know about the hard work, you've done it and the gray hair in the mirror does not lie. You can do the work, but hard work always has a goal, an end, a horizon of hope for which to strive for. But marriage? Marriage has become a life sentence. No way out. Never.

Thoughts of leaving are immediately washed away with the cries of your children, the anguish you would have to see in their eyes. There is no way you say over and over and over.

You make the sandwiches in the morning and little crumbs fall on the counter. You dab one with your finger and look at it. Whatever happened to happiness? What happened to hope?

You vow to try harder. You decide to work more, buy more, plan more, put on a better smile, a better face, get the kids to more and more activities. And in the rear view mirror, the strange, fearful glaze in your eyes will not go away. You make a smile, say something amusing to your kids, and look back. It is still there. It is always there. The beauty in you is gone.

One day you are walking back to the car, pushing the grocery cart, kids tagging at your heels, and a woman you've never seen before gets out of her car and glances your way. The look lasts no more than a second, but she smiles, and you reply with the slightest, send her no messages, acknowledgment. You drive away with the tiniest glow, like one birthday candle on a *middle-aged cake, burning away in the darkness.*

After the groceries are put away you glance at your face in a mirror. The glaze is gone. Your eyes are bright. You notice a smell in the air and it is lovely. You look out the window and see the garden and the leaves on the tree and they too have turned lovely. A song comes on the radio and you want to dance, but don't remember how and would feel like a fool. You dance anyway.

That night you curl up with a small fire warming your heart and fall off into dreams of swimming naked in a warm pool with a stranger sitting at the edge, a ring of keys dangling from her hand.

∧∧∧∧∧∧∧∧∧∧∧∧∧∧∧∧∧∧∧∧∧∧∧∧∧∧∧∧∧∧∧∧∧

I closed my eyes and tried to sleep. The first trickle of cold air found its way around the collar of my condom bag. Within minutes I was clenching my teeth and squeezing my arms against my sides trying to generate some body heat. My mind began racing with a whirling array of where to go, what to do, and how best to deal with being deep in Idaho with no way to stay warm. I began to question my choice to come here. This was nothing new. Every climbing trip I'd ever gone on had its maddening moments, its frustrations, and reasons to make me doubt why I hadn't chosen to go hang out in a warm, friendly, peaceful place or do something sane and predictable like normal, well adjusted folk talked about. I knew the answer to that one. I reached over and grabbed my pad and wrote another page.

∧∧∧∧∧∧∧∧∧∧∧∧∧∧∧∧∧∧∧∧∧∧∧∧∧∧∧∧∧∧∧∧∧∧∧

I have climbed my whole life, and at the top of every mountain is a sense that I wish I were in the arms of someone I loved. And upon returning home, love is busy, and in a hurry to be somewhere else. And I find myself wandering through my own emptiness again, wishing I could be back up on that mountain ridge again, stricken with purpose and vitality again, burning my legs in endless steps to the summit again, only to gain that piece of perfection and admire the view of a world I am missing again.

All my attempts to chase after this myth of happiness and purpose have led me to obsession and control of time. It is this sense of control that provides courage and power and a feeling of being truly alive. Yet, I am a prisoner of my own creation, and the second I reach my goal, there is nothing there on which to rest. All I can do is analyze what I have created, and it is never enough. There is always something wrong with the choice.

BOYD AND OKINAWA

In the morning, I sat staring at my cup of coffee. My throat felt sore and my joints ached. The sky was cloudy, chilly, and foreboding. The air smelled like snow. We went up into the park and climbed the Lost Arrow, but the fun was gone for me as the thought of another sleepless night had drawn a scowl down my cheeks. On the drive back to the dump I suggested to Eric that we take a trip south to Nevada or Utah in search of someplace exotic and toasty. I had just read in *Outside* that our nation's newest National Park, Great Basin, was located in south east Nevada. Given the size of Nevada, and with a name like *Great*, I figured we could wander some rugged winding canyons and endless ridges for a couple of days.

Eric made a face and looked over at me. "Dude, I've crossed Nevada three times and I've yet to see anything I would snap a photo of."

"Well, this *is* a National Park. It *has* to be decent, right?"

"You been to Nevada?"

I told Eric I would pay for gas, and he could buy groceries. That perked him up. We looked at the western states road map, eyeballed a line to Ely and figured it would be little more than five hours to Great Basin National Park.

With the Festiva carefully stuffed, we pulled out of the dump parking lot.

"Which way, Eric?"

"I'm guessin South." He was busy getting *Harvest Moon* punched in the tape deck.

"I know, but left or right?"

"Down"

"OK, smart ass, which way is that?"

Eric grinned and turned up the volume. "I don't think it really matters."

I let the Festiva wheel turn itself, and it went left. So we headed left and blasted off with Neil Young singing: "*On a desert highway...She rides a Harley Davidson....*"

After side one finished, we rolled up to a Post Office/General Store/Cafe, and a sign that read: NAF, Idaho. I was surprised to see that we weren't in Utah or Nevada, so I pulled over to ask for some directions. As I walked up to the screen door, I was greeted by a silver haired woman who boomed: "HI HONEY! Where you headed?"

"Howdy mam. We're going to Nevada. We want to get to Great Basin National Park."

"Well, you're not gettin to Nevada on this road, honey. Not, unless you want to add about two hundred miles to your trip."

"Really?" At that, the energized woman took us over to a huge map of Idaho, Utah and Nevada and showed us our error. We were heading to Wyoming. "Oh."

"You need to turn around and head back to Almo, and then take the fork to..." She rambled off the directions as my head thought about how it was already getting late and we had just added an hour to the five hour drive.

"You know, honey, since you are here, you two might as well sit down and have a hamburger. I make the best burgers in the state."

I could see Eric wince as the thought of spending more than ten cents per meal would break his budget. But, something told me to listen to this woman, so I looked at him with reassurance and said the magic words: "It's OK, I'll buy."

It was late in the day and the lights were on as we settled in to the NAF cafe. There were two older gentleman seated at an adjacent table nodding and sipping coffee. I hoped it was decaf.

The robust woman kept talking, "My name is Pat and this here is my husband Boyd and his adopted half-brother Lewis. You've come on a real special night honey. These two haven't seen each other since 1945."

I looked their way as a gong went off in my head. *1945*? As in World War II, *1945*?

The burgers were grilling and the warmth of the place loosened my shoulder blades. I liked Pat immediately. I liked this cafe. I liked these two old veterans. I listened to Boyd's story.

The two brothers had last seen each other several days before the U.S, invasion of Okinawa. Boyd was a boatswain mate aboard the U.S.S. Coleman and Lewis was on an aircraft carrier escort. Boyd asked his captain if he could visit his brother and was granted permission. Riding over in a tiny motorized raft, he found Lewis and the two talked late into the night.

The invasion of Okinawa began days later and Boyd's ship, which had eight landing craft, took part in the third attack wave. By the second attack wave the Japanese resistance was in full, hideous fury; Kamikazes desperately attempting to defend their last bastion.

Eric and I looked at each other trying to absorb the scale of the story we were being allowed to hear. I looked back to Boyd. Suddenly, his eyes welled up and he pointed and jabbed his finger as his voice became strangled. "For three-god-damn-days-the Japs pinned us down!!! Throwing every god-damn -thing that could fly at us! Every one of those landing craft wiped out!"

"And, and... you made it." I was struggling for words.

He shook his head and his eyes stared out at the beaches and the blood bath he had witnessed as an innocent twenty-year-old kid.

"I'll tell you right now, if Truman hadn't dropped that bomb, there wouldn't have been one American soldier left. There was no way we were getting on that Japanese mainland. They would have killed every last one of us! No survivors! The Japs would have fought to the last man."

"Jesus," I muttered quietly.

"He was a great man, that one. Best decision any President ever made."

There was a long silence. I tried to think of something poignant to say, and offered up, "After all the hell of World War II, how could man have failed to learn his lesson? How can there still be war?"

At that, Boyd practically leaped out of his chair as he jabbed his finger and sputtered:

"Because human beings are rotten, greedy, selfish bastards!! That's why!! Every, goddamn one of them! You! Me! All of us! Nothing can ever change that!"

Another silence, like the hollow after thunder, hung over us. Finally, Boyd spoke again.

"It's what we are. We're all trying to get through this thing, this life. Somehow, ya find a way to do the best ya can. Just try to do whatever you can to help out. Any way you can. Just help out. That's all you can do."

He paused and then looked at me as if he could see through my mask. "And try to shut down your feelings enough so you don't get angry about every-little-god-damn-thing. That's all you can do."

I nodded and looked at my burger.

We slowly finished up our meal, while Boyd and Lewis caught up on lost years. I studied Boyd's face and tried to imagine those three days on Okinawa, his frame pressed against the hot steel of his landing craft, a sitting bulls eye to bombs and hurtling aircraft, mates perishing in the tropical heat, the stench of death floating up from the beaches, the boats, the thousands of miles of Japanese rule. And while he waited to die, Boyd had formulated a clear version of reality, dipped in the clarifying acid bath of war, fully stripped of pretentious rhetoric and posturing. Boyd, the child, had found out that power hungry, self-serving adults controlled the world, held the power, and waved away the fates of millions and millions of peons like himself. That to be a well meaning human being meant that you would eventually wind up being used for a purpose that had nothing to do with being human. That in the blink of an eye, someone's hatred could snuff out your life and your chances of tasting, smelling, hearing and seeing all the beauty and sorrow and blessing and curses that filled each day, each hour, each minute. Boyd knew the traps of being a peon. He knew the meaning of absurdity. And he knew the glory of survival.

My mind drifted away from Pat and Boyd's store, and out to the world, to the villages, towns, and cities where children live in a state of war. How many kids are raised under the ghoulish hand of famine, disease, and brutality? How many Americans had a clue how lucky we were to be stretched out under the red, white, and blue umbrella that blinded us from the grim reality of war. Was there another people in history, so fortunate as we? And how long would the umbrella last before small holes eroded the shield and allowed through what every other human being on this planet already knew. Life drips suffering and grief.

Pat spoke up, changing the subject with questions about my daughters, and where I was from. Finally, the burgers were finished and we got ready to go. We exchanged numbers, hugged goodbye, and Eric and I jumped in the Festiva with promises to call real soon.

We looked at each other and began screaming, "WHOA!!!!"
"DUDE!!!" Eric shouted to the night. "BOYD RULES!!"

We sped back to the obvious fork in the road and headed over the hills to Nevada. We got out of the car on a crest, ran to a ridge and danced as the sun set. I looked at Eric's young face, glowing in the ruby light. Ten years of college couldn't have bought the knowledge Boyd had just imparted.

HAWKIE

That night we drove four hours of dirt roads through the outback wastelands of northern Utah. We raced through the little hamlets of Lynn and Grouse Creek, wondering what kids this isolated had their radios tuned on. Getting low on gas, we eventually wound up on Highway 93 and headed east until we reached the bright lights of Wendover, Nevada, a border-town which Eric promptly renamed "Bend-Over."

He asked me if I had ever been in a Casino and when the answer was no, we hiked to the doors and strolled into the surreal world of smoke and polyester suits and nickel slots and a rock band playing a flawless cover of Eric Clapton's *You Look Wonderful Tonight* to an empty dance floor with every crap table and slot machine two deep in haggard, frenzied patrons, while the Casino employee with the slick hands slapped down the black jack, and eyeballed our unshaven, grubby faces and reckless climbing attire with a smile of envy, and a nod of his head to let us know that he too once knew where to find the door to freedom.

I walked over to the edge of the stage and watched the band. The guitarist was wailing away, pouring his soul through his fingers to the fret board of his Strat', touching my heart with his angst as the last drunken patron stumbled across the dance floor leaving the entire viewing area empty, all eyes on the slots and tables. I stood there, eye to eye with this cat, wondering how far he was from his dreams. How, when his band took this job, they probably thought they had hit a jack pot of their own: a headline gig at a big Casino, a working gig with plenty of cash and time to spend it. I thought of all the primped up dives like this one, filled with desperation, and a band so far from a sense of acknowledged artistry that they probably couldn't recognize their original reason for picking up an instrument. I thought about how playing lead guitar meant so much to me and how writing songs had always been a dream, something I could do, but could never fulfill. The music business demanded your entire soul and I had never wanted to give that part of me completely up.

I remembered a time, in '82, when the phone rang and my lawyer friend Daniel Riviera was on the horn excitedly explaining to me how he'd just come out of the top offices of Capitol Records pitching a song I'd written and recorded called *Liars* and how those heads of state had embraced my tune with overwhelming enthusiasm and a request for more, much more. His advice: Get to L.A. now! I was hearing the exact words I'd wanted spoken to me over a phone since I'd watched the *Beatles* play *Ed Sullivan*. I asked Dan if he could hold a second and then walked into the kitchen and tried to catch my breath. I held the phone in my hand, staring at my "very" pregnant wife, looking down at the teaching contract lying on my dinner table, then back up at the cracked, single pane window, and the peeling wall paper about to fall in to the sink. I knew what I had to do. It was one of those forks in the road... coming fast, where you don't have time to formulate or discuss or even blink, before the *right* words fall out, forever altering your destiny and forever providing you a *what might have been* to carry around like a pet albatross. I told him I was going to sign the teaching contract, try my hand at teaching 6th grade, and watch my first child get born. I'll never forget the silence on the other end of that line.

Now, I stood before this unknown group of fantastic musicians, silently thanking them for letting me see a glimpse of what I might have missed. I turned, nudged Eric away from a slot machine and walked out laughing and reeking of Marlboros. I looked up and read the band's name, written in huge letters, the headline act on the massive Casino Billboard. Within a block, I couldn't remember it.

We headed south, entering the Military Restricted "Biological Weapon Trash" Area, eventually setting up our tent on an abandoned highway which swarmed with gargantuan mosquitoes. There we lay, warm, smelly and peaceful, as a rare light rain fell on those creepy arid wastelands west of the Great Salt Lake. Both of us had heard stories of the atom bomb testing in Nevada and how the inconvenience of ill-timed wind shifts had sent frightening quantities of radioactive fall-out hurtling in to the atmosphere. I'd heard of it landing in quaint farming communities in western Utah, southern Idaho, and just about anyplace you could toss a stick in Nevada. I watched the mosquitoes trying to carry off Eric as he came in the tent door and thought back to all those awesome sci-fi movies of the 50's and 60's, with giant ants, and Cyclops, and Lizards, and *Them* and every other form of monster that might fall out of an atomic hell.

Eric rolled over on his side and propped up on an elbow.

"Hey, do Kris and Kate still talk about that frozen bird?"

"You mean Hawkie?"

Eric burst out laughing. "Goddam, that was the funniest thing, ever."

"Yeah and the best part is, it was all true. Of course it was kind of a sad story because Hawkie never wanted to be a pet."

Eric was giggling, so to humor him, I began telling him the bed-time story I still tucked my kids in with on those every-other-weekend nights when they stayed at my place.

"Hawkie was a sparrow hawk who made the unpleasant decision to fly head long into my bedroom window one night while Zoë and I were in the middle of a lovin spoonful.... You want me to tell the whole thing?"

"Oh, God yeah. This is awesome. I haven't had a bed time story told to me since I was two!"

"Well, just as Zoë was going to start proclaiming her love for God, 'BLAM!!!' what sounded like a javelin banging off our window sent both of us jumping out of bed. Nothing was broken, so I ran downstairs and stuck my head out the door. Same thing. Back to bed we went, rattled, and unable to rekindle the magic. I lay awake all night knowing I'd have to tap dance through a month of mine fields before I could put on that velvet glove again."

"You say this stuff to your kids?"

"Of course. Anyway... In the morning I went downstairs, walked outside and there lay Hawkie. His head was flopping to and fro, but other than that, he looked perfect and I decided to keep him around to show the girls. I was certain that they had never seen a hawk up close, with it's talons and gorgeous feathers. They would be here in a couple of days so I stuck Hawkie in the freezer to keep him fresh.

That next Saturday, I snuck into the kitchen and pulled out the rock hard bird and then handed him to my three year old. Kris took an immediate liking to him and squeezed him oh so tight. Immediately I realized that Hawkie was a keeper as pets go because there was no way little Kris could kill this one. She was tough on pets. Even our black lab eyed her with trembling fear as she threw her tiny arms around its neck and squeezed and squeezed and squeezed. Hawkie was different. There was no way she could kill Hawkie, because Hawkie was already dead."

Eric busted out laughing. My girls loved that line too.

"So, Kris and Hawkie became inseparable. She tucked him under her arm like a football and carried him everywhere. By evening Hawkie was thawing out and his little eyeballs were starting to get a tad milky. Nevertheless, he had been such a hit with Kris that I didn't let a few minor negatives deter from the joy this pet was bringing my child. So, after I tucked the girls into bed, I took Hawkie out from under Krissy's arm and stuffed him back in the freezer.

The next morning her first words were, 'Where's my Hawkie?' I ran down the hall yelling: 'I'll get him for you, Krissy!'

And quick as a running back cutting for the endzone, I had him out of the icebox and back in her vice grip. She grabbed Hawkie with her little hands tightening around his neck. She squeezed and squealed. 'Hawkie like hugs!'

She flopped him by the neck under her arm, locked him in a death squeeze and went off to play with beetles and crickets in the back yard. A happier kid there couldn't have been.

Everything went just about perfect with Hawkie for the next two months. By the end of the fourth weekend, however, poor little Hawkie's left eyeball had fallen out and was dangling by the optic nerve. I kept stuffing it back in but he was getting so mushy that I was afraid repeated attempts might cave in his head if I pushed too hard. Kris didn't seem to notice the dangling eyeball. It just looked like one of her stuffed cats and dogs, which were always missing something. Problem was, she was getting extremely attached to her pet and I wasn't sure how much longer it would be before the wings and limbs would pull off in her hands. What's more, Hawkie was beginning to exude a slight odor. Yes, Virginia, we had a pet problem of the first degree."

"So, what did you do?" I could see Eric's grin in the masked Nevada moonlight.

"Well, that Sunday night, when it was time to run the girls home, I decided to deal with the Hawkie situation in the same way I had learned to handle most unpleasant situations. I stuffed Hawkie in a plastic sack and put him in Kris's suitcase. I'd let their mother be the bad guy and figure out what to do with Hawkie. I dropped the kids off and drove home knowing I had handled one more unpleasant task in life like the man I am."

"Jesus, she must have loved that! Did your kids find out?"

"Oh yeah. They love hearing that part of the story, now. But, to finish the story..."

"Oh, sorry Dude."

"No problem. So, anyway, that night I screened all phone calls, waiting for the girls' mom to call. She did, shortly after 10:00."

"Oh God."

"Yeah. She went off... 'Hello! Hello, Keith, this call is for you. For God sakes, what the hell is a dead bird doing in Krissy's suitcase? Is this the *pet bird* they've been talking about so much. What am I suppose to tell Kris? Great, Keith, thanks a lot. God!! ...click!' When I picked the girls up three days later, the first thing Krissy told me was, 'Mommy let Hawkie go visit his mommy and daddy.' In other words Hawkie wound up in the trash can. How their mom pulled that one off, I'll never know. THE END."

I unzipped my bag and stuck an arm out into delicious evening air. Nevada was turning out to be a great move.

"Night, Eric."

Eric started giggling again, "Hawkie...Jesus..."

Though the air was warm and quiet, the buzz of the evening hadn't left my nerve endings. I kept seeing Boyd: those red, watery eyes and his gnarled finger shaking at me. He had been chosen. I'm sure he wondered why.

I had always marveled at the survivors of life's worst offerings. They invariably seemed to have a solidity, an unmistakable essence. They glowed with a sense of power. These were people who could say "I love you," effortlessly. And they meant it.

I reached over and turned on my head lamp and then pulled out *The Book of Truths* from under my pack. I let the book open itself. Here is what it said:

TRUTH #5:

Because you are human, you will judge others. It is not your fault. Just know that when you judge others you are doing so because you fear that exact weakness in yourself. Look in the mirror and tell yourself you are incapable of sin, or wrong doing, or any evil that has ever plagued this planet. Do not fool yourself: you could commit any crime, could make any mistake. Just remember that you are a walking, tight-roping, balancing act, with sins and evils lurking in the very same soul where angels and healers adjust their halos. The more you deny this truth, the more the universe will unveil the opposite of love.

∧∧∧∧∧∧∧∧∧∧∧∧∧

I thought about the tyrants and judges and the dark messages that filled our daily lives. And then I thought of Coach J. and his message of hope. Of the efforts he made to teach love, despite the pressures to teach fear. This gentle, yet powerful, man was one of those contagious people who appreciated each waking second. He was the maniac who would leap out of his VW in a crowded parking lot and start dancing about loudly for nothing more than the applause of the billowing clouds and his own joy. Coach J. was one of those rare teachers former students came back to see. Throughout his chaotic room were printed words of clarity. One quote I borrowed from him and put on my wall was his philosophy on how to teach. This is what is said:

Lead the people by laws and regulate them by punishments, and the people will simply try to keep out of jail, but will have no sense of shame.

Lead the people by virtue...and they will have a sense of shame and moreover will become good.

- CONFUCIUS 500 BC

"This *whole thing's a circle*," he had told me. "Which ever way you head, you will wind up at the same place."

Back in the day, I had wanted to dismiss him as just another well meaning granola lover who had somehow survived the 60's and Vietnam, who spoke with passion and disdain for injustice, but was too far out there flapping for me to ever take completely serious. Now, camped with Eric in the eerie bowels of Nevada's Atomic Testing Sights, I could see Coach J. looking in my eyes and saying to me for the umpteenth time, "It's all about *commitment to self.* Your survival will depend on it. Just remember: 'To thine own self be true or Dude, you're fucked!'"

On one of our walks, Coach J. had shared a singular story about the nightmare of coming to terms with alcohol addiction. He described a pivotal evening where he had faced down the horror of losing control. He talked of driving home from a social event in his *prized* VW Bug. It was winter, the road icy, and the visibility poor. He said to himself a hundred times to drive slowly, to be careful, to stay in the middle of the lane. And most importantly, no matter what: "WHATEVER YOU DO: DON'T GO IN THE DITCH!!!"

The moral to the story was he wound up in the ditch, wrecking the Bug and much, much more. And as he talked I thought of a recent fight with Zoë, and how I had come home from an exhausting day at work with only one thought on my mind: No matter what, no matter how bad I felt, I would not bring up *the fact* that she was leaving again for another book club meeting. I would watch my every word, control my every impulse, and gracefully allow her to leave in the hopes that she would come back earlier than normal and possibly be talked into some sensual relief.

So, as soon as she got home, and let me know that she didn't want to go for a walk because she had promised her friend a walk, and there just wasn't enough time before she had to leave for book club, I let *the fact* slip out of my mouth. Of course, all hell broke loose and I wound up going for my walk, alone in the dark and rain. I made it four miles that night, while walking as close to the edge of the unlit highway as possible, my thinking being that if an oncoming car were to swerve slightly to its right, I'd be killed. On this walk to nowhere, I went by the house that Leona Quinn had told me about, where a group of recovering souls met twice a week to turn over their pain. It had sounded weird, but nothing was stranger or made less sense than my own life. I could no longer judge or raise an eyebrow at anyone or anything. I was ready to accept the fact that my life had become a catastrophe.

So that night, I hooked a left away from the highway and walked into Leona's meeting where a group of ten women and one man were sitting around talking one at a time. I wound up going to those meetings for the rest of the winter. And things got much, much worse.

Somewhere in January, after another Christmas fiasco and the subsequent fall out, I drove to my parent's cabin and spent several days alone. It was there that I had my first experience with true solitude, as recommended by Coach J. No phone. No TV. No friends dropping by. No distractions to change the channel. It wasn't pretty. I made strange noises and found myself rocking like those cats you see in a psyche ward for the criminally deranged.

As day one bled into day two, I walked into the bathroom and made the mistake of looking in the mirror. Before me was a face I hardly recognized. It was sinister, with down turned lips, and deep ravines cut into my forehead, cheeks and chin. I stared into the eyes of this face, and the scowl grew into a sneer that was like the smile of pure evil. I kept my gaze steady as the face of a murderer, rapist, or war criminal stared back, daring me to look away. It was the most frightening look I had ever seen. Pure sin. Pure evil. It was the dark side itself, standing there with me in the bathroom, ready to snap my soul like a twig. And then the mouth moved... ever so slightly, and the eyes turned a different shade, and they became bigger, opening wide with fear, like that last look of someone about to be crushed in a head on collision... frozen before the oncoming headlights. The eyes could not hold the gaze any longer and they blinked and when that millisecond was over, before me was another face. It was one of those Greek masks used in ancient tragedies. I stared at the open gaping toothless mouth, and the eyes that were down turned and the tears began to pour from the slits, and I stood there wanting to see what true grief looked like. It was hideous and gorgeous as this face bent itself into contortions and the wails demanded a bucket for all the water being drained until hours had passed and there was nothing left behind the mask to cry about. And at the bottom, staring back from the pool of tears was another face. It was the face of an innocent child. It was serene and peaceful and unwilling to hurt anything or anyone. And it was my face. I put it back on and got up and danced through the night like a man released from death row.

THE GREAT BASIN

In the early morning Eric and I headed for an "upscale" grocery store in an "upscale" town. Eric kept going on about SMITHS, a grocery giant which he considered a modern day wonder of the world with its aisles of bargains and friendly service. He had his SMITHS card and carried it proudly.

We passed through several small towns but waited for Ely, which according to our road atlas had *many* people residing there. When we pulled in, Ely appeared a bit stuck in time. We combed the town for a SMITHS, but had to settle on a SAFEWAY. Walking through the milky, tinted doors, I paused to admire the pluck of a local, who sat stuffing nickels in a slot machine, a cigarette in one hand and a stack of change in the other. Her bald spot could have used a comb drug across it, but she didn't seem to notice as she yarded on the handle, her saggy triceps shaking with each mighty pull, her glazed eyes glued to the twirling moons, clovers, and pink hearts. I swore I'd seen her twin walking out of an AA meeting on 90th and Aurora, but wasn't about to blow her zone with so trite an utterance as that cliche bit of coincidental con-foundry.

As Eric combed the aisles, searching for a side dish to go with the 32 cent loaf of bread he'd carefully placed in the Shopping Cart, I kept noticing the blank stares of the patrons and wondered if the whole town was participating in a 20th Anniversary remake of "Dawn of the Dead." I suggested he toss in a jar of Peanut Butter and call it good. He liked my idea and headed over to the Peanut Butter section and then deliberated on which jar offered the most butter per cents. I tapped my toe to the beat of the piped organ music. No one seemed to notice. Five minutes later we headed for the tortilla section, then the refried bean section and on it went, with Eric muttering disparaging comparisons to SMITHS the whole time.

An hour later we jumped in the car, with $5.62 worth of groceries crowding our back seat. Eric could see me eyeing the single brown sack and gave me a big smile. "No worries, bro," he said reassuringly.

For the next two hours our horizon was the same tumbleweed and 'ground zero' brown de jour that we figured had to be the inspiration for the locations shot in "*The Road Warrior.*" Eventually, we could see Mt. Wheeler rising tall in the nuked out distance. We also noticed it was plastered in fresh snow. We looked at each other, rolled down the windows and stuck a finger out. Tepid. Whew. Lucky. As we drove the last hour from the scrubby desert floor to the ten thousand foot camping area nestled amongst meadows and giant pines at the base of Mt. Wheeler, the scenery not only changed dramatically, but so did the temperatures. There was ice in our camp site. Clad in running shoes and our light rock climbing attire, we jogged up the trail to the 13,000 summit, the final mile through knee deep snow. We got back to the car as the sun ducked for cover and headed to camp with temperatures dropping deep below freezing.

I whipped up some spaghetti for dinner, and as I readied myself to strain the noodles in the colander, Eric snapped awake and told me to catch the noodle water in another pan.

"What the ....?"

"Yeah man. For sure. Save the water. It has lots of nutrients in it and you don't waste water that way."

"But Eric, I'm standing next to a water spigot."

I had to watch myself as between the altitude and cold, I was growing a bit testy. Frustrations were certainly mounting. As I knocked the frost off my cup and scraped yesterday's meal off my fork, I knew there wasn't a drop of hope in Nevada.

"Dude, let's use the water to make our cocoa."

"But, Eric, Jesus Christ, there's bits of noodle and stuff and it's all thick and milky."

"That's all nutrients, man. Try it with the cocoa. It's not bad and you get a mass calorie shot."

Eric dug out my cocoa packets and carefully strained the spaghetti water into each of our cups. I slurped my steamy beverage gingerly, and had to admit surprise at the pleasant texture and taste. Two points for the kid. After a few minutes of quiet, I decided to take a deep breath and relax my grip for a sec.

"Hey Eric. Where do you figure they came up with the "Great" part of Great Basin? I mean, if you photographed Nevada from space, this park would look like a green postage stamp on the deck of a beige aircraft carrier."

"The government, dude. They had to come up with something about Nevada that could justify keeping a state this funky in the Union."

"No doubt!" I laughed.

"Nevada is definitely the 'Uncle Bill' of the American family tree."

"You have an Uncle Bill?"

"Yep."

"Jesus, does everybody have one?"

"I certainly hope so," Eric said with a big smile.

"Hey, Eric, I have an Uncle Bill story for ya." I went on to tell him how when my Uncle Bill was a young buck, he enlisted in the Army, and being the wild and reckless sort, volunteered his services as a human guinea pig for the good of our Atomic bombing government. He was one of the soldiers who dug little pits and lay down at ground zero to test the military potential of the A-bomb."

"Whoa."

"Yeah. He said it was awesome. And when they were given orders to charge the mushroom cloud, he said it was the finest moment of his life."

"Dude, how did they clean those guys off?"

"With a broom. He said, they just swept off the dust and then sent them to a shower. They were all told they had nothing to fear."

"So… is your Uncle dead?"

"Nope. He believed the government. He also believes the *Enquirer*."

"I certainly do."

"And you can't argue with him. He's never been sick a day in his life."

"You're kidding?"

"Never missed a day of work. Never had a cold. If you talked to him, he'd tell you that hanging out at an H-bomb blast would be a great place to take the kids for a picnic."

"Well, there ya go. One less thing to fear."

"Yeah. It's all about believing, isn't it?"

Morning and clarity came calling around 1:00 AM, when I awoke trembling in my ultra-thin, ribbed condom bag. The next six hours were spent doing mind control in an attempt to stop my shivering. I found that if I held my breath in deeply, the warmth, somewhere in my lungs, seemed to form a glow that if exhaled slowly, warmed the nylon over my face just enough to simulate a small hand warmer. This was my anchor of hope as I drifted off to thoughts of Zoë, to my daughters, to Uncle Bill, to atomic mushroom clouds, to Boyd, to the beaches of Okinawa, to the Berlin Wall, to the ice crystals forming around my face, to a life spent going down the wrong roads to the right places at the wrong time, to the wrong places at the right time. And then, just before drifting off to dreams of Zoë in a black bra, my mind raced through a random photo album of images: my kids, my parents, my sister holding her cat, and suddenly I felt my stomach quiver slightly, like it so often did, when guilt fluttered through me like a moth inside a light fixture.

I picked up my pen and began to write about an *Eleanor Rigby* I had abandoned. She was suppressed in my soul and showed up at holidays, birthdays, and family gatherings to remind me in her innocence that I was a blasphemy in all my trumped up, glorified attempts to look good before God:

The Brother

My sister has had to endure a life of loneliness and a brother, so much her opposite, that he could never find a bridge back to her world.

She was born innocent to this world, back in the day of RH-factor- back when only the first child was spared the cruel effects of a fetus and mother's blood cells waging war. My sister was born with tumors raging in her body, a condition that would send her to hospitals from the time she was born until she was nearly two.

It almost killed her. It almost killed my mom and dad. They came to see her at Children's Orthopedic every day. Watched her go in and out of surgeries. Watched her turn blue and die in front of them. Saw her fight back at the cost of brain tissue.

But, my sister always smiled with delight at the sight of my parent's faces. Despite the needles, knives and stitches and lying in her crib alone.

Then, one day, my folks came to see her and my sister stopped smiling. She had retreated into a place where there would be no more twinges of joy. She just looked away and waited for the next round of unbearable pain.

Something snapped in my parents that day. My sister finally recovered, but the scars never completely healed and the damage was done to everyone. And by what? By an innocent. By a little child who only wanted to be held and loved and who instead was cut open and forced to lie alone in the sterile comfort of a hospital ward.

I was too young to know that mom stopped smiling because her heart had shattered a hundred times. I was too little to comprehend that mom couldn't look at me with joy anymore because she had fallen into despair. There was no way to know that my father, who could fix anything on earth, could not fix anything that really mattered and was feeling powerless to help my sister, or my mom; was frightened that he might lose this child, and that the woman he loved might lose her mind. The sun no longer shined in our home. Meals tasted funny. There was strange silence. I thought I might have done something to cause all this and tried harder to be good enough, to make it go away.

And my sister, in all her desperate attempts to stay alive, with all the will it took to fight back from death's hand, had no way to know that she was surviving to live in a world of angry and depressed adults. That she would wind up walking through life in the lonely state of the damaged, imperfect, undesirables. Her parents would struggle with guilt and a thousand other issues spawned by her birth. Her "flawless" brother would fall off the same bus and then bloody himself with his own injuries. He would loathe her weaknesses. He would be embarrassed by her inadequacies. He would criticize her shortcomings. He would abandon her. She would never be able to turn to him as an equal. She would never fall in love. She would never be held in the arms of a lover and told she was beautiful. And she would never hurting another living soul in her entire lonely life.

As she lay in her crib in the hospital ward, my sister, in all her beautiful
innocence, must have known she was to blame. For as she grew up, she never
asked for anything, never complained about anything, never cried because
she had no friends, never sighed at the dinner table because no one ever
asked her to a movie, never let a tear fall because she was not included in
activities that every one else went to. She graduated from high school, got a
steady job, bought a house, cared for her pets, traveled the United States,
visited her Grandmother and Great Aunt and helped out the family when
someone needed a hand. She never caused any trouble or created any grief
for her parents. Her brother, "the one with all the gifts, talents, and looks,"
took care of that. Her opposite, but not her equal.

HOVENWEEP

Eric and I didn't talk the next morning as we stuffed the Festiva and headed
out of the Park. I had no idea where to go. I was homesick, but knew there
was no home anymore. Driving by the Park Visitor Center, I spotted a pay
phone and decided to call Zoë. It was a gamble, but I had nothing to lose. I
hoped that some words of kindness might untangle the dusty thorns and
weeds choking my heart.

Incredibly, she was home, and even though she was crying softly, her voice
fell through the wire, perfect and delicious . She told me she was having a
hard time with her three boys, that she missed me dreadfully, that she wanted
me there helping her, holding her. She wished I had never left.

I felt a massive surge of love pump through my heart and told her everything
would be OK, that I would call her back later that evening and if things
weren't better, I'd cut my trip short and head straight home. I hung up the
phone convinced a miracle had finally erupted in the universe, that Zoë was
at long last ready to make room- to open herself- to be there- to want me and
all the good that I had to give. I couldn't believe it. Maybe me being out of
her reach for a week had snapped her awake.

When I had married Zoë, I had done so under the illusion that she would
be at my side, my better half, a compliment of grace and beauty. What she
had failed to inform me during our illicit courtship was that her idea of a
relationship was a peck on the cheek as two cars passed in the night. I'd often
tell her I felt like I was about number ten on her list, right below the dog. She
always laughed at that one, but it wasn't funny. It was true. When I dug
through my drawers and found old notes and letters, written in agony, but
never sent, they always trumpeted the theme of abandonment. Of course, she
thought I had a problem. And I did. I knew that. But did she have to dump
gasoline on my rags and toss burning matches in the air?

Now, something had changed in her; in both of us. I could feel it. I walked
back to Eric with light steps and a song building in my head. At long last, I

felt complete.

Eric asked, "Did you finally call her?"

"Yep."

"Good for you, Dude. I thought you needed to make up with her."

"Really?"

"Yeah. You can't stop love, bro. It's not some faucet that you turn on and off. I mean you can try if you want to, but, if you truly love somebody, you don't just shut off your heart because you got pissed off and left."

I started up the car and glanced in the mirror. My eyes were smiling.

He went on. "I mean you don't have to hang with her, or raise her kids with her, or even like her. But you can't turn off love without infecting the rest of your life. That poison just gets into everything and kills any chance of happiness."

I nodded my head slowly and replied, "I know, Eric. I know. Well, the call went amazingly well. I have this weird feeling like we might be getting back together after this trip. I think she's finally seen the light."

"That's nice." Eric gave me a grin. "Just remember, it gets awful cloudy, real quick, up there in Washington."

As we descended the winding road, the temperatures began to climb and the odor in the car began to rise as well. I spotted a picnic area, whipped in, pulled out my unused "Solar Shower," filled it, tossed it on the hood of the car and flopped down on the picnic table for a much needed nap.

Five minutes of warmth later, a lonely Park Ranger walked up, and having seen my Washington plates, strolled over, eager to chat.

I stared at the friendly, young, bearded Ranger, and asked politely, "Dude, how did you wind up here?"

"Geology major at the U-Dub. This was the only opening in the Park system that met my degree."

"Whoa, too bad."

"Yes, I should have listened to my mother and minored in Law Enforcement."

Rick the Great Basin Ranger was a cool guy, who was making the most of his time in Nevada. He pointed out some first ascent routes he'd climbed on the chossy walls of Mt. Wheeler. Eric and I tried to follow his finger as it pointed out one death-route after another.

"Whoa! Who do you climb with around here?" I asked.

"Oh. No one. I just solo everything," Rick replied.

"Cool!" Eric said. He looked at me and widened his eyes as if to say, 'Rick the Ranger has lost his freaking mind.'

I asked Rick if he had any ideas for beautiful places to hike, and he suggested that we drive to Kolab Canyon, a tributary of Zion National Park, and walk back in to the massive canyons of red rock. He talked about swimming in pools of warm water at the base of giant orange walls. It sounded like paradise.

"So, is there, like, a free campground or something we can crash in if we show up late tonight?"

"Oh, you can just pull off the road and toss your tent anywhere, then go to the Park Headquarters in the morning and get your hiking permits."

It was a plan. He also suggested that we take a short side tour, on a well maintained dirt road that led to some rarely seen Anazi Petroglyphs. He excitedly explained how they were some the finest unspoiled relics of an ancient civilization that once dominated this region of the southwest.

Before leaving, Rick pointed to the *Book of Truths* resting on the picnic table where I had set it before my nap. "You might not want to leave that book lying around. It will disappear."

"You know about *The Book*?"

"Oh yeah. It was a cult classic at the U-Dub. Only something like 400 were ever published."

"427 to be exact."

"Whoa! A fan of Towne. Anyway, there were only two copies on the entire campus. Someone in my dorm had one of them."

"Dude!"

"Yeah, and his disappeared within a month. That's some book." He walked over the table. "May I?"

"Of course."

He thumbed through the pages. "Ah, here we go. I always liked this one."

He turned the book towards me and read out loud Truth #166. Here is what it said:

TRUTH # 166:

Fuck The Ref! *Fuck what anybody thinks of you. It has all been done before and short of nuclear war, what do you have to be scared of? You have lived every second of your life in fear of something: fear of loneliness, of inadequacy, of having no point in life, of having no meaning, no purpose. Fear of not loving enough, not being kind to your sister, your mother, the homeless guy begging for a handout. Fear of not knowing enough, but knowing too much to ever feel safe or trust anyone. Fuck em all before you wind up useless and unable to help another living soul!*

∧∧∧∧∧∧∧∧∧∧∧∧∧

Rick gave us a huge grin, "Geez, I'd never read this thing when I wasn't higher than a kite. Interesting. Well, enjoy your trip and don't forget to check out those cliffs. They're right on your way."

As soon as Rick had wandered off, Eric turned to me and laughed. "Dude, I've been to one too many ancient burial sights. I don't get the fascination with ruins."

"I think these cliffs have etchings, not dwellings, Eric."

"What's the difference? Seriously dude, it ain't worth risking a flat."

"Well, these might be different. I've never seen a hieroglyph."

"They're called petroglyphs, they're all over the southwest and they all look like scratches on rocks you might have made when you were four."

He grabbed the Solar Shower and went off behind a tree to purify.

I lay down on the picnic table, soaking in the warmth and laughing at Eric's disdain for "ruins." My head sprang back to when I was a teenager, driving around in Tim's Ford Maverick on a Friday night, talking about girls and all the sex *Tim* was getting. Lucky Tim was dating a University of Washington History professor's daughter, who's idea of fun was to down one of her mom's valiums and lie on the couch watching Rocky and Bullwinkle cartoons.

One night, while her folks were away on another vacation, he went over there anticipating hours of youthful fun in every room. His gal suggested they dine on a couple of valiums to really loosen up their love joints. Tim, ever curious, thought anything with a buzz could only enhance the evenings performance. They each popped two of momma's little helpers, then turned on the cartoons and waited for the glow to kick in. Pretty soon, Tim rolled over to ask his gal if she would mind not having sex, because it really sounded like such a bother. She was out cold.

After cartoons, Tim awoke his friend and suggested that they watch some of her father's historical slide shows. "NO," was her definitive answer. But Tim, ever thirsting for knowledge, was insistent. Reluctantly, she took him into her father's vault, a walk-in library of slide presentations, with row upon row of neatly arranged carousel trays all specially labeled with trip after trip to the world's most exotic sights.

Tim started reading the titles, "Athens, Parthenon, Rome, Cairo, Pyramids, Machu Pichu, Aztecs, Mayans"… He turned to his lover wanting to know which tray was the most interesting.

She bit her lip and then with eyelids drooping, leaned against the wall and slowly shook her head, "Ruins….." was all she could get out.

Later that afternoon, I followed Rick's instructions, pulling off on the well-maintained dirt road that would take us to the pre-historic slice of Anasazi wonder. It was a gamble. But I had to do it. One thing I had learned from Zoë, was that rather than duck into the bunker of security, one should stay busy and open doors, ready to embrace any and every moment of ecstasy that life could deliver.

"You sure about seeing these things?" Eric inquired again.

I was. We barreled down the rutted road. "It'll be cool. Rick said they were some of the best in Nevada."

"Well," he snickered, "that's saying a lot."

"He said they never get visited, so they are well preserved and unspoiled."

"The road must be bad. Otherwise the place would be visited."

"No. Rick said the road is great. We'll only lose 20 minutes, tops."

"Hey, isn't this the part of Nevada that got fully dusted by Atomic bomb-blast fall-out?"

"Yeah. Dirty Harry. That wayward cloud crossed here on its way to St. George. The other mushrooms supposedly blew north, taking out upper Nevada and Southern Idaho. When I taught school in Howe, I couldn't believe the number of middle aged folk with various forms of cancer. It was creepy. None of the locals suspected a thing. They just thought it was normal to lose your thyroid at forty."

"Well, there ya go, have a nice nuclear day."

A half hour later, I pulled over to check my tire rims, afraid what the last mile of anvil-shaped rocks on an endless moonscape had done. Eric kept asking when the last time was I'd checked my spare tire. And I kept telling him, just before the trip. Of course, I hadn't looked at it since the last tire change two years ago. With every jolt, I was praying to Allah, Buddha, and the Virgin herself that there might be a hint of air in the spare.

The air smelled like the drive to *Hovenweep,* the infamous Anasazi dwellings that had graced the cover of a National Monument brochure that Zoë and I had used years ago as a map to guide our way down endless miles of dusty road in 100 degree heat. The impressive picture that lured us, had been taken in the golden evening light. It showed a triumphant wall of gold adobe brick, etched against a blazing azure sky. And even though we were exhausted from a 'ten parks in ten days' tour of the desert southwest, that photo had been inspiring enough to get us up and heading off to take our rest day in the car. By mid-day, as we drove on through washed out lighting, mirages and tumbleweeds, both of us knew we'd been duped.

"Do you want to turn around?" I'd asked in fear that we were once again heading down the road of discomfort that often precluded a fight.

"No. This is fine," she'd answered back in her best, 'I'm trying to be a trooper,' voice. "I'm sure it will be worth it."

Zoë was doing what so often happens when you take a wrong fork in the road and you get that little click in your gut; you can feel it's wrong but you wait it out a little longer, all the while wanting to turn around and scurry back, until you've reached that agonizing point, where to turn the wheel is to bow before defeat. No one had ever been able to tell me where that fine line was between hanging in there and being a quitter.

As we pressed on past another abandoned Navajo ranch, Zoë, turned to me and served up one of her all time classic lines:

"This *Hovenweep* had better be the eighth fucking wonder of the world."

An hour later, getting out of the car wrapped in wet towels, we stood before several small brick outcroppings. An older couple wandered about poking their canes in the sage.

Zoë and I didn't fight that night. We didn't make love either. Instead, we fell asleep at a slide show, presented by the motel owner who was a world renowned archeologist. The subject of the evenings presentation? Ruins.

Eric and I drove on, a half-hour past the point of no return. Finally, two small dark cliffs appeared in the distance. We pulled up with waves of dust cascading over us like a silt sprinkler. We stared out the windshield at a dark brown rock wall with some scratches that closely resembled a child's interpretation of a tree. Eric and I glanced at each other, as if to say, "Should we get out of the car?"

Eric started to say something.

"What?" I made an attempt to peer out through the dirt.

I could see out of the corner of my eye that he was chuckling.

Unscrewing the cap of his water bottle, he tilted it back, and just before he wet his lips, he spoke deeply into the plastic cylinder, "RUINS...."

I put the car in gear and drove off. After a silent fifteen minutes, Eric grabbed *The Book* off the dashboard and opened it up. Here is what he read:

TRUTH #73:

Once you open the door, there is no going back. Denial was awesome. It was the best time of your life. But Santa Claus just got busted and the Easter Bunny has rabies. The plague is at your door and the smell of death is chasing you around. Now, to survive another day, you must seek light as a drowning man seeks air.

TRUTH #74:

The harder you try, the harder it gets. When you were an ignorant raging slob, adrift in denial, everything was easy. You simply medicated all problems. Everything was cool. A frozen dinner in the oven and a little 'Daisy Dukes' on the tube and you had a fine day. Now that you are trying to raise yourself a few levels up Maslow's hierarchy, nothing you do is good enough. Just remember, that no matter how hard you try, you will eventually fuck up.

^^^^^^^^^^^^^^^^^^^^^^

Eric started laughing. "Where does Towne come up with this stuff?"

"Well, my guess is he's been through a fair share of heart wreckage. You know: a broken heart doesn't lie."

"What is it with love, dude?"

"Yeah, there seems to be two sides to it, huh?."

The sun was dipping behind the Nevada hills, turning the sky deep red. It was the time of early evening when anyplace you stood on earth was a beautiful place. Even Nevada.

Eric broke the silence. "Hey... What's one of the greatest memories of your life?"

"Besides stuff I've done with my kids?"

"Yeah. Best ever."

"Hmmm." I held the question in for a long breath. "Probably brewing up a little cup of coffee in the morning light on Paddy Go Easy Pass, with Zoë's head poking out the door of the tent, her naked in the sleeping bag, and the sun shining on my back. It was perfect."

"Cool."

"What's yours?"

"Every minute I spent with my girlfriend in Alaska."

"Whoa!" I thought for sure Eric was going to tell me of a climbing region, a wall, or a route he'd knocked off. "You didn't tell me about a gal back home."

"Nope. But I was in love once. I've been there too, bro. Gina was her name. She was perfect for me. She made me laugh all the time."

"So what happened to her. Why aren't you with her, now?"

"We were only sixteen and her parents stopped letting her see me."

"What?"

"Yeah, they were freaked...said we were getting too serious, that I was going to knock her up or something; just like her mom had when she was in high school. So they put the screws to her and took my Gina away."

"Jesus, man. You never told me about her... So what happened then?"

"I saved my money and bought a van. The day I graduated, I left home and I haven't been back since."

"Damn. Love is brutal."

"And beautiful... She was something. I still dream about her."

Eric put *The Book* back on the dash and picked up my steno-journal.

"You mind if I have a look at this?"

"Not at all. Go for it..."

He read a couple of pages. "This is sweet!"

FOREVER

She comes to me, always the same. Her eyes are soft, like a creature undiscovered in a wood. She walks towards me, her shoulders a match for mine. Her scent fills my being like a cloud of desire bursting inside my chest. And she brings her face to my lips. And she kisses me... delicious, healing all wounds, all troubles, quieting the sirens, the storms, the shrieks of doubt. Her embrace is a fortress of serenity surrounding my being, indestructible, built on love and carrying the universal truth: love is everything. And I want her forever.

Eric looked at me with a pained expression, letting words form in his head before he took liberty to speak. "Damn, Bro....why don't you talk about that garden more? That makes a whole lot more sense than listening to you hackin at the weeds and thorns all the time."

As we pulled on to the Freeway On-Ramp, the Festiva trailing plumes of dust, I decided not to mention the other dream of Zoë, waiting like a pall of pain on the next page.

ABANDONED

She comes to me in color images, always the same. She is cold and indifferent. My heart bounces off her plexiglas shield, keeping me distant and disconnected. She talks in a voice I cannot recognize as even a distant cousin to love. There is nothing there for me. A stranger in a grocery store would be warmer. Her gaze holds no trace of nourishment, encouragement, or sentiment. She doesn't need me. She doesn't want me. I am expendable. I have served my purpose of building her ego, her worth, her beauty, her belief that she can go on building her walls and her house of Aces and put the Joker at every entrance to point its finger and laugh me off to the dark world- abandoned forever.

∧∧∧∧∧∧∧∧∧∧∧∧∧∧∧∧∧∧∧∧∧∧

An hour later, we stopped for gas in Cedar City as the sun fell like a fireball into the southwest horizon. It was warm and despite the new squeak in my McPherson Struts, I was happy. I could still hear Zoë's airy voice saying my name softly, lovingly, longingly. Life, with all its twists, turns, and ruins, was grand after all.

I called my kids to tell them I loved them. They weren't home.

Then I called Zoë to leave a message of encouragement as billowing dreams of a romantic rescue mission formed in my heart like a massive western thunderhead.

I was surprised to find her home. Her voice answered friendly, polite, and without a hint of emotion.

"Hi," she said, "I was just leaving."

"Well, uh, can you talk for a minute. I'm calling from Utah, remember?"

"Yes, a minute then. But, I told the boys I'd take them down to the skateboard shop so I have to hurry."

"But, ... I thought you were upset with them?"

"Well, I changed my mind."

When I suggested that we meet somewhere in a couple of days, she let me know that she wouldn't be able to, that she had too much going on, and that she wouldn't have any time free until the last Saturday of the next month.

"But?"

"Oh, check that. I won't have all day. Just between three and five."

"What the....!!!"

As I stumbled back to the Festiva, the thundercloud of love revealed itself as a mushroom cloud of doom rising above a Nevada test sight, obliterating any last traces of hope and dreams from my soul. We pulled into Kolab Canyon around 11:30 and sped past park signs that suggested, "No Camping." At the end of the winding road, in an empty turn around parking lot, we pulled out our tent and pitched it next to the car.

THE RAGE

Boyd had mentioned that one of the keys to life was to not get pissed off over every little thing. Well, Boyd may have survived Okinawa, but he'd never had to deal with six years of Zoë's indifference. There was no way I'd be able to sleep. Why God? Why did I make that call? How could I fall through that trap door again? A thousand times I'd opened my heart to her! And a thousand times I'd wound up choking on it! She wanted me until she had me! Same old shit, different day! UNBELIEVABLE!!!! How stupid could I be? I knew it. I KNEW IT!!!!!

I had often heard that a sign of insanity was repeating the same mistake. OK. So? And, *where* did that put me? The answer sparked down my spine, twitching my legs, shaking my toes and cranking up my adrenal glands to a point where I was ready to jump out of the tent and *run* back to Seattle just to tell her one last, final, freakin time that I would never, ever, see her again. NEVER! So long as I should live, so help me God! And, oh yeah, one more f...ing thing...... FUCK YOU!!!! And don't you dare, f...ing call me, or even think about trying to f...ing write me, cuz I'll just throw it f...ing away! Every f...ing word you ever told me was a mother f...ing lie and I'm the stupidest son of a bitch in the world for ever believing a word of what you ever f...ing said!!!!!

The hair trigger to the dark side of my soul fed on rage, was addicted to it, lusted for it. And once again, I'd emptied that gun into my foot, my gut, my head, my heart. Two hours later, the smoking holes of justified anger were filled by a familiar, insidious fog. Once again I was back on the merry-go-round.

People who need control, hate being controlled, and Zoë could control me, had every button wired. Round and round we'd go, with me transformed into a lunatic, spouting epilogues of pain as the painted horses bobbed up and down and the fat lady laughed and the carnies gave me the eye. By midnight, damage total, balance gone, I'd want off the ride, tossing what I could grab in a suitcase, squealing away, tires burning, and falling into remorse the instant I'd reached the end of our block. After an hour of smoldering in a dark, dead-end parking lot, vapors of self-loathing would seep in through the vents, filling the car. On that all night dose of medicine, I would drive to school in the morning and teach a room full of 4th graders hope and fractions.

The rage is what my daughters and stepsons mention when they feel safe enough to share the truth about life with me. Those frightening barks of verbal gunfire are etched in their psyches forever.

They all can recite the look on my face, the cruel words pouring from me, the sickening tension, the threats of harm and devastation hurled at Zoë-smoke and noise to puff up behind, nothing done, nothing ever accomplished from the rage.

Of all my faults, it is my greatest regret. No child should have to be possessed of such fear. And for that chance to unleash my fury and crush the soft-skinned Siren who had dared the unforgivable sin of hurting my feelings, I would ruin a lifetime of memories in the souls of my kids.

Now, as I lay in the Kolab Canyon parking lot, waiting for the sunrise, I prayed for forgiveness. I prayed for my dear children, my mother and father, my two wives, to any human being with whom I had thundered down upon and stolen the light of love. 'Please forgive me,' I whispered into my sleeping bag. 'I'm sorry. I was horribly wrong.'

CLEM

The sun rose before my sunken eyes and shortly thereafter, I heard a car pull up and a set of head lights came beaming through the nylon walls. I waited for the asshole to turn them off, and then noticed that the light was now flashing brightly in reds and blues. I unzipped the tent door and flopped out my unshaven, weary, red-eyed, head.

"Howdy officer."

"Could you please step out of the tent, sir."

"Sure." I stumbled out in my shorts, grimy and cold. "Thanks, God," I muttered under my breath.

"Sir, I'm going to need to see your ID." The ranger had taken his hand off his gun and was now reaching for a pad. "Are you aware of the '**No Camping**' signs posted?"

"Yeah, we saw the signs, but we got in here around midnight, were dog tired and thought it would be OK just to throw our tent down." I tried to flatten down my hair, realizing that the neatly trimmed ranger writing me out a ticket was rapidly judging this book by its cover.

"Sir, you are in violation of Code 7342-1A." He cracked his neck to the right. "I will have to cite you."

The thought of digging farther into my torn pockets to fund this worn out trip sprung my gut into action. I caught the name on his gleaming badge and cleared my throat.

"Excuse me, uh, Clem. Could I explain our situation? We were at Great Basin yesterday and asked the Ranger there for advice on where to hike next. He suggested this park. As the hour was growing late, we also asked him where we might find a camp spot. He informed us quite clearly that we could park anywhere along the Kolob Canyon road. I admit, we did see the signs, but we figured a National Park Ranger would know the regulations of adjacent parks. We are sorry for the trouble we've caused, but, we truly had no intent of breaking any laws."

"Was this Ranger wearing a uniform and badge."

"Yes, and his hat. He was from Washington, like us." Clem's pen stopped moving. "Uh." I stammered. "We could be packed up and out of here in two shakes of a lambs tail."

He looked me up and down with a piercing gaze. "I do not understand how a U.S. National Park Ranger could advise you so irresponsibly."

"Me neither, Clem. But, there is no way we would risk getting a fine. First of all, we're broke. Secondly, we're climbers, not troublemakers."

"Kay." He cracked his neck to the left. "Considering you were given erroneous information, I will forego the citation. However, please obey all signs and park rules in the future. And, do take your tent down."

At that, Clem closed his pad and stiffly made his way back to the car. Before he got in he said, "I'm also from Washington. Grew up in Ephrata.

Beautiful country. Good day, and let's have that tent down by 0700."

Off went the lights and away sped Clem.

Eric popped his head out. "Dude, nice job! What's up with these National Parks?"

"Yeah, give me some more regulations. Hey, did you hear him say he is from Ephrata?"

"Yeah, and did you hear him call it beautiful?"

"Unbelievable."

Eric started to laugh. "I think our man Clem is a couple sandwiches short of a picnic."

We sat in silence on the sidewalks. The sun was rising above the red walls. I kept sighing and shaking my head, waiting for something to clear away the haze. I decided to make coffee and as I hunted for the cone, I picked up *The Book*, letting it fall open. Here is what I read:

TRUTH #65:

Your parents didn't choose you. The people who made you were just a couple of kids trying to steal a few moments of happiness from a life of turmoil and pain. Of course, they didn't choose you. They had a quickie when they shouldn't have. Just like their parents did, and the parents of their parents did, and those before them did, and on and on, and back, back, back; all of them wishing they'd kept their pants, bloomers, kilts, togas, shawls, and/or robes on; all of them forced to wear leaden masks of guilt; all of them ashamed to admit the obvious; that an unplanned child always comes along at the worst possible time to fuck up the works. They could have been somebody. Of course, they didn't want you. Life wanted you. And life is in control. So bitch and blame as much as you want. You're here. They're your parents. There are no single babes. And life doesn't care.

TRUTH #66:

You are either a piano man or a piano key. Odds are pretty good that if you're reading this book, you have been played like chopsticks ever since you were ten. Please remember, there is nothing you can do about it. The only thing you can hope for is to determine if you are a C, E or an F# and then pray like hell that somebody with some fucking talent comes your way.

^^^^^^^^^^^^^^^^^^^^^^

Towne had something there. I knew which key I was. Slowly, creakingly, agonizingly, my frozen wheels began to turn, to grind; to puke dust, silt, and rust, as I forced my inertia to move, to breathe, to absorb the sun, to reclaim something that resembled a life. I needed a sign, a vision, a piece of evidence that there was something of value left in me.

Eric broke the silence. "I wonder where the hike to those pools starts?" That wasn't it. I could care less about the pools that Rick had suggested.

"Don't know."

"Well, what do ya think? Shall we try to find those hikes for something to do?" Eric was treading lightly around my shaky walls.

"I suppose we could drive down and pick up a map of this place." I slumped my way to the car with my camping gear. We drove down to the Visitor Center- which was still closed- and grabbed a 'free' Park Brochure, which included a crude map of Zion National Park on page two. The brochure listed some of the more popular hikes, many of which were accessed through the main (southern) entrance to the park.

We drove back up to our pull out and made some oatmeal. I kept studying the crude map on the brochure and noticed that there was a trail that went all the way from Kolab Canyon to Angel's Landing and the main park entrance.

"Eric, I wonder how far it is across this park?"

We tried to use the little map compass, and guess-timated a distance of anywhere from fifty to one hundred miles.

I felt a chord, the one at the end of the *Beatles*, "*A Day in a Life*," bang down with my piano key. "Hey, Eric. What about this? How hard would it be to hike the whole thing? From here to Zion. Ya know, running shoes. Light and fast."

"Hmmm. That'd be bitchin, but I need to be back to *The City* the day after next. I don't think we could pull off a 100 miler in two days."

"What if it was closer to 50 miles? Just 25 a day? We could do that, huh?"

"Sure. I see what you're getting at. That'd be kinda cool."

"Well?"

At that we began to quickly organize gear for a light and fast backpack. I went over to a garbage can to dump out the remainder of oatmeal from our cooking pot.

Eric glanced over at me. "Hey, wait a sec. Don't toss that."

"What?"

"Keep that oatmeal. We might need it later on today."

I looked at the glued contents at the bottom of the pot, thought about the extra weight, and looked hard at Eric. "You sure?"

He was sure.

We arrived at the bustling Kolab visitor center and waited in line for a permit. We checked out the park topo maps for sale, but they were $2.50 and neither of us wanted to dish out that kind of bank for something we probably wouldn't use anyway.

A nice lady with a round park hat asked if I needed help. I told her of our intent to hike the length of Zion and she said she'd heard of it being done. Eric asked if she knew the approximate length of the hike from here to Angel's Landing. After inquiring from other attendants and painstakingly checking some maps, she came up with a figure somewhere around 49 miles. Eric and I did the eyebrow thing. We could do this!

"OK, honey. Let me just get the Park Ranger to fill out your permit with you. Do you need this map?"

"Is it free?" I asked.

"Uh, no. I am sorry, it is..." she turned it over and checked the price, "$2.50."

"No, mam. That's OK. We already have a map." In my pocket was our little road brochure.

We waited and milled about as the clock began to move more quickly than it had all trip. Finally, the door to the back room opened and the Ranger stepped out. Eric and I did a double take. It was our man, Clem. He walked up to the counter looking poised, ready, and willing to serve the needs of the general John Q public.

Then he saw the two of us. His eyebrow flinched ever so slightly.

"Hi Clem. We need a permit."

Clem cleared his throat and tightened his belt slightly. "Kay. Which particular hike have you determined."

"Clem, we want to hike the whole park. Here to Angel's Landing. That's OK to do isn't it?"

"Whoa, there. Whoa." Clem's wheels were turning. "Yes, there is an established route which is done each year by a party or two."

"Well, then there it is. We'll do that hike."

I could sense that I was really rushing Clem's game.

He put his hand to his chin.

"We were kind of thinking of doing it in two or three days. What do you think?"

Clem jerked his head sharply toward the left, then squinted in contemplation. "Most parties manage it in 5 to 6 days," he began. "I would think four nights would be optimum."

Clem slowly mulled over a park map. I looked at Eric and nodded an affirmative, while holding up two fingers.

"Can you get water on the trail, Clem?"

"You can." Clem looked at me as if to size up the package of trouble he was about to unleash on his beloved park. He nodded slowly and spoke carefully. "It's not always easy to find the springs, but they are marked on the map. So, *yes,* it is possible. Here, I can show you on your map..."

With a slight hesitation, I presented him our wrinkled road brochure, which he pondered without a hint of surprise, before carefully unfolding it and laying it out on the clean counter top.

Clem cleared his throat slightly. "When hiking, you need a minimum ingestion of a gallon and a half of water per day. Therefore, water is your most critical concern on this crossing." He drew out his gold plated pen and proceeded to mark dots and X's on the black line that ran from Kolab Canyon to Angel's Landing. He then added, "There is no shuttle service back to this entrance. You will either have to drop off a car or secure transportation back to this sight."

"We only have the one car, Clem." I talked quickly.

"Be advised, that hitchhiking is prohibited in the National Park."

"We promise not to hitch hike." Eric walked behind me to stop smiling.

Clem was warming up a tad as he turned over the Permit Tag and began reading us the rules and regulations as slowly as words could be formed.

"Maximum group size is 12, (combined total of people and stock).

"It's just us two, Clem. No horses." He looked up and then went on.

"Fire-arms are not allowed in the Park."

I held up my hands, "No guns."

"Bury waste in soil, at least eight inches deep and two hundred yards from any water source." Eric and I eye-browed each other.

"Pets are prohibited in the Park."

"No pets, Clem."

Clem, was in his prime now, cocking and cracking his neck, rambling on in monotone through the abundant inane rules on our permit tag and then turning sloth-like to our map, and drawing circles around the two key springs in upper Zion, where we would find water. At least three times he pointed his pen at the line explaining that a *Minimum of ONE GALLON of WATER* should be consumed by the desert hiker each day. Clearing his throat slightly, he let us know that in point of fact, *two gallons* per day would be a more suitable quantity. At least twice he lifted his eyes to see if we were catching the weight of those words. We were, but by this point, juiced up on pre-race adrenaline, I couldn't hold a focus for anything longer than a wink, and consequently heard little more than my pulse pounding to, "Clem, Clem, Clem," as I smiled, nodded, and fidgeted away another five precious minutes of daylight.

Finally, we signed the last form, Clem dotted the last "I" and we flew out the door for Angels Landing.

CROSSING ZION

It was 1:00 in the afternoon and in the upper nineties, when we snapped a photo and found the trail that would lead us to Zion. We had until about 7:30 PM before it would be too dark to hike without headlamps. Our plan was to move as fast as possible and cover roughly sixteen miles, leaving a long, but doable, thirty miler for the next day. To go light, we'd left most essentials behind. No first aid kit. No extra food. Just enough water to get us to the rest area at mile fifteen. Eric eyed me clutching *The Book of Truths* and my steno-pad and said, "You better bring em. They don't weigh anything."

The relief of that validation was enormous. In the annals of adventure, this hike wasn't going to rank up there with anything more than an extra long bit of scenic wandering. Nevertheless, my heart was pounding, my focus became sharp, my joints stopped hurting and my internal public address system went off, announcing to every fiber in my being that it was *"Show Time!"*

We raced past the trailhead warning sign, stressing the importance of a daily minimum consumption of *ONE GALLON PER DAY*.

The trail wound down into a breathtaking orange canyon, where we stopped once to dip our sweaty bodies in an icy clear pool. Refreshed, we turned a corner and started heading up a wash as the sandy trail grew soft and loose. For the next ten miles, every step required a little calf-pumping oomph at the end to keep our feet making headway. Despite the take-two-steps-to-gain-one terrain, Eric and I were flying. The heat felt great, and the air was so dry that we hardly sweat despite the torrid pace. We polished off our quart of water and stopped once to filter another bottle full. Checking our little map, we figured it was six to eight miles to the next water source, which our road brochure indicated was the rest area alongside a highway that cut through the middle of the park and ended at a camping area high up on the mesa.

The soft, sandy path, began switch-backing up, up, and up and out of the canyon and into pasture land, surrounded by giant red rock formations. There were cow droppings and flies to mark the hot trail as we sped for the upcoming oasis. With an estimated three miles to go before the rest stop, Eric and I killed off our last water just before crossing a crusty looking stream.

Eric spoke up. "Maybe we should snag another quart here."

I looked down at the greenish trickle and was concerned I might clog up my filter in cow slime. "I don't think so. It's only another three miles to the rest area at the highway crossing. Utah rest areas are the best. There's probably a shower. We can make that, no problem."

"You sure? I don't remember Clem saying there was water at the road crossing."

We dug out the little map. There was a penned X at the rest area.

"Yep, look here, Eric. Clem marked it on the map. There's a rest stop so there has to be water…. Right?"

"Yeah, he marked it, but I have this feeling…"

"No, I remember, now. He said something about a road and water. We'll be fine. Let's go."

We picked up the tempo, figuring if we made the rest area before nightfall, we might be able to gain an extra mile or two on tomorrow's tab. The footing remained beach-like and loose, with every one of our steps sucked slightly backward. Despite that, we were making great progress and knew that with a couple more quarts of water, we'd be in good shape for the next day's marathon.

At last we heard a car and sped to the road-side. We broke out of the bushes and there before us stood a lonely outhouse. A dry, single lid, outhouse. We looked at each other, then looked for a water spigot. What the....?!

The car we'd heard grinding up the steep road had stopped and a blonde family of seven were walking over to use the facility. They looked at us like odd curiosities as I stared back wondering how and where this fit into our adventure. They were an odd glitch in my crystal clear game plan. They were alien beings that didn't really belong here, reminding me that I didn't have to be doing this to myself.

We stepped around their van and started walking along the road, trying to locate the next trail. I was still convinced Clem had said something about this spot during his meandering dissertation.

"Wait a minute, Eric. There has to be water here." I walked back to the outhouse again, circling it, waiting for my reality to click and a spigot to appear through the encircling brush. Nothing.

Eric looked at me, looked at the van, then looked at the road. "Maybe, we ought to hitch a ride from those folks up to the camp ground and go at this thing again tomorrow." His words hit hard against my thin shell of toughness.

"No, we're OK. I think we can make the next camp before dark if we hurry."

"Dude," Eric's voice was perplexed, "I hate to point out the obvious, but we've been hauling ass in heat all day on just a couple quarts of water. We have no idea when we'll find any more. It's getting late....This ain't cool."

"We'll find water." My resolve was building like a wall of mud. "We can do this. Come on."

As we marched on, a bony finger of doubt began to scratch my back. It was that familiar little feeling that all climbers know, when a supposedly cake outing changes, like the crack of a hand-hold busting off a rock face, and suddenly, your balls shrivel up and your throat tightens, and your jaw clamps down. It's primal, its real, and its addictive. I had found what I wanted. I was finally scared. This was no longer a hike. I had my mission. I would not give up. I would never surrender. I would defend my island, whatever the cost may be. Crossing Zion was all I had left. I had to pull this off. My salvation depended on it.

For the first time, Eric seemed a bit strained with me. "Which camp you talking about?"

"The one that is marked four miles beyond the road. Right here." I pulled out the tattered road brochure and we stared at the strange markings which dotted the trail. Neither of us had a clue what they meant, except that Clem had been trying to point out water sources. A couple of the dots and X's were a short distance away. It was only seven and there was still plenty of light.

In another block, we found the connector trail and started to haul ass. My calves felt like railroad ties. We picked up the pace to a near run as the trail climbed steeply and nightfall began to cloak the distant forest.

After an hour of uphill jogging, I felt myself beginning to flag and noticed I wasn't sweating at all. A pit of rabid hunger had formed in my stomach and my mouth was a dust bowl.

"Eric, hold up." I stopped us, reached in my pack, and pulled out the pan containing the glued oatmeal. It was still moist. Eric and I scraped out the gooey contents, and sucked on our fingers. Nothing had ever tasted better.

Recharged, we raced up into a forest and darkness, switch back after switch back, until the trail leveled out in woods thick enough to turn away the remaining light. We came upon a sign which I had assumed would be the campsite/water source. There was no water. There was no camp. The trail sign showed that if we took a left, it was only six tenths of a mile to the highway which led to the RV campground. Eric started walking that direction.

"Hey, what are you doing?" I asked.

"Heading for the road, man. We're screwed. We gotta hitch or hike up there cuz there's no water here."

"Well, you go ahead then, but I'm not going."

"What?! Are you kidding me? We need water, man."

"I can't do it, Eric. I want to do this thing clean. No help from anybody. No giving up. I know it sounds stupid, but this means something to me right now."

He walked back to me shaking his head. I spoke softly. "I need this, Eric. I'm sorry. I know it's nuts."

I stood there exposed and naked in the dark, a man at the brink, at the edge of sanity, who knew that to give in and take the easy way, the sure way, the safe way, would be the end of all he stood for. I knew right then why I climbed, why I crawled out on to alpine faces and risked my life when a tourist trail led straight to the top. Tears were forming in my eyes. It was pitiful, but this little trickle of fight in me was all I had left.

Eric walked back to me and looked straight in to my face. "You're not joking are you?"

My lip was trembling. I nodded.

He smiled hard and began to shake his head. Then in his best okie twang he said: "God dam! I want some of what you're smokin."

The way he said it was so funny I started laughing.

"So?"

"So, I'm staying too. I'm pretty dry though."

I was elated. "Great! Here, I'll give you my plums." It was all we had.

Eric took them with a guilty look. "You sure man? I mean, I'm ok."

"Yeah. I'm sure. I had more of that oatmeal than you."

We set up my tiny bivy tent to fend off gnats, and crawled in fully expecting to suffer from dehydration complications. Eric rolled over, then rolled back, trying to find a comfortable position on his light weight-sleeping pad.

I was the first one to break the silence. "Eric?"

"Uh huh?"

"I was thinking about your Romeo and Gina thing today."

"Romeo and Gina...I like that. Cool."

"It seems love bring us whatever we need to smash our heart to pieces. It's like we can only learn the truth from a shattered heart."

"That sounds about right."

"I see whole lot of people going through their rituals, living an illusion of what is suppose to be real. "

"A few years of bummin' will cure the rituals to some extent."

"Yeah... Too bad it takes a tragedy for most people to regain a sense of priorities."

"Dude!" Eric laughed. "That little hike today did you some good."

The tent went quiet. I lay there wondering if we'd find a drop of water before we reached the floor of Zion. How far could we go? And what exactly was I proving to myself this time? The answer came immediately.

Taking risks on climbing adventures was the fastest route I knew of to regaining a sense of worth and confidence. Touching a summit was a valid affirmation that I could accomplish something; that I'd once again gained some control over my life.

Ironically, as an aging climber, an over-developed sense of self-reliance was now the gift and curse of my make-up. I'd learned to avoid a helping hand at almost any cost. I had wanted to be Mel Gibson in the *Road Warrior,* walking away from the wreckage, with the sand pouring out of the tanker, wounded and upright, the last man standing at the edge of the desert. And when I strapped on my crampons, and grabbed my ice axe, I *was* that Road Warrior. Thus, climbing became a religion unto itself and the mountains were the church. And with that juice pumping through my veins, I'd turn my back on the most basic element of humanity, asking for help when I needed it. Better to suffer and beat yourself to death, than to admit weakness and turn to a friend and ask him lighten your load. Better to face the fear alone. Climbers don't admit feelings of helplessness. This is the great evil that must be eradicated. Control is everything.

And then I got older. And I made mistakes. And there were times; cruel, wicked times, when alone, on my knees, with every known survival tool tried and abandoned; unable to out-think, control, buy, beg, borrow, steal, outrun or out-climb the fear; out would come the prayer. Never was it pre-planned. Never was it forced. Just a primal, reflex, knee jerk reaction from my soul, that said, "Please God, help me." Incredibly, it often worked. Of course, as soon as the impending disaster was overcome by one "coincidental" miracle or another, the cockiness would come back and a sense that I was once again the one in control would return to cloud my universe.

It was fun trying to explain my occasional lapses to young climbers on a winning streak. They just wouldn't get it; couldn't get it. All I could say to them was, "Dude, I hope your temporary luck continues, because in this game we all eventually wind up getting our ass kicked. It may be your last day before it happens, but what a last day that'll be- on your knees staring death in the eye- going: "Holy shit, God! Are you there? Wait! I was just kidding, God! I totally think you rule!"

I thought about a recent scare on Mt. Rainier that had rocked me hard; a full on religious experience. The residue of that trip should have been enough to save my marriage, my sanity, and any need to want something more from life than just being able to walk, and breathe, and take a sip of cool water, with all faculties working, and all cares swept where they belong. That trip should have been the one where something clicked so deeply inside, that for the rest of my life, just waking up in the morning would have been reason enough to spring forth with the light of love burning bright.

THE PRAYER

Most climbers are smart. They don't talk about religion, unless it's to lambaste the atrocities committed in the name of our God in heaven, hallowed be thy name. I had always seen religion as a great divider, a wall between peoples rather than the single hand of love, willing and ready to lift and carry anyone with a soul. With that said, what happened to me on Mt. Rainier's Emmons Glacier, was something that anybody who's been knocked to their knees could relate to. Lost in a white out, running out of time and options, I resorted to the only thing I could think of: I prayed for God to help me. I was too scared to care about trivial things like hypocrisy, blasphemy, and spiritual apathy. My rope team was alone and disoriented in a summit cloud cap, cramponing back and forth on a sloping roof of ice, perched above a skyscraper worth of vertical death. So, I prayed. And help came.

[JULY 1992: MT. RAINIER SUMMIT IN A TOTAL WHITE-OUT]

My rope team of four reaches the summit bergshcrund, a monstrous crevasse at the 14,000 foot level of the Emmons Glacier. We are inching along in whiteout conditions. Probing blindly with my ice axe, I wander off to the left and find myself standing on a diving board of ice perched above an abyss. Wrong turn. I tell my team to head the other way and Dustin, a stud rookie, finds a crampon path which takes our rope up and through the wicked ice bridge leading over the crevasse. With him in the lead I fail to notice the absence of wands at the edge of the bridge. I grind my ice axe into the rock hard snow, and make arrow imprints to mark the way back. I am thinking of Messner and Habeler on Everest, not Hansel and Gretl in the dark forest.

We summit with visibility collapsing and winds growing to a howling rage. With me back in the lead, we head down, the gaping, bergschrund just minutes away. My mates behind cannot hear me unless I shriek. At the last wand I notice our crampon and ice axe markings have been obliterated by wind driven ice crystals. The arrows I have drawn in the snow are gone. Hmmm. I head in a direction I hope will lead to the bridge, my pulse picking up speed as visibility drops to about two feet. Everything looks like a swirling white wall. I can't tell if I'm going left, right, up, or down. I walk down a steepening white wall and choke on something that tastes like my spleen as my ice axe begins tracing a line over dead space. It's like a ghost coming out of a haunted house- the dreaded crevasse- twenty feet across and bottomless, sucking like a toothless whore on the tip of my ice axe. I try to make my eyes focus. 'Jesus Christ! Enough is enough! Where is the fucking snow bridge?' I look left and right. No bridge in sight. Nothing but distorted white. Suddenly, my hands start to tingle and I feel my arms going numb. 'What the...?!!' I've been holding my breath in fear. 'Fuck!!!' I bend over and start power breathing for all I'm worth, as a perfect, round, tunnel goes in and out. 'Oh my God!!!! Breathe! Breathe! Breathe!'

The tingling eases slightly and I turn my rope-mates around, trying to find another spot over to the right, then another, and another, all the while I am sucking in O's like a mad man. I crampon down to another spot and it is the same spot as before. It can't be! My hands start to tingle again like someone is smacking my funny bone. I walk back to Molly, the woman behind me who is on her very first mountain climb. I crack a mean smile and offer up, "Welcome to hell, darlin."

I instruct her and then Gary, (forty eight and on his third climb ever) to anchor themselves with their ice axes because I have no idea when I might lob off into the monster gash. I march back to Dustin hoping that he has seen something, anything, remotely familiar. Nothing. But he thinks we should be going the other direction. I have no idea. We hash it over and decide I will walk the opposite way to the edge of the schrund in an attempt to locate a spot we recognize. Visibility fades in and out from two feet to an occasional ten or so. What I would give for a wand! And what I would give to blink my eyes and know that I could be home, safe in bed, and never, ever, have to climb another mountain, ever again.

"HEY!!!" I shout into the greyness. "HEYYYYY!!!" A sharp jab of reality and fear races through me. My cries are useless. Everybody on this mountain has bailed. The cloud cap and crevasse crossings were too intense. We are alone up here.

Wands. There were lots of them on the way up but they were placed at intervals that can't be seen in a whiteout this thick. Spoiled by too many fair weather trips and the usual abundance of wands on well traveled routes on Rainier, I had opted to leave mine in the car, as the weather was gorgeous and the hordes of climbers heading up ensured redundancy in the name of pre-caution on the sidewalk hike to the summit. Now this. Brilliant. My head turns on me, shrieking machine gunned pleasantries, "You freaking idiot!!" I strain to see. Nothing but swirling white mist. "Christ!"

So I start marching back- left and right, up and down. "Breathe, breathe, breathe!" The wind roars making it brutal to hear anyone shouting behind me. Standing close to Gary, I holler for all I'm worth, which makes me lose my breath, turning my arms numb again. This is full on action, like an anvil falling towards my head, right here, right now!

'Breathe! What if I snap?'

'Breathe! What if I black out?'

All we need is a two-second break in the white out and we'll be able to see where we are. But it doesn't happen. It won't happen.

I keep walking to the edge of the schrund, guts in my throat, waiting for the ghost to jump out and give me a heart attack. If I fall into the crevasse, how many will be yarded in with me? Somewhere down there is the body of a climber who slipped and plunged to his death last week. Due to high winds and cloud caps, the rangers still haven't been able to get his body out. We had talked about this poor soul on the way up. What are my mates thinking now?

Molly, bless her heart, has the pick of her ice axe sunk in, ready to save me. Suddenly I see footprints heading down. More prints. 'Yes, these look good. A whole set of footprints.' I turn and march down there, plunging my ice axe into the whiteness, look desperately for something familiar. 'C'mon, c'mon.' Another crampon mark. An ice axe spike mark. 'Please let this be the spot. This is it, it has to be it!' Another step and my ice axe swings across air. The mist opens for ten feet. In horror I realize I'm looking at the same spot I reached a half hour ago!

"Mother of f...ing God!!!" I scream into the white swirling wall. My arms tingle again.

A shot-gun blast of sick scenarios race through my head in a milli-second. I shout at my team to watch their every step. If I fall, they will have less than a heartbeat to arrest. If they fail, we'll all die.

'Breathe! I have met my match.'

'Breathe! I have no answers, no solutions, nothing left in my bag of tricks.'

I suck in another breath and a thought flickers in my chest. 'Please God, help us. Help me find the way across. We need a break in this white out, God. Please! I can't find it God! I can't find it!'

The prayer isn't lengthy. It is to the point and delivered from the deepest, corner of my being. I march on. Resolute. Probing and searching. I am no longer a judging, analyzing, questioning cynic. I am a humbled human being.

I decide to fight. There is nothing left. Options, options, options. Jesus. I know that if we sit and wait, there will probably be a clearing. But what if one of us starts getting sick or hypothermic? And what if this isn't just a cloud cap but the prelude to bad weather? We could be stuck up here. Not an option. With futility gnawing away hungrily, I shout into the void again. "HEY!!!!!"

My innocent mates are counting on me to get them off this mountain. I am their leader and I am failing. Yes I am failing. I didn't pack the wands 'It's Sunday during prime time Rainier season-there's going to be a thousand climbers up here, right?! Right?!' And look at me now. My eyes well up, warm and wet against the chilling blasts of wind and ice crystals pelting my frozen face.

The wind shrieks against my hood. I head back up towards Molly as she and Gary begin shouting and pointing. I turn and there above us is a climber clad in yellow, shimmering through the swirling mist. We are only fifty feet away from him but we can't make out a word he is screaming. In seconds he disappears completely from view. I race towards him and come to the same dead-end launch pad I had tried to cross before. The Climber in Yellow fades back into view, screaming and pointing to a spot to the left from where I am standing.

Even with our savior pointing where to go, it still takes agonizing minutes to find the crossing. Finally, we are navigating our way down, across, up, and over the creepy bridge leading us to the other side of the schrund and the white out descent back to camp. (Later I would learn that the bridge collapsed shortly after we crossed it. We were the last party to get across the schrund.)

There is no sign of the Climber in Yellow.

The way down continues the nightmare as the white out stays with us for 3,000 vertical feet. Not once can I see more than twenty feet ahead. We follow steps and look for an occasional wand that marks turns. More than once I get off route again and start marching up a slope that I thought was down. It is pure intensity all the way down to 11,000 feet. We cross giant crevasses on sketchy snow bridges, but these seem only mildly terrifying after dealing with the schrund. Eventually we come out of the cloud cap to a perfect clear sky. I come across some climbers and ask them if they were with the Climber in Yellow. They say that they were passed by him and his rope team an hour ago.

We arrive back at camp. Packing up their stuff, is a group of four. I ask them if they were the angels who came to our aid. They were. I gush. I want to kiss them all.

The Angel in Yellow tells a story of reaching the schrund, and staring at the bridge, and being too scared to move. Finally he began to approach it, but when his ropemate behind him was knocked off his feet by a gust of wind, the team began to panic and wisely decided to forget the summit and get the hell out of dodge. They started down and had dropped a couple of rope lengths when he was struck by a strange sense of urgency to turn around and head back up to the schrund. "Something, hit my gut and just told me to go back up there." So he marched his reluctant team back up and braced himself at the edge of the schrund. He watched and listened for a couple anxious minutes and then just as he had resigned himself to leave, he heard my last desperate shout. Thus, he saved us.

I shake my head in awe. Already I am questioning whether I have just been part of another surreal coincidence or something divine. All I know for sure is, I love these people. I say nothing to him about my plea to God, but all of us smile and nod at each other in gratitude.

It has taken me a life time to develop the coping skills necessary to deal with the reality of life down here. All the lessons I've learned have come at such a cost: grief and loss chasing down every hint of happiness, the questioning, the groping with the proper this, the correct that, missing my children, missing my wife, financial desperation, working for paranoids, dealing with mean people, assholes, absurdity, my glaring inadequacies, love lost, a heart broken, dreams crushed. I learn and fail and learn and lose and the sorrow chases me around until my life seems so huge, my problems so insurmountable, so out of control, that I run in desperation to the mountains, and climb myself back to a toehold stance, a million steps away from home. Balanced there, stripped to nothing, naked above the abyss, a fleck of insignificance, a coward, a fool, a mistake, I finally know there is nowhere left to go, that I've reached the end. All that is left, is between me and God. It's time to go toe to toe. There is life and there is death. There is nothing more.

Please God, let me remember this when I start to fall. Let me be thankful that I'm being stripped of the posing, pretense, pride, and perfection, down to the void, to this core that is you. Nothing else matters.

That is my prayer.

THE PHOBIC

I lay with the beat of my heart thumping in my ears. Suddenly a light filled the tent and Eric sat up.

"Whoa, bro, you still awake?" I asked.

"Oh yeah. Got some serious chemicals pumping through the veins. We did some hoofin today, Dude. Hey, do you have that *Book of Truths* handy?"

"Right here." I handed it to him.

He fumbled through the little book with one hand. "Let's see, Truth #......I saw it right in the middle, like page twenty or.... ah, yeah here it is. Check this out." Eric read the truth out loud. Here is what it said:

TRUTH #49

You are human. Therefore, you are self-absorbed, greedy, and selfish. Please know that there is absolutely nothing you can do about it. All you can expect out of yourself is to try and get by and to help-out others whenever you can. That's it. Remember, if you completely fuck up on the helping others part, don't sweat it. It doesn't really matter. Because the instant things start going better for the person you helped out, they're going to get a whole lot worse.

^^^^^^^^^^^^^^^^

"OK, I have to admit that's pretty cool. Are you thinking?...."

"Oh Yeah." Eric flipped off the light. "I think our man Towne had a little chat with Boyd before he wrote that book of truths."

Eric handed *The Book* back to me keeping his finger on the page. I turned on my tiny head-lamp and read another truth. Here is what it said:

TRUTH # 50

Those who start wars have not read a history book. Please know it is not their fault. They simply chose ignorance over education.

^^^^^^^^^^^^^^^^

An odd feeling of calm entered my lungs for the first time since Zoë had come over three nights in a row, one magical week... a long, long time ago, in a town far, far, away. How rare was this sense of quiet? For me, only forced marches of pain ever produced such moments of peace. And now, with my ship bashing against the rocks of Zion, I waited in silence for the hull to bust wide open. In that wreckage, lurking in the dark, stood the specter, the damaged child that had been such a disappointment. The boy I thought would be something grand when he learned to sail. I carefully set the headlamp down, opened my steno-journal and waited for the words to flow from a place that had questioned every choice I'd made since I'd put on a *Beatle* wig in the 4th grade, stood in front of a classroom and Lip Synched: *Love, love me do.* This is what I wrote:

Every child gets theirs, their dose of hell to climb through. Mine came quietly and strange. In fact, as it was happening to me I couldn't believe it, thought there might be something I could do about it, that I might have the power to stop it or master it. After all, I was so talented, bright and handsome, so ready to take on the world. I thought I could do anything. I had never failed, never lost control of anything. But as I stood there at a urinal in the PE locker room on the first day of 7th grade, something began to tremble inside of me that I had never known. It wasn't like the embarrassment of failing a test, or losing a race. The sensation climbing up the back of my neck was more like the hand of doom reaching up for my throat and saying, "Pass this test... or we take you away."

I stood there, holding my shrinking penis, waiting for that little click in the urethra to magically happen allowing me to relieve myself. As one kid after another came into the stalls, the cold sweat began to form and the idea that I might not be able to do this came like broken glass under a foot. But, I really had to go. I was carrying a football of piss and needed to unload it before heading out for PE assessments.

I could hear some boys muttering about me, and then I began to hear the laughter, and felt the squirming as they leaned over each other for a better chance to stare at the fag in there playing with himself. I began to pound on my abdomen until the laughter became too much. Finally, I turned around, and with head down, slowly walked back to the benches, shrinking with each step, until I was the smallest kid in the class; and certainly the most frightened.

That was the last day of my innocence. After that, every day revolved around trying to find a way to urinate in private in an extremely un-private world. Heaven was a place with bathroom doors that locked and the privacy of a toilet where no one could hear me go. It was that simple. And that fucked up.

I did not trust anyone or anything. I felt God had singled me out, had chosen to make a mockery of me, to ruin my life and leave me a joke on this planet. It made me mean and unable to love anything. Upon entering adulthood, I knew I was a bottom feeder. I knew that I could never measure up to anyone of greatness. I knew that I would have to fake it my whole life.

This was the world I eventually brought my kids into.This was the space I was crawling in as they began to drool about the furniture and gum anything they could shove in their mouths. I wanted to love them. Wanted to feel soft inside and able to relax. But that wasn't possible for me. I was damned to eternal misery and the best thing for them was to never get too close to me. By the time they were 2 and 5 I had fallen in love with a mysterious, intoxicating woman, and I left their home, not wanting to have them turn out like me.

It was Zoë who showed me there was a way out of my prison cell. I thought that way out was through the look in her eyes, the feel of her skin, the taste of her mouth, and the ecstasy of lying in her arms. This unfortunate, but necessary turn, led me into an addiction to her. She had cured my disease, but I had found another.

∧∧∧∧∧∧∧∧∧∧∧∧∧∧∧∧∧

The Phobic

The child's heart is supple, beating sweetly with hope and spirit
The heart of the phobic is an icebox. It beats with fear and uncertainty
The phobic cries in the night to a God who is playing Gin
The phobic wonders why this creator took away his dignity and worth
The phobic's bedmates are depression, hopelessness, futility and anger
The phobic knows if he gives up his anger he will sink into nothingness
It is the great seductress and it must be battled
But the battle is an endless tunnel and he is forever depressed
The phobic learns to settle for the ordinary.
Builds a life around bathrooms
Safe havens with the door locked. Safe and wretched.
The phobic catches glimpses of his potential on shiny handles
He sees what could have been, then pulls and sees what is
The phobic knows the only cure is love. Perfect, divine unattainable love
The phobic hopes to someday stumble upon this kind and patient force
He hopes to taste, feel, and be love: tender, if only for a moment
He hopes his world will bloom in colors that are now only dreams
He longs to feel the force pour out; unstoppable
To know for the first time what is in every child's heart
To believe he has a right to happiness. To believe in himself
But the phobic is wary. Love, elusive and unpredictable shuns the tunnel
The phobic knows freedom as an abandoned child knows the dark
He knows he must always return to the box, chipping at the ice

101

I turned off the headlamp and laid down to lie awake all night. My phobia had been a life sentence. I could never remember being normal. I could never remember looking at another young man and not feeling envy. Everyone else could. And I couldn't. I was a loser whether I won or lost.

When had I made that intial wrong turn? Was I Five? Four? Where exactly was that one critical moment when, if I could, I would have gone back and picked me up and said, "C'mon my little guy, I am going to save you from harm. I am going to provide you a safe haven from which you may grow to greatness. You do not have to be afraid. I am the light and I will be here. And I understand you completely. I am you. And I am greatness."

I suddenly wished I could call my parents. I wanted to tell them how glad I was they had given me life. I wanted to tell them how sorry I was that I had not been able to be happy. How so much had gone wrong. How it wasn't their fault and that I was trying as hard as I could to get better-- that I would figure this out-- that I was no longer afraid-- that I wanted to love-- that I ... There it was. I was no longer afraid. I lay next to Eric Sloan, waiting for the dawn.

THE ANGELS OF EVIAN

At first light I crawled out of the bivy tent, expecting my joints to crackle and my skin to pop. They didn't. Besides, a general sense of low key fatigue and an acutely dry throat, I felt well. We packed up and started our march, trying to decide if we should add an extra four miles to our day by hiking up to the RV Campground and securing a guaranteed source of water. It was one of those countless little calls climbers have to make- push on with the hope you will find what you need, or turn that ship around and head for security. Feeling like maybe Eric had been right about hiking to the campground, I'd just decided to suggest that we head up there when he stopped in front of me, breaking my concentration.

"What's the matter?" I asked softly.

"Grass." Eric whispered. He was looking at a patch of lush green grass, growing on the bank to our left.

"Yeah… And?"

"First grass we've seen on this part of the trail." Eric walked up the bank a few feet and reached down to part the fine greenery. He smiled, "Oh, baby, that is pretty!"

I walked up and there between Eric's fingers, was a lovely trickle of water. "God that's beautiful."

Eric took a drink and grinned. "Oh Lord," he said, "You don't need a reason to be saved."

I looked at Eric. "Is that Kierkegaard?"

"Nope. Ozark Mountain Daredevils. Best band in the world, bro."

^^^^^^^^^^^^^^^^^

Watered up, we looked at the map. A short distance past the X marking the trail sign, Clem had marked a *dot*. This was the 'water' source he had carefully talked about while I stared out the window and tapped my foot. Now, having broken the code, we studied the map for other dots. There was only one, eight to ten miles farther on. After that, there were no more dots.

We ventured on, with much of the drama vanquished. We would get water. We could hike until the cows came home. We would make it.

As I walked, it occurred to me how often I felt it necessary to under-rate my adventures. I considered the odd dynamics of accomplishment for guys like me. So often, you take a- back of the bus- seat to the super-stars that wander through your life. Rarely do you share tales of daring because those *other* guys have climbed the K2's, and bivied alone at 28,000 feet, and hiked out forty miles on a broken limb and on it goes, and nothing you ever say or do is quite good enough to compared to a legend. So you tuck your victories away, and store them in a closet and never rejoice in the simple fact that you were the best you could be. My sore feet pounding the trail, drove home the sense of never really fitting in: too out there to be *normal*, but not far enough for *glory*.

Our route finally took a sharp turn south and the sign let us know that Angel's Landing was a viable destination: just 18 miles away!

Soon, a middle aged couple, each packing an eight ounce Evian bottle and nothing else, appeared ahead on the dusty trail. They were admiring the view off the edge of the mesa. When they heard our voices and turned to say hi, we could see a startled look of fear overtake their faces. I couldn't help but chuckle at their plight. I must have looked scary with my six day beard, stained t-shirt, and tanned skin. The woman smiled politely, as if to say, "I left my wallet in the car," before shrinking behind her husband.

The trail stayed high on the upper reaches of Zion park, which left one feeling slightly out of touch with the great walls and canyons, yawning far below. After a couple of easy hours we came upon a plot of grass and found our last dotted spring. We sat down for a rest and began filtering the bug-laden water into our quart bottles. We each downed one, and then refilled.

Before long, the couple-- clad in shorts and button up dress shirts-- came by and sat down in the shade of a tree, taking last sips from their Evian bottles. They kept looking nervously in our direction.

"Damn, Eric," I whispered. "I thought for sure those two were just sight-seeing back there. There's no way off this trail except going to Angel's Landing or back to the camp. They can't be heading on with those empty bottles."

"Tourists."

"Well, they're going to be statistics if they don't get some water."

At that, I waved to them as friendly as I could and said in my kindest voice: "Hey, would you guys like us to filter you some water?"

The woman's voice came back with a thick New Jersey accent. "Oh my Gawd, that would that be fantastic! We read you can't drink the watta around here."

"Well, you can if your filter it."

They hobbled over and introduced themselves as Hank and Betty. I suggested they make themselves comfortable and try to down as much water as they could.

"Where you two headed?" I asked.

"Angel's Landing."

Eric glanced my way.

"We wuh dropped awf this morning by friends we made at the Sheraton."

"Jesus," I offered, "that's a helluva ways to hike in this heat with just eight ounces of water."

"Yah, we kinda figured that out. But now if we hike back, it'll be just as far and we won't have a caw."

"Well, there has to be somebody up there in the campground who could help you out."

"Not exactly. The campground is closed for repairs."

"What the...?!"

"Yah, good thing we brought these water bottles. There's no water in the camp. Big signs posted everywhere. No water."

Eric glanced my way again. "Whew." I knew what he was thinking.

Loosened up and watered, Hank and Betty admitted to being completely out of their element. Eric and I shared a few rich tales of adventure and our new friends humbly let us in on a little secret. *They were very, very wealthy.* Betty told us about how she and Hank had met as kids while earning several PHD's in neurological physics and how after years of research, they'd come up with the novel idea of developing specialized computer software for hospitals that, combined with the unimaginable advances in technology, took off like a golden rocket. In no time, their small company in Manhattan, was being hounded by every hospital in the modern world. Thus, they had made their fortune. Now, with money to burn, the two love birds realized that time was running out on them and they needed to get out and see a bit of the world. They wanted to travel, to explore, to have some fun together.

I refilled their bottles, made them drink them down, and then refilled them one last time before bidding farewell.

Eric and I walked the next ten miles in our own worlds. I couldn't help but make comparisons between Hank, Betty and me. In so many ways, they had made it. They were a functional American success story. They had stuck together, with commitments to each other and to a project that must have seemed bold at the time. Their work was helping thousands of people. Their lives had been given to a worthy cause and purpose. And now, close to retirement, they were scrambling around with bodies that had been neglected, and skills that had little to do with enjoying life.

In the same space of years I had managed to walk away from two marriages and a teaching career. I'd gone from mirroring the correct life of my parents, to sailing away from normalcy like a pirate. And for all my laboring, slaving away on mountains and crags, what booty did I acquire to bestow upon my children?

My steps grew increasingly weary as I made my way down a long series of switchbacks, some of them carved into the faces of cliffs. I was ready to be done with this hike now, yet I knew these last miles to Zion were pure cake compared to the journey that waited on the horizon.

I came upon Eric, sitting on a rock outcropping, waiting for me to show up.

"Dude, let's hike together for awhile," he said. "This trail is getting old."

We started up again with me in the lead, and Eric asking questions, trying to get me talking to make the miles go by. He wanted to know how I handled seeing my kids so seldom and what was it like taking them out on Wednesdays, with no money, and no place to go. He asked me questions about how I approached things as their "other" parent; what I thought of having their mom calling the shots and whether I felt I was able to provide a balance to their lives. I told him providing that balance was all I could do.

"Hey, Bro," Eric started getting excited. "Tell me that story about the pet squirrel Kate told me about."

"You mean Fluffy?"

"Yeah, Fluffy. That's it. Did that really happen or did she make that up?"

"No, it happened. Man, those girls never have to make stuff up."

I stopped, took out my water bottle and wet my lips, knowing I would need full use of my larynx for this tale of "how to" parenting. I tilted my baseball cap, adjusted my pack straps, squinted at the sun, and then launched into my daughters' most be-loved story of all time.

FLUFFY

"My kids certainly aren't spoiled. In a land of plenty and every dream come true, my kids have learned to do without. They've been there with me, when we shared a one bedroom condo with another guy. They've been there with me when home was wherever Dad could find a place to stay for another night. They've been there to watch the strings draw tight on an already skimpy purse as Christmas and Birthdays arrived at the wrong time of year. They've learned the art of secretly yearning but never asking for anything more.

Of course, there've been a bundle of plusses to downsizing my life, not the least of which is never having to deal with pets. When home is anywhere with a roof and a phone, showing up towing a critter is not an option. This works for me as I'd rather be off climbing than cleaning a fish-tank or walking a dog. However, my kids certainly wish that weren't true. In fact, just having a kitten would have made my youngest daughter, Krissy, the happiest girl in the whole USA. I knew that. It's taken me years to not be over wrought by her little plea of, "Dad, can we get a kitten?"

"NO."

"Why, dad?"

"Cuz, when you guys aren't here, the poor thing is going to feel all neglected and lonely, and it will probably run right out in to the street and get creamed."

"Oh."

My kids don't even ask anymore. However, *NO*, is a pretty strong word and there was one time, where I caved in completely and let my kids enjoy a happy moment with a pet we will never forget.

The year, in keeping with my cyclical custom, was going straight to hell. On one of my visitation Wednesdays evenings, my daughters and I found ourselves heading for Seattle, with me befoul of mood. Zoë and I had exchanged verbal gun fire the day before and I was lost in swirling thoughts. Like a robot, I arrived at the girls' house, then pointed the car towards Fremont.

When we got to Seattle, we swung by Gas Works Park to stroll up the hills and gaze at the sunset. Both girls could feel my tension and Kate was going off about how she was unhappy that I'd mentioned to one of her friends that her "boyfriend" should call her more often which somehow got back to not only her, but her "boyfriend" who was not her "boyfriend" but *just* her friend because the last three times they were "boyfriend/girlfriend" they broke up right before the holidays.

We crested the hill, nodded at the view, and started walking back to the car, the three of us in our own little worlds. I knew I was floundering, that I was losing precious seconds with my kids, ounces of time that I could never get back. I took a deep breath, looked up from the ground and spotted Fluffy.

Fluffy was a squirrel that had gotten knocked in the head and killed maybe five or six days ago. His little eyeballs were still in their sockets, but the bugs were starting to do their job on his shiny fur coat. The thing I noticed immediately about Fluffy was that he had this enormous bushy tail.

Krissy was right behind me towing a twenty foot length of kite string she had found just moments before. I looked at Fluffy. I looked at Krissy's little serious face. I looked at the string. I looked at Fluffy's enormous tail. I looked at Krissy. I got an idea. I asked her if she would mind if I borrowed the string for a minute. Then I walked over to Fluffy and began tying the string to the base of his tail.

"What are you doing, Dad?" Krissy asked with a, "Oh no, you're not going to do that!" tone.

"Kris, I think we need a new pet."

"What are you talking about, Dad?"

"Well, Fluffy here is very lonesome. I think poor Fluffy would love to go for a walk with us."

"Dad!!" Her voice began to crack in a twitter of disgust.

I started talking in a high, baby-talk voice, "Come on Fluffers, do you want to walk with the girls and me?"

At that I began dragging Fluffy behind me on the sidewalk. A family on their way to fly kites eyed us suspiciously. Kris ducked down and ran to Kate.

"Oh my God, Dad! Stop that! That's sick!" Kate couldn't help but start to laugh.

"Come on Fluffy, " I continued in my high voice. "The nice people are staring at you. Would you like to do a trick for the nice people? At that I whipped Fluffy into the air for a good ten twirling feet. Krissy exploded with laughter. "Fluffers, do you want to run around the parking lot?"

So we began to jog about, around cars and over sidewalk curbs. On every bump, Fluffy would do a head plowing cart wheel. People coming into the parking lot stared at me. The girls were shrieking with laughter. They didn't want to be, they thought what I was doing was disgusting.

"Oh Fluffers, do you want to go for a ride with the girls and me."

"No Dad. You are not...."

I began to tie the string to the bumper of the Festiva. I flipped Fluffy out of the way and told the girls to get in the car. I rolled down my window and shouted out back to Fluffy.

"OK, Fluffers, get ready. This is going to be fun. Hold on Fluffy!!!" We pulled out of the parking space and started motoring through the lot. Fluffy bounced along, perfectly content to just skip behind us tail first. People did double takes as we drove by. No one seemed amused by our new pet. The girls were shrieking hysterically at this point. I looked over at Krissy and she was drooling out of her mouth and nose. Tears were filling her eyes. All these years and I had never seen her laugh that hard: NEVER! And we laugh a lot.

"Oh my God, I'm going to pee my pants, Dad!!" Kate was flopping all over the car.

We pulled out of the lot and onto a two lane highway. At first Fluffy liked the increased speed. With every little bump and hitch in the road he would catch air. After about a half mile of perfect bounding, our car hit a pot hole and Fluffy's little back end caught the lip and the rebound shot him a good eight feet off the ground. The laws of physics took over and Fluffy began a rhythmic eight foot bounce and fly routine that had passing bikers staring at us slack jawed.

"POOR FLUFFERS!!!" I cried. "OOHH, Fluffy, you are really flying!"

We hit the rail road tracks and Fluffy did a somer-saulting, spiro-giro that flipped him completely around and out into the biking lane adjacent to the road.

"FLUFFY!!!!" we all screamed. On impact, Fluffy's tail came loose from his body and continued sailing along behind us. The rest of Fluffy was bouncing amongst the bikers.

"OUR PET IS GONE!!!"

We pulled into the PCC parking lot and fell all over each other in a fit of mirth. "Oh my God, Dad, that rocked!!"

Later on we decided to tie Fluffy's tail to the back of a U-Haul van and say a short prayer of thanks for all the good times we had shared. The girls and I drove away knowing we had done our best to enjoy our pet while he was in our lives.

Kate couldn't stop giggling. "That's going in the book."

That night we walked the streets in bliss. We were making life, with all it had to throw at us, as good as we could. And really, that's all you can ask for. For life dumps on everybody and the happy ones just know how to swallow their pride and accept the ride.

Whatever it takes.

∧∧∧∧∧∧∧∧∧∧∧∧

I looked back at Eric grinning and wiping his nose. He caught up to me, more animated than he had been all trip. "Dude!" Eric exclaimed. "Let's do one of those '*best of*' lists. I'll ask... you answer."

"Cool."

"OK. Let's try it... Best Album ever."

"Which category?"

"There's only one. Rock."

"*Revolver*. The Beatles…"

"Awesome! Best movie."

"*It's a Wonderful Life*."

"No way."

"Yep. That also has the best scene in any movie, ever. It's that part where Jimmy Stewart can't find the money, and he melts down in front of his wife and kids on Christmas Eve. Dude, the look on his face when he was holding his kid and crying was the greatest thing I've ever seen on film. He was perfect."

"I was always too full of turkey to finish that movie." Eric stopped for a second to stretch out his calf muscle. "It's like we always turn it on when George Bailey is sitting around with that Angel in his underwear."

"Clarence. Oh yeah. That movie has it all. I own that one."

"OK. Best Concert."

"Ever? The first time I saw *Grand Funk Railroad* in 68'… Mark Farner jumping off his stacks of amps, his hair flying around… holy shit!"

"Best Comedy."

"Ooh, that's a tough one. Probably *A Funny Thing Happened on the Way to the Forum*. That movie is beyond belief."

"I've never seen it."

"It's a classic. Watch it sometime. Richard Lester and the film editor must have gone insane trying to splice that one together."

"I think Richard Lester did go insane."

We both started laughing. "Oh. Jesus. Well, it was worth it!"

"OK…You're turn," I giggled. "Funniest movie line ever."

"That's easy, bro. Fast times at Ridgemont High. Sean Penn as Jeff Spiccoli, cruising down the ave in the Camaro with the black kid, weaving through traffic, smokin a blunt and poundin brews… and when he runs a red light and almost causes a head on… lettin' loose with, 'Drivers on Ludes should NOT drive."

I bent over and grabbed my stomach.

As the evening began to cool and the light grew more brilliant than any painting, Eric and I suddenly found every utterance falling out of our mouths hysterically funny. If tears were necessary to releasing the pressure of grief, giggling afterward was essential to keeping the heart open and willing to love.

"Hey Keith… I've got something kinda stupid that's been bugging me for years."

"Now, Eric, there are no stupid questions, just stupid people."

"OK. You guys have Dairy Queens up in Washington, don't you?"

"Yeah. What about it?"

"Well, you know their signs?"

"Uh huh."

"What is a *Brazier?*"

"A what?"

"You know, just below "Dairy Queen" it says "*Brazier?*" What's a *Brazier?*"

"Beats me."

"Dang. I thought for sure you'd know. You being a teacher and all."

"Sorry man..."

"It's cool. It's all good."

I closed my eyes for a second and thought of the last truth in *The Book of Truths*: **Truth # 193**. I'd been able to memorize that one. On my first night in *The City*, I'd flipped to the back and read the last page... read the ending, just like Zoë always used to do to bug me. And just like Zoë, I had broken the number 193 up to: 1 + 9 + 3 and realized it added up to 13: her favorite number. That last quote, a single sentence gracing an entire page, had thrown me for a loop that night, as I didn't quite get the importance of it. But, I got it now. This is what it said.

TRUTH #193:

Having a friend to laugh with is the only way home.

THE HERO OF BRAZIER

Later that evening, wincing with every step, I pulled up over a massive sandstone shelf, and there before me was Eric, back lit by the red sandstone cliffs of Angel's Landing. We had done it. Much earlier in the day, we had discussed running up the cable trail, and camping on the very top of Angel's Landing. It had seemed a brilliant capper at the time, but now, unable to bend my knees, I wasn't relishing the idea.

"I don't think I can take another step up hill, Eric."

"Me neither. I think we should camp here. If we go down into the park we'll have to pay a camping fee."

"Great! This spot is awesome!" I tossed down my pack. "God, I'm wasted. I wonder how Hank and Betty did?"

"Oh Man, you would not believe what happened with those two!"

"What?"

"You won't believe this." Eric was shaking his head and grinning, "So, I'm hiking down through the switch backs, just faced, when I look down and here comes Betty with Hank a ways back. She's panting and hoofing up the switchbacks for all she's worth. So I yell at them to wait and I stroll down and ask them what they're doing, heading the wrong way and all. They can't talk, cuz Betty is crying and Hank is completely wasted, grabbing his knees and wheezing. She grabs my hand and starts saying stuff like, "OH ERIC, Thank Gawd! Thank Gawd! You are an angel, Eric! You are our savior!"

So, I gave them a drink of water and listen to this... They'd hiked down to the edge of these cliffs right below us and freaked out. The thing drops off a thousand feet straight down. They couldn't find the trail and panicked. They had decided to hike all the way back up to the campground and the road! Can you believe that?"

"God, Eric. They would have died if you weren't here!"

"I know. So I turned them around and held their hands down the ledges. I mean the trail *is* pretty scary, but, Jesus..."

"Eric, you are a hero! You saved those guys."

"Anyway, they're down in their hotel room right now, doing room service."

"Did you get a number?"

"No. What for?"

"For a college tuition! I'll bet a hundred grand would seem a minimal gesture to those guys right now."

"Whoa. Come to think of it, I think I could have called em mom and dad by the time they got off those ledges. Holy shit, you talk about some happy hikers."

We boiled up our remaining water and ate Top Ramen with whoops of triumph echoing off the walls of Zion.

Later, lying comfortably in bag, I let my lungs fill with the gorgeous air of Zion. Tonight I would sleep. At long last, I was home. I was safe here.

I heard Eric fiddling with his sleeping bag zipper.

"Night, Eric."

"Night, Dad. He, he."

When Eric said, Dad, I burst out laughing. It had never occurred to me that I was old enough to be his father.

Fatherhood. My shoulders tightened. A father. I thought of Krissy and how much I had changed because of her. I remembered how when she was only one and a half, I had to go to the grocery store and for some strange reason I actually looked in her direction and asked her if she would like to come with daddy to the store. Her eyes blinked wide and she began to shake with excitement. She ran to get her coat and hopped back to take my hand. So tiny were her fingers that she could only grasp my pinky. For the very first time in her life I moved her car seat from the back to the front. As we drove away, the look on her face was of that unmistakable joy, where after working so hard to be good, one is finally noticed by the one they love. A year and a half since her mother and I had brought this child home from the hospital, and I was finally willing to acknowledge her. My god. What had I done? The reality started to flood the car as waves of disbelief began to wash over and choke down any explanation for my neglect.

My story was like an anthem for the role of fatherhood. Since the day child #2 was conceived, I had found myself resentful of her mom's new "all things bright and beautiful" solar system. The mother was the sun, with the two girls and the grandparents and aunts being the planets. I felt like a comet and was bewildered by the force of this gravitational pull. So I did what many men do, I slowly began disconnecting from my own family and began looking for something else to belong to. A recipe for tragedy in the making.

As a result, I had gotten even with her mother at the cost of ignoring my daughter's innocence, her beauty, her squealing in delight at the simplest touches and smiles.

I had not wanted this second child. I wanted something else, though I had no idea what that something else was. My sighs and body language let the family know how much I felt the burden, how late night feedings and wake up calls were interfering with my chance to be somebody, my ability to chase dreams and mountain scenes. Somewhere, up there, just over the next ridge, I knew there was a summit waiting to grant me the peace and worth I craved. And then, only then, I too might taste serenity and the blessing of being able to sprinkle love upon my children. Of course, I had never found it.

When Krissy and I got back from the store that night, I walked into the bathroom, locked the door and wept in shame.

Now, resting in peace amongst the striped walls of Zion, I craved to be near my kids. I yearned to tell them I loved them and to feel their little faces pressed against my cheeks. I wanted to bounce with them, to roll with them, to tickle and laugh, and throw myself at their feet in awe of what a miracle life had presented me. I was finally free to love them.

As I watched the colors change on the massive slabs, my heart whispered a truth I didn't want to hear. It had taken me a thousand miles of road and trails to find this moment of contentment. And those girls, who I loved and swore to never abandon, were waiting for me, a thousand miles the other way.

THE ROAD WARRIOR

The next morning we hiked the three miles of switchbacks down into the park, got some water, and then started hitch hiking our way back to the Kolab entrance. We marched along, thumbs out, as car after car zoomed past. We eventually walked the two miles to the visitor center, which we entered like sweaty Lords of the Dance. Tourists kept turning our direction to stare. Few smiled. I eventually went into the bathroom and in the tight, sanitized air, could feel my body odor filling the room. 'Oh.'

I walked out and grabbed Eric, who was busy making points with a shapely young cashier. We walked a couple more miles to the park entrance, as hundreds of cars streamed by our proudly raised thumbs. I felt like Mel Gibson looked, strutting about the 'good guys in white' in the Road Warrior. I liked my beard, my sweat, my dirty clothes. I had never felt this tough, this centered, this certain of who I was. My shoulders were straight, my body cut and solid. Though we hadn't eaten, I wasn't hungry. Though I had no home, no wife, no job, I had never felt more certain that I was exactly where I should be, a thumb out, smelling like salt and garlic, marching down a road with Eric to nowhere.

We sat down at the entrance gate, stuck out our thumbs, and watched as a hundred cars drove slowly past. Now I knew what a homeless street corner person felt like. It was cool. Us against the world. After a half-hour of futility, I marched across the road to a mini-mart and bought a *Bic* razor and some shaving cream. Twenty minutes later I stepped out of the bathroom, walked back across the street, stuck my thumb back out and had us a ride in less than a minute.

An hour later, we climbed out of our third ride, a lonely vacuum salesman's air-conditioned van. He was heading for the soiled carpet paradise of Salt Lake City. We paused at his door, on the noisy, boiling, freeway, to hear him finish his tale of getting all three of his daughters through college and how, now, he was working to keep away from his wife. We all laughed.

We loved the guy. He gave us some Pepperoni sticks and drove off as we jogged to the visitor center, unable to contain our excitement of finding Clem.

I walked in to the Visitor Center, brown and clean-shaven and asked the lady with the National Park Hat if Clem was around. She said he was making his rounds but would be back within the hour.

"We can wait." I said with nonchalance. Within five minutes, Clem walked in and did a classic double take. The trip was worth it right there.

Needless to say, Clem's view of us had transformed. We were no longer neophytes that he would have to scrape off the canyon floor; we were the real deal, a couple of adventurers who had used his park as a back drop to glory. He loved us. He listened to our tale with genuine delight and when we asked him if he would mind giving us a ride back to our car, he turned off his radio, and led us out the door. On the way up the road, he gave us his National Park business card and let us in on a little secret. He was actually considering putting in for a transfer to one of the Washington National Parks. We were stoked. Clem would rock at Mt. Rainier. We got out of the Zion Park Jeep and shook hands with earnest appreciation.

An hour later, coming down off endorphins and starving, Eric shouted: "Jesus Christ it's SMITHS!!"

We whipped off I-15 and peeled into the SMITHS parking lot like famished ravens. He almost giggled as he walked me through its vaunted aisles. When he spotted *refried beans/ 3 cans for a dollar* it was the only time I actually saw him grow misty during the whole trip. And with the purchase of two cans, Eric had just fulfilled his part of the gas/food deal.

Back on the road, we opened and ate those beans right out of the can, shades of the *Road Warrior* and his dog food supper. I was proud, grinning at I-15 with beans in my teeth. Snuggled in the friendly confines of the Festiva, we headed for *The City*, chewing up the interstate for all the little Ford was worth.

Eventually, the glow of the recent victory began to fade, and the reality that I smelled bad, was dead-tired, that it was cold back at the dump, that I probably wouldn't sleep, and that I should head home in the morning began to weigh me down. I thought of how strange it is to work so hard for a summit, always knowing that the state of bliss it earns is just a moment, a blink away from annihilation. I tried to keep my feelings optimistic, but I also knew that October, November, and the dreaded holidays were next up on the survival agenda: dark days, soul sucking weather, climbing would go away, summits would be harder to come by. And where exactly would I be living? And what would I do for work? And how would I finally divorce Zoë?

As Neil Young's "*You and Me,*" played on the tape deck, I thought about our encounter with Clem. I felt sorry for him, stuck in his rigid box, with all its polished, sanitized walls, its rules, and codes, and ethics, which had to be followed to the letter of the unflinching law. I laughed at poor Clem.

And the first jolt hit me. Which of us actually had the upper hand in this life? Me? What a joke. Then the second jolt hit. Clem was like my dad. Or more precisely, my dad and Clem were cut from a similar, dot the **I's** and cross the **T's**, mold. These were the guys who made sure that the bridges and planes and cars, and medical miracles were built right. Nobody was going to crash on their charge. Their world was of the black and white. Either/ Or. Cut the gray bullshit. Just the facts, mam. These were the guys who could handle mind numbing chores that required perfection. They didn't make the world go round, but they made it safe for the rest of us confused souls to stumble through. My dad's gifts of rigidity, perfectionism, and lack of emotion had always clashed with my creative, gushing, chaotic mayhem. We were opposites, and it is hard to be an opposite to your father. Especially if he is always right and never makes any mistakes. You grow up thinking there is something very wrong with the way you are. And it takes a life time of resentment, and going your own way, and messing up the works, to prove that 'lo and behold' you are not like him after all, and that you were just fine being you all along. What a waste of talent. Both me and my father.

What did my dad think of me, now? I knew, besides disappointment, he could not express his feelings for me, whatever they might be. As we approached Salt Lake, I thought of how somewhere down the road, my mom had become my father's emotional voice. Somewhere, way back, he had lost the ability to handle his emotions. Maybe it was watching a jealous drunk of a father abuse his mom. Maybe it was picking up a fire-stoker from a wood stove one night and holding it in that alcoholic's face and offering up the fact that he would kill him if he ever touched his mother again. Maybe it was the unplanned pregnancy which brought me to the world, soon followed by the birth of my sister, who had severe medical problems and would struggle near death for two years. Maybe it was working at a job for thirty-five years that never really allowed him to be who he was.

Somewhere along the way, something broke in my dad. I always perceived that he and I were not connected. It was as if we somehow breathed the air differently, saw the world differently. Things that came out of my head were not like him, and I did not understand the rigid codes that came out of his. God, I wanted the connection, but I kept blowing up the rules with divorce and failures and tragic choices. And he, who had done everything right and me who had managed to find a way to ruin everything, kept the relationship going by the threads of sports, weather, my latest exploits, and the good old times. A short-list.

And now thoughts pounded in my head, that in all my running around, I had made no effort to listen to his story, had cowered before his judgment, had run and ducked instead of asking him what he was about.

I had made a blueprint, based on his inadequacies, and stood fast behind my array of talents, and now nothing was being exchanged between us that couldn't take place between two strangers in a grocery line. Maybe dad had always been ready for me, but I had simply fumbled the ball too many times. He had tried to love me. He had been there every time I ever needed him. Rescued me. Moved my stuff from place to place countless times. Maybe, I was just one more bewildering disappointment, another shining example that life is too absurd to understand, and the only way to get through it, is to find a routine, put your head down, get to work, and do your job as perfectly as you can.

We pulled up to *the* dump and I decided to head for a motel and a shower. I dropped Eric off at his van. The goodbye was quick to keep the emotions in check. After a couple of hugs and a hasty phone number exchange I headed out of Almo to a much anticipated warm room. I no longer cared about the money I'd been saving. I wanted to blow it on a long hot shower.

The sky was black with no trace of a moon and the stars couldn't find their way through the dirt and grime on my windshield. My headlights barely made a dent in the bending void. Used to having Eric glued to my hip, it felt eerie to have him gone; liberating and terrifying at the same time. I drove on slowly, wondering where the courage of the morning had gone.

I turned a corner and a jack rabbit darted across the road, scaring me, and making me hit the brakes. "JESUS CHRIST!!! I screamed at the windshield.

But that wasn't enough. "GODDAMMIT!!!" I pounded my fists into my steering wheel. I was scared to death. I wanted to turn around and head back to the dump. I began to turn the wheel and shifted the Festiva into reverse.... "DAMMIT!!"

I stopped. I couldn't go back. And to go on was unthinkable. I was shaking, gripping the wheel like it were the robe of God. I sat there at the edge, no longer able to defend myself. I dropped my head down into my hands and I began to scream from the core of my being, in fear, in wretched anger, in rage against this God, this creator who had made me imperfect, who had given me talent and then stolen it, rubbed my nose in it, teased my soul with it, and then crushed it before my eyes until there was nothing left in me that resembled the truth.

I could no longer contain the venom of thirty years and it erupted and spewed forth, like molten bile, shit and vomit: "YOU TOOK IT AWAY! YOU TOOK IT AWAY!!! WHY? GOD!! You took my fucking life away! You took everything!! I was grand! I was a gift and you took it, turned me into a freak, a joke, your fucking joke!! WHY?!! What did I do?!!! I was a child!!! What did I do to deserve your fury? Goddammit, I don't want your bullshit anymore! Just leave me here. Fucking kill me!!! Let me die here you all merciful son of a bitch!"

I hurled oaths and shouted into the void until I could do no more and fell over the seat belt and parking brake and lay on my side waiting for the hand of the almighty father to break my spine.

And the air was quiet. And I could no longer speak. I could only listen. And in that moment of calm, out in the middle of the ocean of Idaho, the voice came to me. And this is all it said:

"Pull out your own thorn."

PETERS AND THE DOVE

I found a reasonable motel on the outskirts of Twin Falls. Once in my room, I took a deep breath of Lysol fresh air and heard a high pitched voice screaming in my bathroom. I walked in there and realized I was hearing a woman's voice through the wall. Hmmm. I showered, turned on the news and lay on the bed as: "OH GOD!!! OH GOD!!!" kept overpowering the din of my TV.

Around midnight I woke up sweating and went over to turn off the heat and the blaring TV. The porn stars were still going at it. Sleep was out and thoughts of Zoë flooded in. Yes, I missed her. Yes, I wanted her. As the next door head-board banged against my wall, I knew why I had caved in, folded under, circled back, broken my vows, and broken my heart so many times. It was simple. I didn't want to be alone anymore. I wanted to hold her, spoon against her, roll with her, speak in silence through eyes that matched each other. I wanted to look at her and know that all the trouble of loving me, hating me, fighting me, cursing me, kissing me, was worth it. There was such gorgeous power in that look, when her hair was down and her face was kind. I wanted to know it again, that I mattered again, at that level again, deep, bottomless, with every ounce of what I had to give surrendered gladly- surely- playfully- joyfully, again. Yes, it was play, it was fun, it was from God, it was delicious and it was all that I had never allowed myself to become. It was Love and she, just that one woman, with those eyes that matched my own, was all I believed could ever have me.

Some time after one the air went still, which meant I was finally able to hear the semi-trucks idling outside my window. I sat wide-eyed in the stuffy room, the smell of smoke and disinfectant carving through my mucous membranes. 'I should have stayed at *The City* another night. I should have done a lot of things.' I picked up *The Book of Truths*.. Here is what I read:

TRUTH #85:

The brighter you shine, the more the dark side will reveal itself. You must shine anyway. It is written that the universe is composed of a rigid order of checks and balances. Just remember, you cannot change the dark, but you can keep the light burning for others to see.

^^^^^^^^^^^^^^^^^^^^^^

I set the book down and thought about the way home. A parade of images bounced through until they stopped on my first real crush, a girl named Chris Bostrom. Hers was the first image of beauty that altered my thinking. Three years older than me and the loveliest creature I had ever known, it was she who gave me *The Prophet* on my 17th birthday and wrote the most glorious note on its opening page. But I was 17, didn't understand a word, and tossed the book in a desk. It wasn't until I was thirty and fell in love with Zoë, that I reopened Gibran's masterpiece and saw my life painted in the Prophet's brush strokes.*

I flipped on the ancient Zenith and lay down to wonder if I actually made a difference in anyone's life. Could I make a difference? Or was I too self-absorbed--a suffering clod of ailments--unable to raise up long enough to lend a hand to anyone else?

Coach J had told me years ago that I had to believe things were coming to me for a reason--that I was on a mission from God--even though there was no summit, no ending to this journey.

When he spoke it was with the passion of a coach who knew I had talent, who looked in my eye and asked: "What have you got?" Indeed, it was his caring encouragement that helped me walk away from my job, from Zoë, from the disease-ridden harbor of safety.

So, which way Coach J? Was I supposed to journey-up or journey-down? One thing I now understood, whichever way I went, there was going to be a force of equal and opposite reaction waiting to either shatter my dreams or lift my ruins to the heavens. Both trails would eventually reach the same place. That was the truth. I also knew that the truth inside of me, at the core of my being, was simple: I wanted to get better. I wanted to learn to like myself, to believe in myself, to become the man I had dreamed of being when I was a boy. I wanted to make my daughters proud. I wanted to be able to think that everything would turn out. I wanted to love. I wanted to give without needing anything back.

At that moment in Burley, I truly did not know which side I was on. I had no way of seeing how the universe was stacked, how every positive move I would make in the next decade would be immediately rendered neutral by a force dead set against my progress. How, the higher I climbed, the farther I would fall. How every single time I seemed to be getting ahead, gaining ground, a calamity would come, knocking me back down the ladder. Sometimes I would be able to predict my own demise, but often, it would come out of nowhere: accusations, lies, bizarre evil fingers pointed at me for something I didn't do, but would pay dearly for with the loss of jobs, income, integrity, and at times, sanity. I had no way of knowing that every move was leading me somewhere and the fire that burned, shaped and sculpted my resolve would lead me to the exact spot I needed to be.

And it wasn't until my own daughter and I were riding in our car and talking about my latest tragic love affair, and she read to me the passage about beauty--the same passage that my first love Chris had written in that note way back when getting my driver's license was the ultimate challenge-- that I broke down and wept for what she, and not I, had seen in me 30 years ago. Truth #85 was like that.

I knew I wasn't there yet. I had a million miles to go. But it was a goal.

I heard myself say 'goal' and thought about Tim's advice to me years ago-before my first divorce, before I'd married Zoë. Of course I hadn't been able to hear him. It was always hard for me to hear the truth from someone I loved. At the time, I had thought Tim was a fortunate son and that lofty goals like he talked of, needed equally lofty faith and confidence, something far greater than someone like me could ever muster up. Now, it seemed I had it wrong. Maybe, just the opposite was true. Maybe, faith and confidence were the by-products of straight, unyielding commitment.

I smiled, picked up the TV clicker and flipped through the array of channels. To my astonishment, glowing on the Zenith was a "classics in entertainment" re-run special featuring top live performances of the 90's. Next up was Peter Gabriel, performing, *"Don't Give Up,"* at a concert in Modena, Italy. 'Whoa! Unbelievable!' This was *the* concert Coach J had told me about almost a year ago.

"Secret World Live," he had shouted at me down the hall about eighteen times. "Don't miss it!"

Later on, in the staff room, he'd gone on to say that Gabriel's band featured guest vocalist Paula Cole, and that her voice was THE VOICE of the angels. He said that the first transcendent note that flew from her lips on *Don't Give Up* was like the dove of peace and had made him sob uncontrollably. "It's the best damn concert I've ever heard...period! Sunday night! 8:00 o'clock. Channel thirteen. Don't miss it! Want me to call ya?"

I told him he didn't have to, that I wouldn't miss it for the world.

He gave me a nod then raced off down the hall of need, a light in search of souls to save.

Of course, the night *Secret World Live* aired, I chose to fight all night with Zoë instead.

So, now, on this night, at 3:00 am in Burley, Idaho, I sat at the edge of the bed as Gabriel's opening words poured forth.

"No fight left, or so it seems
I am a man whose dreams have all deserted
I've changed my face, I've changed my name
But no one wants you when you lose"

My body froze as Peter sang of his despair, of being haunted, of being lost, and oh God, oh God was I there. And then Paula Cole's ethereal voice came from the heavens, parting the dark clouds; that same voice I had heard before, spilling from the hearts of my two children who had to watch their proud father crumble, who had seen this great mass of energy and love burned down to the ground and left unwanted.

And it was those two girls, so little and so brave who had taken my hands.

And it was those two girls so kind and worthy of so much better than I could give, who had found the courage to sing to me when no one else would.

"Don't give up...you still have us
Don't give up...we don't need much of anything
Don't give up...cuz somewhere there's a place where we belong."

And as the song played on I wondered how I would ever stop crying. The sobs came from the same place I had felt when Kate was born, when I had been pierced open by her eyes, cut through to my core and exposed before the universe as *chosen*; as the *one* who would love her forever, and because of that, could no longer hide in the shadows and closets.

I grabbed a towel and buried my face as rivers poured forth. *There* was the reason I was here. *There* was the Truth. It was love. Love was everything. My daughters had taught me that. No words, no rhyme, no Prophet's book; just the look of something so much greater than any other force in the universe that its denial led to madness, war, and annihilation of self. I knelt on the ground and felt my soul being knighted by Paula's voice, being asked to deliver the truth:

To love my children and make them strong.
To forgive Zoë and her need to be free.
To honor my parents and all the pain they'd known.
To give and give and love with all I had. It was the truth. And there was no going back.

I sat in silence until the early morn, with my daughters' voices playing in my heart, telling me to come home, that we'd find a place where we belonged.

THE SECRETS OF YOUR HEART

In the morning, I heard the next room door open, and the sound of the porn stars voices chatting on the step. I hopped off the bed and sprinted to the window to peak out at what surely would be a modern day remake of Aphrodite and her lover. There on the lawn, smoking cigarettes in the early morning light was a bald, elderly gentleman and his round and weathered soul mate; he dressed in royal blue pajamas with matching slippers, she dressed in a pink chiffon robe, her hair in curlers.

"Don't give up," was all I could say.

I vowed to call Zoë and tell her I loved her and that I was coming home to

120

pack my things and leave for good. I wanted to try and explain to her what it meant to be cherished, what it felt like to be sent to heaven by her eyes; that because she loved me, I had no defenses against her; that what she thought of me mattered too much; that all my instincts came back when she kissed me... people's faces, the sky, the trees, the shapes of buildings, the expressions of old people, young people, the sound of tunes on the radio, the whistle of the tea-pot on the stove-- all changed when she told me she loved me.

I opened the night stand drawer and grabbed the complimentary AAA stationary and began composing a letter. Here is what I wrote:

Dear Zoë,

Yesterday was a very good day. I learned a ton and couldn't sleep. I am thinking of you and missing you (of course) so I will write you. It's funny, but you know what I miss most? The smell of your neck. Right along your hair line. I love that. It smells like a wheat field, only salty. Anyway, I've been doing a lot of walking, talking, thinking, reading and listening lately. I feel different. Changed. I hope so.

I've been sitting here all night in this funky little motel room, with an old couple screwing like teenagers next door and a million images flooding through my head. And I'm thinking: Is hope real or a fabrication? And if hope springs eternal from the soul, then what is the soul? I mean I know it's there. I have felt it swell inside me after a phone call from you, or after finding a love note left on my windshield on the very day I had finally given up all hope of seeing you again-- your words pouring joy into my heart after I'd walked like a zombie for months, barely able to eat or work. Over and over I have felt this flood of goodness and wellness race through my veins and tell me to get up and try again. Hope felt like a switch being thrown-- from darkness to light with a flick.

Maybe it's just an illusion. But lately, I've seen too many miracles performed under its influence. Something is up. I'm thinking that this ability to generate hope, to walk under its guiding light, to drink it, breathe it, to believe in it; even though it is nothing more than a mind set, a way of looking out through one's eyes, is the key to sanity. And if hope is fabricated, then so is sanity. And that is what life feels like most of the time. This little tight rope dance between two visions: one of despair, a world of fear and disease. And one blessed with light and hope, a world of love and goodness eternal. The struggle feels endless.

Does this make any sense? I do know this. I always wondered if I was worthy of love. But, now, after gaining a hint on how other people carry on and get through, I've turned the whole love idea around. I think we are only given love when we don't need it. We are only shown eternal beauty when we are so beautiful we could take it or leave it. When we need love, we are tortured, played with, given its complete opposite to grind us down and force us to change so that we don't need anyone...so that we are solid, well, healthy, complete in ourselves.

This is the sad truth: If you want love, you will never find it. You will find its opposite. You will find obsession, need, addiction, clinging, abandonment, agony, and cruelty. When you don't need it, you will be flooded with devotion, kindness and beauty. For a week, I have lived this. I think it's the truth.

I also know this. After all the disappointments, I still love you.

Thank you for those times you loved me. I set you free.

I folded the letter and tucked it in *The Book of Truths*. I wasn't sure Zoë would understand. I wasn't sure I understood. I knew that it made no sense to love someone who could not return that gift. I knew it was over. I knew there was no way we could ever work it out. And I didn't care. I was going home to sleep with her one last time, then walk away to start a new life. And because she loved me, she would let me hold her through the night, genuine, close, passionate and dear. And in the morning, she would pull me to her breast and hold me tight, and kiss me deeply, asking me not to go, before getting out of our bed and leaving the house, the covers, and me, forcing my hand, and sending me on my way to the next town, the next job, the next chapter of the wrong life that would have to be the right life for me. I knew I could not give up on this one. I could never give up. Love was all I had left. And that ultimate truth, on which depended my salvation, would have to be enough.

Yes, I would finally give Zoë what she had always wanted. I would let her go and love her anyway. No strings attached. I would leave only a couple things of mine behind. On her bed, waiting for her whenever she got home, would be *The Book of Truths* wrapped in the t-shirt I'd worn *Crossing Zion*.

I rose to make a cup of Boyd's courtesy instant coffee, knowing what I had to do. I was ready to open and walk through the door and commit to becoming a human being. At long last, stripped bare, with no where to go, no plans, no dreams, no vision in white, I was ready to climb the mountain of doubt, and find out what it meant to be me. My hand shook as I poured steaming water into the little plastic cup. I was finally ready to be what I had promised Kate when I had seen her pulled from the safety of her mother and held naked in the blinding light--bloodied and exposed before the world.

> *And the nurse handed her to me, crying and kicking at the air*
> *And I looked in Kate's eyes*
> *And I said: "I love you, Kate. I love you, Kate."*
> *And she stopped crying. Just like that.*
> *And her body went calm. Just like that.*
> *And as I wrapped her in the towel kissing her face*
> *And tucked her in the crook of my arm like a tiny purple football*
> *I understood why I was here for the first time in my life.*

"All these things shall love do unto you that you may know the secrets of your heart." -Gibran

122

Interlude I

Ann

*"Everybody
Needs Somebody
To Lean On"*

"Handle Me With Care"
-The Traveling Wilbury's

From "Sing alongs for a Shipwreck"

A Word About Love Affairs

There is nothing like a love affair to shake you up, to wake you up, to dust off anything about your persona that was gathering mold or disease. Consuming, passionate, and blinding; affairs defy logic, reason and anything you'd want to teach your inquiring four year old about the birds and bees. Some people never go there. They are the smart ones, the sane ones, the well- intentioned, well-controlled, perfectly functional people that pay good money to watch love affairs at the movies.

Falling in love is easy. Love affairs are brutal. Love affairs come when there is something else you should be doing, like keeping your sanity, focusing on your career, raising children with values and functionability, being nice to your mother, and planning trips with your father. Love helps you sleep. Love affairs keep you awake all year.

Affairs are not a recommended part of a healthy diet. Not the kind of affairs I've known anyway: Soul shattering, down on your knees, begging for forgiveness: 'And if you let me live another day God, I promise to change and never do that again!'...affairs. In a kinder, more secure world, there would be a label, a Surgeon General's warning, or at least a three skulls sticker cautioning against the potential dangers of emotional dependency.

I've had the good fortune of participating in three life-altering love affairs. They have come every decade: my 20's, 30's, and 40's and have been the pivotal wrecking point for the next ten years. The one in my 20's was not with a woman, but with a sport that reminds me of a woman, with all those gorgeous trimmings and hidden crevasses, both capable of shaping your landscape forever.

-From **The Shipwreck** *Journals*

ALTERNATIVES TO THE F-WORD

TRUTH #51:

The ordained right to pursue more happiness, while being a blessing, can also be a curse. You need more time to consume. You need more time to drive your large automobile. You need more time to build a beautiful house. You need more time to work to earn more money to buy more toys to avoid feeling lost. You need more time to play with those new toys to justify the price it is costing to buy your freedom. And there's never enough time.

*-From **The Book of Truths** by Langdon Towne*

^^^^^^^^^^^^^^^^^^^^^^^

[AUGUST 2001: CROSSING IDAHO]

"Hey, Johnson. When you were a climbing guide, did you take guys like us on trips?" Jake was chomping on a *Hostess Ding Dong*.

"You mean did I charge kids like you?"

"Yeah."

"Yes, I did. It was a whorish way to make a living. I was a ho."

"That's tight!" Jake giggled. "No, for real, Johns. Guiding chicks musta been hella tight. Right? You know, working it when you wanted to." Jake danced his head left, then right, snapping his fingers. "All right!" He checked his brownie coated teeth in the mirror again.

Alden spoke up, "You were writing for magazines back then?"

"Yep. Writing magazine articles, guiding mountains, recording music, working outdoor retail, parenting my kids, climbing rock, shredding powder, subbing high school, hanging with legends... a real renaissance man."

"Hey, Johnson, what's a renaissance?"

"Never mind. Anyway, my average work-week was 90 hours. My lifestyle sounded romantic, but in reality, I was starving. I grossed about $13,000 two years in a row. I had rent, child-support, and the usual bills to cover every month. On top of that, Zoë and I were still off and on. I was fighting with my other ex-wife's boyfriend over the way he was treating my daughters. My Festiva had 200,000 miles on it. There was no money to fix anything and a lot of mountains to climb."

"Oh."

"After Lopsang Jangbu was killed I started living place to place with friends, just hanging by a thread every damn day. Lopsang and I had made plans to climb in the Himalaya and write of his exploits. He was such a force, the best. An unbelievable spirit. Incredibly strong... all my dreams vanished with him."

125

"That must have sucked."

"Yep. Everything changed on a phone call."

Alden Crag knew all about the Everest tragedy. "Lopsang was the Sherpa who climbed Everest without oxygen on that trip where people died, right?"

"Yeah, that was actually his fourth time up without gas. If you read the *Mountain Madness* section, it talks about him."

Jake reached over and thumbed through the stack. "Hey, Johnson. You got any more funny stories in here?"

"Sure. The *F-word* article is in there somewhere. My friend Mik Shain says that piece is legendary with the rangers of Talkeetna."

"Dude, where's Talkeetna?"

"Denali National Park, Mt. McKinley. The ranger station up there."

Jake searched through the pages until he found the *F-Word*. Ironically, I'd been hesitant to toss my manuscripts in the already crowded Civic. Now I was thanking God as the boys read and giggled away the passing miles.

Ever thirsting for knowledge, Alden wanted to know what the *F-Word* story was about. I explained how, back in the day, mountain guides tended to use a variety of profanity, words as familiar as four square at elementary recess, words as vital as spitting when it came to adding color to conversation and teaching instruction. I went on to say that when driving home a point, throwing up a tough guy shield, or entertaining youngsters, nothing matched the *F-word* for its succinct, attention-grabbing, descriptive capacities.

Jake wanted to know what a *succinct* was.

I added that in a fair world, people wouldn't judge you for being insecure, or limited in vocabulary choices. "But," I reiterated, "this world ain't simple, and it sure ain't fair."

Jake came up with the *'Alternative to the F-Word'* pages and started handing them to Alden. Here is what they read:

∧∧∧∧∧∧∧∧∧∧∧∧∧∧∧

I am more afraid of my own heart than of the pope and all his cardinals. I have within me the great pope, Self.   - Martin Luther

"The F-Word" was written on maps, brochures, and bits of tissue while backpacking in the stunning canyons of Capitol Reef National Park with the equally stunning Jeannie Probola. It was two grim weeks after Lopsang's death on Mt. Everest and we'd taken off for the deserts of Utah to dry out our sobbing hearts. We wandered in silence through red rock canyons and over slick-rock mesas, trying to regain some sense of hope.

One morning, as I sat in the quiet watching Jeannie read a college text-book, voices came to me, bringing up every wrong thing I'd ever done. No wonder no one wants to hold still. Because there was no place to go, I just sat there taking my lumps until a thought came up that actually made me laugh. I grabbed a pen and this is what came tumbling out.

126

^^^^^^^^^^^^^^^^^^^^^^^^^^^^^^

Life and the pursuit of happiness seems to be a process of adjusting and adapting to my bubbles being burst before I even get a chance to blow on them. For example, I recently read an angry letter to the editor in which an outraged reader went off about the overuse of profanity in today's outdoor type magazines. Talk about a load of wet-blanket being flopped on my lap. God knows I'm guilty as a dog for throwing in the *f-word* throughout my articles. It's not that I particularly like talking trash or am abundantly proud that I lack the literary tool chest of a Shakespearean vocabulary. Hardly. I simply find it delightfully easy to pack around my little Swiss Army Knife of descriptors, the *f-word*, and slap it in whenever cracking open the thesaurus might be more appropriate. Can you blame me? The *f-word* delivers. The *f-word* rocks. Everbody understands the *f-word*.

Everybody that is except my mom, my pious friends, and those select readers yearning for something more meaningful than tasteless potty talk. There's no doubt the letter to the editor got under a rib. It made me painfully aware that to have certain folks read my stuff and still be able to look them in the eye, I was going to have to give my communication skills a full on tidy bowl rinse. No more *fuck*.

I decided to adjust my attitude, move away from my Yin, and grab my Yang. I made a monumental decision to take a much needed road trip to cleanse my soul and help me formulate some alternatives to the *f-word*. I filled my Festiva and headed south.

The thirteen-hour drive to The City of Rocks, Idaho was the perfect space to ease in to this project. By the time I arrived I had come up with my list and a plan. I would deny myself the use of the *f-word* when conversing and would rely instead on expressive non-profane words that climbers and wanderers could relate to. I experimented with a five-word vocabulary that combined with winks, blinks, and nods, got the dishes done when communication was the name of the game. I soon found that these single word utterances were all I needed to snag terrific beta, a bitchin belay, score some munchies, and get directions to the nearest jon. The *f-word* was out. *Dude, hey, cool, bummer,* and *man* were in.

DUDE : *Dude* is one of those moronic words that somehow seems to be sticking. Originating from the drug-dazed, riff-raff, surfer culture, it has become a greeting call for comfortably hip climber types as well. Before *Dude, Fuck* seemed the only way to capture any gut-wrenching passion without writing a book about it. Now, with correct intonation and eyebrow lift, *Dude,* like *Fuck,* can cover the intense emotions of love, fear and grief; as in, "*Dude,* this herpes flare-up blows!"

Dude can be stretched. For example, upon greeting a fellow climber, one might give the rock sign and offer, *"Dude."* *Dude* lets others know you care. Or if the greeting is to a female, one might point in the direction of the sun setting behind Asterisk Pass and offer up a melodic *Dude,* which she would appropriately interpret as "My god, can you believe the brilliance of that sunset and the rich diversity of geological formations stretching endlessly before us. I'm overwhelmed by the dreamlike landscape and the kaleidoscope of emotions pulsating from my temples and nads!"

Or, if your belayer looks the other way, locking off the rope, just as you're yarding up several feet to make a clip, *"DUDE!"*, let's him know he's being a total asshole, without *you* getting all ugly about the whole thing.

Dude, is also the perfect greeting for those awkward times when you can't remember the name of someone who was just introduced to you a day or several minutes before. If your brain cramps, greet them with a resounding *"Dude!!"* They'll feel cherished. However, blow the enthusiasm part and those same people will think you're a brain dead rehab project who can't remember names for shit. That could be a black stain on your Karma. People hate it when they think you've forgotten their name. That is why you've been getting called *Dude* for the last several years.

Alas, Dude can look painfully stupid coming out of the mouth of anyone over the age of 27, unless, of course, they're living out of a car with over 173,000 salted road miles on it. Guys living in this kind of space can get by saying just about anything they want because nobody is listening anyway.

HEY: Make no mistake, some chicks hate being called *Dude,* which brings up the importance of using *Hey* if one is planning to score.

He*y*, actually has a kind of hunky ring if offered up with a flip of the head and some James Dean nonchalance. It takes practice to not come off as a total dip, so get in front of the mirror (after you clean it off) and work it.

Hey, if delivered with the right oomph, can say to the gal you're addressing, "I really find you intellectually stimulating and would love to converse at length about philosophical questions concerning Plato's Symposium, but first things first. Would you mind bending over and flaking my rope?"

COOL: If the world were a solely positive place, *Cool* could replace both *Fuck* and *Dude* as the all-around expletive of choice. *Cool* deals with the positive side. Anything around you deserving a compliment or a touch of applause, goes nicely with *Cool.*

If some stranger comes up to you going off about a red-point he just nailed after two solid days of finger tearing dynos, he won't sulk away cheated if you offer up a 'Cool.' Feel free to raise the arch and intensity of the *cool* to correspond to the effort and true value of his climbing status. Indeed, *Cool* makes you and others happy and would work as the number one choice if not for the fact that the world is only half positive. For every Yang sticking his 5.13C red-point, some other pathetic Yin is grabbing a draw and blowing it for the umpteenth time on a four bolt 5.7. If you happen to let go a *"cool"* around this wretch, he'll think you're making fun of him and his obvious inadequacies. He'll think you're cruel and tasteless. He'll think you remind him of the psycho-ex he's been trying to break up with for the past three years. He'll think you've somehow cosmically appeared to twist the screws of his tortured soul and darken the sun.

God knows, *'Cool'* is not what you want flopping out of your mouth if you happen to witness some poor sucker grease off a crimper clipping a draw with 8 feet of slack in his mouth. As he lies there at your feet, writhing with a broken pelvis and shattered femurs, almost anything besides, "Jesus Fucking Christ!!!" would seem a bit sedated. You'll have to make the call.

BUMMER: *Bummer* shows empathy and caring. This is really great with chicks if not overused. Overuse it and they'll think you've got a negative-attitude. They'll think you're carrying lots of cloudy baggage from a former relationship that in point of fact, did butcher your soul like a blender from hell.

Go lightly on the *bummer* and you'll be taken as tastefully dark without being vile. *Bummer,* shows controlled disappointment instead of unfounded rage. It exudes maturity, which is a magnetic turn on for the ladies. Where in the past, a lady friend calling to tell you that she's bailing on the weekend's trip to Smith to go to a friend's tofu potluck and poetry reading would have drawn forth something like, "You've got to be fucking kidding me right? Right?! You're not fu... *click"* The correct alternative response is to mumble *"bummer,"* hang up, then race to the jon to heave. Simple and tasteful.

MAN: To handle utterances of bewilderment and confused amusement, *man* is the word of choice. For example, if someone comes down off a climb and starts telling you how the 3rd and 4th bolt were spinnin, the rap anchors were awkward, some of the moves were chossy, but the climb was still a stellar experience, *Cool* would sound as if you weren't listening to the part about the bolts, the choss, and the awkward anchors. *Bummer,* would express a negative attitude from which you might be perceived as one who sees the cup half empty. This would turn off the chicks who just happened to be walking by smiling, even though they were only smiling because chalk got stuck on your bald spot. *Dude,* would make you sound like an imbecile. *Man,* leans neither way. It lets your frantic companion know you're hip to his scene, one with his bun, flakin' his bacon, and so forth.

Man has come to us from the bad weed days of the hippie dippie sixties. The pot back then was so weak compared to the killer dope prevalent today, that *man* was about all a dude could leak out of his rasty larynx after sucking an hour or two on a joint the size of a Keilbalsa sausage. The sorry hipster would sit there hyper-ventilated, not a bit high, with a wind pipe that felt like a clogged chimney, gasping for breath from lungs plugged full of ash and foul by-products. "Man. I'm fucked up!" really meant, "Somebody get me a fucking respirator!"

Indeed, had the killer bong tokes of today been available back in the 60's, *"Man,"* would have been skipped altogether for more ballistic expletives such as awesome, wicked, and bitchin.

Still, *man,* works. It has managed to be the *F-word's* right hand man for thirty years. People know, *man.* They can dig it. Say you're staring up at a blank wall that is only rated 10b, wondering how to get to the first clip without sketching. *"Man"* is all you need to say to your belayer. Your belayer will know you meant, "Jesus Christ, I know this is only 10b, but this fucking thing looks absolutely blank....not that I want to bail on the sharp end and let you have a go, but I wish I'd been crankin at the gym this month instead of breaking up with my girl friend for the hundredth time!" *Man* is enough.

BONUS WORDS: These words can be used for **occasional** embellishment.

RIGHT ON: *Right on* sounds good about the first 12 times you hear it. After that you just want to slap the compulsive loser back to his defective childhood. Be *extremely* careful you don't flip your hair when letting this one fly. If you do, run right out, rent The Road Warrior and stop shaving for several days.

WICKED: *Wicked* makes you sound like you have nads of steel, that you live at the edge, that you're reckless, fearless, and ready to kick some serious ass. I love this word. Chicks love this word. Use it in response to gruesome, nauseatingly detailed stories concerning body parts that drip or splintered things stuck where they don't belong. "Wicked!" is also the perfect response to watching a buddy take a forty footer in which nothing was damaged except the Metolius shorts he fully crapped in mid-flight. *Wicked* is cool.

AWESOME: *Awesome* is an example of what compulsive behavior can do to a guy. I used to love this word, but I've overused it to the point where I might let it slip carelessly from my mouth, were a friend telling me about a dog down loading on his geraniums. "Awesome, Dude." And he'd look at me like, "What the hell?" Sorry. I've worn this word out. Avoid it.

RADICAL: *Radical* is a pleasant alternative to *awesome.* It sounds a bit goofy coming out of the mouth of anyone over 23, but is hard to abuse because in any given twenty four hour period, there usually aren't that many radical things happening.

No doubt, in a simple, fair world, people wouldn't be offended by words such as *Fuck.* They'd have better things to worry about, such as what their wife is up to on all those lengthy, late-night, milk runs to the grocery store.

Hopefully, you'll find this list of alternatives to the *F-word*, helpful. If you lack friends due to a wanting vocabulary, this list may, in fact, open a few doors and bring a fresh belay slave to your tired and teaming shores. Obviously, one shouldn't rely on this list exclusively if one were say, being introduced to a potential father in law with deep pockets. (If he's a loser, living out of his car, this list is more than adequate). Finally, this list may even help spring you towards a fulfilling lust driven relationship which will eventually consume you, drive you to the brink of madness, then turn on your heart and bank account like Drano in a hair-balled pipe. Whoosh! There go the goodies! Oh well. Yin and yang. Adjust and adapt. Dude, happiness is just a road trip away.

∧∧∧∧∧∧∧∧∧∧∧∧∧∧∧∧∧∧∧∧∧

Alden looked up from the F-word manuscript. "Jesus Tits!!"

I gave him an eyebrow and a nod. There was little else to say.

"Hey, Johnson," Jake Burley yelled from the back seat. "This story is hella funny!" The boys had giggled and snorted as they passed back and forth the pages. I kept thinking *they* were hella funny. I punched a fresh road tape into the deck. We still had another three hours until we'd get to *The City of Rocks*.

Alden spoke above Neil Young's *Old Man*, "Ya know, I think you've been reading too much Langdon Towne. You're starting to sound like him."

"Yeah, a couple of dirt bags in cahoots. I'm learning to tell the truth, anyway. And if you're going to tell the truth, you can't be afraid of losing your job, or pissing off your parents, or your ex-wife, or your ex-wife's husband, or your ex-girlfriend's husband, or his girlfriend, or anybody else who might take offense just because you think you're funny. You have to just say what should be said. Just like Towne. Ya know what I'm sayin?"

They did.

"Hey, Johnson."

"Hey, what?"

"I don't get it. This is one long ass drive. I mean all those trips here to get over your ex #2. Why didn't you just dump her while you were still young?"

Alden turned to me and said, "It does sound like you were always miserable. Why *didn't* you just move on? What kept you coming back?"

I looked at the sun setting on the horizon and turned to the young men who had never tasted a mango freshly fallen from a tree branch.

"Hmmm. It's real simple. When Zoë and I got back together after breaking up for a couple of months or years and we went to the ocean, she would write my name in the sand…. in these giant letters for the whole world to read:

I LOVE YOU KEITH MARK

No one had ever done that for me. No one's done it since. That was all I needed."

THE WINNING STREAK

TRUTH # 2:

If you don't know where to go, go with what you know. Books, fools, and sages will tell you how to paint your face, but you're the one who has to wake up each morning and stare in the mirror.

-From **The Book of Truths** *by Langdon Towne*

∧∧∧∧∧∧∧∧∧∧∧∧∧∧∧∧

When living large you reach a point where your ability to produce on the spot game saving decisions gets tapped out. You can never see it coming. It just shows up like a bad smell in a crowded movie theater. But once it is there, confidence and drive are quick to follow the downward trend.

Since riding the big waves is all about taking risks and facing these trying moments of choice, one must always bank on a never ending supply of 'suck it up' factor. Of course, that's impossible and the fear of losing this power is what keeps us striving and training and attempting to keep our karma clean.

And sometimes the choices come faster than our hope, morals, values or training have prepared us for. Sometimes, these high powered emotionally charged decisions must be processed and dealt with in an eye blink. Sometimes, a choice leaves you gasping in thankfulness for one's blind luck, another time you lay tossed in ruins. And no matter how close you tow the line, there is no escaping the fact that eventually you will fuck up. Eventually you will choose the wrong door. It may be a tiny chunk of undercooked Phad Thai chicken, seeping with salmonella. It may be a drive down the right road at the wrong time. It may be a careless comment emitted in a state of glee to a pair of ears straining to hear you make a mistake. All you can do is strive for absolute control, with all your little eggs lined up in a row.

Meanwhile the universe is waiting to find a chink in your armor, a moment when you breathe in and announce to yourself: "Damn it is good to be me." And then wham! The channel of hell will open wide to suck you down into the bowels again.

So how do you know when a streak is about to change? How do you know when 'for better' is about to turn 'for worse?' It can be as simple as driving up the Alaskan Way Via-duct at 70 MPH, with "Keep on Rockin in the Free World" blasting on the tape-deck, clouds billowing up over the Olympic Mountains to the west, the sun sparkling off Puget Sound reminding you there is a God, and then looking to your right to give yourself a couple kudos on what an awesome decision maker you are since I-5 is a stalled heaping nightmare and you are heading north like the speed of light, and then looking back at a set of tail lights and a Taxi bumper approaching your windshield as fast as your 2001 Civic can decelerate with your foot punched full tilt on the brake, no time to check the rear view mirror for the semi-truck that was tailing you, while the shriek of Les Schwab's finest Z-700 rubber burns over the top of "...one more kid who'll never go to school, never get to fall in love..." with your fate already sealed by the simple mathematics of a single statistic you can't remember right at the moment that states specifically the number of feet required of a 2001 Civic to stop from 70 to zero. Of course there's no time for a prayer, just the usual four letter word of alert confirmation that might hint to God or whomever might be interested that the number of that braking statistic rhymes with nifty and not heavenly. And in that space of three adrenaline laced heart beats your winning streak either ends or begins.

-From **The Shipwreck** Journals

∧∧∧∧∧∧∧∧∧∧∧∧∧∧∧∧∧∧∧∧∧∧∧∧∧

[AUGUST 2001: AUSTERA PEAK, NORTH CASCADES]

"You are never going to get up the Grand." Langdon was laughing.

"Jesus Christ, Towne. It rained one day out of forty-nine! What are those odds?"

"About five per cent."

"Dammit. If it wasn't for bad luck…"

"…I'd have no luck at all." Towne took a pull off his Slim-Fast. "Best song *Cream* ever did."

"The sad part is, I really could care less if I ever climbed the Grand Teton. But you know how it is, you get on a road trip and you need these little goals sprinkled here and there to keep your mind on a mission."

"Oh yes. And how quickly those peaks can turn from mission to obsession. And oh what a price will be paid if said goals are not met."

"That's the problem with any mountain. Once you lock it into your sights, it does become an obsession. It changes from a mundane inanimate, to something brilliant and worthy of devotion."

"Sounds like love to me." Towne squinted at the sun.

"God yes. The hell of unmet expectations."

"Exactly. Better to toss the bar out the window. If you don't expect anything good, anything at all is fine."

"Yeah. If you got nothing, you got nothing to lose. That's easy to say and pretty hard to do."

"10/4 good buddy, c'mon."

"Like that second attempt at the Grand Teton. Anything short of the summit was unacceptable. How could Craig and I fail? We'd done our homework. We were in shape. We'd prepared every last detail. We went to bed without a cloud in the sky. And then 'ka-plink' the first raindrop hits my head."

"Sometimes all you get to do is dream of a summit. Sometimes it just isn't meant to be. There's a reason in there somewhere."

"Right…"

Towne started chuckling lightly at my tale of woe and misfortune. "Hey," he smirked, "did you ever consider the reality that climbing the Grand is less important to the balance of the universe then a single snowflake dropping from the sky." He began to laugh out loud.

∧∧∧∧∧∧∧∧∧∧∧∧∧∧∧∧∧∧∧∧∧∧∧

The mood was jovial now, but the summer before it hadn't been so funny when Dear David and I had mistakenly crossed the little foot bridge in the dark and taken the wrong trail through the Meadows that soon ended in snow fields and boulders that we hopped and slipped over in the dark until we arrived at the wrong col between the Middle and Grand Teton. Had we stopped and taken five seconds to pull out the map stuffed in my pocket, we would have taken a step to the right instead a hop to the left and kept going up the well worn trail until we reached the correct col with its running water source and our shiny objective looming above us like the Taj Mahal. Instead we had stumbled up that loose boulder field and those icy snow slopes in our running shoes, all the while going, "Where is the freaking trail?"

When we arrived at the lonely, wind swept gap between the Middle and South Teton, we were in shock. No tent sites. No climbers. No running water. We stared in horror at the jumbled walls above that loomed in the darkness like the Castle Dracula. What had we done? There was no laughter in the morning when we descended the three thousand erroneous feet of loose boulders and snow fields in our running shoes and started limping our way back up to the correct col between the Middle and Grand Teton. We got there, but I was toast. My ankles were hammered and my drive was yanked out of the wall. I sat down on a rock and quit. I'd never done that before. For the first time in my memory, I felt the shame of turning around because I didn't have the will to keep going. I put my head down and headed for the valley floor as wave after wave of cheerful climbers, hikers, and babes kept storming past, heading up on their way to fulfill their dreams. On that day in July, there were no thunderstorms. There was nary a cloud. It was the most perfect summit day of the entire year.

∧∧∧∧∧∧∧∧∧∧∧∧∧∧∧∧∧∧∧∧∧∧∧∧∧

I looked off in the distance and sighed. "Oh well, it's just a mountain."

"Yeah, yeah. Sure. It's just a mountain. It's just a woman. It's just the barrel of a shotgun stuffed in your mouth with your toe on the trigger."

"Uh…"

"Dude, I'm laughing, but it isn't funny. I know that. Once we goal-oriented, risk-taking, addictive-types lock in, it's not just a mountain anymore. It defines who we are. It's the canvas on which we paint our worth. To have God intervene and decide we're not worthy seems a nasty attack on our perception of order."

"So, Langdon. When will it change? When will this losing streak end?"

Towne took off his sunglasses and cleaned the lenses, staring long and hard at my face. "In about two and a half minutes."

"What?"

"Let me take your head and hold it under some water. In a couple of minutes you'll want that air pretty bad. That's how much you gotta want change. Until then, it's all just smoke and bullshit."

∧∧∧∧∧∧∧∧∧∧∧∧∧∧∧∧∧∧∧∧∧∧∧∧

A few days before the morning Craig and I got douched on the Grand, I had found myself atop a giant boulder, deep in the Wind River Mountains of Wyoming. But it wasn't far enough. I was watching the sunset, off to myself, out of sight from Craig and Kristan. The familiar sickness of heart had followed me. I now understood that no matter how far I walked, no matter how much my legs and feet hurt, no matter how hard I laughed with Craig, no matter how long the road trip lasted, this aching in my deepest corners would be there to invite me home. And I sat in the silence and looked at the jagged peaks etched in red and this man of constant sorrow that I'd become. And I wept for what I wasn't and for all I had not been. So many holes to fill. So many moments wasted. So much time lost to nothing more than my own emotional garbage. And now I was middle aged and felt like a middle aged child, still scared of the loneliness, the alienation, and the sense of having no home. And it was there, on that ridge watching the sun fall behind a row of dagger like peaks, that a thought whisked through: "My God you should be thankful for this life." And in the space of thirteen desperate breaths, I finally said goodbye to Zoë. My heart emptied and she went with it. I knew I was going to be utterly alone. And I didn't care. I couldn't care anymore. Alone was going to be wonderful.

And three days later, as Craig and I headed to Jackson, for the second attempt at the Grand, I knew that for the first time in my life I felt solid. There would be no more agonizing over Zoë. There was nothing left to work on. There was nothing waiting at home to worry about. There was no one to disappoint me. My world would be what I created. No one was going to be indifferent to me anymore. I couldn't believe the relief. And just like that, the weight of depression vanished.

Once I got back to Kent, I stopped and saw Kate. She hardly recognized me. I was young again, vibrant again, and in love with life again. My grin was infectious, my eyes gleamed all knowing. I finally had what I'd always wanted: confidence and serenity.

So there it was. Three weeks on the road, no phone calls home, climbing ten vertical miles of rock, running ridges at altitude, laughing with Craig, and staring down into the great-wide-empty had done it. I had finally crossed through some barrier, purged the demons, and entered a new zone. I felt it in every cell. I feared nothing, not even the fact that there were a ton of desperate messages from Zoë on my answering machine. Not even the sight of the card in my mailbox, sealed with a lipstick kiss, altered my inner sense of clarity.

I still felt confident when I hopped upstairs wondering if I should actually dial her number. And when her voice answered ecstatic and she came down four nights in a row to make love, even then, I simply accepted those moments of rapture as a product of commitment to self. And on the fifth night, when I left for a three day traverse in the North Cascades with Zoë in my pulse, I knew she and I had finally become one. It wasn't until I came back triumphant and drove up to her house unannounced to surprise her and was treated to a predicatable, yet painful surprise myself, that I realized the planets weren't aligned quite as perfectly as I'd imagined.

And that was that. I presumed my winning streak was over. Our hastily planned trip of rest and love making to the ocean was spent sprinting alone up various peaks in the North Cascades in a vain attempt to remove the bile coating my every cell.

The following week I picked up Krissy from her mom's and took her climbing. I chose a secluded crag so we could clip bolts in late afternoon solitude. Krissy led everything in style and we were doing laps on a favorite route when a group of climbers came wandering up the trail. The late afternoon light was filtering through the tree branches, lighting up the shape of the woman in front. She was stunning and my first thought was: "Oh my God, she is a vision." My second thought was an immediate recognition of the man walking close behind: Dr. Orval Faubus. The woman was his wife, Ann. Oh well. Taken goods.

Ann sat down next to me and laced up rock shoes on feet attached to legs so perfect I could not swallow without turning everyone's head. So innocent was she of her magic that it hurt to pretend to not look at her. The shape of her shoulders, her waist, the richness of her olive skin, the shine on her chestnut hair... I found myself gasping and embarrassed. And when she opened her mouth, smiled at me, and began to speak, it was the voice of the woman on the *Herb Albert and the Tijuana Brass* album cover that I had pinned up in my bedroom at the age of seven. Now, she was before me, witty, funny and holding court as she drew her bow and shot an arrow through my chest. I sat smiling with *Neil Young's: Heart of Gold,* playing in my head.

As I watched Ann turn in the streaks of filtered light, I suddenly knew why I hadn't met anyone I'd truly wanted in the ten long years since I'd left Zoë. The voice came up gently: "She's the one." And right then, I knew I was still on a winning streak.

136

A harmless little crush of course. She didn't know me, but I knew her husband: a physician, a man of steel, adored in the community, revered by friends and compatriots. He was a legend, a hero figure. The two of them made a silhouette of marital bliss and I admired what they had achieved from my lonely little perch of envy.

I purposely belayed Ann on some climbs so I could stare at her shoulders and hips. Eventually, Krissy let me know it was time to go. As I flaked my rope, Ann walked over and thanked me for the belay and asked if she could ever go climbing with us again. She informed me that her husband would be out of town for the next two weeks and she'd be without a climbing partner. I offered up a 'yeah, sure,' but quickly round-filed it, certain I wouldn't see her again any time soon. After all, two of my best friends were due in town in the next few days to wisk me away on another North Cascade binge. But God, she was divine. Her husband was a winner and one lucky dude.

And a week later, when Kate left for college, and Kris went back to her mom's, and every single friend who had promised to head up into the mountains to binge had bailed, and I sat down and called information to get Ann's number, I knew, no matter what, I should not make that phone call. I knew I was trouble with a very capital: **T**. I knew that my heart had finally healed for the first time in my life and that I should try to enjoy this winning streak and see where it took me. It took me straight to my phone.

And that is how winning streaks end. You push it just a few minutes, a few moves, a few mountains, or one phone call too far, never satisfied with sitting on contentment, never satisfied with a sense of peace, just upping the ante as soon as you can muster the strength, just a little more, ever so slightly, until the cup is too full and there is nowhere for the juice to go but down.

ANN

Sometimes there is no way of explaining why we do what we do. There is no way of explaining standing alone for ten years, while your youth goes by. There is no song that carries the weight of opening your bills alone, and staring at bad news with no one there to look at should your heart fall. There is no book out there that has the answers for fixing your second cup of coffee, knowing there is nowhere to sit in your apartment that doesn't feel empty and that the warmth of the steam on your face is the only comfort your skin will know, and you know, you should be thankful for even that. Sometimes there is no good reason why you pick up a phone and dial a number you shouldn't, or say hello to a pretty face with a ring on that one finger that says you shouldn't, or get in your car and drive back to a grocery store in the hopes that maybe, just maybe, that one face that you were too scared to approach, will miraculously appear to give you a second chance. But she never appears. And, thus, with no explanation that could ever make sense to anyone in their right mind, you call the number you shouldn't.

*-From **The Shipwreck** Journals*

∧∧∧∧∧∧∧∧∧∧∧∧∧∧∧∧∧∧∧∧

[AUGUST 2001: KLAWATTI PEAK]

"So when does it turn? When does it go from attraction to addiction?"

Langdon turned to me as he emptied a packet of GU in his mouth. "That depends," he said.

"On what?"

"On how strong the attraction is." He chased the GU with a sip of tea.

"Hmmm."

"And that, my friend, is why we are so susceptible to beauty, so moved by it, so afraid of it, so in need of conquering it. For we know it is crush or be crushed. We know those eyes will soon control us."

"That's extremely cheerful."

"Well, think about it. Who is your harbor, your plate of joy, your garden of paradise for the first bazillion seconds of your life? The eyes of your mother are everything. They are life and death. They determine every ounce of your joy and suffering. You are a sponge, and she is the water, or the darkness."

"I see where you are going with this."

"And what if mom is on a downer? What if mom is lost in grief? What if mom is doing evil to her body? And you are the tender sponge waiting for nourishment, not just your belly, but your heart and soul and every belief you will ever carry about yourself forming like a thundercloud billowing to the sky. And how many of us were looked at and treated with the softness and patience and tenderness we seek so dearly from those women we chase, that one pair of eyes we yearn for until the grave."

"God."

"Hey, this ain't rocket science. We need her. So we carry on like we don't. And we grow old and our joints hurt, and we beat out fists to death to prove that we could have done it without her, and all the while the truth is something different. We would have died without those arms around us, would have died if she didn't care for us."

Towne paused as his voice choked up and tears welled in his eyes. Suddenly he was alone with the music in his head playing a love song he would never sing to anyone but his walls.

∧∧∧∧∧∧∧∧∧∧∧∧∧∧∧∧∧∧∧∧

Ann did not belong to me. She did not belong to anyone but God and the spirit of love and beauty. For she was the face of beauty and holy light and I have never been so drawn to another human being in my life.

A giving soul, Ann did not know how to ask for help. She did not understand that if you ask for help, it will come. She thought that to be strong meant to be self-sufficient and ready to be there for others. She gave and gave and asked for nothing in return. Ann had hidden in the shadows of her famous husband, working in the dim light behind his great presence. She was the keeper of his flame, tendering it, making sure his fire was in good order. And her hands were dark with soot and ashes; her gaze longed for beauty and color and she stoked the fire and chopped the wood and dug out the splinters and cleaned up the mess so that he might shine and bring honor to his name.

I came to her as a beacon, recently purified of my sins, cleansed and rejoicing in truth and freedom for the first time in my life. In this gorgeous space I held up a mirror to her and said: "You are the most beautiful creature I have ever seen on this Earth. More beautiful than any flower, sunset, or fawn standing in a forest."

I spoke the truth and I fell in love with her. My words were the music she had yearned for all her life. They came and swirled into her heart, filling nooks and crannies of doubt and darkness, bringing joy and light to places that had been lost along the way. She rejoiced at the sight and thought of me and I became her love.

One day I took her hand and we stepped into a warm pool of perfect clear water. We let ourselves float in beauty and embraced as one while the world stopped moving and the universe shut its eyes for a moment. And when the eyes opened again, there in the pool was the reflection of his angry face, the one who was entitled to her name, the one who claimed to possess her body and her soul. The look was terrifying. We hid our nakedness and scrambled from the pool in horror at our selfishness.

Fear came like a vacuum to empty our hearts. Ann trembled before his hands, which trembled at the thought of me touching her skin, the skin which he claimed as his own. And he swore vengeance upon her and me and the children she had borne him, swore to crush all hope and spirit from her if she ever contacted me again.

And she turned from me in holy fear, fear of the sin, fear of the father she had never known, fear of a God which had always shunned her light, and kneeled before the King to kiss his ring and praise his mighty nobility, while truth and beauty and love vanished from her world, and death overtook her gaze: invaded her thoughts, invaded her dreams, stole her sleep, stole her appetite for nourishment, stole the memories of me as the last petal of her heart, which had only moments before risen in full glorious bloom, rippling in the breeze of love's ecstasy, trembled dry and lifeless to the ground to lie in the ashes with all her other dreams.

-From the **Shipwreck** Journals

THREE NIGHTS

We humans need affirmation, a look from another set of eyes that says we are loved. It is a driving human want and need, close behind air and water. And it comes at such a cost. It can lead to prison cell relationships. It can lead to soul shattering affairs. It can lead to an eternal searching for that one true soul mate; that kindred spirit out there somewhere.

There was a day not long ago when my daughter Krissy and I drove back from a climbing trip and her breath came in tight, compressed fits, little gasps of forced pain, mouth open, head down, body contorted, the language of the un-loved. She knew she was unwanted. She ached every second, and I knew that ache, knew it was why I had risked everything to see Ann once in awhile.

*-From **The Shipwreck** Journals*

∧∧∧∧∧∧∧∧∧∧∧∧∧∧∧∧

[AUGUST 2001: CAMP #34, THE CITY OF ROCKS]

Kristan looked up at me. She had been reading since first light and having worked her way through most of the *Shipwreck Journals,* wanted to know more about my love affair with Ann, wanted to know why, after finally getting over Zoë, I had put myself through such madness and heartache again.

"I'm not sure why it happened, Kristan. I go back and forth between believing in fate, in the whole star-crossed-lover thing, and thinking Ann was just ripe for an affair. I know for me, I fell in love with her instantly. And she says she did with me. But, I don't know."

"I can't imagine trying to parent, teach and coach through all that."

"Oh yeah. It was a work out. Best weight loss program in the world. Ya know, when you awake each day, for years and years, and there is always a hurt, a dryness, an ache that you know full damn well a single look would take away, you become vulnerable. Your shield goes down slightly. Your reflexes become awkward. You find yourself needing love, and that need is dangerous. It is far better to be a rock, never in need. But, the heart is not a rock. The heart is soft and willing to open the instant someone comes along with the right watering can."

"It shouldn't be so hard to find love."

"No. But once you *do* find it, once you feel the change and the immensity of the difference, once you walk in a room and after a simple smile, see how the view has changed, how everyone looks more approachable, more forgivable, where suddenly you understand the meaning of it all, and the voices in your head change from losers to angels, just from a single glance from a face that pleases you; how can one pretend there is anything else in the universe more wonderful than being adored? I mean it. Is there anything better than that?"

"There isn't."

We got up and walked across the granite outcroppings adjacent to Campsite 34 searching for the perfect place to sit and catch the sunrise glow. The air was ideal, warm, with nary a breath of wind. We sat down and let our legs dangle over the edge of a cliff, the light turning the rock golden. We were bathed in the best of early morning Idaho.

"You know I was out of my mind all last year. And I was trying to keep up this healthy appearance for my daughter, the kids at school, my athletes. But I was sick of heart, just dying the whole time. It's unreal how much turmoil you can endure."

Kristan smiled in her peaceful way, reached over, thumbed through the pages of the *Confessions* and read a journal entry called *Three Nights*.

Friday Night

I stagger around my apartment. I am completely fucked. I can barely get air. My life plug is pulled and sparking all over the rug. I feel like my heart is being vacuumed out through my ribs. I want to talk to you and tell you I cannot see you. I want to talk to you and ask you to come here and lay in my arms. I know you must not see me. I cringe at the thought. How again does one live with this kind of pain? I want to scream at god for showing me perfection. I want to praise god for letting me glimpse that which I always dreamed possible. I am not insane. It does exist. I am insane for thinking I could touch it. However brief.

I'm scared. Scared of being alone the rest of my life, like the feeling of walking down a busy sidewalk and everyone has their hand in another's, and you catch your reflection in a window and your eyes are sad and sunken and the light is going out.

Ann, you are what I have dreamed of my whole life, described you to my heart, my friends, and my children. I asked God to deliver you. And he did. I simply forgot to include one detail on my wish list. I am humbled at the power of this force and the agony of its absence. It is like the brighter the light, the darker the emptiness.

Please know that I am so thankful you exist. You are an answer to countless questions. I could not help myself for falling in love with you. Though I knew better, I couldn't stop. You are that remarkable.

Saturday Night

The pull toward you is the greatest force I have ever experienced. I am so humbled. I do not write these words to pull on you. I write these words to express truth, as I cannot stand pretending everything is fine, or that I'm supposed to stop loving you now. How do I stop this river flowing through my heart? What am I suppose to say to these forces that wake me every night, that have stopped me from eating, that have shot my mind into hyper-space, a vacuum for truth and spirituality? What can I say to this force so much greater than myself? I have tried to stop it. No chance.

My mind races with questions. Am I an awful man to feel how I do? Is love like this purely obsession, or is it true, and valid, and as important as the air. What are the laws and rules of this universe that dictate love and who we can be with? How can something so strong come from such a short amount of time in the presence of another? Why do you feel like the one, the one I could grow old with and take care of? How can I think these things when we have never even spent a night together? I wonder what forces have grabbed me that I am shaking now uncontrollably as I write to you? I have not seen you now for weeks. Every second has been painful. I have rejoiced in the pain. Given thanks that I can feel this deeply. Crawled in and out of fear, agony, despair and bliss. You have swelled inside my heart, and I have to write to relieve the pressure or I would burst.

Sunday Night

I sit on my perch, begging for wisdom, begging not to repeat mistakes, searching for clarity, trying to distinguish between the fire of lust and the dedication of love. I have attempted to be noble, saintly in that I will sacrifice being happy so that you might be. My heart is wildly tender and it speaks so highly of you, and yearns for you so deeply that I lose my ability to think clearly. But when clarity does come, what speaks to me are these incredible feelings: that I will soon lose a love who unlocked my soul, that I will wander alone for the rest of my life as a result, that If I could take you away without harming anyone's spiritual self, I would do it, that I feel I am here to bring light and truth, not to darken, that I know I have work to do on this planet.

Every day I look in hundreds of eyes that need me. But, to do it always without someone to love me back, I wonder how deep is my well?

I believe I am tapped into a force and that sometimes it shines from me and is too blinding to ignore. You saw it, you felt it, you touched it, and you loved me because of it. I have given you that. It is yours. You too are the light. I saw it in you and wanted to touch you as well.

I will not live a lie. I will always search for truth, no matter where it leads me. I believe there is a greater purpose for me, for all of us. I have seen people's worlds rocked by me, simply because I was willing to look at them and acknowledge their beauty. This is the truth. Remember, there is nothing you must do. Nothing. Simply be. And someday what you always dreamed of will simply walk down a trail right into your arms.

^^^^^^^^^^^^^^^^^

I sat waiting for Kristan to look up, or at least breathe. I felt embarrassed, felt this might be the stone under which she finally realized I was unworthy of her devotion.

"So?"

Kristan looked up at me with her mouth ajar. "Sheesh! Your poor kids. Their dad is a madman!"

"And a loser, don't forget. Don't worry. I'm not going to put that in the story."

"You're joking?! I love this stuff! God doesn't give points for boring people to death. Have you got any more?"

And with that affirmation, I handed her the rest of the *Confession* and let her read the truth.

∧∧∧∧∧∧∧∧∧∧∧∧∧∧∧∧∧∧∧∧

THE CONFESSION

[October 2000: Kent, Wa]

Krissy and I were on our way to meet Kate and my cousin, Craig, at a climbing area in eastern Washington. I got in the car with a bone of love-sickness stuck in my throat. Just the day before, Ann and I had come to the same, healthy conclusion. Despite being madly in love with each other, there was no safe way out of this. She needed to fix her marriage and raise the children with their father. Love was a grand thing, but sometimes timing was a cruel affair. She would talk to me soon to let me know how she was doing. Knowing her, "soon," would be anywhere from a day to a year. I was shattered.

Kris climbed in the car and studied my wooden face. I could sense her body tightening. I did not know how to explain to her the madness of what I was grieving about. My head went back and forth. "Jesus, she is going to be with me all weekend. Now that Kate is gone, it will be just the two of us for the next two years."

Kris and I weren't used to talking much as her sister had been born with a gift for gab even more profound than mine. Kris had learned the fine art of tuning out and heading into her own world while Kate and I ranted. But that was before all this. Now there was the thing with Ann. And no Kate. Just Krissy and me.

'She's fifteen' went the voice, 'does she need to hear this? Are you going to damage her or help her if you reveal what the hell you are up to? Christ! In love with a married woman, again? Not once, but twice in your life.'

I couldn't do it, so we drove for a half-hour with me making small talk, trying to be cheerful through a clenched jaw. I felt myself growing wooden, wanting to protect her from me, to keep her safe from the realities of my dark side. We drove another mile in agonizing silence and my voice said to do it, to drop the bomb. It was time to be real with my kid.

"Kris."

"Yeah, dad?"

"I got something troubling me."

"Yeah, I can tell."

"Well, you know it has nothing to do with you, right?"

"Yeah."

"Honey... you know I'm sprung over Ann. Bad. Real Bad."

"Oh dad, I'm sorry."

"And ...."

"Yeah?"

"And... she's, she's just as sprung over me. She's in love with me, Kris."

At that her eyes went wide, her mouth dropped into a smile of disbelief and she began to scream.

"OH MY GOD!!!" she wailed. She looked at me again."OH MY GOD!!!"

This went on for ten minutes. Her looking, then screaming with amazed, disbelieving, wild delight.

When she finally settled in and quit laughing, the talking began in earnest. How had it happened? What had happened? Could she stay married? What about her kids?

Finally she said, "Well, at least you didn't kiss her, Dad. Dad? You didn't kiss her right?"

I sheepishly looked straight ahead.

"OH MY GOD!!!" The screaming began anew.

The rest of the drive to Vantage was a delirious revelation of twisted tales and Shakespearean tragedy in the making. It was the first time in her life that she and I had talked at such a level.

It had not been long ago that I sat at the kitchen table of one of my runner's mom's, listening to her scold me for my choices, for not being a good role model for the boys. We talked on and I asked her some things about her son and realized that she knew virtually nothing intimate about him, that at seveteen he was a stranger in his own home, that I knew him better than she did.

After dinner, I drove back to my apartment, walked across the stains on the carpet, stains on the counter, a half-ton of left over undesirables festering in my fridge, and thought about it all. The truth was, her son told me everything. I knew his fears and his dreams. I had shared mine with him. We were both transparent, vulnerable, real. Sometimes it was ugly. Sometimes it hurt.

I picked up last night's cereal bowl, bits of granola dried to the bottom. I was a loser, a mess, a bad role model, a soldier of misfortune. And her son loved me. I stared at the clutter piled on my 12 inch Gold Star TV and made a promise: I would make my daughters proud. I vowed to be me. To not quit. It was all I had. It had to be enough.

A year after my *Confession* to Kris, on the black Sunday morning when I had met Ann to say goodbye forever and I came home to stumble through my apartment, unable to support my own weight, leaning on my daughter's 5'2" frame, broken and reeling, no longer able to form words from a mouth bent in horrid despair-- Krissy was an eye of calm. She understood it all. She had seen the whole ride. She knew I was the man who had shattered a family. She knew I was the man who had run her sister's boyfriend across the state the day before to save Kate a few hours of agony. She knew what love could do. She had heard about little else for a year.

Krissy had grown up over the year. As we grew closer and talked more about life's realities, she learned not to worry about my sorrow. It didn't bring her down. But there was more to it than that. During the spring she too had fallen in love. For the first time in her life she was rejoicing in every breath, wanting to leap and dance with every step. Song lyrics made sense. Every flower was a delight. Every ray of sun was designed to make her world shine brighter. Krissy knew that I knew about love, and so she shared every detail of her delight, talked of her tortures when he didn't call, laughed at her meanness and revenge tactics when he let her down, was amazed at the similarities between me and her. Unbelievable. She talked and talked and it was music to us both, salve for a wound that would never heal in me.

This was the child who rarely spoke, who was shy and introverted. This was the child who had to watch me struggle as I shoveled my way through two marriages, two divorces, losing my job, guiding mountains for cash, money desperations, moving thirteen times in one year, fighting for another dollar while trying to stay alive with a slight amount of dignity.

This was the child who now discussed morality, spirituality, right, wrong, and the plague of indifference. This was a child who rarely judged and who said to me the day I lost my heart: "Dad. Look at it this way, you have produced two kids who can love in this world. That is something to be proud of."

This was the child who now read me passages from *The Prophet* about *Beauty,* and with me knowing that the words were about her, that she was beauty itself, smiled at me as the tears fell, thanks filling my heart for the miracle next to me.

This was the child said, "Ya know, I wonder how many dads and their daughters are driving in a car right now, reading pages from *The Prophet.* How many have ever done that?"

And for those words, I owed her my life. For it was that acknowledgment of my worth in her life that rang in my head the day I sat on the ridge not knowing if I would ever get up again. I didn't want her, did not want that second child, and now without her, I would have died.

YOUR LUCKY DAY

TRUTH #190:

Enjoy the moment. Yes, enjoy it and then knock on wood. At the very least, pick up a lucky penny and point to the sky in thanks. Because just as soon as you gain something stable, sensible, and fulfilling; as soon as your world begins to make sense, with hope and dreams blooming like red Indian paintbrush on a marbled mountain side; as soon as song and laughter return to your heart with a warm confidence you haven't felt since playing kick the can as a child; as soon as you can say the words 'you like me, you really like me'; say your prayers. For, like a pigeon from hell, out will pour the dark forces, the sirens of evil, the haters, the wannabes, the jealous, the needy, the tyrannical promoters of fear, the puritanical stealers of joy; all for the sole and explicit purpose of reducing your joyous dream world to rubble.

*-From **The Book of Truths** by Langdon Towne*

^^^^^^^^^^^^^^^^^^^^^^^^^^^

[AUGUST 2001: AUSTERA PEAK, NORTH CASCADES]

Langdon sat on a tilted block of rock on the summit of Austera Peak letting his feet dangle over the void. 'You know what I love?"

I just looked at him knowing he would answer his own question.

He took the lid off his water bottle and took a sip. "The fact that there is no one up here to take a shot at you. It's just you and whatever beats within your soul. It purifies the spirit. Ya know what I'm saying?"

I did.

"Yeah... gaining some space between what is good in yourself and all the trivial shit back home does help the head."

"And the heart." There was a long pause with a quiet hanging that gave new meaning to the term *dead silence*. "You know what just popped into my head?"

"Hmmm. Olive skin?"

"Dude, good guess. Actually, I was thinking of Lopsang."

"Jesus. Where did that come from?"

"The quiet made me think of silence... like being buried in an avalanche silence."

"That's why I hate holding still."

"You and the rest of us. Ya know, you never did finish telling me what happened up there."

"I told you a hundred times. It's all I talked about for a freakin' year."

"I know, but every time we'd get started talking about Everest the subject would switch to Zoë."

"Ouch. What were you just saying about getting purified?"

"Hard to purify your blood. And you're the one getting purified, not me." Towne chuckled as he pulled his Harvard baseball cap down over his nose. "So… What happened up there?"

I let go a huge sigh. "I'm not sure about this. Talking about Lopsang kind of feels like a favorite album with a scratch. No matter how bad you want it to play, it just keeps skipping back to the same spot- over and over."

"Yeah and this time we're going to blow on the needle and let the song play through." Towne took a long pull of water. "Hey...we got all day and no where to go but down."

And there it was. I took a slow breath and let my mind shift back to the darkness of '97. It was the wettest winter since the Ark, I was house-sitting in a lonely mice-infested farm cottage, and every dreary night was spent hunched over a keyboard writing in defense of Lopsang Jangbu Sherpa. I never showed the stories or journal entries to anyone. I didn't publish a page. I just wrote for me and whichever God was in charge of this theater of loss and absurdity. Lopsang was dead, Zoë was gone, my daughters were a long distance phone call away that I couldn't afford to make, and my good buddy *Angst* kept me company as sorrow poured from my icy fingers.

∧∧∧∧∧∧∧∧∧∧∧∧∧∧∧∧∧∧∧∧∧∧∧∧∧∧∧∧∧

[SEPTEMBER, 1996: ISSAQUAH, WA]

I got the call at High Mountain Rendezvous on Friday, Sept. 27ᵗʰ, 1996 from the senior editor of Climbing Magazine that my dear friend, Lopsang Jangbu Sherpa, had been killed in an avalanche somewhere on Mt. Everest. There were no details on how or where, just that he was dead.

Before hanging up the editor asked in a matter of fact tone, "Oh, since you're the one who knew him, could you write a brief epitaph? Oh yeah, and could you fax it to us by Monday? Thanks. I'm real sorry." Click.

I sat down, stared up at my boss, and burst into tears. Later that night I drove up to Zoë's to sleep with her one last time. In the morning, I asked her if she would come with me to Hidden Lake Peak as I wanted to write my goodbye to Lopsang from that beautiful summit. She told me there was something else she needed to do first.

Thus, I left for Hidden Lake Peak alone-- having no clue how I would say goodbye to Lopsang and Zoë at the same time. A surreal eels' tune was repeating on my tape deck and in my head as I slowly made my way to the summit of ten years of despair:

"This could be your lucky day...in hell.
Never know who it might be... at your doorbell."

I knew that with all the recent hoopla over the May 10th Everest tragedy, Lopsang's death would most likely register back page news. Tragically, the media and viewing public's memory of him would be the slandered versions they read about in <u>Outside</u> magazine or saw on ABC and NBC specials. As it stood, no one had gotten the facts straight or told the whole story.

The next day, as I sat on a rock, trying to write about the loss of an irreplaceable light in my life, I was overwhelmed with the fact that I alone knew the truth about Lopsang's ordeal on Everest. Everybody who had been up there and knew the score was dead. I finished writing the goodbye and waited in silence for most of the day, waited for a reason to move my legs. And then it came to me. It was Jeannie Probola's lovely face. I wanted to hold her. And with that image lifting my feet, I got up and headed back to let her know our friend was gone. Three weeks later I asked her to marry me while climbing the second pitch of Tammy Baker's Face at Smith Rock. She just looked at me and laughed in that gentle way of hers. Of course, I wasn't joking. I had nothing left to lose.

^^^^^^^^^^^^^^^^^^^^^^^^

Act Two

EVERYBODY OUGHT
TO HAVE A GUIDE

Sung to **"Everybody Ought to Have a Maid"**
-A Funny Thing Happened on the Way to the Forum

From: "Sing alongs for a Shipwreck"

"The only decent perk of being a mountain guide is that terror is a bitchin aphrodisiac. Silly moral restrictions and frigid self-denial tend to fall away as the fear meter goes up. Every guide knows this. That's why they're guides."

-Langdon Towne

WALTER BO-MITTY

A Word About Home

You know when you've made it home. You can feel it in your bones, your teeth, your hair, your heart, and your organs. It is a sense of completeness, of belonging, of the molecules that surround you being aligned in your favor.

When you've never been comfortable in your own skin, it's pretty tough to earn that feeling of home. You can try. You can climb your mountains and rest in the arms of your woman, but when standing alone, that familiar gnawing sense of things not being quite right rises up to shift your balance. And it is that desire for balance that becomes the elusive song to which you dance. And the morning after I'd returned from Zion, after having that cup of coffee in Zoë's bed, I knew I hadn't made it home. Thus, I climbed out of bed and into my Festiva and headed off to find a place to rest my head. I wound up walking into a climbing store in Issaquah called High Mountain Rendezvous, (HMR), hoping one of the nice sales people needed a roommate. Nobody did, but the owner recognized me and asked me if I needed a job. I did. And so began the next chapter of my life.

That first month I pulled in $800. $450 of that went to child support, $550 went to rent, another $300 for food, car insurance and so on. Starting the next month I was looking at $800 in the red, with no benefits and a car that was just a tossed clutch from putting me out in the street.By December I was approaching financial ruin.

*-From **The Shipwreck** Journals*

^^

Spurred on by the prodding genius of financial desperation, I started bootleg guiding in the winter of '93. The retail sales thing was fun but it didn't cover my child support, rent, food, or Q-Tips, so with the gnaw of necessity keeping me awake at night, I came up with the idea of offering custom guide services to friendly customers who were too scared to give climbing a try on their own. It turned in to a sweet gig, in that I could talk at length with a person, size them up, and if I liked them, offer to teach them whatever they needed to know. By being selective and careful with each client, I created a rewarding little guiding niche where I could help people gain some knowledge and overcome their fears while keeping the wolves of poverty from chewing through my door.

After a stretch of desperate months, I felt myself emerging on to a winning streak. By busting my tail I'd earned my way to a momentary glimpse of that precariously delicate wing which most forty year olds desire more than sex, money, or power, and yet find as elusive as that butter fly of happiness. *Balance.* There it was, shimmering on the other side of a tight rope I'd been creeping across forever. Finally, at my fingertips was my one and only dream: that proverbial sense of solid ground.

Though HMR had a parcel of timber to knock upon, I gleefully sidestepped all wood products and pounded my beats on plastic and synthetics. Confidence was soaring. And rightfully so. I'd earned my moment. And so, with a smile of joy, I stepped on to the *winner's* platform, then turned around to see what that familiar noise behind me might be. I should have known. It was the universal truth of cosmic alignment, zeroing in on my light like a kamikaze aiming for landing craft on the beaches of Okinanwa. *Truth #13. If you ever have five minutes of happiness...*

One of the beautiful ironies of bootlegging was watching people who came to you fearful of their own shadow-- too scared to even leave a trailhead parking lot without you there to hold their hand-- return from a summit convinced they had what it took to be a mountain guide. "Dude, this is easy money!"

Of course, the guy had no clue the trip was easy and fun because, you the guide, did everything but lace his shoes in an attempt to justify the fee you charged. The dude tagged his summit but never once had to make a decision or risk anything. Meanwhile you were watching his every step, hoping he didn't catch a crampon and fly off, cart-wheeling through your rope team. This guy built his mountaineering resume by plopping down on a toilet seat with a copy of *Climbing* magazine and reading about all the bitchin' places he was too scared to visit.

Now all that former baggage didn't matter a bit. Something about those twelve hours you spent inside this cat's head, helping him overcome deep seated fears, thereby allowing him to unlock the door to his phobic prison, launched him into a delusional state of grace. In fact, you did such a grand job, he swung by work the next day to ask how he could start a guide service just like yours.

This must be what every psychiatric therapist experiences when his psychotic, tic-ridden clients stop therapy and head straight to the nearest University to get a BA in clinical psychology. Now free of the chains that bound them all their lives, they too will finally have the balls to charge some twitching, closet-case $100 an hour for their services.

Of course, I didn't see that my boot-legging bubble of happiness was about to burst. In fact, until it was gone, I never even knew I had a bubble to blow on. But I should have known something was up the day my checking account came up with a few dollars left over at the end of the month. Maybe it was because I turned around from the cash machine and felt the warm sun on my skin and actually smiled. I don't know, but it was that very same day that I decided to be a nice guy and take Walter, who I worked with at HMR, along for *free* on a guided alpine climb. Though Walter knew little about the actual tendon crunching process of mountain climbing, he was hilarious, a virtual stand up comic who could make me double up anytime, anywhere. To his credit, with the aid of friends, he had climbed a couple of low angled walk ups in the Cascades and could get up a rock climb without killing himself. But, for the most part, he just memorized Black Diamond catalogs and spewed forth a comical wealth of climber jargon and trivia.

On that infamous day, when I had noticed the sun kissing my skin and decided to take Walter along on that joyous guided winter alpine romp up the West Ridge of Red Mountain, he was in prime form, strutting about like a banty rooster, decked to the nines in the latest, top of the line, North Face mountain wear, quoting Don Whillans and Rheinhold Messner and driving in boot axe belays every nine yards. He had me bent over and drooling. It was an alpine laugh-in.

I stopped laughing when he showed up to work five days later with a brochure, professionally done, explaining the merits of his new climbing company. The wording had been plagarized off an American Alpine Institute pamphlet and the picture on the cover was the one I took of him when I led him up the alpine classic four days before. My gut turned over and the light began to dim. I knew what was coming. Within two months, *Walter Bo-Mitty Adventures* had organized a trip to Ecuador and was taking most of my rock and alpine business.

Walter Bo-Mitty Adventures was the main reason I drove to West Seattle after Scott Fischer called me for an interview. Financially, working for Mountain Madness made even less sense than working retail, but pulling that Mountain Madness T-shirt over my head brought me some things I needed:

1. I was finally backed by insurance, so that if one of my clients lobbed off a cornice and blew up an internal organ, I wouldn't wind up in prison.

2. When trying to pick up chicks at a party, I had learned that if you used the, "I'm a mountain guide" line you lost them as soon as they saw your duct taped shoes and figured out which car was yours in the parking lot. But, *if* you mentioned you were guiding for *Mountain Madness* and did a quick squint towards the North, the babe would sprint for the bar, grab another round and race back to ask you if you'd ever rappelled off the REI wall.

3. I wouldn't be lumped in a heap with the all the other Walter's out there ripping people off.

Integrity. The pay is shit, the honor... priceless.

DUDE BOYS

"Dude, happiness is not a state to arrive at, but a way of traveling."

-Langdon Towne

When you're a non-custodial single-parent, there's something cruel about the dynamics and the importance of vacations. Because you don't get to see your kids much, the bit of time spent together becomes compressed and intensified; hyper-important. You want every second to be the absolute best moment you can make it. For when the trip is over and you've dropped the kids off at their mother's, all you'll tuck in to bed and kiss goodnight are the memories of joy you hopefully brought to your children's hearts.

-*From the* **Shipwreck** *Journals*

^^^^^^^^^^^^^^^^^^^^^^^^

JOHN

"Dude, I want to do Smith!" John was adamant.

Though he had only been rock climbing since getting hired on at HMR a couple months before, the guy was a natural. A National Ski Team mogul racer, John was used to pushing his limits. He was more than ready for the world class sport climbing at Smith Rock State Park.

"All right," I sighed. "I'll go, but I want to ride together to split expenses and I know we can't all fit in my Festiva." I was still trying to get out of it.

"Dude, I can drive."

"But, I thought you said your buddy Steve wanted to go?"

"Dude, he's got a motorcycle. He said no problem if we wanted him to come down separate. Dude, SMITH ROCKS!!" John thrust his hand in the air, gave the rock sign and started head banging about HMR until his sunglasses went flying off his head.

Part of me, the part that has a smidgin of inner intelligence, started going off like a climatic crescendo in a Beethoven symphony, "Keith, get out of here now! Run for it! Bolt, while you still have a chance!" The other part of me, the part that likes women, leader falls, and stuffing my toes into rock shoes, revved up like a Van Halen guitar riff and screamed: "C'mon, you uptight sack of spuds, live a little, hang with young studs. Oh my my, oh hell yes, be the rock, SMITH ROCK no less!"

You know which side won; the side that has ensured the continual repopulation of the earth.

Departure time was set for 6:30 sharp Sunday morning. My last words to John had been: "John, don't be late."

He replied with his huge Cheshire cat grin, "Dude, SMITH ROCKS!"

COFFINS AND TANTRUMS

Getting gear ready for the girls and me took some doing. By the time I picked them up from their mom's, fed them dinner and got everything thrown out of the closet and onto the bed, floor, and kitchen counters it was after 11:00. In a state of befuddled indecision, (the absolutely disorganized mental condition I'm always in getting ready for trips), I called Zoë to try and patch things up before I left. Instead, we wound up in the same hapless conversation we had been shredding each other with since we'd uttered: "Til death do us part." By midnight I had wound myself into a fit of wild cursing and rock shoe throwing. With the coffin of divorce nailed a little tighter, I walked out to stare at my innocent kids, who were thankfully sleeping through my tantrum. Had they ever spent time with me when I hadn't been pulled apart by some absurd set of circumstances? I stood there with nerve endings sparking like I had fallen on a high voltage power line. There'd be little sleep for me tonight.

At 5:45, I arose painfully and finished the last bit of packing. My inner voice said to call John to make sure he was up and moving. I ignored it and quietly cooked up some breakfast, letting the girls sleep to the last minute. At 7:15 I called John.

His voice sounded groggy, "Dude, Steve just got here, we'll be right over."

By 8:00, I had everything out on the side walk, had fed the girls, taken two agitated dumps, one long shower, wound myself into a state of nail spitting fury, meditated on the good things in the universe, resigned myself to the beauty of patience and tolerance, let go another round of anxiety induced diarrhea, thrown a full rope bag hard enough to tear a rotator cuff, screamed til I choked, tripped over the rope bag, and went sprawling under the questioning stares of my neighbors and children. Wiped, I sat deep breathing on the sidewalk. "I feel good, I feel great, I feel wonderful...."

I looked up to the heavens. The weather was cool, about 41 degrees, with rain filled clouds grumbling along on their way to the mountains. June in Seattle. I hoped that the warmth of Smith would once again do its magic and restore my faith in the universe.

Around the corner I could hear the rumble of a motorcycle as John's beat up 76' Scirocco came into view. I wanted to tear both of their heads off but instead graciously stood up and introduced myself to Steve, plunked down on his 450 Kawasaki, no fairing or windshield to protect him from the numbing temperatures. Dressed in light clothes, wind breaker, scarf, and ski gloves, he was all set for a delicious summer day. No worries there mate. He'd be frozen to death in twenty miles.

"John, you're an hour and a half late."

"Dude, sorry. We just kind of spaced last night. We stayed up jammin til 4:00. I didn't hear the alarm, or I turned it off or something." He looked at the parking lot full of gear and then at his hatch back Scirroco. "Okay. Dude, is all that stuff going?"

"Yep. Don't worry I'll get it in." I walked over and opened his hatch. Inside were two small daypacks. "John, where's your stuff?"

"Dude, it's all there. Steve and I travel light. Smith ROCKS!"

"You mean to tell me Steve's stuff is in here too? John, we're going camping for 4 days. Are you guys bringing a tent? Sleeping pads? A cup? Spoon? Bowl?" He shook his head to each question. I told him to run up to my apartment and grab some more ensolite pads, eating utensils and another tent. I began loading the car.

Turning to Steve I queried, "An hour and a half late?"

Steve grinned from behind his goggles and helmet chin strap, "Dude, that's John."

By leveraging with a large stick I was able to force the last sleeping pad into the Scirroco, leaving minute spaces for my two girls and me. The only way we could all fit had us sealed off in our own compartments, surrounded by cooking gear, sleeping bags, clothing bags and tents. Under my feet and legs were the climbing gear and cooler. This meant that I would have to prop my legs and feet up on the dash for the entire 6 hour drive. At least we were on our way.

"Dude, where's the nearest gas?" Aah, spoke to soon. We drove two blocks and gassed up. Steve sat behind us, idling away on his Kawasaki. No fairing. Jesus Murphy, what kind of nut case road show had I strapped myself onto? There was no doubt in my mind that Steve would soon be a textbook study for extreme hypothermia. The only cheering factor was that he would most likely maim and destroy just himself when his brain went numb and his Kawasaki jumped the guard rail and pitched off some 90 foot bank. Sour and precocious was I, sitting there with my knees tucked beneath my chin. Finally, we were off.

VAN HALEN AND KAWASAKIS

Twenty minutes out of Issaquah it began to rain. Hard. We climbed up Snoqualmie Pass and the rain looked like it could turn to sleet or snow any second. Steve chugged along beside us, rain slashing into his face and jeans. "Hmmm, that looks like fun." Dull amusement soon turned to horror as Steve would ride his tiny Kawasaki directly into the blind spot of the clueless free way motorist ahead of him and plunk along ready to get flattened in a heart beat should that hapless Winnebago or Geo driver decide to change lanes.

"Christ, has he ever heard of the word blind spot?"

"That's two words, dad." My eleven year old Kate spoke from behind the gear out of the back seat. I couldn't see her, but her muffled voice reassured me that I was not alone.

156

"Jesus! What is he doing?" Steve looked oblivious to the rain pelting his chin. He looked equally oblivious to the trucks lumbering along inches from his goggle strap. In the comparative comfort and safety of the rattletrap Scirroco, my buns began to throb. Twenty minutes gone and we were all in hell. I looked away from Steve, unable to stomach the certainty of him being hammered sideways into our lane, our front end bouncing over his head and shoulders as the bike spit into the air. "Christ."

"Dude, I'm starving." John broke the silence. "Is there any place to eat in Cle Elum or Ellensburg?"

"We can do McDonalds, eh?" I had given up on the concept of reaching Smith anytime close to our original early afternoon idea. My innards grumbled, 'Let's see, we ought to be in Smith sometime next June....'

"John, shall I tell Steve, what's up? Hey, where's Steve? Oh no. Oh god." Steve had disappeared from view. "Jesus, I'll bet he's getting drug underneath a Semi! Dammit. You better slow down John and see if he comes into view."

An hour later we pulled into McDonalds with no sign of Steve. Fairly certain he was now spinning donuts in the great Kawasaki moto-fest in the sky, we could only hope that he had come to his senses and headed back home to warmth and safety. The rest of the drive was a blur of Van Halen riffs, sore butt cheeks, and occasional utterances from my poor sardine canned kids. Kate's head was wedged in between a box of cooking wear and her suitcase. Her pigtails rested on the back speaker, where distorted Van Halen songs bounced them to and fro. Every hour or so, as John changed Van Halen tapes, I would hand the kids back a soda with a straw. I could hear their muffled remarks and could touch their hands so I knew they were still there. The sounds of their lonely slurping struck melancholy chords in my heart.

SMITH ROCKS!!

We pulled into Terrebonne with John going on about which Van Halen album had been THE album of the eighties. We had already covered the Sammy Haggar versus David Lee Roth thing, with DLR getting the nod due to his climbing interests. Five straight hours of Van Halen trivia and fun facts left me misty at the first glimpse of the Monkey Face.

The glorious sight of Smith Rocks and the promise of warmth, nobs, and blue skies helped ease the shooting pains roto-tilling up my right butt cheek. We drove around the parking areas; no Steve. Oh well. Like some ripe June bug that had picked the Scirroco windshield for a mating partner, the intitial vividly sickening images of Steve's splattered remains had become just part of the view. *"First there is a Steve, then there is no Steve, then there is."* We pulled into the bivy sight parking area, hastily set up camp under a blazing sun, loaded up the quick draws, and headed down to the Dihedrals.

John got on his first Smith lead, a sweet little 5.8 nob climb called Ginger Snap and began shaking like a spanked chicken. "Dude, these nobs are weird."

"You'll get used to em." John was already knocking on the 5.11 door back home, and I knew he would take to the nobs in no time.

"Okay." Big pause. Much chalking up. "Dude, these suck!"

"John, stay over your feet. It's all balance."

John pinched his way up the remainder of the climb shouting, "Dude, watch me! Watch me, Dude!"

Within an hour we were on a 5.10 and John was waving his rock fingers in the sky. "SMITH ROCKS!!"

UNDEAD DUDES WALK AMONG US

We sat in the fading sunlight below the Peanut when who should come sauntering up out of the golden rays, but freshly undead Steve.

"Dude." Steve began a jolly tale of his epic adventure to gain Terra Firma at Smith. "Dude, I'm coming down to Easton in that heavy rain and I run out of gas. That's when I lost you dudes."

My mind flickered with a, "But why didn't you gas up in Issaquah?" type question but I remained outwardly quiet.

"Dude, I should have gassed up when you guys did, but I thought I had a full tank. So, Dude, I push my bike to the exit and into town. Dude, it's raining, I'm soaked and it's then I realize that I forgot my wallet. Dude, I got like 10 bucks on me. So I sit there and think, 'Well Dude, whatever.' John, I'm going to have to borrow some money. Is that cool, Dude? So I fill up my tank and I'm all wet but I can see the clouds are thinnin. I head on. After a bit my chain starts to make a funny noise. Dude, I pull over and it looks like its going to fall off. Keith, dude, did you bring any tools? Well, whatever. So, that kind of blew, because I kept waiting for the chain to pitch and lock up my rear wheel."

On my lips were words something to the effect of: "Did you think to pull over at a service station you blinking moron?" Instead, I suggested he ask Dan at Redpoint Climbing Supply if he might loan a crescent wrench for a minute or two.

After his story, Steve got on our rope and did a good job on Pop Goes the Nubbin, 10a. We headed back to camp. The girls took an immediate liking to his easy going manner. I started to get dinner ready, hinting lightly that I was cooking for the girls and me, not for the whole show. With all the sour messages banging around in my head, I was beginning to feel like the sheepish asshole, but I had to draw a line somewhere with the Dude Boys.

John and Steve headed into Terrebonne for sustenance and socializing. The Kawasaki's chain clanked and clattered wildly on the sprocket as they sped away. I figured at any speed above 15 mph the thing would hurl itself off the sprocket and onto the axle wrapping tightly enough to send the dudes sideways in a last wild, high-siding, head-smashing dive to the expecting asphalt. The girls and I finished up and then retired for the evening. Snuggled in my bag, with the long day at last behind me, sleep was gently feathering my ears and face, when....

"Dude! Ha ha, hee hee. Dude, I think its over here."

John and Steve were stumbling through the dark, jam packed bivy area, searching for their tent, while babbling at the top of their lungs about Dude this and Dude that.

"Jesus H" I muttered into the nylon. They wandered here and there, their voices rising and falling, and sometimes echoing off the great walls of Smith.

"Dude I see it."

"Dude, are you high? It's over here. Ouch. Shit! Dude watch out for that dude's stove." Boing. John fell over a tent guy line cratering in the dust. As the tent quickly collapsed on the unsuspecting innocents slumbering inside, there was much gay laughter erupting from the happy Dude Boys. "Hee hee. Ha ha. OK. Whatever. Dude, this is hopeless. Let's just sleep in the car."

"Dude, how do we get back to the car?" More laughter.

After ten minutes the joke was up and I crawled out of my tent and told them where they could find theirs. I also informed them that there were about 200 tired climbers who would love to string them up by their ball sacks if they didn't shut the fuck up in a heart beat. I bade them goodnight with a, "Jesus H Christ, get a fucking clue!" and zipped their smiling faces inside the tiny tent I had loaned them.

DUDES AND DUDETTES

During the summer months, one must climb early or late in the day to enjoy the spectacular and easily accessible southern faces down along the Crooked River at Smith. Out of bed by 6:30, on the rock by 7:30. By 10:30 your sliming off holds, sweat dripping out of every pore. At first light I was up, making coffee and getting oatmeal ready. I got the girls up and told the Dude Boys that they ought to be getting up as well. By 7:30 there was no movement so I went and roused them. They were cheerful and easy to get going but the clock was ticking. We got to Phoenix Buttress just as the temp climbed to about 90. Within an hour we were all baked and the mornings climbing was over. We decided to go for groceries and wait for the afternoon cool.

I saw Steve eyeballing his bike, so I offered, "Dude, we can take your bike over to Redpoint." What?! The **D** word had just slipped out in front of that sentence like warm butter off a knife.

"Dude, Dad, can we get some licorice at Redpoint?" Kate asked. God, my first born child was doing it!

While I picked up some groceries, Steve tightened his chain and picked up his helmet (he'd forgotten it there the day before) and licorice for the girls. Climbing later that afternoon was splendid. Both Krissy and Kate flashed

the Smith classic, *Bar B Que the Pope,* 10b. John and Steve were dazzled by
the girls' abilities and were not the least bit afraid to praise them.

From the orange walls one could hear, "Dude, belay on?"

"Belay on, Dude."

"Dude, these holds are way thin."

"Lookin good, Dude."

"Dude, tight! Tight, DUDE!"

"C'mon, Dude! Stick it!"

"Dude, you got me? You got me, DUDE?"

"Gotcha, Dude."

"Dude, Falling!"

Krissy stopped calling me Dad. Instead it was, "Uprope, Dude." We were
a show.

DREAMS AND UNDERPANTS

We got back to camp just before dark. Steve suggested that he and John
ride into Bend or Redmond to go out for dinner. This was a cool idea except
that they would have to ride on the inter-state and John didn't have a helmet-
which is illegal in Oregon. They solved this dilemma by grabbing my plastic,
lime-green spaghetti colander and tying it to John's head with twine. It was
one of those sieves with little round legs poking up in three spots. Combined
with John's tiny sunglasses and permanent grin, the odds of them coming
back alive were thin.

"Dudes, where are your coats?" They were heading off dressed in T-Shirts.
The desert nights in the area dip down into the low 40's. Combine that with
a 60 mph wind chill and you could bet they'd be packin donuts of frost on
their nipples within five miles.

"Dude, my coats at the bottom of my pack. It's too much hassle."

"John, get your damn coat. Steve, you're going to freeze to death."

Reluctantly, the Dude Boys put coats on and headed off to spend John's
money. Before parting I told John no less than three times to be double triple
sure to put money in the camp fee deposit box for the nights camping. It was
his turn. Forget to pay and as soon as the sun has popped up over the horizons
of Nebraska, the Smith Rangers come and wake you to collect their money.
Standing there, shivering in your underwear, digging through your pack for
the wallet that got left in the car, the ranger talks about cheerful things as
crust falls off your eyelids.

The Dude Boys pulled away, the green strainer plopped on John's head, a
big grin on his face. We gave each other the ROCK sign. As they left the lot,
Steve's towel, which he had set on his luggage rack, unraveled and fell onto
the rear wheel. John grabbed it just as a corner caught in the chain and a pair
of Steve's under-shorts went flying out into the middle of the parking lot
road. The Dudes sped off, John holding the partially torn towel like a banner.

It flapped madly behind them as the sieve flopped over to the side of his head, knocking his sunglasses sideways. I looked at Steve's undergarment lying there in the road and decided to wait and see how long it would take for him to realize it was his and pick it up. The girls and I walked off to our tent to sleep. My gut told me to go ahead and pay the camping fee. Oh well. Whatever. John said he'd be sure. Somehow I knew I would be shaken awake by the ranger.

I bolted upright from a nightmare at 6:00, the sun streaking into my tent. In my dreams, the Smith Ranger, fed up with the absence of camp fee payments in the little metal box, had pulled me from my tent. A group of bitchin euro climbing babes sat sunning themselves, stretching their buff thighs, backs, and butts, and flipping their wild hair this way and that. I yearned to know each and every one of them deeply, to learn their languages, to father many of their children. However, the upset ranger, to the delight of the babes, threatened me with a cavity search if I didn't immediately come up with the camp fee. Standing there shaking in my skivvies, I tried to explain that John had the money, that John was supposed to pay the camp fee. The whine in my voice was pathetic and I ducked my head down in shame only to notice I was naked save for Steve's Tidy Whities. Jesus! Handcuffs and rubber gloves dangled from the rangers back pocket. The babes giggled and twittered in several foreign tongues as the ranger marched me off to the bivy parking lot at gunpoint. Where in God's name was John? The lot now resembled a busy street in downtown Seattle. People were stopping and gawking at me, the barrel of a .44 Magnum planted at the back of my cranium. John was nowhere to be seen. I looked around frantically until I spotted a note written on a McDonald's burger sack, taped to a light pole. It read, "Dude. Gone to the valley. See you in the fall. SMITH ROCKS! John." The ranger unfastened the cuffs and started pulling on the squeaky glove.....

MEANNESS AND MAGIC

Coming out of the swirling fog, I could hear my little daughters snoring lightly. Whew, reality was just another brilliant day at Smith. All was quiet. All was peace. I wandered out to the car. There on the front seat was the camp fee envelope and John's money. Well, at least he had gotten that far. I deposited the money and got breakfast ready. The quiet felt good. I decided not to wake the girls as we would be climbing on the shady backside today. Mesa Verde and Screaming Yellow Zonkers. Yes! Moons of Pluto. Yes!! As I sat sipping coffee, the ranger pulled up in his truck and stopped smack dab on Steve's underpants. **Action!** The sun was up and cooking by the time Kate, Kris, and Steve rolled out for breakfast. John was still slumbering. After everyone had eaten I headed over to wake him.

I looked in at the Dude brother. He was out like a lump. "John. Hey, dude, we have to start hiking over to the wall before it gets too hot." John started awake but didn't get up. He looked wiped.

161

Still face down, John tried to form words. "Dude. Umph. Ow. What IS that?" He was feeling through his sleeping bag at the mound of pointed rocks he had been sleeping on. "Dude, um. I couldn't find the tent last night. Steve left with the flashlight. I went to take a leak and when I came out he was gone. Okay. Thanks Steve. Whatever. Like, Steve, Dude, are you mental? Sheesh. So I wander around in the dark, tripping over rocks, freezing my ass off. Ouch! What the hell IS that under my knee?"

Looking at the tent floor I could see the outline of large rocks poking into the nylon and ensolite pad. The day we set up the tents, John had disappeared leaving me to do the setting up solo. I had purposely placed their tent on the biggest mound of protruding rocks I could find. It was supposed to be a sick joke. For reasons unknown, the Dude Boys hadn't thought to pick up and move the tiny tent.

"Well. OK. Whatever. Anyway I couldn't find the tent so I had to sleep in the car. It was way cold. Dude, I just sat there freezing til first light. As soon as I could see I went for the tent. Dude, what AM I lying on?!" I had to look away as a tiny smile flipped across my lips. God, I was mean.

The day at Mesa Verde was sweet. We cranked up Screaming Yellow Zonkers, 10b. Both Kate and Kris nearly top rope flashed the 100 foot route. After that success we headed back to the Dihedrals to find shade and perfectly delightful summer temperatures. That was what we had come for. The girls looked so beautiful in the sunlight, bouncing down the trail, full of power and confidence. Once again the simple magic of Smith had overpowered the chaos of my life and eased me into a space of quiet contentment. The impending divorce, my rocky financial position, all my longings for peace and security no longer mattered. We were here. Life right now was sweet. As an exclamation point to a fantastic day, I ran a rope up Wedding Day, 10b. As everyone took laps, I marveled at the power of this great sport.

WHITE FLAG

That evening, Steve headed back to Seattle. I voiced concern about the strong head winds blowing off the mountains and down the exposed eastern plains of State Route 97, and suggested he head home via Portland and the more temperate coastal climate along I-5. He thanked me for the advice, hugged everyone goodbye, and sped off into the gathering darkness, leaving yet another skid mark across the tattered remains of his wayward underpants.

The next day we learned that the west side was being blasted by a wintry June typhoon. There had been coastal flooding and road washouts. The mountains were being rocked by blizzards. Sickening, visions of Steve frozen to his Kawasaki, winding around the slushy hair pin turns of Mt. Hood, water and slush streaming off his back, a last bit of change vibrating madly in soaked pockets, drenched ski gloves wiping globs of rime off his goggles, while a crazed redneck 4 x 4 madly hugged his twin tail pipes, left me once again doubting the value of my advice.

162

"John, you think Steve will be OK?"

"Dude, Steve is probably in a Denny's sippin a thirty five cent cup of coffee and talking to some local about entering holy nirvana or something. Sheesh. Whatever. Dude, do not worry about Steve."

John was right. Like a fresh piece of driftwood, Steve could float and ride the currents and storms and land wherever without feeling the least bit displaced. He traveled free and light because he knew there would always be a safety net out there to catch and protect him. Dude, no worries.

The next day, Steve's long abandoned underpants dangled from a tree branch next to the bivy restroom/shower complex. Crisscrossed with countless tire-tracks, they took on the image of a war torn white flag. I thought of home, my need to fight, to take charge and get my way in this world. I looked at the walls of Smith. I looked at my kids. Dude, maybe surrender was sometimes the only sane way.

THE RENAISSANCE MAN

TRUTH #31

There is no point to anything you do. Please know that everyone is making everything up. The rules could change tomorrow, with sin seen as virtue and virtue seen as an uptight prank. Just remember that what we call molestation, Plato called enlightenment. The only voice you can trust is your own and you do not trust yourself.

*-From **The Book of Truths** by Langdon Towne*

∧∧∧∧∧∧∧∧∧∧∧∧∧∧∧∧∧∧∧∧∧∧∧∧

[WINTER 1994: ISSAQUAH, WA]

A year and change after my first trip to the City of Rocks and my subsequent move away from *The Valley of Tears* I was staring down the cocked, cold-blue steel of financial necessity. Completely on my own for the first time in my life, I had become a creative dervish of earning power, punching out articles for climbing magazines, bootleg guiding on local mountains and crags, working retail at a local climbing store, subbing at high schools, writing and recording songs on my guitar, part-time parenting my two adolescent daughters and divorcing the love of my life, Zoë. I was dirt bag poor, always hustling a buck, selling my soul and ligaments in the name of creative freedom: a true Renaissance man.

One dark, rainy, winter day I was holding down the stool at High Mountain Rendezvous, when Jim Nelson called offering me a position as a guide for Scott Fisher's budding outdoor adventure company called: *Mountain Madness*. Jim knew I was doing some successful bootlegging and wanted to employ me legally. What's more, Scott insured his guides. If you killed somebody in the mountains, the lawyers wouldn't be able to steal your children in the night. Jim knew that umbrella of insurance was all the carrot he needed to draw whores like me in.

MOUNTAIN MADNESS

Zoë and I had broken up for the hundredth and final time since getting divorced the day Scott Fischer called me in for an interview to guide for *Mountain Madness*. I had been stranded by my phone all night, waiting for her to call back so I could tell her off and hang up. By the time the phone finally rang, there was nothing left of my nerve endings. *RING ...RING ...RING...* I let it ring three times just to show her I no longer cared.

"Yeah? "

"Keith?"

"Uh hum?"

"Hey, this is Scott Fischer."

"Uh..."

"Your... Jim Nelson's friend, right?"

"Yeah."

"He mentioned to you that we're interested in you as a guide for our Northwest programs, right?"

"Well...uh.."

"Could you make it down for an interview?"

"Sure... Uhm... Like, when?"

"Today at 11:00 would be great. I have to catch a plane for Kathmandu at 2:00."

I exhaled. My tongue felt like wet wall board. This was a joke right? Today? Now? I hadn't slept a wink or eaten a thing in two days. "Yeah, sure," I replied. "No problem." What I wanted to say was, 'Let me just lift this ton of bile off my soul.'

"Good. I'll see you at 11:00, then." Click.

∧∧∧∧∧∧∧∧∧∧∧∧∧∧∧∧

In the spring of '94, *Mountain Madness* was getting a ton of good press. Scott had bagged Lhotse, K2, Everest, and Broad Peak and was becoming a Seattle alpine star. His picture was in ads touting "*Scott Fischer won't sleep with just anyone.*" *Mountain Madness* was cleaning up mountains and raising money for AIDS. Scott was cool. With the financial backing of a new co-owner they launched a campaign to raise the Seattle area's consciousness about its legitimate guiding company, nestled up in West Seattle. It seemed to be working as *Mountain Madness* was becoming fashionable with clients from all points of the country. Scott had earned connections and coveted permits to everything from Mt. Baker to Everest. *Mountain Madness* guides, "Made it Happen," for a lot of people who never thought they had what it took to climb a mountain.

The day of my interview, I climbed up the creaking stairs to the *Mountain Madness* office with lead filtering out of my stomach lining. Zoë hadn't called me back. This time we were really through and every cell was varnished with grief.

Up the stairs I went, one step at a time, an aging, bootlegging nobody about to talk to super-star Scott Fischer about being worthy of a legit guiding job. I stood at the door, pinched my cheeks, told myself it was "show time," put on the 'electric guide' smile and tried to look confident as I walked into a throng of sweaty, pony-tailed climbers, scurrying kids, and shapely women. I could see the back of Jim Nelson's head as he sat punching out a program itinerary, his face staring into an antiquated computer screen.

Jim waved and went back to work. The co-owner, whose face I'd recently seen in an article in the newspaper, gave me a smile and introduced herself. She then went on dictating a fax to another employee who was about to ring up a Sherpa-superstar named Lopsang Jangbu about his availability for the upcoming Himalayan season. Scott came bounding in, looking the alpha male stud, a mountain movie star, his eyelids squinting under the weight of apparent exhaustion. He looked at me with a slightly confused, "I have no idea who you are, but I guess I'm glad to meet ya, blah, blah, ...next."

'Jesus,' I pondered in awe. Lopsangs, Sherpas, Everest, Himalayan heroes: this was prime time, top of the pops, mountain guide real estate. The gilded confines of the elite guided world. 'What was I doing here?'

I bounced off a couple of elbows and bumped up next to a stunning beauty named Gerri. I instantly appreciated her incredible smile and calm eyes. One quick look told me she could easily make me forget my pain. She introduced herself as the secretary in charge of paychecks, then floated across the room like a muse. I decided right then that I liked *Mountain Madness*.

The party moved into a room with a futon couch and a giant desk. Scott had me go in with him. Gerri took out a pad of paper to take notes. Jim Nelson came through the door with several other important folk, all of whom had me wondering what kind of vitamins they were slipping into their morning rations. Everybody, except Scott, seemed amped to the nines. I sat there, feeling small, wondering if my hair looked as bad as my stomach felt, or if my fake smile and canned enthusiasm were as transparent as my fractured heart.

Scott introduced me to everyone and gave a spiel about how *Mountain Madness* was trying to make inroads on the Northwest climbing market. So far so good. He then talked briefly about the local programs, how they needed someone able to work with teenagers. I babbled something about my experiences teaching kids. He then reached over to a box filled with new climbing gear, pulled out some harnesses and asked one of the employees to try one on. Scott turned to me, "So, when you're tying in all these kids in, to save time, you just tie into this belay loop, right."

I suddenly felt the little spotlight on my face. All eyes were on me as I rolled out a firm and educated, "No, I wouldn't do that, Scott. Though belay loops are quite strong and suitable for belaying and rappelling, they are not intended as a tie in point. I never tie into the belay loop." I then showed him how I would tie the kid in.

Scott gave me a smile, "I was just testing you." He stuck out his huge hand, "Welcome to *Mountain Madness*. Let's go get some sandwiches."

Gerri gave me a grin and got up to get cold beverages. I loved her already.

We stepped out onto the bright streets of West Seattle and I noticed Scott, the *Lord of the Madness*, looked completely wiped out. I tried to make chit chat.

"Looks like you got quite a show going on up there."

He took a breath. "Love it, love these people, but what a fucking money vacuum."

"So, you going to climb while you're in Nepal?"

"No time for that anymore. Eighteen hour flight to Kathmandu. Take care of business and fly back."

I went home that night signed on as an officially insured guide for *Mountain Madness*. And legitimacy felt strange. I knew I was a personable, competent rock and alpine climber, and after twenty years of trials and learning, well versed in fast, light, Cascade travel. But Jesus, I'd never been up Denali or climbed abroad. These mountain guides were bad asses with resumes of stunning alpine suffering.

As a bootlegger, I'd always made sure my clients felt they'd gotten their money's worth. The clients liked me because I was real with them, because I understood how insecure they were. I made sure we never went in deeper than they could handle. If they were coming apart, half way up a climb, I knew that they weren't risking enough money to push them any farther. On the other hand, *Mountain Madness* Clients would be paying big, first class bucks to bag summits and my job was to make sure it happened come hell or high water. As the 'well-paid' *Mountain Madness* Guide, doubt, fear, and financial sensibility were to be replaced by honor, character, and adrenaline laced denial. I now would have to be *somebody*. A true leader. A real life hero. And who exactly was that somebody supposed to be?

COFFEE WITH BILL

TRUTH #89

Assume nothing. *Even if you have convinced yourself that thinking positive and looking on the bright side are beneficial to your outlook on each day, you have made the giant faux paus of thinking the universe could care about your pretentious attempts at mind control. Just know that if you are temporarily in luck, you will think your mind control works. If you are currently out of luck, you will think the universe has the upper hand. Please remember, either way you look at it, you're wrong.*

*-From **The Book of Truths** by Langdon Towne*

^^^^^^^^^^^^^^^^^^^^^^^^^

In a state of delusional grace, I sign up to guide back to back, five day, glacier climbing/mountaineering courses on Mt. Baker. There will be twelve teenagers, two adult group leaders, another Mountain Madness guide and me. I've never met the other guides, but have heard plenty about their hardcore lore in local climbing circles. The first of these trips features postcard perfect weather with climbing conditions to match. The two young adults in charge of the twelve kids on the trip are saints, treating me like a king. In the morning they bring me breakfast. In the evening they bring me vegetarian cuisine. I decide then and there that guiding is the life for me. The evening sun, shining on the shapely female leader's tight capilene top, convinces me I wouldn't want to be anywhere else. I soon put to rest the reality of making under $2.00 an hour for the privilege of leading kids up 7,000 feet of trail, snow, and crevasse strewn glacier. That night we sit out under the stars with the pretty lady asking me all kinds of: "Gosh, being a guide must be cool!" questions. It's an outstanding trip with kudos to all, and to all a good night.

Five days later we are waiting to meet our second crew in a Burlington parking lot. The second guide on this trip is a local alpine hard man named Bill Pilling. We don't know each other and probably never would except he got stuck with me on this trip. The weather begins to cloud up as we stand around waiting for the Longacres' Van to show up. They arrive and out fall fourteen, very unhappy looking people. Their three-week trip has been filled with bad luck and trauma. The two young adults in charge are not getting along with each other and know they will be sharing a cramped, damp, smelly tent for another five days. I look at rings of moisture forming around the sun and wince.

We hike for five hours until we reach a campsite right at tree line. The first drops of rain begin to fall as the kids start pulling out tents. Unlike the over-kill Everest worthy tents of the previous group, these kids have smaller, two season, duct-taped specials. Within an hour the rain is coming down in horizontal sheets. Bill and I have a tent designed to be stable in high winds, with its low profile ceiling and rather cramped environs. I notice the tent smells brand new and ask Bill if the fly was ever seam sealed. He looks at me with wide eyes and says, "Man, this thing has never been out of the stuff sack. It's still got price tags."

It rains hard all night. I keep waiting for drips, but the fly holds steady. In the morning Bill makes coffee. He boils up a quart of water then dumps a hand sized package of gourmet French Roast into the bubbles. I stare on as the brown mass coughs and hisses then bubbles all over the place. Bill frantically grabs a sock and lifts the pot off the burner, then sets it back on, lifts it, then back on for a couple of minutes. Grounds are spilling over the rim onto the nylon tent door, packs, and boots. Finally, satisfied with his creation, he sets it down and pours a little water in to make the grounds settle.

He fills my cup, black and hot. No sugar or creamer. I'm sipping straight coal-tar and can barely choke down half a cup. Bill, agrees the stuff is nasty and has about the same amount. Left in the pot is a quart of steaming brew that doesn't get touched until the next morning, when after staring at the tent walls for twenty four straight hours, Bill dumps out the pan of black-water, boils up a quart of water, dumps in a package of French Roast and goes through the bubbling mess and sock ritual. It is a full on De Ja Vu.

After two sips of the liquid charcoal, I busy myself reading the contents of my first-aid kit: reviewing my CPR card, and going over First Aid manuals. Bill, a veteran of Alaskan doldrums, lies quiet and content with a book he brought.

As the rain and wind roars through day three, we begin discussing the realities of our situation. The duct-taped tents are leaking like sieves, and the kids are all soaked. Only one out of the five white gas stoves they brought is still working. The young adults in charge, who are providing us meals, are no longer talking to each other and have decided to fast. The meals they begrudgingly prepare us consist of pasty beans wiped on cold burritos. Bill has his NOAH weather radio with him, (thank god) and we spend the day glued to it. The forecast is frightful, save for a tiny silver window. It is supposed to clear on Thursday afternoon, remain clear and cold through Friday morning, then cloud up and spew again. By Wednesday night things are desperate and Bill and I make the decision to hike these folks out to drier ground. It rains all Wednesday night and doesn't stop until shortly after Bill brews up another quart of coal-tar in the morning.

By noon, the clouds have broken up and the sun has worked its way through. We run around, getting everyone out and ready for a quick ice-axe, crampon, self-arrest, crevasse rescue, seminar. We cram two days worth of experiential training into about three hours. Bill is a great teacher and everyone but one kid, Jimbo, is intently absorbing our instruction. Jimbo doesn't listen to anything we say. He talks and laughs while we teach. He goes through the motions as we talk about potentially life threatening situations we may encounter. He's an asshole and he's on my rope team the next morning as we slog our way up the soggy Easton glacier.

Things go well, until we get to our first big crevasse at around 8,000 feet when I notice that the lip of the yawning crevasse is encased in water ice. I look up the slope and notice that the whole upper mountain is also encased in water ice. Three days of rain have soaked the glacier through, and the clear and freezing skies of the previous night have turned the upper reaches of Mt.Baker into a giant inverted hockey ring. Our crampons nick into the gentle slopes. We make our way for the 1,000 foot, 35-40 degree headwall, wind gusts slapping at our parkas. Normally, this part of the climb is the fun part, with the rising steepness accentuating the fact that every step is getting you closer to the summit. But things have changed. The headwall is glistening in the cold shrieking wind, and the crevasses at its base are yawning huge and deadly.

My mind does a quick run through. A slip on this wall by anyone in my party would result in a hurtling mass of sliding death. To self-arrest with our ice axes would require the strength and reflexes of Bruce Lee. With my heart in my throat, I crampon my way up to the summit following Bill's rope team. Bill clicks off step after step, never pausing to discuss our situation. I follow him blindly, with my guts fluttering and every fiber in my soul questioning what we are doing dragging these kids up here in conditions this dangerous.

Little do we know that on Mt. Rainier, glistening to the south, and coated in the same water ice as us, two park rangers on a rescue mission are sliding to their deaths unable to self-arrest on the slate like surface.

We tag the summit and I turn to my rope team for a serious pep-talk. I look down at Jimbo sitting in the snow and notice that his crampons are laced so poorly that they have almost rolled off his boots! I know better than to scare a client, but my golden rule doesn't apply to this kid. I tell him point blank that we are in a very serious fucking situation! If anyone slips on the face and we don't self-arrest in a milli-second, we will probably die!

I bend down and properly lace up his crampons. He looks terrified. We start for the headwall. I am at the back watching every client's every move. Tensed up and ready to stab my ice axe into the sheer ice, I know the chances of me pulling off that super-hero miracle are slim. We march diagonally out and down the steep face. The 16 year old girl I have in the front needs to turn and wind her way back, creating a sort of Z. This is the kind of maneuver we would have practiced repeatedly had the weather not kept us in our tents for three days. Now, she is fumbling with her ice-axe leash, frozen in terror, afraid to lift her feet to turn. She is scared to death and doesn't move for over a minute. The wind is hammering us. I try yelling instructions to her, but she can't hear me. I yell again, emptying my lungs completely. Suddenly a black tunnel begins to form inside my eyeballs and rapidly starts to close. Panicked, I start breathing as hard as I can as my arms begin to tingle and go numb. I grab my axe for all I'm worth, bend over and breathe. The tunnel begins to open up. "Christ!!" Meanwhile, the girl is making her move. I breathe like I'm in labor in order to stay conscious. Every time I have to roar encouragement, the tunnel comes quietly back.

For the next hour, I breathe, yell, move my ice axe, and breathe, over and over, all the way in, all the way out, as hard as I can. My hands are tingly numb. It is a nightmare that I cannot awake from. It is unreal, surreal, and inexcusable. It is so unthinkable that I'm unable to stop thinking about it and the thin veneer that separated us from a place in 'Accidents in North America' infamy. Through another sleepless night, I question everything I am doing and whether I should ever guide again. Maybe this is the end of the line.

The next morning it is snowing sideways. After a couple sips of black tar, we walk over to the young adults in charge to see about hiking out early. They don't feel like they've gotten their money's worth and want us to take them over to some nearby crevasses and practice ice climbing. I spend the entire day on the lip of a crevasse in a blizzard, lowering and raising teenagers. I feel like a cheap hooker giving up my health, body and spirit for the delight of others. This is not who I am. This is not where I want to be. By the time we hike out, everyone's lips are blue. I've made up my mind not to guide volcanoes anymore.

SEX AND RUBY TUESDAY

TRUTH #101:

*If you are ever overwhelmed with temptation, simply dump your lover.
Please know this is all you must do to restore order to your life. For the
moment you slam that door shut, all beauty will vanish. Soon, you will be on
your knees, alone with your God, shrinking and wondering if you are emitting
an essence that only Missionaries and Black Labs find attractive.*

*-From the **Book of Truths** by Langdon Towne*

∧∧∧∧∧∧∧∧∧∧∧∧∧∧∧∧∧

[JULY 1995: GUIDING MT. BAKER FOR MOUNTAIN MADNESS]

When I met Ruby Tuesday and Mik Shain, I was coming down off a three
day mountain buzz and feeling an almost radiant glow that would last another
five hours before the bottom fell out. But for those last few pain-free hours,
I felt I could hold my own in most crowds and arrived at our appointed
rendezvous feeling comfortably casual in a jean jacket and shades.

Ruby and Mik showed up with their hair pointing in assorted directions
having just done a shot-gun two hour shopping blitz of REI with the twelve
teenagers they were about to take on a six day back packing expedition. I
didn't envy them one little bit and wanted to leave before I started getting
depressed. I gave them my rehearsed two bit spiel about what they could
expect on Mt. Baker and reminded them that the last group of Longacres
guides had done the cooking for me and I preferred a 'south of the border'
cuisine.

A week and a half later we were all at the bank of a swollen creek, trying
to find signs of the washed out trail. Being the guide, I was 'spose to know
the way and was faking it for all I was worth, but nowhere in the guide
manual did it mention losing a normally well marked trail one had walked
up five other times when the suspension bridge was still in place. Everybody
was too tired to notice my anxiety, but I couldn't believe how quickly things
had gone from comfy to intense. I eventually located the trail and we were
able to head up the lower flanks of Mt. Baker with relative ease. But the bug
of worry had begun it's work and I couldn't sleep and spent the night thinking
about how my ex #2 had nastily hung up on me for the last time the night
before and how horrible I felt knowing I was going to have to spend the rest
of my life coping with never having her hang up on me again. The thought of
schlupping this group up the mono-syllabic Easton Glacier, packing a ton of
leaded futility, seemed an unthinkable hardship.

In the morning, I walked over to Ruby and Mik, sitting out in the chilly morning air to see what they intended to feed me for breakfast. Stumbling over, blowing on my freezing fingers, I spotted something that changed the whole meaning of the trip. Ruby was seated in her camp chair wearing ultra-thin, white, long underwear, with no bra. I heard a chorus of angels and felt a delicious smile sprinting out of my heart. My head switched channels to super-guide mode, and suddenly I really liked these two strapping young people. I liked the fact we were here together, doing something positive for kids, and that we were all so lucky to be getting paid so little to hang out together in God's kitchen. I thought life, with all its ups and downs, presented a wealth of possibilities, with most of the ups visible in the reflection of my sunglasses.

Two days later, after an uneventful summit climb in a roaring fog bank, the cast of twelve teens and Mik nestled down into their tents for a much needed nap. Meanwhile, Ruby and I hiked to a flat bit of shale and with me still playing the part of the guide, I carefully organized us a little spot, using ensolite sleeping pads to block the wind.

With mountain high pumping through our every cell, we snuggled up on one sheet, then propped another over our heads to fend off the mist and wind. We were playing house like little kids. I pulled the ensolite shield tighter wondering if Ruby wanted to play doctor. We talked and laughed and I felt us growing more and more intimate, like we'd known each other all our lives. I shared dark secrets, she shared dark secrets. I talked about my ex # 2, she talked about her ex #2 through 17. I rubbed her sore shoulders and neck, she rubbed my sore shoulders and neck. Relaxed and secure, I asked her if she wanted to sleep out under the stars that night. She thought that sounded, "awesome, " except there might not be stars with all the clouds and mist circling about. I spit and gave a non-chalant guide look, and said it would clear by late afternoon. Of course, I had checked my NOAH weather radio earlier that morning and the forecast was for late afternoon clearing. The mist cleared on cue. She loved me even more. So we did. I was charged. So charged that after my mountain high wore off, I lost my nerve and didn't make a pass at Ruby all night. Nothing happened. We spooned. Nothing more. Sporting the grime of four days facial growth, and the bad scent of four days without a bath, something inside me grew shy at the thought of scratching off her face or rubbing off this thick layer of body oil. It just seemed kind of filthy.

On the way out, Ruby and I exchanged hugs, numbers and promises to call. We set up dates to meet and my mind raced at the speed of light with the endless possibilities of what I could do with a bar of oatmeal soap, a shower, and Ruby. Of course I kept my promise. I called her every other day for a week. I kept calling until I got the news she had left for two weeks to go kayaking with her boyfriend. Later that night, slumped against the shower wall, I tried to wash Ruby away, the smell of oatmeal dripping off my neck.

172

GUIDING GUMBY

The whole thing that happened with Sandy Pittman on May 10th, 1996, where she climbed Everest while jacked up on maximum bottled-O's and a short-rope tow from Lopsang, then published exclusives with no acknowledgement to the fact that Lopsang gave her his personal emergency oxygen bottle at the south summit, that he took the time to re-set her oxygen regulator to a level that would allow her to summit and get back down to another cannister, that this act did in fact preserve her life-- is just another prime-time example of guided mountaineering's Catch-22. The better you are to the spoiled and pampered, the quicker they'll forget you existed once they're safely back in their opulent world.

The Gumby trip was typical of most of my bootlegging adventures. I didn't sleep for two nights prior to the outing, turning over in my head the endless possibilities of unforeseeable disasters that there was no way to ever predict or prepare for. And then because I had the 'Lady who would be Gumby' inside my tent, spooned and safe from the building gale, I didn't get a hint of sleep that night either.

-From **The Shipwreck** *Journals*

∧∧∧∧∧∧∧∧∧∧∧∧∧∧∧∧∧

[JULY 1995: JUST ANOTHER NIGHT ON MT. RAINIER]

The last week in July, with rent and child support due, I have $23.71 left in my checking account. If all the clients show up for the guided adventure up Mt. Rainier, I'll be able to pay my bills and buy some bread and peanut butter. However, the weather forecast is grim. Several clients call complaining of sore throats and back problems and the fact that the weather man is predicting a cyclonic hell. I sweet-talk them into believing that they can do it. I don't tell them I've had a sore throat and a bad back for the last two years. I don't tell them that I will be homeless if the weather caves in before I can get them to the crevasses at 11,000 feet.

By the grace of God, no clients bail, and we spend the day gaining 6,000 vertical feet in perfect weather. Later that night, camped on a ridge above the Emmons Glacier, I talk the *fox* who would be Gumby into sharing my tiny duct taped Bibler tent. Of course, I play the part of the alpha-male protector, hoping the snuggle will become more intimate; two lonely people facing danger together, drawn close by the unfolding drama. The wind picks up on cue and is soon shrieking. Our tent flaps all the way over and then starts lifting off the ground. The *fox* starts asking me poignant questions like, "Are you sure we're going to be all right?" and "Have you been in winds this bad before?"

In the mean time, there are at least four tents being flattened and climbers' inner boots getting air mailed off the ridge. I snap to attention when I hear the tent next door erupt with laughter. The wind has just lifted Sue and Cindy's tent and turned their whole deal upside down. They are laughing so hard I start laughing. They are loving life. They think being upside down with all their gear piled on their heads is a riot. "God, this is just like Everest!!" they keep screaming with mirth and merriment.

I hear people cussing in another tent and decide that duty is calling. So, I unspoon myself and head out into the gale. As soon as I'm out of our tiny Bibler, it lifts up and flops over, terrifying the little *fox* who has no idea she will be doing a righteous Gumby impersonation in about seven hours. I straighten her out and head over to examine the mayhem of broken poles, missing inner boots, scattered pots and pans. I spend the next two hours hiking up and down a loose scree slope, trying to find a missing Koflach boot liner. We finally give up and fill the client's plastic boot-shell with extra socks and an insole. Everybody is dressed and tying into the rope. Actually, everybody is dressed but no one can remember how to tie their knots so they're bracing themselves next to the rope, waiting for me, while I storm around like a pit bull, tying and double checking knots, prussik cords, crampons, ice axes, and gear. One of the climbers has dropped his pack and is up behind a rock, crapping himself to death. Just as he starts back down to join us, he turns and sprints back for his rock and reluctantly hollers out that he isn't up for a summit push just now. Wish we could all be so lucky.

The wind keeps gaining in velocity, with pieces of ice and rock crystals pelting our faces. This is day three of minus zero sleep and counting, but my mind is set on overdrive as wicked bursts of 100 proof, endorphine laced adrenaline, superman, stud-complex vitamin T-for testosterone, pumps through every cell, enabling me to stay up forever if there is any chance of getting some action off the *fox* I have tied in behind me.

∧∧∧∧∧∧∧∧∧∧∧∧∧∧∧∧∧∧

Of course there will be a price for this lunar launch. Universal laws of physics do not lie. For every up there is a down. This trip's mania will get stacked upon last week's molar grinding agony and those impulses will be stretched over the near miss, flash backs of the previous four outings. After one "close-call" trip after another, you become convinced that if you don't lay awake all night trying to figure out how to cover every base, something that you didn't expect to go wrong will go wrong. You become afraid to think happy thoughts because that last time-- four weeks ago-- when you had a happy thought, something bad immediately happened. You develop superstitions. You pick up every penny: heads or tails. You knock on wood every time you even hint of happiness. You don't bring a camera, because every time you do the weather turns bad. You don't say, "when we get to the top," you say, "if, we get to the top." You start wearing certain pieces of clothing over and over, eating certain things over and over, and filling your first aid kit with an eclectic assortment of 'thank god somebody packed that' fix it oddities that only MacGyver fans could appreciate. During the trip, you never allow yourself to relax or let down for a second, because you're not sure the people on your rope team know how to walk and chew gum let alone back step across a two foot wide snowbridge clad in Plastic boots and crampons. The only let-down allowed occurs shortly after the last check is handed to you by the last client as he stumbles off, lock kneed to his Volvo, leaving you suddenly aware that you haven't slept in over 80 hours and it's still a three hour drive home.

So you wire yourself up on a six pack of coca-colas and fly home screaming to *Rage Against the Machine* with your head hanging out the window and bugs in your teeth. You park outside your apartment and grab everything you can, because the last time you parked out there you forgot to knock on wood and all your climbing gear was jacked. You climb the stairs, balancing against the handrail, doing one arm pulls with a lucky penny between your fingertips. Pushing through the door you collapse on to the bed, wired out of your skull on a thousands grams of caffeine. You fall asleep around three AM and awake in a dark hole that feels like Mexico City smells.

Which is why within seven brutal hours, you'll be on the phone planning the next epic. Addictive? Three sleepless nights from now you'll be up on a mountain, doing wind sprints underneath a corniced ridge, bounding over boulders, jumping over crevasses, one arming a babe up to a ledge. The eagle will have spread his wings and landed; powerful and mercifully blessed.

But right now, you're nobody, sitting next to a pile of garbage, with a bad mountain hangover and no where to go but down.

^^^^^^^^^^^^^^^

We punch our way up the Emmons Glacier, with winds knocking each of us out of our steps and out of our rhythm. A piece of flying ice finds its way into my cornea, rendering one eye useless. We arrive at Camp Schurman, and a Park Ranger friend comes out and lets me know that everyone is bailing off the mountain. No one is going up. I give him that look, of, "Got to get these folk to 11,000 feet to guarantee payment." He knows. So off we go. As the dawn breaks, black saucer plates stack one on top of the other over Little Tahoma. Lightning is streaking through the clouds and a cap of doom is pouring off the summit of Rainier. The wind is so wild that I cannot make headway. I take a step, get knocked left and right, and then take another, fighting to keep my balance. We cross a crevasse that gives everybody a grand ole 'crap your pants' scare. And then, at precisely 11,000 feet, I turn to the crowd and play the part of Moses. I raise my arm and point at the saucers as the cloud cap unleashes a volley of snow that steals my voice. I signal for us to go down and everyone cheers a wild affirmative. We sprint off the mountain as the sideways snow turns to sideways rain and the wind picks up another couple notches.

We reach the flats above Camp Schurman and pause to catch our breath. It is the same spot where an hour earlier we'd watched an amusing show put on by two RMI guides who were towing a young client suffering from acute altitude sickness. The Guides, out of necessity, had the client strung tight between two ropes and kept him upright and walking like an overheated GUMBY, ice axe flailing wildly at the end of his wrist loop- his head flopping back, left, right, and forward- his long legged stumbling gait, stick-like and uneven. It was so funny at the time that I turned to the *fox* behind me, gave her a "thumbs-up" and then a cynical, "Hey, don't laugh. That's going to be you in an hour."

Call me a prophet, but in an hour the *fox* behind me is doing her own GUMBY impersonation. One minute she's standing there looking like a potential long term, cash carrying client, and then "wonk," she's slurring words and falling over. As my rope team gathers around, I grab her, look in her eyes and know she and the rest of us are in deep wang doo. I try talking to her but she keeps mumbling incoherent nothings, like her tongue is too thick for her mouth. When I get her to her feet, she can only walk with assistance. I quickly retie in closer and grab under her arm to keep her upright as the winds and rain open up to full hurricane fury. My rope team scampers down and across a crevassed slope. The complete novice at the head of our rope team keeps coiling up tons of rope to ensure that he will plunge to his death should he fall into a hole. I scream at him through the wind to: "Drop the fucking rope!!!" then turn and scream at GUMBY to "Fucking breathe!!"

On like this it goes until we reach the base of the ridge that leads to our high camp. My brain is surging into a space I have never known. I am wired, clear thinking, and convinced that I am strong enough to carry GUMBY on my back if I have to. I will do anything to save this girl's life and in my deepest heart there is no doubt I will.

Several clients help carry her up to the tents, where, after grabbing what I can and giving clear orders to Leland, my second guide, I clip a long cord to her harness and then proceed to haul ass down the 3,000 vertical feet of glacier in order to get her to richer air. She is a rag doll as I drag her like a sled through the rain and slush. I am running for all I am worth, then jumping behind her and glissading down as fast as we can go. Her head flops around and she is moaning.

Coming to a stop at the end of a glissade track, she is flopped on her side whining. Then, in a soft voice she whimpers, "You are trying to KILL me." I burst out laughing with relief. When we get down to around 6,000 feet she comes to, begging me to stop so she can go pee. Rejoice! As soon as she stumbles off under her own steam I sit down in a lump and start to sob.

At this point the team shows up and several studs help haul her out. I am no longer needed and find it hard to get up and walk. The four mile hike to the car seems to take forever, as my legs will barely move. Back at the parking lot I figure the clients will be pissed off and disappointed. They aren't. Everybody is high fiving and hugging. It's a mountain high, adrenaline, love fest and for a few moments I'm a mountain superstar. Sue and Cindy are still laughing as they come up to hug me goodbye. "My god, that was just like an Everest video! He He he. It was *SO* cool! Thank you! Thank you so much!!"

Later that year, I have a Rainier reunion party and my "Gumby Gal" shows up. To everyone else's surprise she doesn't want to talk about needing assistance getting off the mountain and laughingly insists that I had forced her to be towed down behind me. She doesn't remember laying there in a lump at 9,500 feet, or being unable to stand on her own feet. Oh well. As anyone who's ever stuck his neck out for others will testify, most adults are basically self-serving children who will believe whatever they want to feel they're not a loser.

A LITTLE VISIT FROM ERIC SLOAN

At the end of the summer, Eric Sloan shows up and decides to live with me for the next month. I enjoy our reunion and love having him around, but soon my skimpy income isn't balancing out the double drain of two mouths to feed. I eventually drop a hint that he might think about helping out, so he promptly goes down to the food bank and brings us back blocks of orangish cheese and cans of chunky tuna. That's nice. Eric, concerned about my stressed out countenance, suggests that I start saving money by finding a cheaper place to rent. He tells me that renting a room in a house is the way to go, because, then you have access to all the amenities. Desperate for a change, I give notice and move in with the first guy that comes in to HMR looking for a roommate. His house is tiny, with no amenities and unbeknownst to me, is a hang out for all his AA friends who sometimes sleep under bridges and shrubs when not sleeping on his floor. I like these people, but having them walk in during the night when my daughters are in the hallway next to me, and listen to them get pissed off because we didn't leave space for their sleeping bag, is more than I can take. I save about $200 the first month and another $200 the second. My car promptly pukes a clutch, taking $500, and on it goes like Murphy's Law. These are desperate times for my little family and me. I am scrambling everyday for something, anything I can think of, to keep us going.

*-From **The Shipwreck** Journals*

LEONA QUINN

I was on the phone with Tim, reminiscing about our favorite alpine outing of all time. Hundreds of climbs, a million hours of five star visuals, and we both agreed our visionary winter ascent of Mt. Stuart in 1977 was our crowning moment. It wasn't that we did anything special on that climb. We climbed Cascadian Coulior, Stuart's easiest route. It wasn't because we did the climb in record pace. Nope. Encumbered by monstrous packs and a lack of showshoes, we waded through waist deep snow and could barely move. Exhausted from the all-night approach, we wound up over-sleeping and ran up the route in panic. The winter sun was already going down when we reached the false summit and decided to press on. The summit for me was absolutely terrifying. I nearly dropped my ice axe stepping around a boulder and the traverse across the headwall was an ice sheet which, having never worn crampons before, tested my mettle about ten thousand times more than I thought necessary for a good thrill. Tim and I stood on top long enough for a single photo of fear, then bolted. We wound up making it back to our tent in total darkness. I was so strung out I couldn't sleep and asked Tim to hike out that night. All he said was "what the...?" The tone answered my question for me. I was nuts.

Twenty-five years later, what has etched that climb in our psyches was the fact that we had the balls to be there at all. It was our first climb of a Grand Mountain. We had no idea what we were doing. It was the middle of winter and just the drive up the icy North Fork road in my '65 Rambler was an adrenaline-laced gamble. And we did it anyway. Stuart was our first sampling of sheer intensity, our first commitment to total risk, our first awakening into the beauty of the alpine world. It was the beginning of a long march to something more splendid than the fleeting desperation of that first love affair.

-*From* **The Shipwreck** *Journals*

^^^^^^^^^^^^^^^^^^^^^^

Leona Quinn, who worked the night shift at the *Elliot Bay Book Store*, was one of those "cool" single moms who had raised a child as a child. Now that she was ready to be healthy around her 'dove,' the dove had flown off to college. Like me, Leona was lonely and sought the comfort of rock climbing as a source of healing. Like me, she had that 'I'm hitting 40 disease': afraid to date, yet desperate as sin for a warm hand to rub your neck. She was one of those fallen angels who still had her sights set on something grand she might never attain. She had watched too many movies, seen too many happy endings. She was a romantic who still believed in the myth because she knew that reality sucked.

Leona had told me she couldn't meet anybody she considered in her league. I liked that one, because who exactly *did* she consider in her league? Who was an eligible mate for her madness, insecurity, charms, and wit? I knew that she knew there was no one. I knew, she knew, she was stuck. But she kept pretending anyway. Sad, sad, Leona. Too out there for most, not far enough for the one she wanted. I knew her league well. Like me, Leona climbed a lot.

Between occasional climbing encounters and late night conversations on the phone, we'd become comfortable around each other. The Mighty Quinn was one of those people who always had her hair down. No games. No secrets. Friends had suggested that we hook up. But Leona was smart. She knew the shadow of Zoë was still blocking out the sun.

One summer morning the two of us linked up at our favorite sport climbing area, Smith Rock State Park, and hiked up Misery Ridge just as the sky began to change to hues of salmon and gold. We sat down on a large hunk of flat rock and rested our hearts in the immeasurable comfort of a friend who, despite knowing your flaws, likes you anyway.

"Oh my God!" she began. "Yesterday, before you got here, I was coming out of the urinal and up walks this gorgeous man. I did one of those classic double takes-- my jaw just hanging open. And you'd think I could get a word out! I just stood there pretending to sort through my pack, hoping he'd say something. He had that certain thing... dark, curly hair, a poet or musician, with thin fingers. I'm sure he plays guitar. Jesus, I wanted him."

"Leona you want every body."

She laughed. "No love. That's not true. Just this one dark hunk and you."

I chuckled. "Well, Leona, if you didn't keep changing your hair style every month, you might just steal my heart."

"You big tease. Don't get me thinking again. You'd just dump me the second you had me."

"No that's Zoë's trick."

"Oh my God, Keith! Are you still going there?"

"Well... Only every other month or so. Just enough to stay a junky."

"Good."

The sun had risen and the air immediately gained a warmth to match the temperature of pumping blood. Leona and I headed out with a plan to climb on the shady backside of Mesa Verde Wall. We crested the mesa and stopped to appreciate the massive upside down exclamation point called the Monkey Face. As we scooted down the loose trail towards Mesa Verde, Leona began to talk fast about her life:

"God, I look at this face in the mirror, and wonder what's happened... if I've become like the rest of society? I don't get it! Why the pain? Why these feelings of misery? I look at the desperate situations in Africa and Asia and think of the millions who are truly suffering and fighting for survival. And then I think of my problems: stuck in a shoe box apartment, unable to meet anyone who's appealing and has a brain in his other head, nights filled with books and emptiness, days crammed with pointless projects and the distraction of buying stuff. And…and, I know I shouldn't complain. I know I have it so good compared to the rest of the world. And yet, most of the time I feel useless and unwanted. Like there's no meaning to anything I do. And it feels like shit. It honestly does."

I answered with: "The key my dear, is taking action and gaining some confidence. You move with confidence and things take care of themselves."

"And what if you never feel confident?" she asked.

"That's why we climb. It takes away the fear for a day or two."

The temperature was getting warm and Leona stopped to take off her sweatshirt-stuffing it into her pack. Our next steps took us down into the shade and the morning chill worked its magic inside the Mighty Quinn's tank top. I looked at her and gave a "Thank you, God!" smile.

She smiled back and rubbed her shoulder up against me. Thus inspired, a series of abnormally profound thoughts poured forth.

"Ya know, Quinnster, when I'm alone at night I battle this dance. What is right once you blow up the rules? It's like I tell Zoë, I don't care if she gets married, please just keep having sex with me once in awhile so I don't dry up and blow away. Is that asking too much? That way I don't ever have to fall in love again. Me and Dionne Warwick. Does that make any sense?"

"God, yes! My ex wants me to meet someone, so I will quit pestering *him* for sex!"

"Hmmm?" A huge smile broke across my face.

"Now, now, no teasing. And really, all kidding aside, how do I explain to him how complicated meeting someone is? How sex leads to so much trouble."

"Jesus, you sound like me."

"And you read *The Prophet* and it says, 'And think not that you can direct the course of love, for love, if it finds you worthy, directs your course.' Well, maybe that's my problem."

"What?"

"Maybe I'm not worthy."

"Oh, Leona, please!"

"Well?"

"Jesus..." Leona was buckling up her harness. She started to cry. I placed my fingers under her chin and lifted her face.

"My God. Leona. You are beautiful! Thanks for all you've done for me. Thanks for letting me flirt and be myself with you. I can't tell you how much a little of your attention has helped. I'm lonely too. And I swear... you've saved my life a few times. Trust me. You're worthy."

At that she flung herself around me like a child.

180

THE ANNIVERSARY

I'll never forget a moment back in my late thirties, when Tim and I were hiking into a climb, and I was talking about my second failed marriage and he pointed out that my life did look bleak, but in all truth, we still had our health, still had our parents, and still had our kids. "These were our golden years," he said.

∧∧∧∧∧∧∧∧∧∧∧∧∧∧∧∧∧∧∧∧∧

[August 1995: Seattle]

I arrive home from guiding Mt. Baker and collapse on the floor, too tired to unpack my stinking, soaking gear. I had a bag of chips and a coke on the way home and am now way beyond mustering up the strength to fix a plate of spaghetti. I know I should have picked up a hamburger, but it's hard to justify such a lofty expenditure when you're scratching and clawing to save every dime. I want to call somebody, want to talk to Zoë (it's our 10th anniversary) but she's not home. I don't call my kids because I don't want them to hear the fear in my voice. I grab a pad and write down the thoughts that swirl from my head, much colder and desperate than the snowstorm I cursed earlier in the day.

WELCOME TO MY HOLE

The meaningless absurdity of life is the only incontestable knowledge accessible to man. -Tolstoy

At some point, after all the divorces and counting of losses, you wake up on a Sunday--alone. Your kids are at their mom's. Your climbing friends are out of town. There isn't a woman to dream about. You have given up on meeting anyone you might have peace with. No one is going to call you today; you can feel it. Waves of emptiness, regret and pain come washing over your bed. The futility of your life, your efforts, your attempts to make something of yourself trumpet from a frightened heart. Lying there with the covers drawn tight, you are twelve, a boy who has always come up short.There are a million things that you should be doing today, and twice that many that need to be done, but you're not sure if you have the will power to brush your teeth. You finally make a cup of coffee and sit down heavily to contemplate your own nothingness. There will be no climbing today. You have been there, touched the summit, and even that was not enough. For inevitably, the path leads back down. Your cup is warm in your hands, a touchstone to a world outside this place. But not today. Today you will be descending, into the darkness, into the abyss of self.

∧∧∧∧∧∧∧∧∧∧∧∧∧∧∧∧∧∧

I sit and stare at the phone, still shaking from cold and nerves. There are thirteen messages on my answering machine. Not one of them is from Zoë. I sit in agony knowing that had I not told her to *never* call me again, there might be a message from her and I would have an excuse to call her back. But I can't call... not without her calling me first. That would be weak. I can't go there.

The thirteen calls are from Smith Rock clients and a guy I met at HMR who wants me to lead his party of seven up Mt. Rainier in a couple of weeks. I call the guy back and tell him I'm flattered, but am taking an extended break from volcano guiding. He begs me to reconsider, guaranteeing a superb cash-paying crew. I let him down easy by telling him I'll think about it while guiding at Smith. I call back the Smith clients and find out that most of the cash-paying crew have bailed. This is extremely bad financial news. (Concerned that I wouldn't be able to get everyone on enough ropes, I had asked Leland Windham to come along as my second guide for the trip.)

I call Leland to discuss the reality of client to guide ratios. Leland doesn't take the hint, but instead spews gleeful anticipations of curdling epitahs over the record heat wave predicted for eastern Oregon. I rub my forehead trying to find words to explain the dire straits of my financial position. Soon I figure out I'm wasting my breath as the dismal figures of my pathetic income make me look like the *Duke of Windsor* compared to Leland's net worth.

"So... speaking of nightmares, some guy I met at HMR just got off the phone wanting me to take him and seven guys up Rainier."

Leland had been my second on the Gumby trip. He was the stud who got all the clients safely down in a hurricane while I drug the altitude stricken Gumby to lower elevation. Neither of us had slept for three nights on that trip and the stress of the rescue had left both of us barking up trees with post-trauma syndrome. I thought he'd never want to guide with me again.

"So, when we goin?" He sounds thrilled.

"Are you kidding?"

His voicé bounds up high. "I'm serious! I can't wait to hear you yell at some client: 'Dude! Drop the fucking rope!!!' That was unbelievable!"

"Yeah, what did the guy have in his hand... like twenty feet of coiled slack? Standing at the lip of a crevasse? Jesus! Anyway, I think I'm done guiding volcanoes. I'm shot."

"WHY!!! Rainier is AWESOME! Let's go. I love your guiding style. Just cussin, screamin, and yardin clients the whole way to the summit. Sign me up!! He. He.... Hey, I know." Leland starts giggling. "We should start our own Rainier guide service. We'll call it: *Mountain Fucking Hell.*"

"Yeah, that would sell."

"Our logo will read. *Mountain Fucking Hell: An Epic Waiting to Happen.*"

I burst out laughing. And with that shift, I know that despite every ounce of common sense screaming 'NO!' I'll soon be yarding bodies up to the crater rim of Rainier.

THE CIRCUS

The secret source of humor itself is not joy but sorrow. There is no humor in heaven.

- MARK TWAIN

She hasn't called me now for five months. She isn't going to. There isn't a quiet moment that doesn't wind up flooded by memories of her laugh, her smell, her skin. I can't get anything done. Can't eat. Can't sleep. Miss her with every breath. My heart is gone. My laugh. My humor. All gone. My wit and sense of timing are off, taken and tossed. I can't write. Every thought is something trite and over done. I am not original. I am a repeat of the same song and dance being played on every block, in every town.

-From **The Shipwreck** *Journals*

^^^^^^^^^^^^^^^^^^^^^^^^^^^^

SKIP

June in Seattle had been wet, cold and miserable when Skip, a gregarious and delightfully animated fifteen year old called to make plans for our return climbing trip to Smith Rock. Skip had been a client on a three day guided excursion in May where he had been fortunate enough to have "the absolute-bichenest-time-of-my-f...ing- life-ever, man!!" Besides his staggering energy, what I enjoyed most about Skip was that he was financially lucrative. Like many spoiled kids, his parents couldn't stand what they'd created, and were constantly seeking expensive ways to unload their *trouble*. Skip was bright and knew how to manipulate disadvantaged,cellar-dwellers like myself with a baffling array of freebies and handouts. On that wonderful trip in May, he was constantly tossing snacks, iced teas, and future guiding enticements my direction. Skip knew the score: as long as he kept the dollars coming- I was a happy ho. In point of fact, that wonderful trip in May had been such a well-paying love-fest that I'd told my daughters we might go back to Smith with Skip in August.

Now, as Skip rattled on the phone about being 'so sick and f...ing tired' of having to spend his free time on the equestrian circuit, and how only climbing really pumped his nads, I gave no thought to the fact that August in Central Oregon could be a blistering hell. Not a thought. For in June, any place being too hot to enjoy seemed simply absurd. And a well-paid vacation to Smith with a rich kid my daughters would adore? What could be better?

LAKE

The week before my *paid vacation* found me guiding a group of twelve teenagers on Mt. Baker in heinous, wintry conditions. Thoughts of Smith, warmth, knobs, and fun with my daughters and Skip kept me going.

When I got home Sunday night, bone weary, there were at ton of phone messages from Lake, a kid who had been on the May love-fest with Skip.

"Keith, I've got four people that want to go to Smith and they're all ready to pay. Two of them are total babes with a car. They can drive."

"Sorry, Lake. No can do. This is my one and only vacation with my kids."

"But." I could hear him fidgeting.

"But, what?"

"Dude, these chicks are bitchin. All you have to do is string up ropes for us. We'll belay. It's easy money."

"That's nice of ya, but no thanks, Lake. You know what it's like with that many kids. It'll be a freakin Circus."

"But, but, these guys are so psyched. What am I supposed to tell em?"

"Tell em, tell em we'll do it another time. I'm sorry man, I'm exhausted."

"DUDE!!" The phone went quiet, like Lake had put his hand over the receiver.

"Dammit, Lake. Are those guys there right now?" I uncurled the arm holding the phone and felt cramping in my bicep. The silence on the line was painful. I did some mental math as sweat ran down my collar. "Listen, Lake. I've got a buddy who's a great second guide. I could call him."

"Really?! Thanks dude!! You'll love these guys."

"OK. Now, who all do you have signed up to go?"

"Tammy and Linda are down for sure." Cheers erupted. "And Stan is in."

"No Stan. No way! He always looks pissed off."

"Yeah. OK. Right. And my friend from Montana wants to go."

"What?!"

"And his uncle."

"Wait. Wait. Hold it a sec. You said you had four people. Now there's an uncle from Montana?

"Bo's uncle wants to help out. He's been teaching Bo to climb."

"Uh huh. Well, Bo can go, but bag the Uncle."

(A long silence.) "OK... That's cool."

"Lake, tell the *babes* and Bo I'll give Leland a call." Cheering erupted. "Tell em the costs and when we're leaving. Make sure they bring plenty of money for food and camp fees. You got that? I don't want any hassles. This is the only vacation I get with my kids all summer."

I hung up the phone and limped off to find the Advil and dial up Leland Windham.

"Sure." (pronounced sshheeerrrrr in Leland speak) Cooooolll! Guidin' at Smith ought to be *real* fun. Yeah, about 105 in the shade. Right ON!" Leland's voice rose and fell like a Chopin sonata.

"You think so, Leland? It won't be that hot, will it?"

"Have you heard the forecast? He he he. We're going to ffrryyy!"

"Oh God." I rubbed my temples slowly waiting for the Advil to kick in.

"Yeah. It's going to be awesome! What should I bring? Do I need food?"

"No, no uh, well, yeah. Throw in whatever you've got."

"I've got a carrot and half a can of tuna."

"Perfect. At least we've got the food handled. Yeah, you throw in that and I'll bring the rest of the stuff."

"RIGHT ON!! I'll bring the carrot, the half can of tuna, my balaclava, rock shoes, and a chalk bag. That's it. Nothing else. He He He!"

I hung up and called Lake back. The kid talked fast. "Well, OK, here's what's going on. Linda and Tammy are out...."

"What?!"

"Yeah, I know, bummer, chicks, man. What can I say? They forgot it was cheer camp week."

"Lake! I just got off the phone with Leland. He's packin his carrot and balaclava right now. I don't need him for just you and this Bo. Dammit!"

"Wait! Stan's still in. And Bo's uncle still wants to go real bad. My dad says we can use the Suburban so we can all ride down together."

"Wait, wait, wait a minute. I said no Stan and no uncle!"

"Dude, I couldn't tell Stan. It would kill him."

"He was never invited!"

"I know, but we kinda…"

I had been duped. Full on. My specialty. After another half hour of run-around, Stan was going, but I had held firm on Bo's uncle. I called Leland back to tell him the news.

"Wow! He He. We just planned this trip an hour ago and people are already bailing. He he he. Did we get their deposits?"

"Well, no. The good news is the uncle from Montana isn't going and we can use Lake's parents' Suburban."

"Uncle from Montana? What?!! No WAY!!! That's it. I'm bailin right now! I'm out of here!"

"So do you just want to bag this thing, Leland? I wouldn't mind."

Leland burst into a fit of mirth. "He he He. No way. This'll be a pARTy. MAN, am I desperate for cash! Oh MY GOD! Man, it's going to be hot! A full on bake-fest, makin twelve cents an hour. RIGHT ON!!"

"OK, then. I'll see ya at 4:45 tomorrow."

"4:45??!! 4:45 in the morning? What the hell?! Are you serious?"

"Yep. Six hour drive; meetin Skip and his dad at noon; you do the math."

THE BURB

Lake's pious parents walked out on to their farm house porch at 5:44 AM.

We roared up at 5:45, dead on time. The August sun was rising over the distant ridges and the air was already warm. Introductions were made between the three teenage boys, Lake, Bo, Stan, my two daughters Kate and Kris, Lake's parents, Leland and me. His mother's hand trembled as it lightly touched my palm. Both she and her husband looked like deer caught in the headlights, fixated as they were on the back of Leland, who with lengthy dreadlocks and tattered threads was popping his Kodiak can and humming "Dee de, de." Their silent expletives fell like dandruff to the shoulder as Leland pulled his lip out several inches and stuffed in a pinch of chew.

Meanwhile, I was trying to fully register the Suburban that Lake's parents were lending us. As I took inventory, a foreboding flutter whipped through my bowels. When Lake had said Suburban my mind had instantly locked in on a late 80's model, two tone, door dings, with good rubber. Reality was a '72, rattle trap with towing mirrors bail wired to tweaked doors. Cracks in the windshield intertwined with other cracks. I crawled up into the spongy driver's seat, pushed in the clutch and felt a pop in my upper thigh. "Nice action." The tattered cargo area behind smelled of a cat litter box, making me gag slightly every time I forgot to breathe through my mouth.

The kids and Leland crammed in five days worth of gear. Bo and Stan brought out a queen sized mattress to use as the boys' sleeping pad. We bent it in half, stuffed it in, and were ready to go. I leaned out the window and inquired nervously: "How many gallons does the gas tank hold?"

"Counting the reserve, 40 gallons. Yes, you ought to be able to get all the way to Oregon on that." (Oregon was two hours away; Smith Rock another two.) A quick flutter of dreams gone by flickered in my heart: Driving the Festiva, the girls and I could have made it to Smith on 10 gallons....met Skip, gotten paid, and headed home with cash and smiles bounding. I quickly flushed that happy thought and grabbed the wheel.

We hit the road and I shifted the Burb into high gear. At 52 MPH a shimmy started and the twin towing mirrors banged madly against the ill fitting doors. At 57 MPH, the exposed steel cord of the tires hummed almost loud enough to drown out the voices of Lake and Bo shouting in the back. Blissful, they arched their voices up over the stifling din and burst into a song they had recently learned at a church camp.

(Sung to "*Row, Row, Row Your Boat*")

> "*Fuck, Fuck, Fuck a Duck*
> *Screw a Kangaroo*
> *Finger-bang an Orangutang*
> *Support your local Zoo*"

BO MONTANA

As we rounded a corner, the sun hit us full blast, creating a pattern of refraction's and reflections off the myriad of cracks. If I squinted and turned my head slightly, only one eye was completely blinded. Unable to see which lane I was using, we blasted over a nasty pothole, and the Burb caught air. Heads banged loudly against the metal roof as dust and shit flew everywhere. I floored the gas pedal as the Burb shimmied back up to 63 mph.

I'm always on time. That's my rule, hard and fast. We were to meet Skip and his golf-hungry dad at noon in the Smith Rock bivy parking lot. I did some mental math and had us pulling in to the bivy area 15 minutes late. Not good. I pushed down harder on the pedal.

In the town of Toppenish, we slowed to stop at a traffic light. Leland fidgeted nervously with his can of Kodiak, pulled his lower lip in and out, threaded his dreads, and sang the "I Dream of Genie" jingle."

Behind us, Bo was wrapping up a set of Cheech and Chong skits. The kids were all weeping. A low-rider Pontiac Bonneville, filled with Mexican migrant workers pulled up along side us. Bo rolled down his window and shouted racial insults at our brown neighbors. Leland and I looked at each other in horror.

"Whoaaa!!! Hey, Bo!! Get back in here. What the hell are you doing?!!"

"What?!" He looked at me with a questioning glance.

"What?! What the hell do you think? Are you fucking nuts?"

"They're spics, man. Gimme a break." His sulk showed he hadn't the faintest clue what I was talking about. It was obvious that in his heart of hearts he thought giving the finger to diversity his God-given right. He took the wrapper off a Butterfinger and tossed it out the window.

"HEY!!! Bo! WHOA!!! The Mexicans rolled down their windows. I raised my hands over my face.

"Jesus Christ, Bo! What year do you think you're living in?"

"Hey, Bo." Leland suddenly piped in. "What part of Montana did you say you're from?"

"Butte." He hocked up a wad and spit out the window. "Why?"

Leland turned to me, wide eyed, and slowly mouthed: "BUTTE. Oh my God!! Butte, Montana?!! THAT's it. I'm outta here!!! Did they pay? Let's bail right now while we're still alive!"

LIPSTICK ON MY DIPSTICK

Cruising down the road, we had happy youngsters singing, crowd surfing, and head banging away as the boys slammed CD's in to Lake's Boom Box. "Get down tonight," was on ten as we passed the town of Goldendale.

Leland stared out the side window, before letting go a long painful, "Ooohhhh Mmmyy!!!!"

Despite the din, I focused on the job at hand. The proud mental image that we were right on time and that I was a dad who went the distance to bring joyful adventure to the lives of his children, fluttered like a shiny bubble. Once again, I had overcome doubt and the odds to provide an experience my kids would never forget. And that positive, little, thought made it all the way from the back of my skull to behind my left eyeball when the Burb suddenly lurched out of gear with a loud clunk. I shifted and gassed it and shifted again as we coasted to a stop. My heart began to beat inside my tongue as I jumped out into the sweltering heat and popped the hood.

"Oh dear God! Oh dear God! Lake? What the hell is going on?!"

Lake sounded scared. "I don't know man. Check the oil."

"Oh my, oh my God. I think we just dropped the transmission." I began to feel sick. Kris and Kate got out and took my hands.

"Dad. It's going to be OK. We'll get to Smith." Krissy was trying her best to reassure me.

"Oh, girls. OH, OH, OH!" I started rubbing my forehead with both palms. Every fear I had ever felt in my life started whooshing up my pipes like a vacuum cleaner bag blowing in reverse. Broken down in a borrowed vehicle. A client and bucks three hours away. 100 degree heat, five kids and no phone. "Oh my god. Oh my god. I won't cry. I won't cry!"

"Dad, it's going to be all right." The girls walked on either side of me holding me upright as I tried in vain to collect myself. A Mazda pickup with a tractor engine in the back pulled off the road and parked in front of us. I turned around and couldn't help but notice the license plate. Here is what it said in big bold lettering: **HAPPINESS IS LIPSTICK ON MY DIPSTICK!**

I walked up to see what the driver might have to say. The little truck door opened and out stepped a huge brick of a man. His crewcut glistened in the sun and his belly rode well over a suspendered pant line. Printed boldly on his T-shirt were these words: **EXPOSE YOURSELF TO THE WEST!** On closer examination, I saw that the print below the slogan was of a man flashing a cow. I wanted to hide Leland, afraid of what our truck drivin son of a gun might think of alternative life forms.

"Uh, hi sir." I grinned. "We're in a bit of trouble here."

"The names, Merle. What seems to be the problem?"

I flipped a switch in my head, and cranked out my best redneck accent, adding a little okie twang to get the flavor just right.

"Well, Merle." Leland caught my eye and mouthed back at me, 'MERLE?' "The deal is, we're neck deep in it as far as I can tell. I think we just dropped the tranny. One minute we're drivin along, then I hear this here clunk and then nothin. I got five kids with me, Merle, and one waitin for me down at a little town near Bend, Oregon. This is our vacation, darn it. We're rock climbers. We climb rocks for fun. I borrowed this here rig from that there kid's parents and now I got us in a heckuva mess."

Kate looked at me funny, "Dad, you sound just like Eric Sloan."

Merle took a quick peek at the engine, pulled out a rag, wiped his brow, and turned to me. "You're looking at three days to get a new tranny in. Maybe two for a rebuild. The wreckin yard up the ways sometimes has these models, but you're still talkin two or three days by the time you go up there, pull out the tranny, get it moved back to town and stuck in this rig. You better get a hold of that friend in Bend cuz you ain't leavin town for a spell."

"Oh, dear God!" I almost passed out.

Merle mopped his neck. "Well, there's nothin we can do here." He blew his nose. "Now, let's get you towed into the Chevy dealer and see about startin there."

With that he grabbed a cable, crawled under the Burb and hooked us up to the little Mazda. Risking his life, jerking and shuddering along, Merle yarded six tons of worthless scrap iron into town. The quiet in the Burb was painful. Krissy kept looking into my eyes to check for tears. She'd look up, see no tears, and then smile a little smile of hope and cheer. The way I figured, this little fiasco was about to suck dry my entire earnings for the summer. My one vacation with my daughters was officially ruined. Soon, Skip would be driving away from Smith, an irate wealthy parent screeching obscenities. In tiny oven baked Goldendale, I was looking at four hell-bound days with the Circus.

Merle pulled us into the Chevy parking lot and went over and said something to a mechanic wrenchin on a GMC 4 X 4. I told the kids to go across the street to find some shade in the little park and headed into sign my financial future away to the Parts/Labor man. I gave him my song and dance about climbing, kids, and limited dollars. I was beaten, defeated, and I'm sure I looked it. Leland came up and we started talking in the soft tones of the thoroughly thrashed. A few minutes later, I spotted Merle walking briskly down the sidewalk and went out to thank him for all his trouble.

I looked up to see a dirty, junk heap of a rig go by. The Burb was moving! "Merle, hey Merle, what the hell?"

"Hey, kid, I'm not sure. Kenny just jumped in, fiddled with something for a second and took right off."

Kenny came roaring back up main street trailing dust and droppings and whipped the Burb into the Chevy lot. He jumped out and beamed, "Shoot, somehow your 4 by lever got knocked into neutral. Gears don't work with the 4 by in neutral. So there ya go! Ain't nothin wrong with her at tall. Har Har." He spit onto the Chevy lot and slapped his oil stained overalls.

Merle whacked me on the shoulder, "Well I'll be a son of a gun! There ya go, kid. How about that?!"

I wanted to bury my head in his big burly T-shirted chest and sob with unabashed gratefulness. We shook hands instead and I raced in to pay the labor charges for the dealer's efforts.

"You get those kids back on the road and go have some fun with your rocks." With that, the Labor/ Parts man tore up the bill and sent us on our way.

MURPHY'S LAW

Everyone in the Burb knew a miracle had just taken place. My head did some quick math. We had lost an hour in Goldendale, but if we drove like hell we could get to Smith only a half hour late. Skip's smartly attired dad would be miffed, but still there.

In the back of my mind, I knew that somewhere in Murphy's code of law was an axiom about being behind schedule when traveling by car: [If you absolutely, positively have to be there ....] However, feeling the tide had turned, I was ready to defy the odds. I punched the Burb and whipped out in front of a pack of Manufactured Homes crawling down Highway 97. "Yes!!" We all screamed.

"Right on!!" Leland was getting chirpy. "Ooohh man, the Mobile Home Parade doing 25 MPH all the way to California. Man, did we score, gettin by that show."

I goosed the Burb as we crested a rise, our voices exploding triumphant with *Nirvana's* ultra-anthem*: Smells Like Teen Spirit: "*

"IN DENIAL!!! IN DENIAL!!! IN DENIAL!!!!"

Before us was a row of stopped cars and a flagger, tiredly waving her stop sign. We slowed to a stop. And sat. My stomach lining fluttered. Ten sweltering minutes later we were off.

"OK. OK, we'll be an hour late." I passed cars in a desperate effort to gain back precious minutes. A half hour later, after taking the Burb to the limits of bald tire adhesion, we came upon the next flagger. As we sat at the head of the pack, I watched as the eighteen wheelers we had blown past came sidling up, three or four cars behind. Over the horizon soon appeared the Mobile Home Parade.

Leland slumped over, resting his forehead on the crusty dashboard. Chossy (Leland's nickname for Krissy's nickname: Koss) played with his dreads, twirling, braiding, and stacking them. She kept saying, "I like your DANGLE-RODS Leland."

It was 11:30 and we were at least two hours from Smith. As I sat there mulling over every mistake from every ill fated trip, I quickly ran out of the will power to go on another wretched second.

"Ooooohhh mmmmyyy!" Leland looked over at me in off-green anguish. "We're partyin now!" Chossy had lumped his DANGLE-RODS on top of his head in a decent replica of Stonehenge.

"Hey Leland." She took one of his long dreads and creeped it down her arm. "I've got a sluggy."

At 1:47, we roared in to Terrebonne, dropped off the boys at the grocery store and sped off to the bivy parking lot to meet Skip. Mirages shimmered on the road. I pitched the Burb sideways into the two lane gravel driveway and almost fishtailed in to a gorgeous 1995 green Suburban coming the other way. It was Skip and his dad. Whew!! I dove out of the car, apologies and nervous exhaustion pouring out of my sweat glands. Talking as fast as I could, I laid out the game plan, the forecast, the meeting places, synchronized our watches and bid Skip's-- already late for his golfing date-- dad farewell.

We had made it! It was hot but Smith could be done in the heat. Skip started passing out iced tea and doling out hilarious tales of fights with father and other horrors of family life. Good ole Skip. Yes, we would be all right.

I roared back to Terrebonne to collect the boys. Tired of watching the tar bubble in the grocery store parking lot, they'd started hoofing it toward the State Park with grocery bags. Stan's pearly white skin was turning a lush scarlet and Lake's frown spelled trouble.

"Hey guys, pile in. Here's the plan. We're going to set up camp. Keep poppin in to the showers to cool off. It's not bad when you're wet. Keep drinking tons. We'll eat some lunch and head down in to the canyon as soon as there's some shade. It'll be great. Lake, what's wrong?"

He leaned over and whispered, "Man, Bo's only got about ten bucks left."

"Huh? Well did you tell Bo that he's going to go hungry? I told you I'm not funding your buddies, Lake. I hope they like Top Ramen. And what about camp and guide fees?"

"Well, Stan's cool, and Bo did have enough until he spent it all on webbing and carabiners."

"I told you I had enough draws and stuff for all of us."

"I know. I know. But, he really wants to lead. His uncle thought he should use his own gear."

"Hmmm." I turned around to change the subject. "So, Bo, what level are you leading?"

"Well, back at Castle Crag near home I've led all the 10s. I been working out on the 11's and 12's. I like the cracks the best."

"Wow. I'm going to be putting you on the *sharp end* then."

"So you bein the guide and all, what you leadin?" He asked flatly.

"Here at Smith? Oh, mostly 10's, sometimes harder. Depends on the day."

"That's all? We should have brought my uncle, he leads harder than that."

"Hmmm," I thought, "and tactful too."

THE SHARP END

At long last, the sun had ducked behind Asterisk Pass and the time had come to pull down knobs. Leland walked over to *Double Trouble*: 10a and with Skip belaying, started clipping bolts. I took the Circus over to Dancer, 5.8, one of Smith's most gentle routes. Bo was bouncing up and down to lead.

"Man, I want this one! Let me lead it man!! Can I?"

I told him to rack up the draws and tie in. I was curious to find out just how much this kid had learned from his uncle.

"I'll use my draws." I waited patiently as Bo dug through his pack and started yarding out piles of bright green 1" webbing, tied into three foot slings. With oval biners attached, the draws swung half way down his calf.

Leland spotted the show as he was about to make the sick move from the first block to the second block of *Double*. "Wow. Cool! Now those are some sport draws!"

Bo looked up. "What? These are what me and my uncle use. What's wrong with these?"

"Nothing, Bo," I explained, "we're just not used to seeing draws that touch the ground while hanging off one's harness."

Bo had no clue what he was being ribbed about. I refreshed him on how to tie in and gave him my chalk bag as he didn't have one. He let me know that his uncle and him didn't believe in using chalk.

"FUCK!!" Leland's voice ripped past our heads like a stray bullet. Sliming off a greaser, he had just grabbed a draw to make a clip. "I HATE this Fucking HELL HOLE!!"

A solid 5.12 climber back home in the misty cool of Washington, Leland was reduced to dogging in the sauna-like heat of Smith.

"Looking good, Leland! Right on! Now, Bo, seeing how you are a 10+ leader, and judging by Leland's performance over there, maybe the most capable climber in this Circus, you'll probably be a bit brought down when you knock on this little 5.8. But, sometimes it doesn't hurt to warm up on something easy. Hey, Leland! Are ya lovin the heat?"

"FUCK!!! I can't fucking believe this!!!!!!!"

Leland was sticking his whole hand in his chalk bag, trying to gain the courage to continue.

Bo fiddled with his slings and biners. "No. No.. This climb looks fine."

Leland continued to scream every few seconds. "OH MY GOD!!!

The Circus, with its wholesome family-like exchanges, had people staring.

"How many slings do I need?" Bo inquired.

"Take eight, Bo. Here's two of my draws for the anchors. You ready?"

"Yeah, I'm on it."

"And you know what you're on it like?"

"Huh?"

"I said... You know what you're on it like?"

"What?"

"A bad smell."

"Huh?"

"Just climb, Bo. Belay on."

Bo inched his way up the beginning knobs, chalking up madly. He got to the first bolt, clipped it and grabbed the draw. "Geez."

"How ya feelin, bro?"

"What's this rated? He asked with a dry rasty voice. "Take! I gotta hang."

"OK. But clip the rope into the biner first....Bo, you haven't clipped into the biner yet. You'll deck if you let go." He grabbed the rope and fumbled it up to the carabiner. "Clip it the other way, nope, the other, not that, nope....Jesus Christ! Just get the rope in that biner!"

"Dang. These bolt placements suck." Bo was still fiddling, trying to get the rope into the carabiner, which would get him safely on belay.

Skip leaned over and muttered: "5.11 my f...ing eye."

For the next half hour we watched Bo Montana scratch, hang, and claw his way up the knobs, shaking and sweating, pissing and moaning. I was kicking myself for letting this kid off the ground on lead. Normally I would check him out on a safe top-rope to make sure his skills matched his mouth. But with all his bravado, I figured an easy 5.8 would be a walk for him. Duped again. Bo's calve's were doin the sewin machine. At every clip he ran the rope the wrong way through the biner. His Uncle, I'm sure, would have been very proud.

THE CIRCUS

Within an hour we had three ropes and six climbers teamed up and cranking routes. The plan was simple; for the next four days we would beat the heat by climbing where the sun wasn't. We would spend our every waking moments seeking out all the shade Smith could muster.

Soon, the dynamics of the Circus began to swing into full gear. Skip treated the experience like it was his last five days on earth. He wanted to be on as many routes as often as possible. I kept putting ropes up harder and harder climbs hoping to God his tips would trash or his arms would cramp into knots. No way. He just wanted more. I had him carrying his rope, my rope, Leland's rope, water for seven and treats for eleven. He ran everywhere. He was a machine.

Stan whined constantly that he wasn't getting to climb enough, which was partially true. Everyone of us balked at belaying him as his climbing technique was like a sloth on downers. Every move took minutes. As Stan quietly shouted down for more tension on the rope, belayer's fingers and joints turned purple and disfigured. By day three, only Lake would still belay Stan.

Lake was in 'pig pie' heaven. He was lovin' the heat, the knobs, the dust, and the sweat runnin' down his butt-cheeks. From the second his feet hit the dirt at 6:00 am, 'til the last bedtime story somewhere around 11pm, Lake was a whirl of high fivin', revved out of his mind energy. He didn't care what he was climbin' or who he was belayin'. He was diggin' every second of every day. With boundless patience, he would talk Stan up climbs. With unabashed enthusiasm, he threw out move by move, sequence-by-sequence beta. He had come to Smith to have the time of his life and by Joe that is exactly what he was havin. What heat? By the start of day three, the sound of his positive, cheerful voice screaming, "Hey, Dude, you're on this like a bad smell!" was making us all wince.

Kate was digging the boys. Their constant attention, however, made her even more self conscious about her hair. I like her hair. That, of course, mattered not. She was twelve. It had become her obsession. The poor thing spent every moment combing and straightening, combing and straightening.

"Kate, your hair is fine. Leave it alone."

"Dad, my hair sucks. I can't believe this. It won't lay straight."

"Wash it."

"I did and look at it."

"It looks fine."

"You're just saying that to get me to shut up."

"Yeah, so?"

"See?! You don't really think my hair looks good."

"No, really Kate. I love your hair. Hey, try washing it and then rolling the ends up in the window of the Burb and hanging there for awhile. Maybe that'll straighten it out. We could drive around town with you dangling from the door."

"Dad, you are such an asshole!"

"Yeah, and my hair looks good."

By day three, her brushing and fussing was getting too annoying, even for me, so I took her hairbrush when she wasn't looking and stuffed it in my pack. When she found it, I stuck it in an empty hamburger wrapper and hid it under the back seat of the Burb in a dirty clothes bag placed under a set of tire chains. When she found it there I decided to let it go.

Kris/ *aka* Kossy/ *aka* Chossy was content to just pester Leland. She could not get enough of his Dangle-rods. Moreover, she could entertain herself for hours by sitting with her stuffed toy cat with the missing eyeball named, Julius. Julius had been around since her birth. Krissy would go nowhere without him/her. (Kris says he's a girl, but I'm not sure.) Julius accompanied Kris up climbs, lashed to her harness with a carabiner and sling,

Leland thought 'Chossy' was radical and loved the way she delivered one-liners out of the blue. Every so often, she would blurt out something totally unrelated to anything we were involved in such as: "Dad, when dogs drag their butts around on the ground do you think it hurts their nards?"

Bo was busy alienating himself from his peers with a constant barrage of ignorant put-downs. He had particularly bad timing and the remarkable ability to utter statements that poured salt into open wounds. Of course, there were positives about him. For example, as the only member of the circus who completely ignored my warnings about swimming in the agricultural drainage ditch: 'The Crooked River,' he hardly complained about the rashes and blotches erupting on his Montana-brown skin.

Leland ran ropes up climbs: in the heat, in the dust, not enough water, not enough sleep. Sitting there humming with a plug in his lip, he was being rendered senseless by the eighteen hour days of climbing and belaying. Earlier in the summer I had seen him laughing and cracking jokes in the face of hurricanes as gear blew out of our ravaged high camps. Smith was another matter. Leland was gassed, and couldn't keep his mind off black suicidal thoughts of steaming, melancholic bliss.

As for me, I had lost my sense of humor somewhere on the icy, storm swept flanks of Mt. Baker about a week before Smith. I was no longer a 'fun' guy. I was a water sucking robot, trying to keep everyone alive til I could pack them back in the Burb and get the hell out of Central Oregon. By day I kept the Circus oiled and rolling. By night I kept the circling boys at bay, shooing them away from our food. I tried to keep my heart sealed from the piercing reality that I was losing money, losing any joy I might have felt with my kids, and slowly and steadily losing what was left of my mind.

THE CHURCH CAMP

On the second day, a Holy Mother of Jesus Church Camp bus pulled up. Out stepped twenty enjoyment starved teenage girls and their two overheated male camp counselors. In an act of blind irony, they set up their city of tents all around the queen-sized mattress the Circus was using for a bivy sight.

The twenty teenaged girls soon knew the four boys by name. Any signs of physical let down evaporated in the desert night. Out of our sight, the boys spent every waking second til dawn trying to sneak into tents and cop a feel under the paranoid eyes of the exhausted church camp counselors. Lake collected phone numbers. Bo and Skip's foul mouth, nasty, antics excited the girls creating wonderful middle of the night dynamics. Occasionally, a wild eyed adolescent would come running up to my tent, babbling incoherent nothings about the babe he was just about ready to jump behind a bush with. I would shoo him away only to have another gleeful voice appear out of the darkness.

For the boys, pursuing babes and making out was all about bragging rights, and the farther one got, the more esteemed was the glory. A hand on bare skin was a major deal. A hand on bare skin while horizontal was full on action and could be embellished as long as there were no witnesses. Lip to lip contact, however brief, was X-games material. If you weren't slapped, it meant she wanted it and that you could have gotten it had she not had to leave so abruptly. Tongue was the gateway to the promised land. Anything beyond tongue and horizontal was a guaranteed wet-dream of legend and lore.

In the morning, the Smith Ranger received a rash of complaints about the boys from the overly exhausted male counselors, but couldn't locate them to serve citations since the Circus was up before the sun in order to escape the camp fee payments. Other than Skip, none of the boys had any money left. They didn't care. This was no ordinary road show. The Circus was having the time of their lives.

DAY FOUR

Driven by tiny glands secreting hormones from the backs of their skulls, the boys had managed to stay fired up by chasing the Church Camp girls by night and scarfing Skip's supply of Hostess treats by day. Nevertheless, by day four, the Circus was beginning to feel the effects of heat exhaustion.

The fourth day dawned stifling and grim. Stepping out of the tent at 6:00 am, the air was already a touch too much. During the night, The Church Camp had abruptly packed and fled. Each boy blamed the other for this disaster. There was much grumbling as they eyed my pot of oatmeal. By early afternoon, out of options for climbs in the shade, the show began to unravel.

Kate and Koss, subsisting on little more than pasta, cantaloupe (it was on special for 15 cents/pound) and Skip's Ding Dongs and Cupcakes, were shot. It was their unfortunate lot in life, to have a dad who was always living on the edge of poverty, and therefore shopped for deals, even on food. If cantaloupe was 15 cents a pound this week, we would be eating cantaloupe. Next week it might be broccoli. The girls had to wonder if they were the only kids around whose dad bounced into the produce department going, "Look kids, Yams are 12 cents a pound!"

"Oh my God, DAD, that lady is looking at you!"

"I don't believe this!! Kate, grab a plastic bag!!"

"Dad, we had Yams last week with you."

"Yeah, but Yams go good with chilli. We didn't have them with chilli last week did we? Or did we? How about with chilli? It's marked down to 79 cents a can."

"Mom fixed chilli last week."

"Spaghetti then. Yams and spaghetti would be awesome!"

"Dad, we have spaghetti every time we spend the night with you."

"I could eat spaghetti seven days a week."

"We know. You do. And you say that every week."

"I do?" My girls knew where the edge was.

On the fourth day, everybody was trashed. Everybody that is, except for

Skip. Skip still wanted to get his twelve routes in--the sooner the better, because then he might be able to bag another couple routes before it got too dark. And since it was Skip's dad that was funding this trip...Well? After three days of dashing for the shifting shade, stringing ropes, belaying youngsters, cooking and cleaning in the dark, Leland and I were physical and emotional wrecks. We decided that Skip could lead everything since our fingers shrieked just trying to unwrap a Twinkie. He loved the idea and raced off to rack up draws.

Under normal weather conditions, sport climbers tend to be neurotically chirpy sorts, skipping about camping areas, flexing, stretching, twisting, and flipping hacky sacks. The mood around Sport-ville is always full of cheer and goodwill. But not in the heat. As the temperature soared, Skip's hyper-antics, hilariously endearing in the cool sweet air of the spring trip, now seemed dreadfully demanding. Stan's permanent bad smell facial expression seemed reason enough to send him packing on a north-bound cattle truck. Leland was delusional, right on the edge of launching gear or Lake and his back-flipping enthusiasm into the abyss. Sitting beneath a tree, spitting cantaloupe seeds, my girls' smiles melted into the mirage of another epic vacation with their dad. I tried to remember what had been so bad about the rain and ice storms on Mt. Baker.

And then there was Bo Montana. Normally we could have forgiven his adolescent put downs, his mindless redneck manner, his tactless hits below the belt, his pilfering through our coolers for savory delectable treats. But, not in this heat. By day four, everybody was ready to chain him to the back of the Burb and watch me drag him down the road.

THE SHOW

The *Circus* ended up at Phoenix Buttress, the smell of anger thick and foul. For the umpteenth time, Bo had said something moronic to piss off one of the amigos. They stomped over to me, looking for leadership.

"Give it a rest you guys. It's hot... The kid's pathetic. Ignore him."

"Yeah? Well, he's pretty pissed at you, Keith."

"Yeah? So what else is knew? What did I do this time?"

"He says you won't let him lead any 5.10's"

"That's cuz he can't lead a 5.8. Hey, Kate, throw me the bottle of Advil."

"It's gone, Dad. We've been eating them for snacks."

"Keith, you've got to let Bo lead a harder climb so he'll shut up."

"Chill out, guys. You've seen him climb. He still isn't clipping the draws right. He won't listen to a thing I say. I don't want him getting hurt. You know that."

"He says that you let Skip lead the 5.10s."

"Yeah, and did you tell him that Skip is funding this trip? And did you point out that Skip can lead 10's? Hey, Kate, look through my first aid kit and see if you can find me some of those little packets of Aspirin."

"We ate those too, Dad."

Skip added, "He says this trip sucks."

'Bong!' Something went off. All of us, including the kids, had busted our butts to make the best of our time at Smith. Everyone was cranky, and they all had a reason to be. But hearing the suck word was too much. What more was I supposed to do for this kid?

I thought about it as my gaze fell upon some climber, clam-baking on the ultra-classic *Light on the Path*. It had to be at least a 130 degrees on Morning Glory Wall. I wondered what that man's finger tips were made of.

Chossy, working with Leland and Bo on a 5.11 behind us, let go a torrent of violent curses as an arc of 4:00 o'clock shade suddenly creeped near the "*Light.*"

"Hey, Bo!" I shouted with a plan forming in my head.

"Yeah?" Bo walked down from his perch next to Leland.

"Listen. I know you're feeling bad about not getting to lead many 10's. I know you're psyched to go for it, so I'll tell you what. Ya see *Light on the Path,* over there? It's only rated 5.9, but it feels more like a 10a. It's a classic. If you could run a rope up it, the gang could take some laps."

"Cool!!"

"What do you think, Leland?" I shouted. "Don't you think that '*Light*' is a pretty stiff, 9?"

"Oohhh maannn. For sure! Sick moves. But, that things been bakin all day in full on sun. There's no way I'm climbing it."

"Yeah, I know that. We're gonna wait til it gets in the shade and then let Bo have a go at leading it. What do you think?"

"Yeah, it'll only be 110 in the shade. Right on! Man, I'd clip the first bolt for him, though. It's a ways up there."

"Gotcha." I turned back to Bo. "Dude, I'm going to clip the first bolt as it's about thirty feet off the deck. If anything went wrong you'd be toast."

"That's cool. How many bolts after that?"

"Five and then the anchors. You'll love it. Pack up a rope and head over there. I'll get these guys rounded up and we'll let you be the show. Cool?"

As soon as Bo was out of earshot, I huddled the Circus together.

"OK, guys, here it is. '*Light*' has been in the sun all day... It starts with thirty feet of Heuco jug hauling and then suddenly blanks out on a vertical wall. The holds are crimpy and painful, and in the heat, they'll be a living hell. Bo is going to get to the third or fourth bolt, slime off, and come whimpering down like a spanked dog. 5.10: see ya fuckin later."

LIGHT ON THE PATH

Everybody started singing and jiving, "Do a little dance, make a little love…."

Our united group marched to Morning Glory Wall where Bo was lacing up his rock shoes. I handed my best draws and biners. I didn't want him blowing a clip and falling too far.

"Bo, give me a belay up to the first bolt, then the sharp end is yours."

"Yeah, sure, that's cool. Thanks, man."

Constantly dipping, I climbed to the first bolt in heat so thick that chalking up did little more than coat my cuticles white. I clipped the bolt and lowered off. The show was now Bo's. He tied in. "Ok dude, you're on it. And you know what you're on it like?"

Not saying a word, Bo scampered up the giant holds of the first thirty feet, seemingly unaware of the heat. He quickly reached the pre-clipped bolt and made the moves to get above it. He was now officially on lead. Climbing with great focus, he rapidly reached the next bolt and slapped a draw onto it. When he went to clip the biner, he ran the rope the wrong way again.

"The other way, Bo," I yelled up in a quiet voice. "Reclip with the rope running from the rock out to you."

"Oh yeah. I forgot." He re-did it perfectly and started up. "This is cool!"

The kid was focused. He was climbing better than I had seen throughout the trip. Leading could do that to you. Suddenly you were playing for real. You could rise to the challenge. Or you could get your ass spanked. Bo was climbing into that space that lead climbers know about, where the rest of the world and all the bullshit, drops away. All that is left is you and a series of holds you have to climb. Nothing else matters. Nothing ever mattered. It was all an illusion. This is real. This is all there is. Bo was right there.

Bo got to the fourth bolt and let go a, "OH MY GAAWWDDD!" He clipped the hangar, slapped the rope into the bent gate the wrong way and reached up as if to grab the draw and hang.

"Bo, do you want me to take?" He couldn't hear me. Instead he searched frantically for the next holds above. We all knew he was done. The Circus looked amongst themselves smugly, waiting for the words "take and lower," mission accomplished. The rope began to move. Bo was going up.

"God, he's got nads!" Skip was craning his neck, watching Bo's every move.

"I would not want to be on that wall right now." Lake added.

"Me neither." We all agreed.

At the fifth bolt I thought my prediction would finally come true. Bo was shaking so badly he could not make the clip. The Circus forgot about the heat, the hate, the wrath of ages, and began feeding Bo beta and encouragement for all they were worth. Little palms sweated with grip, watching him fight to make the clip.

"C'mon, Bo. You can do it!" Kate yelled.

Kris, holding Julius above her head, cheered: "Stick it, Bo! C'mon stick it!!"

Bo would let go of a crimper to reach for a draw, just about peel off, then repeat the process. I was braced and ready to catch his fall.

"Man, reach up with your left hand for that good edge." Leland was soloing up an adjacent route, trying to get within ear shot of the trembling, Bo. "Yeah. Reach up with your left- clip the draw with your right."

That sequence worked and Bo got the draw clipped to the bolt. He still needed to get the rope clipped into the carabiner to be safe. He pulled up slack and then dropped it. He looked down from fifty feet above me.

"Fuck man! Which way do I clip this thing, again?!"

"Rock-then-OUT-Bo!"

"I am so FUCKING stupid." He tried and failed again, shaking wildly.

I hollered up, "Grab the draw and clip it for Christ's sake!!!"

He did and hung there, sweating and scared.

"All right!! Nice going, Bo. That was awesome!" The Circus breathed a collective sigh and high fived Bo's great effort. I looked down to rest my strained neck. I waited for Bo's command to be lowered off.

"Well, gang." I whispered, "He didn't pitch, but I think we did the job. And to tell you the truth, the kid did good."

I felt the rope tug and looked up.

"Holy shit. I don't believe this."

Bo had hung just long enough to chalk up his drenched hands. Now he was inching upward for the sixth bolt. Somehow he had calmed his shaking limbs. Leland had climbed up about twenty five feet and started giving, move by move, beta. Shortly, Bo was at the sixth bolt and ready to clip. Little stomachs gurgled in the anxious quiet. He desperately slapped on a draw, threw the rope in the biner and yelled, "Take!"

"YEAH!! Oh my GOD!! BO, you RULE!!!" screamed the Circus.

"Bo, you ROCK!!" shouted Lake.

Before I could collect a breath, the rope went slack and Bo started up again, the anchors only fifteen feet straight above his head. With adrenaline roaring, he climbed quickly to the chains, pulled off a draw and clipped it into the anchor. Everybody on the ground went nuts, cheering him, waiting for the rope to be slapped into the draw in a triumphant act of finality. Instead, he reached back up and grabbed a tiny crimper three feet above the anchor.

"What the..." I shouted up, "Grab the anchor Bo! Get the rope in the draw!! You're done!!!"

Not hearing me, he reached down and took off another draw. Shaking wildly he clipped it into the second anchor chain.

Leland spoke emphatically, "Bo, grab the chain and clip the rope into the draw. NOW!!!"

Completely in his own world, Bo reached back up and pinched the crimper, his feet doing a sewing machine on the relatively large knobs he was standing on. The anchor chains were at his crotch.

"Bo, grab the fucking chain and clip the rope!!"

He looked up. He looked down. He looked up and… "AAAGGGHH!!!!!!"
Bo was airborne, arms, hair, and legs whipping about! For thirty feet he flew
screaming. The rope finally went tight and yarded me off my stance.

As soon as I could see he was OK, I yelled up, "Nice air bro!" There was
a long silence. "Hey, Dude. You want me to lower ya?"

"Yeah," he spoke limply, "just give me a second."

The Circus cheered. Leland and I looked at each other in disbelief. I looked
at the kids, "Oh my God, I do not believe how far he just fell."

"Uh. You know." Bo looked back up the thirty plus feet to the anchors, "I
think I can finish it, just give me a minute." He hung high above us, limp as
a rag. "Actually, I don't think so. You can lower me. I'm sorry."

Relieved and with humor restored, I turned and asked Stan if he wanted a
crack at it. His eyes were the size of tuna cans. He took a huge gulp and
sighed, "Yeah, sure." I had forgotten the power of teenage hormones.

Stan climbed the route in his usual sloth-slow style and did the finish.
Lake belayed him. I later cleaned the anchors and took a look at the draw
Bo had fallen on. With the rope clipped the wrong way, the biner had twisted
around when he fell, bending against the bolt, and crushing the gate shut.
Leland took a quick look at the damaged biner, handed it to Bo, fished for his
Kodiak and walked away mumbling.

We walked back to camp as the evening air began to cool. The Circus
burst into song as they skipped up the trail: *"Do a little dance…"*

That night we all ate together. Later, Kate, Stan, Lake, and Bo lay on the
top of the Burb talking, watching shooting stars, and sipping Skip's root
beers. Leland, Skip, Kris, and I sat in the parking lot, sharing stories and
dreaming. The night air was perfection-delicious against our weary skin.
From across the parking lot, Kate's constant giggling glided past like ripples
of joy.

Kris and Julius crawled onto my lap. I stroked her hair until she fell
asleep. Roars of laughter kept dancing off the Burb. Kate was doing a dance
while the boys pounded rock rhythms on the metal roof. I looked over and
felt a strange, gentle wave wash over me. It was that elusive emotion I rarely
embraced; that wonderful by product of life's toil, that feeling that cannot be
faked, forced, or wished for: happiness. For me it could only be fumbled
upon while I was busy doing something else. All the absurdities, all the weary
struggles now laid down before me like a pathway of gifts on which to stand
and find my way back to me. Life would never make sense, but if I tried,
there would always be a way to find this place. I stretched out on the gravel.
Kris snored softly on my leg. "Life doesn't miss a trick at turning my head
around." For the first time in memory, I was home.

A thought sifted down through me: "If I added up all my failures and
stacked them up against all my wins, I'd probably look like the all-time loser.
But, God, thank you for this moment. Thank you."

IT'S NOT WHO YOU BLOW

A WORD ABOUT SEX ON EVEREST

I'm not sure if God cares whether you have sex in the mountains with anyone but your married mate or not. Maybe you can have tons of sex with anyone you want to, anywhere you want to, as long as it's not at the Everest Base Camp. I don't know. But, with that said, if I was about to attempt Mt. Everest and every Sherpa with a prayer flag warned me that by having extramarital fing- fing I would severely up my odds for getting the chop, I'd definitely take a note and keep the barn door closed.

So why do expedition members repeatedly throw caution and other things to the wind? Maybe they can't help it. I, for one, understand the need for mountain sex. I've been a guide. I know what it is to have a body full of endorphins and adrenalin pumping up my receptors morning, noon and night. I've seen the look women give you when they realize you are the alpha-male and with a little rearranging of client lists, a potential tent-mate. It's the best part of waking up.

However, during the spring of '96, the Karma minded Sherpa, including Lopsang, were spooked when the Everest expedition base camp busted out a mother load of bad luck, with a whole lotta ficky fickin going on.

-From **The Shipwreck** *Journals*

∧∧∧∧∧∧∧∧∧∧∧∧∧∧∧∧∧∧∧∧∧∧

[WINTER 95/96: WEST SEATTLE, WA]

I don't know why, but I was there the day Scott Fischer and Mountain Madness, Inc. fired his close friend and veteran Everest climbing partner Rob Hess from the upcoming 1996, 'Sagarmatha Environmental Expedition.' Like most prophetic events that come in like a slight haze and wind up wiping out people's lives, the import and wording of the decision and subsequent phone call seemed rather matter of fact, strictly business, we can make this work, at the time. It was indeed, nothing more than a tactical business decision, and guiding in the death zone had become a big business.

It was necessary. It had to be done. Rob had fucked up. He had hurt a client's feelings on the Broad Peak trip. He had not presented pleasant enoughbed-side manner to be trusted with the likes of Sandy Pittman and her Satellite Phone and On-Line Chats. Rob, was old school; a no-bullshit-mountain-guide-tough-guy. Scott knew Mountain Madness needed great Public Relations to earn that monster slice of the Adventure Outfitter's Pie and Rob was a political liability.

I was sitting in the Mountain Madness office, making a few bucks, writing up the "Yellow Brick Road' Expedition Manuals for all the $65,000 Everest clients. Researching to be accurate, I was doing what I could to make the Everest trip sound organized and fun: kind of like a 'Snorkeling Cruise' to the Bahamas except these $65,000 clients would be donning Down Suits, Crampons, and Oxygen Masks, and taking dumps in sub-zero temperatures at 26,000 feet. Problem was, while sitting there getting paid to write about scuba-diving up Everest was cool, I had to be careful. I didn't want the trip sounding too fun. I had to find a way to say a few things about possible mild discomforts and the chances of a little altitude sickness. On the other hand, painting the cocked gun-barrel in your mouth reality of coughing until your ribs crack while humping a load at 25,000 feet in an icy hurricane, with bleeding lips and lungs, your skull and heart pounding apart, no sleep, no appetite, piles, blisters, dehydrated, frostbitten and dying, might have been a bit too much color for the: *What do I get to look forward to when I leave Camp Three for Camp Four?* section on page thirty-three. I kept shaking my head, trying to find a way to explain that this trip was designed to guarantee you a crack at the summit and: *"Oh by the way, if you forget your mittens, you'll get frostbite and lose your hands."*

So, there I was, writing away, trying to focus on my project but fully aware of the conversation going on next to me between Scott and the MM co-owner. She made it clear that it was purely good business sense to fire Rob.

Scott agreed but was having a hard time with the decision. His words were heated and prophetic: "All right. All right. I understand and support the thinking behind this. But…but, what the fuck am I going to do if something goes wrong up there? Rob has been up there, he knows what to do!" He looked over at me and continued, "Keith, you know what I'm talking about."

I nodded like I did.

"I can't be everywhere on the mountain."

I nodded back with a "Yup."

I wanted to help him out, but I'd never been on an Everest or K2. All I could think was I *did* know what it felt like to be spread too thin, way beyond my limits, to feel pressure and expectations mount with no one there to help me. So I offered, "You're going to be trying to keep a lot of people safe… with all this pressure on you to not get sick."

Scott nodded back. "I'm not worried about getting sick, but what if somebody gets in trouble up there and I got people all over the fucking place! People could die up there. If the shit starts coming down, I better have somebody up there who knows what the fuck they're doing!"

Scott said his piece and the decision was finalized.

Sitting there, finishing up the itineraries for Caribbean Cruising in the death zone, I suddenly felt the slightest bit scared for Scott. This Everest business was still about human beings: fragile, vulnerable, fucked-up, and error prone. I continued typing in silence while Scott went in his room, shut his door and contemplated his company's decision to knock over the first domino that would lead to a ton of tragedy on May 10th, 1996.

CLIMBING AND DYING IN PRIME TIME

On June 9th of '96, I met Lopsang Jangbu Sherpa at Scott Fischer's memorial service held at Camp Long in West Seattle. With hundreds of sobbing family, friends, and acquaintances from all over the world present, the tribute to Scott showed how much the guy had meant and done for so many people. There was also a throng of copy hungry NBC, ABC, CNN correspondents milling about, probing for a hardline exclusive that could make a buck off this dizzying Mountain Opera. There were articles and books to be written, made for TV movies to be produced, 20/20 prime time stories to be aired, millions of bucks to be made off the public's insatiable craving for details on the fall of kings and the failure of heroes

It was just over a year since my interview in the formerly jovial rooms of the Mountain Madness office. There was no joy anymore. Lives, careers, friendships, and marriages lay in ruins after the May 10th, '96 fiasco swept away Scott's dream.

Sitting there in the sun and looking around at the eclectic crowd, I knew I'd gotten off easy. I'd never climbed or hung out with Scott and wasn't stricken with the bottomless grief his many close friends and climbing partners were battling. I was on the loose familiar turf of the wandering, alienated cynic, studying the human spectacle yet still unable to connect the dots on how I'd managed to wind up here.

After the services, I spotted a dark skinned young man dressed in a bright yellow t-shirt, jeans, sunglasses and an NBC baseball cap. He had a long pony tail and two tiny golden hoop ear rings and it dawned on me that this must be *the* Lopsang everyone at the office was always talking about. At that moment, a friend came by and asked me if I might loan him some of my climbing gear so that he and Lopsang could climb Mt. Rainier the following week. I said that would be fine and then walked over to personally offer the Sherpa-Star my gear. His sunglasses were off and he turned to me with one of the most remarkable faces I'd ever seen. His cheek bones and face structure reminded me of photos of Apache Indians. His eyes were incredibly kind. He smiled at me with a gold tooth flashing and then bent close trying to figure out what I was saying. I was nervous, and feeling completely undeserving of being presented the honor of loaning such a legend my stuff. After a few fumbled attempts to explain myself, he figured out what was going on and made it clear that he would not need any gear because the friend he was staying with had loaned him everything. He was very polite and thanked me for my kind offering. So that was that. I didn't know what else to say so I said I was sorry he had lost Scott.

"Mmm. Bery bad luck on expedition." He shook his head sadly. "Bery Bad luck."

I stood there feeling celebrity tongue tied, then walked off and into a series of intense conversations with motivated media people who exchanged numbers and cards with me knowing that they would fly straight back to their gilded offices and never call.

∧∧∧∧∧∧∧∧∧∧∧∧∧∧∧

A week after Scott's memorial service, I was putting on my rock shoes at the Vertical World Climbing Gym when in walked Lopsang with two Mountain Madness employees.

Those two went off to climb, leaving Lopsang standing by the counter, sipping a soda. After a few minutes, I nervously walked over to see if he might want to climb. He recognized me, smiled and held out his soda to me.

"Want juice?"

"No. Thank you." I slowed down my words and made hand signs. "Do you want to rock climb."

He looked down at his feet. "No shoes."

"I have an extra pair. Would you like?"

He pursed his lips together and nodded, OK. I flew out to my car and got him my extra pair. I tied him in and had him climb some juggy 5.8's which he seemed to enjoy. He then looked over at a route rated 5.12 and asked if he could give that a go.

"Sure. That is fine. But, very hard climb." I was already talking Sherpa.

"He, he, not problem," he laughed and flexed his small arms. He stepped up on the first hold, lunged for a nub and swung off spinning. He looked at me sheepishly and giggled with a girlish sounding laugh. "No rock climb in my village. Too dangerous." He pointed to his tiny arms. "Sherpa, not strong."

I already liked this super star. With my courage up, I asked him what he was doing in his spare time in Seattle and he made a face like he wasn't doing much. I mentioned that I was going hiking with my two young daughters in the morning and asked him to come along. I was surprised when he said he wanted to go. That evening I called my kids and told them that the next day we were going hiking with Lopsang Jangbu Sherpa, a four time summiteer of Everest without oxygen, and considered quite possibly the greatest high altitude athlete in the world. They were thrilled.

I picked him up at his friend's, Peter Goldman, beautiful home on Alki. We couldn't leave until we had set the house's alarm system. Lopsang pushed at knobs trying to set the correct beeping lights. Being the American, I should have had a clue, but provided little help. We fumbled around until several lights were flashing, then sprinted for the car, laughing.

"Come on, let's get out of here before the police come!" I joked.

We took off with me gripped at the wheel. It was quiet in my car and quiet makes me nervous. I felt wildly self-conscious of a need to say something, but had no clue what that something was going to be. I had never talked to, let alone sat next to a real sherpa. The Everest story was the hottest thing going. It was on the cover of every newstand magazine. People were talking about it in check out lines. And I was sitting next to the guy who had risked his life trying to save Scott. I was in awe and fumbling to form a question that would show how sincerely thankful I was for the opportunity to be here. I knew one thing for absolute certain; I wasn't going to talk to Lopsang about the disaster.

It soon occurred to me, that trying to have a conversation with someone who understands only a smidgin of English is challenging. First of all, it was hard to understand Lopsang. His English was extremely broken and he couldn't say "F's". Instead he put a "P" in its place. Thus *fight* was *pight*. I couldn't use slang or off-color language. My vocabulary was thus reduced by 75%. Every phrase had to be clear, precise, with no double meanings. It dawned on me as we drove that ninety percent of what I yak about is slang ridden, cynical humor, that only a jaded American who grew up in the sixties would find amusing. I wanted to blurt out a question or two about what had happened on the May 10th tragedy, but controlled my selfish, greedy, tabloid tendencies and asked instead the typical, "How are you liking the United States?" And the Sherpa, with animated, loud, emphatic words, shouted about how it was nice here. And how he liked to play BINGO, a lotto gambling game, and how he had lost much weight because of his depression. And how he had cried for two days after Scott died. And how Sandy Pittman, who's life he had saved by giving her his own personal emergency oxygen bottle and then turning down her flow to 2 instead of wide open, enabling the bottle to last long enough for her to summit and get back down to the south summit, had returned the favor by ignoring him at parties he had attended here in the U.S.

Whoa!! Lopsang was intense. So we started talking about the Everest trip. We were buzzing down I-5 and I tried to explain that we were soon going to be meeting my ex-wife #1 in Renton so that we could pick up my daughters and then drive another half hour out to North Bend to meet my ex-wife #2, who was going to join us on our hike up on Snoqualmie Pass. Trying to get all that out in plain English seemed to take a week.

"You divorce two time?"

"Yep."

"You no like tese women?"

"No. I like. But we have many problems." I made a face of bewilderment and said the first of the many cuss words I would teach him, "Shit." He seemed to understand it's meaning, laughed, and said in his best english,

"Sshhiiittt.".

I was overcome with a sense that he would be bored hanging with me and would probably want to get back home fairly soon. I pointed to my watch. "Do you need to be back to your house at certain time."

He didn't understand the meaning of *back* and *certain*. He stared at me then raised his hands and said, "Not problem."

I tried to explain. "This hike is long. We gone all day. That OK?" I was already dropping conjunctions and adjectives.

He nodded and made a soft hand gesture that said, "Dis is all good."

Next, he spotted a Freeway Sign and asked me to read him the words: *Martin Luther King Way.* He practiced as we headed down to Renton.

When we pulled up to the girls in the Fred Meyer parking lot, they burst out of the car and bounded up to Lopsang. He grinned and hugged them dearly. Kate babbled about how cool this was. We headed off to pick up Zoë, then drove up to Snoqualmie Pass.

Kate, with no qualms, asked Lopsang question after question about life in his country, his Buddhist religion, what kind of food he liked, and on and on. I was saved.

Getting out of the car I set our packs on the ground and prepared to load up some wind jackets, lunch, and water bottles. Lopsang started grabbing everything and placing it in his book bag sized backpack.

"No. No. I carry my stuff, Lopsang."

He looked at me, smiled, nodded, and proceeded to empty the contents of my pack into his pack.

"No. Lopsang. No need. I carry too." The girls looked at me wondering why I was omitting 50% of the words necessary to form correct sentences.

"Not problem." He pointed to the mountain and gave a thumbs up.

On the trail Lopsang brought up the rear, hiking with the bubbling Kate. Kate was at a gangly age where she would trip and fall all over the trail. Every time she slipped, Lopsang would catch her, always smiling and joking.

"Whoops!" he'd say.

We cruised to the top of Guye Peak where the five of us sat and ate lunch. Lopsang pulled out scrap books and journals from his book bag and proceeded to show us pictures from his various trips to Everest, Kachengunga, Broad Peak and Cho Oyu. He explained that the first time he climbed Everest he was only 19 and summitted dressed in multi-layers of cotton sweatshirts, a cheap borrowed wind suit, and borrowed boots that were too small; permanently damaging his toes. He talked about that first trip, carrying eighty pound loads without oxygen twice from Camp Two to Camp Four at 26,000 feet. How he had to wait at the South Col for three days before the weather improved enough to go for the summit. How he had summitted without oxygen that time and every time since then.

Since he'd mentioned Everest again, I asked him a question that I thought might be safe. It concerned the much-published heroics of the Russian guide, Anatoli Bukoreev, who the media had heralded as a real life hero during the May disaster. I figured Lopsang would have great respect for this powerful climber.

"Anatoli!" He sneered in disgust. "Sherpa, no like. Anatoli, climb for Anatoli. Not pix rope. Not pix camp. Very bad for Scott! Sherpa not climb wit him!"

My jaw fell to my knees.

"Hey, Lopsang, pass the M&M's." Kate plopped down next to my hero.

KILLING IN THE NAME OF...

So you want to be a Sherpa-Superstar? Try this one on.

Your mom leaves home when you are an infant and your aunt keeps you alive by chewing up rice and placing it in your mouth. Your father marries an angry woman who beats you from the time you can remember. Terrified of her, you leave home at thirteen and work in hotels and inns, chopping wood, cleaning and cooking. You study karate earning a black belt and because of all the travelers, you learn to speak eight languages. At nineteen you are allowed to join your first expedition. You are so poor that you climb in borrowed sweatshirts and boots, badly damaging your toes. By age twenty three you have been to the summit of Everest four times without the use of supplemental oxygen. You are such an incredible worker, so fantastic with people, so likeable and intelligent, such a gifted climber, that one of the leading expedition outfitters in the world has plans to let you run it's Himalayan operations in order to allow it's aging founder a chance to rest. You build your life and future around this man and his company. You want to ensure that his company has great success and agree to haul a satellite phone and brutal 80 pound loads up the flanks of Everest to heights of 26,000 feet in order to ensure great PR for your friend's company. A fellow guide, being paid $25,000, does little more than prepare himself for a summit bid, which tires your boss/friend immeasurably. On the ill-fated 10th, you summit and partake in a terrifying epic trying to rescue your boss/ friend. He dies. You earn a total of $1500 for your services. $350 of that went to your emergency oxygen bottle which you gave to a client so she could make it up to the summit. She never repaid you. She never thanked you. She never acknowledged that you helped her up the mountain. There is no signed agreement about anything in the way of a future or support for you. Your name was Lopsang Jangbu Sherpa. You were twenty four years old. You left behind a wife and a child without financial support. You left behind friends that thought you were the greatest human force they had ever known.

-From **The Shipwreck** Journals

KISS THE LIGHT GOODBYE

It wasn't until I spent the summer with Lopsang that I believed I might just fit into the "top of the world" climbing club. It wasn't that I had gotten that much better, it was that Lopsang made me believe I could do anything. He and I made plans that summer to climb Cho Oyu and anything else we felt up to. We were going to go for it, light and fast, just the two of us. We would have made it too. Lopsang was that good.

*-From **The Shipwreck** Journals*

∧∧∧∧∧∧∧∧∧∧∧∧∧∧∧∧

Late in July, Lopsang and I spent a Wednesday with my kids, then drove them to their mother's house and dropped them off. As usual I wouldn't see them for a week and a wave of deep sorrow flooded my heart. As soon as I'd kissed them goodbye and watched the door shut I drove off with tears flooding my eyes. Lopsang was sitting there in silence, and I tried not to cry, but couldn't stop the tears from dripping down my face.

I had to stop the car for a second because I couldn't see. I muttered to Lopsang, "I'm sorry."

He turned to me, and with a gentle wave of his hand, offered, "No, no. It is OK. I cry too. I cry easy. Dis is bery sad ting for you. It's OK."

That day he and I drove into Seattle to exchange his brand new Nikes that were losing a thread. We began to open up, both of us talking about life and loss.

"When I am just six munt old, my mot-ter and pot-ter pight. Bery bad pight. She leave me and my pot-ter. She go to Tibet. Never come back." His voice was animated.

"I am baby. Still on breast. My aunt chew rice and put in my mout. She save Lopsang."

"So, did your aunt raise you? Or your dad?"

"My pot-ter marry a woman, bery soon. She bery mean to me. Beat me everyday." His voice would rise and fall like a melody when he was animated.

"Why? Why would she do this to you?"

"I do not know! Why?! She no like me. Treat Lopsang bery bad."

"So what did you do?"

"I leave my pot-ter's house and live wit uncles in Kathmandu. I learn Karate. Earn many black belt. I learn to pight. When tirteen years, I go to Lukla and work in Holiday Lodge. Learn many language. Work bery hard. I cook, clean and chop wood. Bery hard work. Bery poor."

We pulled up to a Mall where we would go exchange his Nikes. When we got back in the car he pulled the new pair out of the box and gasped, "Oh Shit!"

"What?"

He was incensed. He held up the shoe. "We take tese back."

"What?"

He pulled the tag in the shoe out so I could see it. MADE IN CHINA. "I no wear tese shoe. Chinese government bery bad. We take tese back."

I let him know I didn't want to run back to the mall again.

"No can wear tese shoes. Chinese government bad." He shook his head sadly. "Tese shoes no good. I give tem away."

Lopsang had seen first hand what the Chinese government was doing to the people of Tibet. Supporting the Chinese economy did not make sense to him.

"So did you learn karate for fun or to fight?"

"One time I have big pight. In bar. Put pive guy in hospital."

"What?" Lopsang was not very big, maybe 5'9" amd 135 pounds soaking wet.

"I have bery expensive watch. Six bery bad mans come up to me. Tey want watch. But, I say no! One man shove me and six mans stand around me wit stick. Tey all want to pight me. But I just one. I very scared."

"So how did you get out of that?"

He made a face, biting his lip and flashing some Bruce Lee moves. "I pight them. Pive go to hospital. I run and get away on motorcycle. I lose coat, helmet, watch." He giggled, "Pive guy in hospital."

I asked him if he got in trouble.

"No...Police know me. In my country I bery pamous. When guys pind out it is Lopsang, tey bery sorry to me. Lopsang, we buy you drink."

We discussed his goals. He had a plan to scale Everest three times a year for enough years to break the oxygen-less ascent record held by Ang Rita Sherpa. I asked him about money and material wealth and being famous.

"In my country, I bery pamous. My picture in newspaper. King and Queen of Nepal know me."

"What about the money? Americans make so much. Do you want to be rich?"

"I no care por money. I no climb por money! Money mean nutting to me!"

"But you, the Sherpa, are being paid poorly compared to American guides."

"Yes, but $1.00 American, same as 70 rupee. Good money por me."

"You're still being ripped off, though."

"No. Money mean nutting. When I climb Everest eleven times no oxygen, and I bery pamous, I build school in my village. I give money to my people."

Lopsang explained how his drive to climb was centered around a desire to be the best in the world, to be loved and admired. He was very proud of being the first to scale Everest 4 times without oxygen by age twenty three. In many ways he was typical of any young athletic superstar who sees the world has his oyster. These athletic phenoms, i.e. Gretzky and Griffey, are rare. Lopsang was in that class, except his arena was in the death zone.

SEVEN SHERPA

[August 1996: Mercer Island, WA]

After the Outside Magazine article, *Into Thin Air*, hit the newsstands, the '96 Everest fiasco reached a tabloid summit of its own. In a Seattle apartment, Lopsang, five Sherpa friends and I gathered to read Jon Kraukauer's version of 'what happened up there.' In anguish, we watched him go from shock, to tears, to rage. He had been referred to as a "showboat," a "goldbrick," and "a vomiting mess." There was no mention of his supreme effort to save the life of Scott Fischer, just slanderous allegations that would soon be read by millions.

One of the Sherpa showed me a rebuttal he was already composing.

Lopsang, finally had heard too much and exploded in rage. I tried to calm him down, but he knew full well that these damaging allegations would soon be his epitaph.

In his pocket was a fax from a Japanese expedition begging his services during the fall on Everest. They were offering him $2500 for two months of labor. Lopsang was still undecided about going. His friends in Seattle were advising him to take the season off. To all of us who knew him, it was obvious that he still wasn't over Scott Fischer's death. "*Into Thin Air*," made his mind up for him. He would go back.

He turned to me, shaking his head in agonizing despair, "I don't believe it!.... Por times I summit Everest wit-out oxygen. On all expedition I do my best. Help all expedition member summit. I pix line. Carry heavy load. Tey respect por me. Tey say good ting about me. Who is tis Jon Kooker to say tese tings! I give him interview! Why tis!? Why he say tese tings? It is wrong!"

In Jon's defense I tried to explain he'd written the article before their interview. That he had not intended to harm anyone, that Jon was a great writer, a great, guy, and guilty of having to meet a *Outside's* deadline. Lopsang would hear none of it.

"Jon Kooker on New Zealand expedition. He not on my expedition. He not know me. Tis is bad!" He sat down and stared at the magazine.

Lopsang had me read the article to him again, slowly, section by section. Kraukauer claimed that on the summit climb, Lopsang was sick, lethargic and shirking his responsibility to be out front fixing lines. Kraukauer then criticized Lopsang's decision not to use supplemental oxygen. When I read him the part about being referred to as a Goldbrick and a Showboat, he didn't understand. I tried my best to explain what it meant. He was sickened.

Lopsang recounted with the obvious, pointing out that he was the expedition member coherent enough at the summit to converse by radio with on-line expedition members at base camp, that he had waited on the summit for three hours to ensure that every member from both expeditions tagged the summit and got down safely, that he spent the rest of the night dragging Scott Fischer down from the south summit through the deadly storm, that he had done all this without the aid of bottled oxygen and therefore, could not have been suffering from altitude sickness. He also reminded us that on nine other 8,000 meter expeditions he'd never used supplemental oxygen. Not once. He wasn't arrogant about it. In fact, Lopsang was acutely aware and respectful of the effects of high altitiude. Because of this, he always carried a bottle of oxygen and a mask just in case he were to start suffering from edema. He had never used it.

Lopsang went on, "If I have sickness, how can I wait tree hours at summit? If I have sickness, how can I spend all night wit Scott Fischer?"

Lopsang admitted he was very tired and that he did puke on the balcony. But, he insisted this was not a problem, that he often threw up when exerting himself to the limit. "I vomit. It is my habit. I breete very hard. I vomit at Camp 1 and 2 and 3. Always I vomit. It means nutting. It is my habit."

Lopsang certainly was sick and tired on the May 10th summit day and had every right to be. We had talked over the summer about the lengths he and Scott had gone to, trying to make sure Sandy gave a glowing report on *Mountain Madness.* One day before the summit climb, Lopsang had ascended the Lhotse face packing an eighty pound load, including 40 plus pounds of Pittman's gear and a satellite phone. Lopsang knew what was at stake for Scott. He wasn't doing it for a fat tip. He knew that Sandy and her high profile PR would make or break the future of Scott's business. He didn't want to let his best friend down.

I read on, getting to the part about Anatoli and Neil sitting at the South Summit, waiting for Lopsang to come up and fix the lines for them. Lopsang couldn't believe this twist of facts and asked me to read it again. Kraukauer described the horrid frustration of waiting as the seconds ticked by and Lopsang didn't appear. It was the crux of the story. Lopsang nearly blew apart. He slammed his fists down repeatedly. "No! Tis is wrong! I do my job!!! Anatoli and Neil go out pront to pix rope to summit!"

I read the paragraph again, trying hard to picture guides sitting with the coil of lead rope in hand just a short distance from the Hillary Step. What could those guys have been thinking? Were they following Rob Hall's orders? We know better. Everest could care less about Rob Hall's rules and orders. Suddenly my head was spinning with memories of *Mountain Madness's* firing of Rob Hess, Scott's long time friend and Everest veteran who didn't pass the PR requirements necessary for such a high profile trip. Rob may have lacked bedside manner, but he could kick ass up where it was needed. Scott's prophetic words had been, "What am I going to do if something goes wrong up there?"

The Sherpa were shouting and handing me a pen to write their rebuttal. Lopsang explained emphatically that Neil had taken the ropes from him when he went out in front. That at the balcony he saw Lopsang vomiting and thinking him altitude-sick, opened up the Sherpa's pack and took a coil of rope.

As he told us: "Anatoli and Neil go in pront. When I go, ten no one stay wit clients. Bery bad ting! When all guide summit and no expedition member summit, tis bery bad! So, I stay. Tat is my job! Everybody summit! Tat is what I want. Ten everybody happy. Tat is my plan."

I started writing down notes. "So, Neil had the lead ropes, not you? Then what were they doing up there?"

Lopsang went on, "When Neil want me to go in pront I go. But, Neil open my pack and take rope. He come to me and say, 'Please Lopsang. You are sick. Let me take rope.' I tink, tat is pine. Neil and Anatoli go in pront now. I stay back wit expedition member. I get everybody to summit. Tat is my job."

The Sherpa sitting around me made it clear that many of *Outside's* views of them were racist and not based on the reality of their culture. They explained that for any westerner to order a Sherpa around like a laborer was a remarkably colonial viewpoint.

Lopsang continued telling his story. I tried to write the words down as fast as I could. He explained that just beyond the Hillary Step, slightly below the summit was another exposed, very dangerous section. He had fixed a small length of rope there and secured it with his ice axe so that other expedition members could safely pass up and down without incident. Thus he put himself in a position to wait at the top until all the bottlenecked party members had summitted and descended. He wound up waiting three hours without oxygen while Scott Fischer slowly approached. Upon Scott's topping out, they descended to Lopsang's ice axe only to find Rob Hall and Doug Hansen still heading slowly up the fixed line. After those two struggled up his line, Lopsang sent Scott down and then waited next to his ice axe in the building wind and intense cold for another forty-five minutes until Rob and Doug had tagged the top and started back down. Recounting this, Lopsang shook his head, "Tis was very cold, very bad time."

When Rob and Doug finally were down his rope, Lopsang freed his axe and raced past them to catch the ailing Scott just below the south summit. The situation immediately turned desperate as the storm built in fury and the sky began to grow dark. Scott sat down and told Lopsang he was dying and that he was unable to walk.

Had Scott Fischer lived through that horrific night and been able to descend to Camp Four with its oxygen and tea, Lopsang Jangbu Sherpa would have been a celebrated hero: a legend in Himalayan lore. Scott would have seen to that. But that was stuff for Hollywood. Reality was brutal.

Earlier in the day, Lopsang had given up his personal oxygen bottle to Sandy, enabling her to safely make the summit. Now, without the gas to help his dying friend, Lopsang turned to his unbelievable strength and proceeded to drag, push, and carry Scott down the treacherous terrain into the dark and deadly storm. Lost, alone, and praying for help, he fought for seven straight hours. He was ready to give his life for his friend. Over and over, Scott screamed, "Lopsang, go down! Save yourself! I can't make it! Go down!!"

Lopsang ignored him. "He is my brutter. I cannot leave him to die alone. I must try to save my brutter. I make up my mind to save him or die."

Finally, off route in the blinding conditions, they wound up in a rock band that would have to be negotiated to reach safer terrain below. Makalu Gau, from a Taiwanese expedition was also stranded there, unable to get down. Try as he might, Lopsang could not get Scott to descend any farther. He tried to get him to move. Carrying him was out of the question. Lopsang sat down next to his friend and prepared for death. "I wait to die."

Suddenly, Scott started tearing at his clothes and screaming at Lopsang: "You go down now or I will jump. Go down, Lopsang, right now or I'm going to jump!!"

Lopsang cried, "Scott, my brutter, I stay wit you! I die wit you my brutter!"

Scott would have none of that. "Go down, now, Lopsang!!! Now!!!"

"So…I go down. I leave my brutter. I cry and cry. I cannot stop for tree days."

The final copy of Lopsang's rebuttal was faxed to *Outside*. The Sherpa in Seattle now knew they were being exploited by the Western world and that they were viewed as being in service to the wishes of the guided elite. They knew that the guide services were dependent on Sherpa labor to do the dirty work of fixing ropes, setting up camps, cooking the food, carrying the oxygen bottles up to the south summit, and even stringing the fixed ropes through the dangerous sections of the route. These Sherpa, with degrees in physics and chemistry from the University of Washington, could do the math and questioned why Lopsang earned $1,500 for the Everest expedition while the Russian, Anatoli earned $25,000. They wanted answers.

Lopsang, who was becoming increasingly despondent, told me how he had come to the states to honor Scott and heal. He had also hoped to make some connections and possibly work for some of the Americans who had made promises of loyalty and support to him while in Nepal. Sadly, he soon learned what all climbers know. That promises made on mountain flanks were quickly forgotten once the passion of the summit had faded. Scott Fischer was the key to Lopsang's future. "Scott and I have plan," he said. "We have puture. Now every ting gone. All plan, every ting, gone. I have nut ting."

Lopsang was never the same after Outside's article. He returned to the great mountain trying to regain his rightful position as the finest high altitude athlete in the world, out front, breaking trail and fixing ropes up the Lhotse face of Everest. It was too soon. He was still too fragile to be there. For him to have been killed in an avalanche on a route he knew so well, seemed an obvious indicator that he was unwell, knocked off his game, fallen from the thin line between brilliance and the abyss. Lopsang was the most brilliant person I'd ever met, with instincts and judgement to match. He should still be here. He left behind a wife and child who are struggling to survive in the poverty that is Nepal.

NICK NORTH FACE

The universe took everything from me but the one thing I needed:
Love.... And, Dude, I've been happy ever since.

  *-From **the Book of Truths** by Langdon Towne*

^^^^^^^^^^^^^^^^^^^^

[AUGUST 2001: DRIVING TO THE CITY WITH JAKE AND ALDEN]

"Hey, Johnson?" Jake was chomping on *Cheetos*, downing bottles of vitamin water, and turning pages of my *Shipwreck* manuscripts.
"What, Jake?"
"Are you going to put me in your book?"
"Oh yeah. You'll be the human highlight reel."
Alden turned to me. "Whoa! What's this *Clockwork Brown* about?"
"Hmmm...*a colorful guide to pooping regulations in the National Parks.* I thought you'd like that one."
The boys were all ears so I went on. "During the spring of '95, after becoming a legit, insured, Mountain Madness guide, I noticed that the basic mountaineering questions asked about climbing hadn't really changed. Invariably, the first question out of every rookie's mouth was: "Hey, Dude, how do you take a dump up there?"
It's a strange concept for anyone who grew up going #2 in the outdoors to think that adults can't figure out how to squat and go without leaving a trace. But, as a guide responsible for the comfort and well being of his clients, I learned early on that one needed to provide education about the varied and often bewildering requirements necessary for downloading in particular parks. For example, when I guided Mt. Baker for Mountain Madness the downloading formula went like this: You were handed a large Mr. Coffee coffee filter, a brown paper lunch sack, a hefty garbage sack and a four foot section of eight inch diameter PVC tubing with a screw lid and told to go over there. The plan was that you'd squat over the filter, package that event into the brown paper lunch sack, and then stuff it all into a black hefty garbage bag inside the tube. Drawn on a chalkboard back in the dust free confines of Mountain Madness gear storage, it all looked simple enough.
The day I finally went for it, our tube had been used by four climbers for three days in ninety degree temperatures. By that point the tube weighed about forty pounds When I undid the lid, I was hit by a stench that seemed to glue itself to the lining of my nose. Three weeks later the smell would still come wafting out of my sinuses in quiet moments. Despite the pain, I did manage to bulls-eye the coffee filter and got the paper bag thing going, but when I tried to push the prize into the garbage sack lined cylindrical opening,

all hell broke loose. I wanted to leave the mess and run for it, but I soon remembered I was the guide and had to make a good impression on my clients if I were to get a fat tip."

Jake and Alden were slapping the dashboard and headrests, so I kept going.

"Back in the good old days, legendary mountain guides used the flat shale-like volcanic rock as BM receptacles. They would then burn their paper, light a doobie, walk to the edge of some abyss and frisbee off the morning offering. Out of sight, out of mind. Now, we had poop tubes. These were especially troublesome with chatting up trail babes. It once had been that upon descending the railroad grade, one could overcome the pain of sore feet and metal to metal knees by talking, squinting and flexing at all the day-hike babes wandering up to have a look at the mountain. Between an overdose of endorphin's and a killer suntan, one imagined oneself attractive in an irresistible manly way. Instead, there I was, slumping down the same wretched trail with the same sore feet and the same screaming knees, squinting and flexing with a fifty pound tube of shit tied off the back of my pack. I no longer was going to pull over and chat up every gal on the way back to the car. I could just see it: "Hi there!… Yeah, we climbed it… Oh, that smell?… Gee, could you check to see if the lid of my tube came loose?" Now, I just pulled my base-ball cap down, kept my shades on, and bee-lined for my '85 Camry with the missing door handle. Nice call. Leave it to the Park Service. Now there was no reason to climb."

"Oh God, oh God!!" Jake screamed.

"On the upper flanks of Rainier, with its glaciers and climbers by the thousands, toilet etiquette is a major drag. Rainier's vast seas of tilted snow and ice create a landscape sorely lacking in appropriate places to duck one's buns. Talk about cruel irony. Most Rainier summiteers, crampon their way to glory possessed by either the worst fear of their lives, or extreme altitude sickness, both of which are classic inducers of the runs. In fact, unless one can arrange to be lowered down into the depths of some bottomless crevasse, there is virtually no place to take care of business discreetly. Imagine those of us who have 'bathroom stage fright' trying to deal with this hostile environment. Because we don't like the exposure, we're going to hold it-- even though we don't want to-- until we're at 13,000 feet, stepping over the third terrifyingly thin snow bridge in the last five minutes. With the gun cocked and pointed, it's either stomp a hole in the ice and squat, or fill your windpants. That's Rainier reality."

Jake was flopping about the back seat like a drooling fish.

"The Mt. Rainier Park's solution is the 'blue bag.' The Park Service wants you to download your business in a plastic blue bag. The bag issued would have a hard time containing half a small swirl ice cream cone, let alone the cow pie brewing in most climbers' GI's. Nevertheless, one is supposed to bend over and hope the first shot is a good one. You then get to tie up the bag with a little plastic tie that probably fell off somewhere, meaning you'll just have to roll up the thing and stuff it next to your sack of bagels."

Alden was banging his head against the head rest.

"Of course, I've tried the obvious: holding it for three days. If you can avoid scary crevasse crossings, this technique works. That is, of course, as long as you don't have to engage in anything but bed rest for the week after your Rainier epic. Between dehydration, the fiber-less diet, and the altitude related dry heaves, you'll head for home packing a prize that'll feel like a prickly pear cactus chose to hibernate in your colon. When you finally make it home, you'll unload your Outback, partially paralyzed and reduced to speaking in winces and gasped utterances. Instead of the usual: "Hi, honey I'm home! Boy did we kick that mountain's ass!" It will be: "Uhn, uhn, uhn, … gasp! Oh my God! Gasp. Uhn, uhn, uhn!

At Camps Muir and Sherman on Mt. Rainier, outhouses are provided for guides and quests of the mountain. These Sani-Kans make sense, except for one slight problem. If you're ever sitting in a Porta-Poddy read the little label next to the door. It will inform you that any number over forty persons using this facility in a five day work week is illegal. At Camp Muir, the sani-kan you are entering was used by over two thousand nervous climbers in the last six days. If you are truly blessed, you won't have to squat with both feet perched on the rim to keep your cheeks from touching the void. Imagine the mental gymnastics that poor woman next to you is trying to make. Yesterday she was seated at a Micro-Soft luncheon, a loaf of bread away from Bill Gates. And now this. For the rest of the trip, she'll reek like a blue-bag."

Jake grabbed his stomach and told me I was killing him. The boys' laughter was like a cup of perfect mountain water brought to my parched heart. I paused, took a long drink and smiled. We were half way through Idaho.

"Hey Johnson!" Jake sputtered through a mouthful of bright orange powder, "when you were guiding, I'll bet you scored with lots of chicks, huh?"

"Well... I'm not sure if I ever really scored, Jake, though I came close to copping a feel a couple of times. The deal was, I always stunk so bad, hadn't shaved, and was so stressed out that scoring wasn't my main concern."

"Were the clients cool?" Alden started thumbing through the pages of *Nick North Face.*

"Most were. The deal is, adults are just children who've grown old. Most jerks with attitude don't change as they get older. They just wind up in control: either at work or in their home. I did find that if you can get adults out of their little boxes and in to the mountains, most become decent human beings."

"Cool."

"The best part about guiding was being able to say and do whatever you wanted. You didn't have to censor your mouth. You just had to look confident and in control and the people would follow.

Alden wanted to know more. "So, how did you find these clients?"

"When I worked at HMR, I would meet people in the store and feel them out."

"Whoa, Johnson! Chicks let you do that?"

"Yeah, Jake. Guiding babes was pretty cool. It was nice getting to call the shots. It was different with Mountain Madness though. I was assigned trips and would meet the clients for the very first time in a parking lot. That was scary, a blind date type of feeling. You never knew what you were going to get. And man did I learn you can't judge a stud by his cover. So many times clients would show up and the guy who looked the least likely to succeed would wind up right behind me at the summit. Invariably, the dude who got out looking like a pimp, was the biggest puss. Just like high school, huh?"

Jake piped in, "Hey, Johnson? I don't look like a pimp do I?"

Alden answered for me, "Dude, you don't look like a pimp. You look like a ho."

I told the boys to read *Nick North Face* to gain an appreciation for the romance of the mountain guide's life. I told them that I had once been a lot like Nick and that only through the good fortune of meeting top climbers like Jim Nelson and Steve Swenson and adopting their "*Light is Right*" alpine religion, did I emerge from a gear-head mentality.

I rambled on about climbing with Steve Swenson back in 1977 and seeing him stuff a ragged *Sacs Millet* daypack into the hatch of his Volkswagon Bug. "We were on our way for a winter ascent of Mt. Rainier, and when I questioned him about what that tiny pack was for, he looked at me like a grandfather would to his little boy and said: 'We are going to be climbing close to 9,000 vertical feet in a day and a half. I don't want to carry a single ounce more than I have to.' "

I went on to explain how Steve's words were a gong going off that something was amiss in my approach to alpine climbing. I simply didn't know any better. I'd truly thought that loading my pack and strutting about the living room, staring at my image in the windows and then talking on the phone to Tim about climbing was how I'd get to the top.

"Steve knew the truth about traveling light," I added.

Jake leaned over my car seat. "Hey, Johnson? Did Swenson ever climb Everest?"

"Oh yeah. Everest, K2, and so many other major peaks that it's unbelievable. And the best part is he is still alive."

"That must have been awesome... climbing Rainier in winter with him."

"It was an experience all right. You know what I remember, though? Shrieking winds, golden light in the morning, and stomping uphill with a bladder full of piss. I couldn't find a place to hide and pee."

"What?"

"Back then I still couldn't piss in front of anybody. And on that mountain there is no place to be alone."

"But, Johnson? I don't get it. Couldn't you just turn around and go."

"No. I had a phobia. A mental disorder. I couldn't have gone in front of anybody if they'd put a gun to my head. I would have just told them to pull the trigger. I'm not joking. It was unreal. But that's what I was... And still am, actually. I just don't care about it anymore. I've got other problems."

The car went quiet.

"That's how I spent my life guys. Climbing and ducking behind a bush to take a piss. Pee shy. And terrified to admit it. Some warrior, eh? Life is strange, isn't it? You just never know what lies beneath the surface of the people you meet."

"Why couldn't you piss, Johnson?"

"I don't understand phobias, Jake. But I know what it is to have one. It's like sticking a vacuum hose on your self-worth about five times a day. Whoosh."

"Sorry, Dude. God, that must have sucked." Alden looked at me with an understanding I would have given all the dimes in the world for back when I was fifteen.

The boys grabbed some treats to munch and then went on passing pages and reading about the wonderful life of a mountain guide. I told them to start with the story about the Rainier climb with Steve.

A WINTER RUN WITH STEVE SWENSON

When I met Steve Swenson in 1976, he was only twenty-three, but had already been climbing at a high standard for eight years. Like every other budding alpinist he had learned the ways of the steeps through trial and error and watching the best perform their craft. Amazingly inquisitive, Steve was not afraid to ask questions and learn. Thus, at the age when Tim and I were just getting started, Steve had already bagged McKinley and El Cap, plus an astounding assortment of classics in the Canadian Rockies, the Sierras, and the Cascades. Now, he had his eyes set on bigger prizes in Alaska, Canada, the Himalaya, the Karakoram-- Everest and K2.

As we drove up to Paradise, Steve said something to us that made little sense at the time, but makes a whole lot more now. He was watching Tim and me, and our obvious child like joy of heading off into the mountains. He smiled and in the kindest possible way said, "You know, you guys are at that ultimate place in climbing... the true golden years. It's that time when every climb is such a big deal. All the classics are there, waiting for you, and your skills will be tested to their limit every time you go out. There's nothing like it."

Steve's comments pretty much summed up the process of getting old and losing your way in sameness. The giant firsts: falling in love, climbing Stuart, having a kid, having a love affair, getting fired, getting hired; they are the landmarks, the life changers, the hubs from which the rest of the days spin and swirl, with our eyes always searching for the next prize.

By 1977 it was clear that Steve was going to some day stand on top of the world, and most likely by a difficult route. He was driven, confident, and kind; an amazing combination. When he asked Tim and I to tag along on Rainier, we were ecstatic. It was our chance to see how the "big boys" did it.

Our eyes and ears were open wide; we literally hung on every word and action Steve emitted.

When we got to the Paradise parking lot, Steve assessed our enormous packs and without being the least bit arrogant or uppity, asked us flatly why we were bringing so much shit. Tim and I looked at his tiny ruck sac and laughed to ourselves. This was obviously one of those cases where the bright new student knew a tad more than the teacher. But we didn't say that. We just marveled at how someone who had climbed so much, could possibly not know what to bring on a winter ascent of Rainier. Our attitudes were quickly adjusted about a hundred meters out of the parking lot, when Steve, clad in snowshoes, went sprinting off, talking and smiling to skiers and hikers wandering by. Tim and I, determined to make a showing, pushed ourselves hard, giving all we had to keep the pace. Steve was oblivious to our pain, and kept up his banter with stories and lessons to be learned all the way to Camp Muir, 4500 feet above.

We pulled into camp and set up residence in the Muir Hut. It was early and Steve suggested we sprint over to the Nisqually Icefall and see if his friend Todd Bibler was over there. Since jogging would take too long, the three of us ran over to the snowfields below Gibraltar Rock. We found Todd, setting up camp with his newly designed, homemade Gore-Tex tent. The thing looked tiny and flimsy. I mentioned something to Tim about my A-frame tent back home being a lot more sturdy and well thought out in design.

Todd and Steve talked about legendary climbs Tim and I had read about, drooled about, but never dreamed of actually doing. We did our part as humble guests, smiling and nodding and pretending we had a clue.

Back at camp, Steve cracked open tins of greenish clams and other moist delicacies that Tim declined with a look that even a sniff of the brackish morsels would send him running for the door. Wanting to be like Steve, I choked down anything he handed me. The sun dipped away and we pulled out extra clothing. Steve spotted Tim's bright yellow foul weather jacket, guaranteed to keep out moisture or your money back. Steve picked up the heavy piece and gave Tim a strange look and then let go a classic-

"Why did you pack this thing?" He gave us a big smile. "Man- it's Rainier- it's winter-- there won't be any rain happening up here."

Steve put on his little blue cap, cinched up his smallish wind breaker and then headed over to chat with some Alaskan veterans camping on the snowfield out back of the hut. He soon came back with tales about how those guys had been weathered off McKinley last year and were up testing out gear for a return trip.

We crawled on to our beds, with the Muir mice soon scampering over our sleeping bags. Tim rolled over and said to me, "A note for next time: no rain gear and bring lots of DECON: rodent killer."

I was having a hard time getting my feet warm in my -25 degree four-season bag. I found that the roomy cut would fill with cold air, freezing whatever part of me wasn't snuggled in nylon. Tim's bag was even worse. He had gone out and bought a brand new Polarguard bag that promised to be warm when wet. Earlier that day, the ever-clever Todd Bibler, had heard of Tim's latest purchase and offered up his summary of a polar guard sleeping experience, "Real nice bag...sleeps cold when warm." I could hear Tim's teeth chattering like the beat of a hummingbird wing. I pulled my bag over my head as the temperature plummeted and the wind picked up to an incessant roar.

In the morning, the wind sounded like someone had pinched their hand over a vacuum cleaner hose, turned it on high and stuck it next to my temple. As we prepared to leave, Steve told us to dress so that we were a little cold at the start, but with the potential to warm up as we got moving. I looked at the shrieking nightmare outside and decided to put on everything I owned.

We stepped out of the hut, and were met by the party of Alaskan veterans, tuning up for the return gig on McKinley. They informed us that the winds were too severe to go any farther- that they had been practically blown off the slopes above, and that they were getting the hell out of dodge.

Steve thanked them for the beta then turned to us and grinned like a little kid about to chuck a water balloon off a building, "This is going to be cool!"

He explained the proper techniques for dealing with "extreme" wind. He said that during the normal gusts we should keep our heads low, our stance a little wider, and our feet nimble in case we got jostled around. And then he said, "When you hear this real low wail coming, drop down into self -arrest and hang on with all you've got."

I looked at Tim and realized I was already sweating.

We raced up the steep snow slopes below the Gibraltar ledges, sprinting and dropping, as the wind battered us. The sound was a steady, wild, drone, with intermittent shrieks of cyclonic terror. We arrived at the shoulder next to the Gibraltar ledges and received our next set of instructions. Steve pointed out our line. It was a series of narrow, snow filled ledges in the rock, with a couple thousand feet of exposure on the left and a constant shower of falling rock cascading down on our right. We were tied together (an act of courage on Steve's part that I still shake my head at in utter amazement) with no chance of survival should one of us trip and pitch off. Steve explained that the only way to not get killed by falling debris was to run like hell in our crampon clad boots for the small indents in the rock, a couple foot ball fields away. I felt my bowels come undone.

Just the day before, he had shared a gripping tale of snagging a crampon on his gaiters while ascending Rainier's Ptarmigan Ridge and being saved from certain death only when he and his mate's rope hooked around an ice formation and stopped their slide. On that jarring thought from memory lane, Steve took off and the three of us sprinted as fast as our legs could move.

Running full speed at 11,500 feet is trying on the best of days, but holding my breath in fear as I ran, with my eyes straining to focus on the rope, and the rock, and where to put my feet, certainly didn't lessen the pounding of my high altitude headache.

Just as we popped under the rock lip of the indentation, a blast of smoke bit in front of our feet, followed by a crack and then a shower of brown, as layers of Gibraltar came hurtling down upon our trail. The three of us pressed our backs practically inside out, as we screamed in jubilation. It was awesome! We were still alive.

We peeled ourselves from the wall, and sprinted off for Camp Comfort, so named for the same reason low income housing tracts and asphalt hood projects are called Emerald Shires and Waterford by the Lakes. Where's the Shire? Where's the Lake? Exposed on a naked ridge in the puke zone of 12,500 feet, Camp *Abysmal* might have been a bit more appropriate. At the moment, we were in the lee side of the wind, so standing erect was no longer a problem, but seeing above us was. A cloud cap had encircled the summit obliterating the view. We were much relieved.

Tim had a little plastic thermometer on which he was trying to compute the wind chill.

"What's the temperature, Tim?"

"Zero."

"What do you think the wind speed has been."

"Oh, anywhere from forty to ninety."

"So what does that make the wind chill?"

"Fucking cold."

At this point I wasn't sure what the next move might be. Down? Not by way of Gibralter Ledges I hoped.

Steve came over to talk summit plans. With a big smile, he let us know that these were the strongest winds he'd been in since the killer storm on McKinley where a bunch of people died. I tried to see if he was joking but the ice riming my sunglasses only allowed a fuzzy gray hole from which to view the remains of my life.

Tim turned and walked over to a pile of marker wands partially buried in the snow. He grabbed a bunch then walked back over to me and said prophetically, "We should bring these. If we get lost up there in the cloud cap, I think we might survive the night if we can find our way back to a crevasse and get out of the wind."

It was a good thing Tim couldn't see through the frozen lenses of my sunglasses. My eyes were two cue balls of terror, stuffed in gaping sockets.

Steve then informed us that we could still make the summit-- that he'd done it before in a cloud cap, although not in winds this bad. He was smiling again. There was no way to deny that Steve looked as happy as a black lab rolling in a pile of manure. He took the bamboo marker wands from Tim and set off for the top.

My glasses were blinding me completely, which I was thankful for, as it kept me from having a heart attack every time Steve or Tim plunged up to their hips while crossing another hidden crevasse with thirty feet of slack in the climbing rope. Steve had gone out of view, meaning I was basically by myself, waiting for the rope to tug at my harness.

And that is how it stayed until I saw Steve step out of the fog and tell us to turn around and get the heck out of dodge. We punched steps down the Nisqually Icefall Coulior and then spent the afternoon with Todd Bibler's rope-team, lowering Steve into the Bergshrund at the bottom after his favorite hat blew into it and disappeared. Steve was all smiles as we lowered him down, down, down. At the 120 foot mark on the rope we heard a scream coming out of the black hole and began to heave him out of there. Chuckles resounded from the merry crew....

∧∧∧∧∧∧∧∧∧∧∧∧∧∧

"Hey, Johnson? Where's the rest of the story?"

I told them the next page was missing because I'd never finished the article. The boys paused, grabbed some treats to munch and then went on reading Nick North Face.

NICK NORTH FACE

[AUGUST 1997: GLACIER PEAK WILDERNESS]

Note: The Glacier Peak trip was one of my last guided outings. Mountain Madness was drowning in Post-Scott mayhem and I could make more money boot-legging. So I did. Shortly after this trip, I packed my car and moved to Kent. That would be the official end of my guiding chapter as well as many other parts of my life.

Mountain Guides often get to meet their clients for the first time in a trailhead parking lot. Anxious clients, paying the big bucks, hop out of their Outbacks and Pathfinders, staring in disbelief at their 'fearless leader' falling out of his rusted '85 Camry with a missing door handle. You can see them looking at me, thinking, "*Jesus, Mother of God, he didn't look like this on the brochure.*" After nervous introductions, with all eyes checking out my "thrift store " robin's egg blue, polyester tights, the clients pull out their monstrous and meticulously packed Dana and Gregory packs. After all, they've had months to analyze, fuss, plan, and fret over what to bring on this three day volcano slog. They've read every manual on how to prepare for mountain adventure and they've packed every safety precaution in the Campmoor catalog to ensure they'll make it back alive. They are scared. They are doubting. They especially doubt me. I know the routine. I know that I have about forty-nine seconds to make them believe in me. I square my shoulders and walk up to each and every client, firmly shaking their hands with a grip strengthened by a dozen vertical miles of rock climbing. I flash my grin of confidence. It is pure acting, something I've learned to do well over the years. And now with that out of the way, I turn, hock up a wad of bronchial bile, and tell them to take everything out of their bulging packs and dump it on the ground. They all look at me with a: "What the...?!"

∧∧∧∧∧∧∧∧∧∧∧∧∧∧

"Hey Johnson. You really made them do that?" Jake was laughing.
"Ah huh. I had to. You can't believe the shit people would pack along. I mean everything looks fun when you've had three beers and you're sitting on a couch watching the *Discovery Channel*."

∧∧∧∧∧∧∧∧∧∧∧∧∧∧

I'm not phased a bit by the grumbling. I go into my climbing-coach mode, looking intense, squinting at the sun, "Trust me on this guys. We gotta get light or we ain't gonna get there."

I start circling the parking lot, using tact and delicacy, trying not to piss on the parade of these aspiring alpinists. They are new to the sport. I understand their pain. I know it hurts like hell to let go. I know that. I've been there. I remember well the joys of acquiring excessive baggage. Like these folks, I once thought mountaineering was a bitchin sport where you read colorful books about crazed Europeans climbing nordwands and then went out shopping for gear to look just like them.

I remember training for arduous Cascade classics by sitting on a couch and eyeballing my monstrous pack and trying to figure what else I could cram in it. Back then, gear was my mark of success; the bigger the pack, the newer the boots, the flashier the outer wear, the shinier the hardware; the better the climber.

I walk around the parking lot like an amiable drill sergeant. The ladies are all packing three changes of clothes, extra bras, three types of hiking boots, make-up kits, deodorant, mirrors, and *expedition* weight Gore-Tex sized to cover their car. All the fellas are pulling out every present and birthday gift they accumulated over the last year; all weighing ten times what is needed on this low angle snow climb. Their 6,500 cubic inch capacity packs are big enough and high tech enough to be comfortable packing a hippo. The problem is their knees and achilles will explode nine miles down the road. In comparison, the 4000 cube pack I bought twenty years ago, after the trip with Steve, looks small. And it is. I'm carrying as little as I can.

Everybody looks gripped. They needn't be. Climbing Glacier Peak via Kennedy Hotsprings, though arduous, is not technical. The key is to go super light, set a turtle pace, and enjoy the changing views. I walk around explaining *the plan*, but, except for the Canadian client, they're all still gripped.

I know he's a Canadian because several minutes before he got out of his rental SUV wearing a Maple Leaf hockey jersey and packing a half rack of *Labatts* under his massive arm. His first words to me were "How's it goin', eh?" Whereupon he offered up a warm beverage. I passed on the brew and didn't say a word when he took a presto log shaped polish salami and shoved it in his gaping pack. I figured the half rack, minus a few, would be going in as well. He let me know that, being from Toronto, he didn't particularly find climbing mountains an aspiration of choice, but was here to lend physical and moral support to his weak kneed brother, an aging neurologist from New York who had aspirations to scale the Seven Summits of the Seven Continents.

Standing next to my aging Camry is Zoë, who I've invited along to be my second. Now that we're divorced and seeing each other every other month or so, we get along great. The way it works is she sees me just often enough to ensure that I can never fall in love with anyone else. Zoë's a tall, gorgeous, auburn-haired, olive-skinned, charming, witty, scorpio lady. Condor Lange, the hulking Canadian, like any guy with his loins intact, lights up like a Christmas Tree around her. He starts cracking jokes, and when Zoë laughs, he cracks a few more. It's perfect. This trip will have comic relief.

After a half-hour of sorting and dumping, everybody's load is trimmed and ready to go. Everybody that is except the sparky who just pulled up, fashionably late in his White Lexus RX SUV. He jumps out decked in fresh *North Face Extreme* fleece top and bottom and matching rafting sandals. The guy is sporting my monthly income on his casual wear alone. He beams at all of us, shouts a mountain cliche, and then pulls out his Mountain Smith expedition pack, loaded to the hilt. After a quick introduction, I suggest that he follow everyone else's lead and take out any *"extras"* that might slow him down. He does a double take and then let's me know that he's in shape, that he sure as hell won't be slowing down, and that his Mountain Smith is packed just fine, thanks. He also lets me know that he's got exactly what he needs, nothing more, nothing less. He sounds impressive. I know better. So I start in with a friendly, "Dude, I can see that you're well packed. But I need to see what gear you brought so that you don't end up with too much stuff. This approach hike is a bitch." To add effect I spit and wince at an imaginary sun.

He looks a bit perturbed. "Man, I'm telling ya, I went through everything. There's nothing in here I don't need.

"Yeah, I know. I know." He's not getting it. I decide to use the broken record approach. "Dude, you've done a real good job of getting ready, but this approach trail is thirteen miles and the last few miles up to our camp are steep, slippery and brutal. We're all going to be hurting and Dude, you're pack looks way too heavy."

"It's cool. I can handle it."

He looks over and smiles at the petite little fox who is busy unpacking her stuff next to him. I look at her too, and then look at God and ask him a simple question:

"OK God... I guide twenty trips without Zoë along, and not once do you let a girl like that show up. NOT ONCE! And now, Zoë's here, and this girl is a babe, with no ring on her finger, and, and, and....Jesus CHRIST!!!!"

I turn back to Nick North Face. "What's that black thing sticking out of the top flap of your pack?"

"Oh, that's my camp stool. I'm not going anywhere without that, man. No way." I can see his jaw clench into a fist.

Now, Nick is paying me $300 dollars for this trip and the sadistic part of me wants to let him suffer under the load of his new toys. As a guide, I'm not worrying about this cat falling off anything or getting killed. I'm worried about him spraining an ankle or a blowing out a knee. These are the things that can kill a trip. These are also preventable if Nick North Face isn't packing a ton of trouble. I've been here before and I know this guy; he's packed his closets and chest of drawers and is a *mountain rescue exercise* in the making if I don't convince him to shit-can about 50% of his bulging load.

Nick is a high power bank executive used to making high power decisions. He is not exactly feeling in his comfort zone taking orders from a stooping guide, with a rotting pack, dressed in bright blue, retro tights and a polarguard vest climbed in since the Disco era forced me to give up my rock n roll career. Nick's read all the Outdoor manuals and has a layer for every situation. He is sizing me up and questioning my judgment on everything from my car to my duct taped sunglasses. He has learned to not trust the world, and he certainly doesn't trust me. After a couple more attempts to break through his barriers, I give up. I walk off thinking I better throw in a ton of MoleSkin.

Condor walks over to offer Zoë a beer and asks us how the marriage is fairing. When we tell him our status, he lets us know he's in our boat, but wishes his ex looked like Zoë, eh? He cracks a beer, and cuts off a slab of red meat, offering said pre-hike morsels to all.

He turns back to Zoë and me. "It's all about having too high of expectations, eh?"

"You mean in marriage?" Just the sound of his Great White North Canadian accent has me giggling.

"Right. You gotta lower those expectations, eh? Get em down where they belong. Like, if you're above ground and the sheriff ain't at the door, the day is fucking awesome, eh."

Condor picks up the half rack and tosses it in his pack. I just look on in awe.

THE COACH

Only one guy isn't quite ready to go. He's the old guy who showed up by himself in an even older Datsun pickup. His door creaked when he climbed out, and his knees seemed to creak just as loud. Several times during the *dump out* exercise he comes up to me, asking if his borrowed gear is suitable for the climb. I finally go over and sort through all his stuff. It's all good-well used, but perfectly fine for this trip. Nervous as hell, he says something about hoping he's up to this. I give him reassurance and then head for my pack to double check that I've brought along my MOFA (Mountain Oriented First Aid) manual with step-by-step instructions for CPR.

After a few parking lot photos, we pack up and I gather everyone around to give them the "hike at your own pace-- tortoise and the hare"-- speech. Nick isn't listening to a word as he helps the Little Fox with her sternum strap. It starts to rain as we leave the lot and head on down the trail. Nick sprints off in front, decked to the nines in matching yellow and blue North Face Gore-tex from head to gaitored toe.

I stay back, walking with Bruce, Zoë, and the Doctor from New York. We get talking about life and the aging process as the rest of the group, trailing Nick, races rapidly out of sight. I'm not worried as the trail is wide and flat for the first five miles. I gave specific instructions for the group to stop at the first bridge crossing in two miles.

Bruce is a great guy, using this climb as a gear up for Mt. Rainier. He's smart, listens well, and has no problem hiking in at this comfortable pace. The Doctor is a breathing medical journal, suffering from a multitude of ailments, already convinced he won't make the summit unless his brother carries him. Back at the car he informed me that his bum knee was flaring up and he'd awoken with a sore throat. Just completing the eleven mile hike to camp is his goal. Forget the summit. Knowing this, I have Zoë hike in front of him, a sensual carrot, dangling just out of reach. Within a mile, he is walking up-right, chest out, belly in, his noticeable limp noticeably absent. Zoë, using her gift of being able to turn any man's attention away from obsessing over trifles to obsessing over her, produces an endless line of questions which fluffs up the good Doctor, his peacock feathers bristling in the mist. This guy will summit. He's got to. I'm his coach. He is my mission.

∧∧∧∧∧∧∧∧∧∧∧∧∧∧∧∧∧

My first true coach was Dear David, a young Mormon kid I worked with at HMR. Though our ages were twenty years different, he embodied all that was good in a human being and we became inseparable climbing partners.

I had always believed that good guys finished last and that greed, power, and brute force were going to win out in the end. Since childhood, I had watched the world around me, like an alien, wondering how the wrong people were always in charge, and how the right people were always ridiculed, crucified or assassinated.

David turned my head around. He was faith personified. He believed in his book and didn't question an ounce of that questionable truth. And it worked. I watched dumbstruck as miracle after miracle unfolded before him for no other reason than that he believed miracles would happen. I watched him help others unselfishly, giving his time and energy with vigor to any and every project. I watched him jump out and help a stranger change a tire, with the same intensity that he would have led the first pitch of a rock climb. Life to him was about doing the right thing twenty four hours a day, and on the seventh day he'd rest, re-juice, and recharge in his Church.

Climbing with Dear David was like walking under an umbrella of safety. Standing next to him gave me a sense of having a guardian angel at my shoulder. I told him I thought a hilarious short story would be to die and find out that only Mormons were let in heaven. David smiled, nodded his head and said: "That's true. But you can come too, Keith."

After a short time, I began to experience something I'd never had happen before. My luck changed. Around David, things began to work out. Every moment spent with him brought something out of me that seemed better than what I was made of. And two years later, it was his comment to me when I was reeling from another round on the roller coaster, that changed me forever. I had done it again, stumbled again, fallen back into Zoë again, I had no one to blame but me again, I was ashamed and distraught with self-loathing again, and I knew I had a ton of "I told you so's" coming from anyone who needed a target again.

Sitting in despair at the base of a climb, I told David why I was so sad, ending it with: "I'm crazy, David."

He started coiling the rope, looked straight in my face and said softly, "No you're not, Keith. You are the sanest person I know."

Those words shocked my heart. For if David was anything, he was truth and sincerity and virtue and kindness and goodness and all that I was not, and for him to see me, this struggling wad of grievous errors as sane, was an unbelievable validation.

Amazing what one voice of love can do.

A coach needs a mission. At times it has been as simple as accomplishing one positive thing in an entire day, a compliment to someone, a phone call to someone; one thing, anything that justified that I took up space on this planet. Other times life has abounded with purpose, with every second spent giving forth with every fiber in my being. Guiding was my staircase to that mindset. It was the road to being something of importance to someone. Every guided trip had an event, a purpose, some special significance that let me know that someone was better off because I had lived. If I came back from a trip without this feeling in my gut, I knew I had failed.

Over the years I figured out the role of a coach was to allow an individual to release the true power of their gift, to create confidence, to make them better, to make them believe they had a chance, to make them see in themselves what they could not see before. You had to tell them things you wished a coach had told you.

These were the lessons I learned while guiding in the mountains. The stakes were much higher up there. It wasn't about winning some game. It was about staying alive. You had to look your athlete in the eye, tell them you believed they could do it, and then set the example and lead them to victory. I'd always felt it would be a treat to take a tyrannical coach into the mountains and let the steeps reduce him to a bubbling ball of tears. And then, while he was on his knees praying for mercy, teach him how to motivate and produce miracles in someone who'd lost his confidence. Talk about changing a tune.

EVERYBODY OUGHT TO HAVE A GUIDE

Eventually, we get to the bridge and everybody, though worked into a lather, smells terrific. Sweat is running, smiles are shining, Power bars are chomping. Nick North Face is adjusting his shoulder and waist straps. The Fox has taken off her Gore-Tex shell and is standing in her tight fitting capilene underwear. Just as I offer thanks to my higher power, a ray of light penetrates the old growth canopy, forming a beam around her, as if she were on stage. She is a sight worth framing.

You can feel the optimism filtering through warmed up muscles. Off we go again, Nick in the lead, Bruce and me bringing up the rear. My troop has that look, the one Tim and I used to get, that child-like enthusiasm of pushing the envelope to a place it's never been. I'm sure they all wish right now that I wasn't here, taking their money, walking them somewhere they could have found on their own. They don't need a guide to do this. They know that now. But they didn't know it an hour ago. And that's the difference. Everybody can talk a mean game. But the truth is, some people need a guide to be brave.

The next mile goes by flat and easy, with time to stare at Zoë and time to think about the excited faces of my clients. How long has it been since I felt such joy? Climbing for pay has taken much of the fun away. I know I'm a whore. But I'm broke and the bills don't stop just because my moral flag is wanting to change from red to white. But it's more than that. Truth is, getting old has taken much of the joy away from everything. I don't laugh as much, dance as much, make love as much, sing as much, dream as much. Getting old is a constant broadside of random shots from all angles that you never have enough shields to deflect. It is a workout, day out and day in, and if you wind up on a losing streak, it is all you can do to keep those weary feet moving. As I walk at the back of the pack, heading for Kennedy Hot springs, I wonder when the streak is going to change, when the tide will finally shift, when my head is going to come up for air and not plunge back under, when the car repairs will quit eating a hole through my bank account, forcing me out on another climb for cash, and when Zoë will finally wake up, smell the coffee and realize she wants me in bed with that cup each morning.

At mile four, we come upon Nick, by himself and grimacing, his Mountain Smith pack tossed off to the side of the trail. "What's up?"

"Man, it's this freakin pack. It's riding really bad and I can't get it adjusted right."

I have him try it on. It looks all right. "Dude, buckle up the waist belt and lets see where it rides."

"I don't use the belt, man. It doesn't fit right."

"You're shitting me."

"Nope. I've never used the belt on this pack. It hurts my hips."

"Well you're going to use it now or you're not going to make it. We have another seven miles to go before we get to camp." With great reluctance he buckles up, and I tweak a few straps. His pack weighs a ton. "What the hell have you got in this thing?"

He adjusts the matching bandana around his forehead, and heads on, his face the study of determination. I look at Bruce and shake my head.

At mile seven, Nick is being treated for blisters. I cut him little donuts from my mole skin stash. He's flushed and complaining about his bad knee. Bruce, the Fox, Condor Lange, Zoë and I crowd around his pack in order to divvy up some of his load. After prying off the three legged campstool, I open up the Mountain Smith and discover why *Marmot, Inc.* turned a profit last year.

"What's this?" I pull out a white plastic sack. It weighs about five pounds and feels like a piece of wet clay. I open it up and there at the bloody bottom is a Filet Mignon. "What the....?!!!!"

I turn to the Fox who comes to my shoulder and hand her Nick's Waterfall Ice Climbing Footfangs. Bruce, Zoe and I split the rest. Condor Lange offers to carry the whole thing, but I decline the offer, as he already had to tie his brother's pack on his backpack with bungy cords. It's a disgrace to everything I hold sacred, but Condor isn't phased a bit. He slices off a round of salami and offers some to the group. I decline as I don't want to eat up his food supply. Little do I know he has two more foot longs packed in his top flap.

We head out with the group behind us now, Bruce in the lead, me shaking my head.

The rest of the approach hike is spent slowly emptying Nick's pack of one useless item after another. The approach boots he had picked up at REI on his arrival into Seattle yesterday, don't fit him properly and have worn a hole though his heel pad, grinding away at his Achilles tendon. We stop a couple of times to empty our first aid kits of athletic tape and mole skin. The wad is so thick that his toes are scrunched into the toe piece. He's trying to act tough, but I can see the guy is on the edge of tears.

The hard part of the hike is still ahead of us. A vertical mile of hand over hand clambering up a muddy trail laced with roots and vines. We're extremely fortunate that it isn't raining, which would render the trail more muddy, slippery, and treacherous than it is. Nick's pack only weighs about thirty five pounds now, exactly what it should have weighed at the trail head.

Even Condor is working hard on this phase. I ask him if he's OK, and he explains that it's just an old hockey injury: no ligaments in his left knee, a couple of screws in his right. He'll be fine.

He asks me loudly, "Do you know why Canadians do it doggie style during the hockey playoffs?"

"Nope." I start to belly laugh.

"So they can both watch, eh?"

I hear Zoë snorting behind me. Condor goes on about the girlfriend he's dating back home.

"Geez, I got it good, eh? I got her talked down to twice a week. I mean this chick calls me and gets off on my answering machine. You got to love her enthusiasm, eh?"

Condor says he's focusing on beers in camp. I readjust his gangling bungy cords and move on, trying to catch up to Bruce.

As we grunt and labor, Nick catches a second wind and begins moving at a better pace. He starts talking to the Fox about leading a trip up Rainier next summer. He then explains that Mt. Rainier is really just a walk up and that he's only climbing it to tune up for McKinley-- next on his tick list. He tells her all about the training necessary and what kind of gear one needs for high altitude snow slogging. I'm praying to Allah and the Virgin herself that we spot a bear so something will shut him up.

A LAST SUMMIT KISS

We arrive at Glacier Basin, expecting to see glaciers. We're wrong. Glacier Basin on Glacier Peak is one of the most disappointing hangouts in the Cascades.

We set up camp, as dozens of Marmots lounge on rocks, waiting for the evening meal to begin. I've heard of the notorious Glacier Basin Marmots, but I am not prepared for the frenzied feeding that is about to be unleashed on our high camp.

As we scurry about, the Marmots move to this rock and that, watching our every move with the banality of vultures. They are looking for angles of penetration and succulents to gnaw. Nick is setting up his four season Everest Expedition Tent, designed for 100 mph winds and snow drifts. I am hoping Marmots like the colors blue and yellow, because, Nick's tent matches his azure/amber outer wear and head band, complete with complimentary gloves and cap.

Zoë and I move our tent, to a secluded sheltered spot slightly below the Marmot Zone. I have two things on my mind.

One: To be out of ear shot so that Nick and anyone who wants to can vent about what a jerk I am.

Two: Is all about Zoë.

Before retiring for the evening, I hike up and warn all the clients to hang food bags and put camera cases, climbing boots, packs, and clothing inside their tents.

I awake the next day to the aftermath of carnage. Marmots have nibbled through the night, chewing up anything worth a good gnaw: boot laces, boot tongues, boot collars, neoprene crampon straps, pack harness systems, and tent walls.

The Fox storms up to me and blurts out the only thing I remember her saying on the whole trip. "I never thought I would ever want to kill anything cute and furry, but give me a rock and those motherfuckers are dead."

Unshaken, I round up the team and give them orders for the morning's assault.

"All right, here's the plan. You guys are to follow me up this low angled slope, practicing the rest step, as well as handling your ice axe. Use it in cane position until the slope steepens, then turn that pick around and keep it in arrest grip. Do not set anything down on the snow, as it will take off. It's a little windy today. Be careful if you take anything off that you carefully tuck it away in your pack. Otherwise it will be air mailed to Tacoma. Everybody got that?"

They all nod 10/4.

"All right then. Let's do this thing."

At my feet are two 150 foot ropes, each weighing about ten pounds. Condor Lange walks up to me and looks down at the ropes. "Who's packin those, eh?"

Before I can get a word out, he reaches down and tosses both ropes in his pack. I swallow my words and give silent thanks for Canadians in general and hockey playing Canadians in particular.

We head out, everyone in a line behind me. Nick pants as he takes six quick steps, then stops to rest. I eventually turn and remind him that we are practicing the rest step. He lets me know that I am messing up his rhythm because I am going so slow. The slopes above us are safe as a bunny slope, so I tell him to go ahead of me and then wait for us at the top of the first shoulder. He sprints off, camera bag attached to his front, snapping photos of us like a hyper photo journalist.

I keep a slow pace, with the rest of the F-troop behind me, breathing and stepping in a comfortable rhythm. As we crest the shoulder, we spot Nick on his knees, blasting through another roll of Kodak 64. His camera case and extra lenses are resting on the snow next to his pack. Just as I reach him, the camera case tips over and begins a bowling ball like descent down the thousand feet of snowfield we've just climbed up. Nick screams but there is nothing he can do.

By the grace of whichever God Nick supports in cash donations, a wandering solo traveler goes sprinting out of his way, intercepting the flying debris half way down the mountainside. We all cheer, hurrah. Nick, though greatly relieved, has a funny look on his face, a look that I don't ever remember being able to put on my own face. As he accepts the bag from the passing stranger, he smiles in a way that lets me know that this kind of thing is routine stuff for him; that he spends most of his high powered life at the top, making messes for others to clean up. It's his role.

I look around me and notice that Glacier Peak has suddenly transformed from a hunchbacked hag to a voluptuous princess. The views from the shoulder are staggering. I make a note to camp up here next time I make a go of this. Then I pause to think of the approach hike and make a note to get back into rock climbing.

The sky is brilliant, and the snow is wind whipped and lacy. We start our march to the next shoulder, not a hint of a crevasse in sight. Everyone is having fun, and appreciating the spectacular views. Bruce has a look on his face that sums up why we keep climbing. He looks rugged, confident, and ready to do whatever it takes to keep punching steps to the top. The Doctor is behind him, moving along nicely, using ski poles instead of an ice axe to keep his shaky knees happy and his feet moving. He too has been transformed from the nervous, twitching, batch of ailments back at the trailhead, to a pleasant, peaceful warrior, stepping in rhythm to the beat of his heart.

Nick, is off to the side of us, and can't see more than a rectangular view of the mountain, with one eye glued to his 35 mm camera viewing lens, and the other eye closed. He keeps slamming in rolls of film, switching lenses, changing F-stops and snapping away. I'm reminded of Mr. Woo in Caddyshack, stepping out of Rodney Dangerfield's Rolls Royce and shooting a roll of film in the parking lot. I figure that when Nick's done, he'll have every foot of this snowfield documented for no other reason than to turn to a board room full of executives and say: "Why did we climb it? Because it's there."

I can't help but laugh as the North Face jacket Nick bought three days ago, goes zipping off into the jet stream winds after he takes it off and sets it down next to his pack. His wild attempts to skewer the $400 jacket with his ice axe are priceless. Miraculously, Nick's face doesn't have that *high powered look* when he limps back up to us, minus his coat, wallet and gloves.

I turn to Condor, who is packing extra everything, including one of the foot long salamis. It is so humbling to climb with a rookie hunk who breaks every rule of alpine travel I've painfully learned over the last twenty years and then proceeds to non-chalantly climb me into the ground. I love the guy. He is carrying his expedition pack with food and beers for five, both of the team climbing ropes, and all of his brother's essentials. Raw hide tough and twice as fun, he is the perfect compliment for wanting to kick Nick North Face in the nuts the other half of the time.

I ask Condor if he has an extra wind shirt and gloves. He asks me which color I want. I eyeball Nick in his blue and yellow, and ask him for the fluorescent bile green pull over.

Condor turns to Zoë and starts talking about his girlfriend again. "Jesus, the whole first month we never made eye contact cuz she doesn't have eyes on her boobs, eh?"

Zoë falls over. As we head on, I ask him about his family and he tells us that mom is getting up there in years, that she knows her time is coming: "She doesn't buy green bananas, eh?"

He starts talking about his daughters and the line he uses on the young suitors coming over to visit his house. He says he takes the kid out to the porch and tells them: "I got a shotgun, a shovel, and five acres, eh? If you make her cry, I'll make you cry."

The winds are picking up and the terrain above is steep. I pull the ropes out of Condor's pack and form rope teams. I tie Nick into Condor's. I tie Bruce, the Doctor, the Fox, and Zoë on mine. We head up, the ex-hockey player dragging his team much quicker than my rope. As we crest one of many rolling false ridge high points, I see that they are racing for the wrong side of the summit dome-- bolting right when they should be bolting left. My team starts screaming at them, but the wind is whipping our voices back in our faces. Only when Nick gets the team to strike a pose or two for an action photo sequence, are we able to make up ground and avert their attention to climbing the easier, northerly side of the dome.

The traverse around the dome gets a bit interesting as the snow has turned to bubbly ice and the wind is making movement a chore. Even Condor finds the gusts a tad unsettling. I gather everyone and inform them that snagging a crampon point on their pants or gaiters and tripping is Bad Ju Ju #1. We review the importance of instant self-arrest, proper rope spacing, and correct climbing commands for both teams. We weave our way in a series of Z's, winding up the steep icy slope like a precision marching band. Everyone is in a groove. Thankfully, Nick has transformed, putting his camera away to fully concentrate on safely negotiating the steeps with his ice axe at the ready.

At the top there are hugs and high fives, with Zoë and me kissing on the only Washington Volcano we hadn't previously climbed together.

The summit is memorable for four religious reasons.

One: The kiss.

Two: The view.

Three: Condor's beers are frozen solid.

Four: Nick runs out of film before he snaps a single summit photo.

Maybe God is a woman after all.

The descent is fun and disappointing. Fun in that we get to glissade on perfect corn snow for 4,000 feet. What took us five hours to get up takes less than a half-hour to get down. Disappointing in that:

A. Nick finds his $400 North Face Jacket snagged on an outcropping of pumice, a mile down the glacier.

B. I know that as soon as we get off this mountain the feelings of power, self-trust, and confidence I had marching up the summit ridge will vanish from view, just like Zoë.

Interlude II

The Gift

"So your life's become a catastrophe
Well it has to be
For you to grow...boy"

"Take the Long Way Home" -Supertramp

From "Sing alongs for a Shipwreck"

The Guide

When clients and friends would see me stumbling out of my car, sucking down a Powerbar and racing off to climb with friends half my age, they'd ask me how I kept it going despite the constant setbacks and frustrations of poverty, divorced parenting, and the on again/off again cycle with my ex #2. I wasn't completely sure, but I knew a few things were saving me as I approached forty. I had learned that you could toss the pursuit of money and material gain. Enough money to meet your needs was a necessity, but more than that was just one more thing to worry about losing. I had learned that the point of being here was to do your best at everything you took on. David had modeled this. After watching him take turn after turn in the right direction, I became convinced that he was on to something. From Boyd I had learned to try and help out rather than sit around stewing over my woeful condition. From Towne I had learned that there were words of inspiration out there, to turn to in times of need. Zoë had taught me forgiveness: that you can despise and hate someone and then turn around and crawl into bed with them and see God in their eyes. From Lopsang Jangbu, I discovered that the mightiest are the kindest, the most giving, the most unselfish. He let me see that there were always deep-seated reasons why certain people became the best. On my own, I learned that the sun always comes up and that if you hang on, pray your ass off, and ask for help when you need it, things will turn, often when there's seemingly no way out.

*-From **The Shipwreck** Journals*

THE GIFT

You awake one day, thinking you'll see her again, that you'll hear her voice, taste her lips, look in her eyes to the well of youth, to a fountain of joy that will water the gardens of your heart forever and ever.

And the phone rings--her voice is trembling and she tells you she cannot see you again, that she cannot love you anymore-- that it is wrong. And you try to say the right things-- try to figure out what you said, or did, and why it turned. You were so close, had taken her to the gates of paradise. The two of you touched the handles adorned with jewels. And you laughed and held each other and felt the power of love-- all love-- from the ages to the present filled your heart and expanded your vision to see the truth stretching across the wastelands, over the mountains, out into the heavens.

And then the door shut and sealed-- her words snuffed away into a box with a lid of lead and chains of steel. And the crush of that lid closing down stole your breath, stole your heart, stole your hope. And when you inhaled, your lungs filled with fear, insecurity, and need-- every blood cell craving for what was lost.

*-From **The Shipwreck** Journals*

^^^^^^^^^^

TRUTH # 186

***No matter how many times you say you're sorry, you will quickly forget all lessons learned**. Please know it is not your fault. You are human. You will fall in the same traps. You will forget, forgive, and be burned again and again-- only to rise above it all again and again. It is your blessing. Your spirit is alive and hope springs eternal in the heart of man. It is your curse. You are a fool, borne to repeat mistakes-- willing to forget the most horrific pain to ensure the continuation of life. And that is the gift. You will choose life. When hanging by a finger tip from a hold on a cliff you will choose to cling on.*

*-From **The Book of Truths** by Langdon Towne*

^^^^^^^^^^^^^^^^

Kristan and I sat in a dish of rock at the top of a route called *Carol's Crack*. The topic of the moment were the problematical odds of ever meeting someone one could truly be compatible with. My comment had placed the odds slightly worse than winning the lottery, but a tad better than being struck by lightning or marrying Larry King.

Kristan talked excitedly. "I was just reading this article in *Time* where scientists think falling in love is an explainable, chemical imbalance."

"Yeah. Leave it to *The Scientists* to take the fun out of love. Oh well, it doesn't matter a bit what they think. I still believe in love at first sight."

"You certainly do. Ya know, I wonder if I'll ever get so lucky?"

"I don't know about luck. And I'm not saying I've done anything right."

"But you've had passion. You've had romance. You've known rapture. No one has ever loved me like that."

"Or... maybe you've never allowed yourself to love anyone like that. You have to be ready to take the risk to get the good stuff."

"It *is* about risk, isn't it?"

"Uh huh. Risk and passion go together I think."

"That sounds dangerous."

"Yep. You *will* know pain. There's no way to be safe enough, or to cover your bases enough. You have to risk everything. You have to open your heart and expose your fragility to the care of another flawed human being."

"Unbelievable." Kristan held up a finger to signify she got it.

I took a long breath and rubbed my fingers over the warm rock. "Yeah, passion is awesome. It guarantees that you'll want to love somebody. *But*, it doesn't guarantee much else."

Kristan laughed.

"Ya know, a month ago I was rummaging through some old journals and I found a page I'd written back when I was seventeen, before I ever had a girlfriend, ever'd fallen in love, ever'd made love, ever'd missed a woman's neck more than air. And there on that page was a quote from Saint Augustine with all the answers I've been searching for ever since.

Kristan smiled. "Do you remember the quote?"

"Oh yeah...

> *Too late I loved you*
> *O Beauty, ever ancient and ever new.*
> *Too late I loved you*
> *And behold, you were within me,*
> *And I, out of myself*
> *And there I searched for you.*

Later that evening, as we made dinner at Campsite 34, I told of a late winter miracle that happened after I'd recorded several songs I'd written for Ann. Kristan wanted to hear them so we walked to my car. I explained the songs were written in a three-day binge of grief and inspiration; that after five months of longing to hear from her, I had all these emotions banging around and blocking me. I needed a release and music was the only way. The pain rolled out through my fingers as I played my guitar. The lyrics flowed out with a sweep of my pen across the page.

We punched in the tape. The first song was called: *I Wait For You*.

Are you scared before you sleep?
Is there a place you'd rather be?
Close your eyes, fall and dream of me
I wait for you, I wait for you
Come to me, rest your head
Let your tears fall on my bed
There's so much room left for you here
I wait for you, I wait for you
Days get lost, fill with rain
Finger prints on a window pain
Close your eyes, fall and dream of me

'I Wait For You' was a combination of hypnotic rock guitar and hip-hop, with Asiki laying down a rap over the top of a melancholy synthesized melody. While I sang of waiting on love, Asiki captured the pain of being a refugee, with flashbacks from the war in Sudan.

Kristan looked off at the clouds rising from the desert floor. "Honestly? I am not sure I have ever been *in love.*"

"You would know. There is no mistaking it."

"Do we really have any control over love finding us?"

"Probably not. And what do you do if it finds you and it isn't right? What if you wake up with someone else's heart in your chest and it can never be yours? How do you turn away from the light and turn off those feelings and just say no and do the right thing without shutting down your whole being and drowning in your own sorrow?"

We laid pads down on a rock next to my car, listening to my tunes and staring out across the moon-lit *City of Rocks*. I started getting excited with the memory of those nights of music dedicated to Ann.

"I don't even play keyboards and I came up with these killer chords and melodies that stick in your heart like honey on your fingers."

I told Kristan how the guitar part on *'I Wait for You,'* was intricate, with all this jumping around, hitting notes all over the neck.

"Five minutes of fingering and no mistakes," I said. "I'd never done that before. I wrote the lyrics in a single sitting. Just sat down and poured them out. The chorus hook came to me as I fiddled with my mixer, trying to sound a bit like John Lennon."

"You do kinda sound like him."

"It's crazy, huh? It was like I was lifted to another level, another dimension. Maybe, for a few moments I actually got to feel what it was like to be a *Beatle*. I was just so tapped into the channel of love. I was trying so hard to be good and true to her and true to my heart. It was an awesome time. Painful, lonely, desperate, and awesome!"

The tape played through to the next song, a B-side tune I'd recorded during the same binge session. It was a soft, slow little ditty, with some sweet, sensual synthesized chords and a bluesy jazz guitar lead, setting up a background for a love letter I had written to Ann.

The moments go by, in a state of confusion
I can't believe this is my life and what if will be
How can I regain a sense of appreciation, for what I have without you?
You showed me, what I dreamed was possible,
Happiness the joy of breathing in a way I can't replace
Nothing compares to you, nothing comes close
To just pickin up the phone and talkin to you
To hold you in my arms, see you smile and leap through the air
Hair flyin, bouncing down on the bed, My God!
My God, I miss you. I miss you
I weep for all I missed, and have given away, waiting to meet you
You are the one, the one I dreamed of
There is no one who makes me laugh
Irreplaceable, insatiable, pleasurable
Like a wave of warm water that takes you down
And makes you let go, let go, let go

Kristan liked this song even more. I told her the true miracle happened when I sensed something right as I finished singing the last chorus of '*I Wait for You*,' and after taking off my head phones, heard this voice playing over my answering machine. My ears were so hammered from all the hours of recording that I couldn't tell who it was.

"This voice kept saying her name. But I couldn't hear it! When I found out it was Ann my knees buckled. We hadn't talked in two months and she picked that moment to call me."

"That's some kind of coincidence, eh?"

"Oh yeah. *I believe in miracles.*"

"So you think there *is* a pull, a force that the ones we love can feel?"

"Definitely. It's like I can sense something when my kids are having a hard time. I'm not talking when they are with me. I am talking when they are far away."

"That makes sense, but would be hard to explain scientifically."

"No harder than trying to explain how the hell a salmon knows which creek to swim back to from the ocean. There's something a lot bigger than profit margins out there controlling the universe."

HENG YOM

TRUTH #148

You can wander the desert in search of truth. You can find your caves, holes, and cliffs. All empty. All stone. Or you can laugh again; a friend's smile pointing the way back to the heart, the dream, the one home you can never leave.

-From **The Book of Truths** by Langdon Towne

^^^^^^^^^^^^^^^^^^^^^^^^^^^^^

[WINTER 1994: SUBBING AT SAMMAMISH HIGH SCHOOL]

I awoke at three in the morning, hoping like hell I wouldn't get called to sub. I'd had a fight with Zoë and was blistering up with guilt. Naturally, at 5:00 am the phone rang and I was offered a job I couldn't refuse at Sammamish High School in Bellevue. Subbing Sammamish was usually a cause for celebration, but this was one of those mornings where a breakfast with *The Beatles* would have had me bummin'. I arrived at SHS hoping to find an easy day ahead of me, maybe movies or quiet worksheet activities, thereby allowing me a chance to fester in my pool of angst. Much to my horror I read the day's lesson plans:

Dear Sub:
You will be having a guest speaker today. His name is Heng Yom. He is Cambodian and a student at this school. He speaks broken English and the students may not be able to understand him so please keep them quiet. He will talk the whole period. Do not issue any bathroom passes.
Thank You,
Ms. Ballard

I put the paper down and headed to the 'teachers only' bathroom to heave. It was my worst nightmare. No sleep, no movies, and a kid named Heng Yom in charge of a room of teenagers. It couldn't get worse.
I walked back to the room and entered the world of thirty six sophomores crammed in a sweaty box, waiting to be entertained by a teacher who had to be part Confucius and part Eddie Murphy not to be devoured. I fumbled through the plans hoping I'd read the wrong day. I hadn't. As the back of my neck began to moisten, in walked Heng. The universe must have been listening...because, it got worse.

Before the class, stood a young Cambodian who looked like he was all of thirteen, fresh off the boat, four foot nothing, with a row of bottom teeth that swerved up like sickles towards his upper lip. His polyester collar was buttoned up tight. His pressed slacks were faded and a tad too short exposing white socks that shined a little too brightly against the sheen of cheap black leather loafers.

"Good God!" cried my soul. "Welcome Heng," cried my mouth. "OK class. Today, you have a guest speaker. He is from Cambodia and will share some stories about his experiences there. I see that you have been reading, *The Clay Marble*," and I would like you all to please pay attention. Thank you for your good listening skills and cooperation."

At that I sat down and watched the room squirm in discomfort as Heng opened his asymmetrical mouth and the first broken word came out like a scratch on the chalk board.

"Christ almighty." Cried my soul. "Forgive me for all I've done! I'm sorry I can't stop fighting with Zoë. I'm sorry I left my first wife. I'm sorry I never call my sister, or visit my Grandmother. I'm sorry I stole that record album from *DJ's Sound City* when I was twelve! I'm sorry God! I'm really sorry!"

The young Heng began his story, and I tried to focus through eyes that needed sleep more than a pay check. His tale started slowly, with a bit about his loving family and how happy they had been, despite hard times in Cambodia. Then he told of how the Khmer Rouge entered their world like the forces of pure evil unleashed; how they persecuted and murdered 1.7 million innocents; how they executed anyone with an education, money, or political status; how they sent all the young people to work in the killing fields until they died; how his parents, terrified of their children being killed, had sent Heng and his sisters and brothers to a refugee camp to await a chance to come to America.

The Yom children rode away from their parents on buses and went to a loading dock where they would be placed on boats and sent to their internment. Heng, the youngest child, got in one line while his brothers and sisters got in another. Soon the older childrens' lines were loaded and gone and only he remained. It wasn't until he boarded the next boat that he realized he had stepped into the wrong line, that his boat was going to the Thai refugee camp. There would be no Cambodians there. He was nine years old. He did not speak Thai. He would be alone: no toys, no family, unable to share a word of kindness or a story with another soul.

In the barbed wired complex, Heng was fed one bowl of rice/soup a day. His body received insufficient minerals and nutrients, which stunted his growth, emaciated his muscles, and made his teeth grow crooked.

For two years he suffered at the camp, waiting to hear of his placement abroad. Shortly after his eleventh birthday he learned he had been granted a VISA to Canada.

He decided to wait. He wanted to join his brother in the U.S. For two more years he waited in the camp. Finally his papers came and he was able to join his brother in Bellevue, WA. He was now 14 and ready to enter high school.

After a year of adjustment to America, Heng made a friend. One friend. The next year, Heng's brother found a better job and moved them to Bothel, fifteen miles away. He had to enroll at Bothel High as there was no way his brother could provide transportation to SHS.

It was at this point of the story that Heng looked in the faces of the kids before him and with eyes glistening said: "I cry at school everyday. Everyday I cry. For I miss my friend. I have no friend in school. No one know me. I am very, very sad. And I cry." He paused to wipe his eyes before going on.

You could have entered a tomb and not heard air as still.

He continued with his tale. Unwilling to endure the loneliness any longer, Heng took it upon himself to re-enroll at Sammamish High. He got up at 5 each morning, walked a mile and a half to the Metro Bus ramp off I-5, then rode the bus to Bellevue, where he hiked another couple of miles to SHS.

"I do this everyday because of my friend. I am so unhappy without my friend. So I come here everyday and I am happy."

And at that point I broke down... trembling for all the people out there, in here... wondering how to go on, forsaken, and friendless.

And Heng, the graduating honors student, stood before us the most powerful force in the room, another saint borne of suffering-- on his way to Washington State University on an academic scholarship.

And my soul cried for all that it is to be human, the glory of hope, and never giving up, and believing in goodness when evil is sweeping away the sky, and thinking you can make it when you are starving and sick and terrified, and clinging to dreams when all faith is being tested second by second.

And my heart cried with the truth that I had no one who really knew me, who could tolerate my whims, who thought I was the answer, who would catch a bus and walk across town to be near me. And right then I knew that all the riches and opportunities of kings meant nothing when a heart was missing that one most noble and essential thing.

Heng Yom was a light. He helped show me what the door to manhood truly looked like. And once you open a door of truth, there is no going back.

THE DEAD LADY OF DEL CAMPO

TRUTH # 77:

Only the woman whose child has grown, can fathom the emptiness in the heart of every man. Women have children to stop the bleeding, and the control of this child keeps the band-aid firmly applied. In the end, however, the child moves on, the band-aid rips off, along with the scab, revealing the wound that never healed. And the woman, with purpose lost, must re- learn what you knew when you were three, playing in the dirt with rocks and sticks, talking to yourself and your imaginary friend in your imaginary world, as happy as a pig in shit every second of every moment.

*-From The **Book of Truths** by Langdon Towne*

^^^^^^^^^^^^^

It is one of the perversities of life, that the sanctities of safety which we hold most sacred often harbor the greatest damage and pain. In the photo albums of the mind, all is safe and beautiful in love and nature. In the uncaring reality of the universe, one is only a careless step off a boulder from writing a definitive narrative of one's journey straight to hell. The trick to the blissful life is to never acknowledge how close we are to the snapping of the twig.

I don't mean to be mordant, but there is a scene in the movie Silver Streak, where a shattered Gene Wilder confesses meekly to another train passenger that he is taking a train excursion because he is in desperate need of some rest. Of course, he no more than gets the words out of his mouth when he witnesses a dead body being tossed off the train and winds up spending the next 72 hours fighting for his life. Much to our relief, Hollywood transforms Gene into an ass-kicking hero who outsmarts the bad guys and gets the girl.

*-From **The Shipwreck** Journals*

^^^^^^^^^^^^^^^^^^^^

[SEPTEMBER: DEL CAMPO PEAK, NORTH CASCADES]

In the fall of '99, I'd greeted the sunny morn by slamming my phone down on Zoë. It was a Saturday and she had just called to bail on the afternoon's date. She informed me that her women's group had rescheduled for that evening. When I said, "So..." she let me know that they hadn't met for over two weeks. When I told her that she hadn't seen me for two months, and what about meeting for a morning hike, she cheerfully let me know that she was leaving for her Yoga class. When I told her that she had attended Yoga classes the last four Saturdays she got huffy and gave me her patented, "All right. I get it, already!" It certainly hadn't been my intention to come off as demanding, but as truth would have it, the singular image of dropping one of Zoë's black bra straps was the only thing I'd been living for over the last two weeks after I'd made the cyclical mistake of agreeing to meet her for tea and pending *treats*. So much for the fickle flutter of hope.

Because it was the fall, I was over committed with teaching, coaching, parenting, and climbing. To add fuel to the fire, I'd made a reactionary decision and gave notice to my apartment manager after they raised the rent for the second time in a sleepless year. Now, I sat frozen at the edge of my bed, staring at Rental Want Ads, trying to pick from a thousand shades of ghetto.

To maintain mid-life sanity, Tim and I were climbing as often as we could and he called to make plans for Sunday. I told him, I was up to my neck in decisions and how about he came up with the plan? He called back later to suggest we do Del Campo Peak. "Yuck," I thought. I didn't care. I needed a long peaceful walk. I wanted to see beauty. I wanted to find clarity. I wanted to believe in goodness. It didn't matter where.

The next day was gorgeous. The whole hike in was a needed therapy session. A single glimpse of peace was all I needed to justify the day's effort and I'd almost found it while navigating past an alpine lake. It was close. It felt like that look Zoë used to give me when I'd asked the question: "Well, uh, did you?"

Tim's walk in had been different. His life was business as usual, same old smell, different week. He talked of needing some spice and adventure. He ran ideas by me that ranged from Himalayan treks to wandering in the Andes. It all sounded complicated, leech infested, and crawling with dysentery to me.

The climb up Del-Campo proper was quite pleasant for a Cascade scramble. We summitted in t-shirts and shorts, lusting at the massive west face of Sloan Peak. On the descent of Del Campo, we chose a fast and direct route back to the main trail that ended up on a steep, dangerous, rock-hard snow slope. We paused to contemplate spending a couple of minutes to strap on our crampons. The slope looked easy so we declined the *safety first* mode and headed down, our crampons strapped to our packs, carefully kicking micro edges as the tongue of white narrowed down and steepened into an hour glass which revealed a nasty thirty foot drop-off on either side. White knuckling our ice axes, we knew if we slipped and flew off the edge we would be plunging headlong into a black icy moat with fatality written all over it. It kept us acutely focused and we both made it down, relieved, but feeling moronic for not taking the extra minutes required to stop and buckle up.

We stomped on down the trail muttering oaths to-- pull our heads out -- before we wound up a Mountain Rescue body bag statistic. We reached a bend, just a mile from the car when we noticed something odd. A giant ice cave which we had walked in front of that morning, had calved off and there were refrigerator sized blocks of ice stacked on the creek bed. A few hikers were milling about talking casually. Another hiker was next to a young woman, who's face looked ashen. I could feel my skin begin to crawl.

Tim hurried down and walked up to the men. I undid my pack and started putting on some warmer clothing since the breeze coming out of the tunnel was chilly. No one except Tim was moving very fast. 'Maybe there was nothing wrong,' I tried to tell myself. Tim's head shot up above a block and he waved at me to come over quickly. 'Oh God!'

There was a woman under the ice. Tim was asking questions of the men, trying to get a sense of how long she had been pinned under the massive blocks. As best we could tell it had been around 45 minutes, part of which she had been able to communicate. But there was silence now, and the men who had been taking turns hacking away at the tons of ice with only a single ice axe adze, were all weak with exhaustion and the weight of the inevitable. One guy was in the hole, his legs and rear sticking out. Soaking wet, hands frozen, he inched back out revealing her gray-blue legs. One of her lower legs was snapped and pointed at a ninety degree angle. I felt my guts go numb. I did not want to be seeing this. I did not want to be here at all. It was obvious that the lady had expired, that the situation was brutally hopeless. There was nothing we could do but help reveal an obvious tragedy. I wanted to go home. Tim took the axe and went down in the hole. It would be my turn next.

Talking quietly with the group standing on the ice, the world still seemed fairly normal, but that illusionary view changed dramatically once I was handed the ice axe and headed down into the hole. There was a creepiness that I had never experienced before, like standing in a dark, steamy bathroom with a specter hunched over the sink and trying to ignore it while flossing your teeth.

I thought I had become pretty tough, had even begun to trust my courage in moments of crisis. That was gone now. I wasn't trusting anything. I wanted someone else to do this. I wanted to walk away and pretend I'd never gone hiking up here. I didn't want to take a turn in the hole. I wanted Tim to say it was pointless and tell us to let the *Search and Rescue Team* come up here and finish the job.

Tim dug away, driven by his belief that there might be some micro-thin chance of saving her. He had to get her out. He kept digging and chopping until his hands and bare knees went numb. He slithered out and handed me the ice axe. Oh God! Oh Christ!

I hunched down, tried to breathe around a chunk of heart in my throat, and entered the hole, doing my best not to touch her as I crawled on top of her gray legs. One of her shins was snapped like a straw, the foot lying up by her thigh. She was wearing shorts and a T-shirt and I could see half way up her torso. I tried not to put too much weight on her legs, but had to kneel on them to get the leverage to hack away. Her face was behind a thick block of gray ice and I started to chip at it, trying not to hit her shoulder in the cramped quarters. Her arms were resting in a palms-up, bent at the elbow position. I glanced down at her shorts, and could see her hip had been split open like a

246

dropped cantaloupe. I noticed yellowish gel-type matter creeping out. Fat cells, the kind of stuff you see under chicken skin. My whole body revolted as I chipped weakly at the block of ice hiding her face.

I hacked a couple more times and thought about the reality of being down in that dark hole and having her face pop out. What would her eyes look like? What would her mouth be doing? What if her face was all crushed or mutilated like her leg and bottom? What if I broke off the block and she fell toward me, my head just inches from hers? God! I couldn't do it. No more hacking. I wormed back out and Tim plunged back in.

I didn't know what to say as he took the axe. I knew I had failed. I knew I could forget all those climbs to glory. At age forty-four, I was still a scared boy standing back on square one.

Tim dug like a mad man. He wasn't afraid of her face, but that there might still be a chance of reviving her. He grabbed her legs and lifted them up until he could free her buttocks from the rocks she was flattened on. He jerked her up and down like a stuck sled, until her body swung over and her head, with eyes blank, mouth wide open, and a face of alabaster, fell dead against the wall of the hole.

And there it was. The face of death. Empty. Nothing. No hope. No love. No sense of anything human. Just a mouth opened wide as if singing the "Ah," of "amen."

After all that horrific build up, hers wasn't a face to be frightened of and Tim must have known that when he climbed down in, shook her body, and revealed the blank eyes that came up behind me later that night in my bathroom as I tried to take a leak. In my bedroom, in the kitchen, any time I was alone or walking into a room, there she would be, with those blank eyes and those alabaster cheeks. And I would tell her to go away and as soon as she was gone, drop and give thanks to Tim for forcing me to stay and help dig her out. My God, if I would have just walked away...what then? What if she came up behind my back and I had left the scene and not known if she was really dead or not? What if I would have had to walk into dark rooms for the rest of my life with the weight of her gray nails scraping down my psyche?

My initial thought upon seeing her broken corpse was a flash to how only a few minutes back, Tim and I had been edging down the hourglass, our fragile bodies just a fractional misstep from hurtling off to a bone snapping end. It could have been us. Dropped melon.

The next impulse was one of complete awe at the miracle of creation. I was staring at a carcass. Whoever this person was, had been, believed in or dreamed of, was gone. Without her spirit, this body lying on the ice was just a vessel comprised of molecules and atoms, stacked in a precise manner to ensure that all parts functioned. Yes, this thing still looked human, but it was not human. Minus the light, her body was a piece of organic matter waiting to rot. And where was her spirit now? Was she staring at us?

I kept thinking about her spirit staring at us. What explanation, what data, what blueprint was out there explaining that force?

Now that we had her free of the ice, Tim kept mulling over whether we should administer CPR. I suggested that if *he* was going to undertake that heinous task, it would be best if we moved her over to the dirt trail and off the ice. Not wanting to touch her, I looped some of my climbing webbing around her legs and with Tim grabbing her shoulders, we yarded the body like a sack of spuds over to the trail. Her back and lower end had received the brunt of the damage and there was much clotted blood dripping out. Just as we were setting her down, a doctor showed up and took over the task of pronouncing her officially dead.

The next order of business was her unfortunate friend. Even in her gray state of shock, I could see that she had a nice face and kind eyes. Several people were at her side and began walking her back to the cars. The dead lady left behind in the dirt, who just over an hour ago had innocently walked with joyful curiosity into the ice cave, was her best friend, a grand and irreplaceable force in her life. I wondered if one of the men helping her down the trail, would wind up attached to her, a sort of miracle replacement, a weird and sick way to find true love. I hated my mind for all its perversities.

Suddenly, there was the sound of a chopper approaching and Search and Rescue people began coming up the trail. With the scene completely taken over, Tim and I began our departure.

The ride home was grim, with curses and sighs inadequate for the situation. Without warning, Tim and I had entered a channel that neither of us were prepared to handle. Our emotions had no way of processing what we had just witnessed. I wanted to crawl out of my skin and bathe my soul. And the question began to race up, into my chest, into my throat, into my hands that pounded on the dashboard.

'Why? Why her? How could she have known that the ice cave would collapse during the handful of seconds it took for her to walk in and snap a photo?'

I thought about the time my climbing buddy Carl yelled: "Rock coming down!" just before two rocks the size of anvils bounded by my ear. Upon hearing his cry I had stepped to my right, thereby avoiding having my head being taken off and my body hurled into a moat fifty feet below. I never step right, but in the blink of a blind eye, I stepped right instead of left. Why?

And do these brushes with death, if fairly common, support the theory that it simply may not be one's time to go? So? Was it the Lady's time?

Or was God in the heavens so callous that we were allowed to stumble in and get blasted while chatting with a friend? Was life that irrelevant? Were human lives that meaningless? Was all the worrying, all the ethics, all the codes of conduct, all the morality, just so much rhetoric?

Tim wondered out loud if there was something more he could have done. After dropping him off, I drove home to my empty apartment and a sense that once again, the rules of the universe had changed. Things were different.

Anxieties considered paramount earlier that day, now seemed as trivial as whether to place one's toilet paper facing in or out. I knew I was supposed to care, but I wasn't quite sure what I was supposed to care about.

The Lady of Del Campo's image showed up in my bathroom within an hour, filtering up behind my ear, with those blank eyes and gaping mouth. I got out of there, sat on my bed trembling, and wondered what I would see when I closed my eyes and lay down to sleep.

The next morning the papers were filled with the tragic story. The ill-fated lady had been a respected leader in her community, a caring, giving person who had worked incessantly for the common welfare of all people. Typical. A rapist could have spent two months inside that ice cave playing a boom box at full volume and the dripping ceiling would have stayed together. Why? And why had Tim and I gotten there when we did? Of all the five star places we could have gone on a perfect fall day, why Del Campo? And come to think of it, had we not taken that wicked short cut down the hourglass, we would have gotten to the sight long after the doctor and the Search and Rescue hordes had inundated the area, saving us from the up close and personal encounter.

I talked to Tim and he said that though he wasn't experiencing her presence, he was plagued by a sense of guilt over having not been able to save her. All I could think to say was what more could he have done? I told him I could only imagine what it would have been like for the lady had we been able to get her out in time. With her body so completely smashed, what kind of life could she have led? Would she have wanted to be saved with her shattered limbs, hips, and organs damaged? Dumb question. Of course she would have. For life, any tiny spark of life was better than nothing.

My guilt swirled with a torment of questions centering around the fact that in that moment of trial inside the icy hole, I had shriveled to a child-like state of wanting someone else to come in and take care of the mess, the bad things and the scary things. I questioned whether all those hard years of living and climbing had really taught me anything besides the ability to distract. Yes, my path had led me to some magical moments, had unveiled some of life's most golden treasures: falling in love, the birth of a child, triumph over adversity, working with purpose, and achieving lofty goals. Yet the road kept going round and round, eventually leading me back to nowhere, back to a black hole, and now back to this: the futility of death and a gnawing sense that in a moment of truth, I was nothing more than a coward.

As I sat in grief, I felt finished. I had lost my fight, my courage, my ability to play the game of justification anymore. How different I was from Tim, who had the guts to dig away with all his might, who shook her body until she flopped over and her face revealed those blank eyes. And with that image, the truth came clear. Her light was gone. But, mine wasn't. And right then I knew why Tim had handed me the ice axe and why I'd climbed down in the icy hole to become the Dead Lady Del Campo's last act of good will on earth.

[December 2000]

Oh, if only life were that simple. If only I could remember anything I learn. A year and change later, I sit in the darkness of a lonely December day, trying to figure out why I am here. Every day I battle myself. Every day I question whether my life is a beacon of light or a quagmire of desires. I am trying to master these things called hope and faith, but can never quite remain on any plane of contentment. Life has become more intensely precious than ever and yet, though I am busting to do good in this world, it rarely feels like I am getting it right. I'm still second-guessing. I continue to be caught in a struggle of climbing up or climbing down, with brief summits providing rare glimpses of inner completion. Those hard won summits are, in fact, mere turning points. To wait there and enjoy them is to become irrelevant. I have to keep climbing and descending and learning and risking and paying the dues and it gets old, and you get old and wonder how much more you can take, how many more times you can jack yourself up, knowing full well that your days are numbered and that getting to the top is really just a half-way ticket to the bottom. It's all the same thing.

And then I catch my self and a shiver runs through my shoulders. I think of how I swore I would never waste another second of my life playing in this loser's bracket. How, just to breathe and feel warmth on my skin was reason enough to rejoice and give thanks. How there was only one way to truly become real and worthy of divinity in the eyes of the universe.

Thank you dear lady for that gift. I won't give up. I can't give up.

THE PURPLE PAL

TRUTH #76

Thanks is the only prayer you need to know. If you added up all your failures and stacked them against all your wins, you'd look like the all time loser. Please know, it is not your fault. Just, give thanks you can still count.

-From the **Book of Truths** *by Langdon Towne*

^^^^^^^^^^^^^^^^^^

"Hey, Johnson, how the heck did you wind up coaching in Kent." Jake was slumped in the back seat, checking his hair in his sunglasses.

"I had no idea I'd wind up a coach. I'd moved down to Kent be closer to my girls. They were both entering secondary schools and I knew I'd never see them if I didn't fit my schedule around theirs."

"That was the summer after Lopsang died, right?" Alden asked.

"Right." (Alden was a very bright track star.) "I'd lost him, HMR had gone out of business, Dear David left on his mission, and Zoë announced she was getting married to a local psychologist. So much for my five year plan. I still believed in silly things like that back then. Now it's more like five weeks."

"How about five days?" Alden smiled.

"Oh yeah. Lately, it's been more like five hours... wait, no make that five minutes." (much laughter) "So, with nothing left to lose, I moved to Kent, found a tiny apartment and began subbing. I was so scared. I remember lying awake at night thinking 'How in the hell am I going to pay my bills?'"

"Hey, Johnson. I know how to pay some bills?" Jake danced his head on his shoulders and gave us a slick smile. "All right. All right."

"Of course, it all worked out. Within a few months, the principal of KM asked me to develop a program for "at risk" kids. That spring I asked Erickson if I could help out with the track team, and the rest is what you know."

"Hey, Johnson. Let me show ya my program for at risk females. I'll fix em up straight. All right. All right"

Jake was on a roll.

"Hey Johnson."

"Hey what?"

"You know what I was just thinking about?"

"Hmmm."

"That the first porno I watched as a kid was with two chicks going at it."

"Jesus Jake, what kind of a Mormon are you?"

"It scared the holy crap out of me. No lie. I remember telling my friend to turn it off. Damn, Johnson! She was making all these noises. I thought they were hurting each other!"

Alden looked at Jake and then me. "Glue," was all he said.

"Ya know, Alden, for some reason, learning the details of Jake's early childhood development seems to ease my pain."

"Hey, Johns, ya know what I just thought of?"

"No, Jake. But, I'll bet I could guess."

"No, for reals, Johnson. Seriously. When I thought of those chicks in that movie, it got me thinking of that story Krissy told me about the Purple Pal they found in your closet."

"What!! Oh my God! You're kidding? You mean the bag of porn toys that Kate found in the attic?"

"Oh man!! So it was true? I knew it!"

"Yeah. Oh that's a good one… What exactly did she tell you?"

"Just that you were making out with some chick from Argentina in the living room and Kate jumped out the window after finding a stash of porn toys."

"DUDE!!!!" Alden Crag was laughing, all ears.

"OK. Let me tell the real story. God, I love how these things get twisted around. Anyway, it happened during the first year I moved to Kent. I was subbing and making a name for myself by helping out athletes and volunteering for everything at your school. I'd met an olive skinned, Argentine woman at Alki Beach and took her with me to chaperone a high school dance. Kate decided to have a bunch of her friends over instead of going to the dance. Right before I left, I noticed that the attic crawl-way lid was slightly ajar, and some fiberglass insulation had fallen out. I told her to stay out of the attic. I didn't tell her why.

So, curious as to what I wouldn't want her to see up there, she and her boyfriend pushed aside the lid and snooped around. They found a hefty bag and pulled it down as her group of girl friends circled around them. The contents inside the bag were the stuff from which legends are born. The first thing they pulled out was a 12 inch purple rubber penis. After that came Lover's Package panties, and vaseline, and a stack of hard core girlie mags that made Hustler look like family reading. Of course, Kate's imaginative boyfriend immediately put two and two together and condemned me as the closet fudgepacker of Kent."

The boys burst into hysterics.

"Yeah. It's funny now…Jesus Christ. So I get home from the dance and everyone in my tiny apartment was looking at me strangely and the girls that were going to spend the night had called their parents for rides home. Lena and I laid down in my tiny living room to have some time alone. The next thing you know, Kate heard us kissing, freaked out, crawled out the 2nd story window, jumped into the bushes below, and ran to her boyfriends apartment. All the while I was out there having a good time, thinking life had really turned a corner. At some point in the morning, I got a knock on the door and it was Kate's boyfriend's dad bringing her back. She was trembling like a leaf. Of course I had no idea what the hell was going on. I thought she was cold. I didn't have a clue her mind was running wild with the image of me out in the living room having butt sex with Miss Argentina."

Jake was flopped over, crying and drooling.

Alden was laughing so hard that sound was no longer leaving his larynx. "Jesus, Johnson," he finally blurted, "you are sick!"

"Thank you. In the morning I sent Lena packing and went for a walk with my exhausted kids. Kate unloaded the truth on me and I just about shit. I tried to explain to her that I'd never seen that bag of trash, that the person who lived here before us must have been into kinky sex, that I was completely innocent and what could I say? For the first time in my life, after all we had been through, I could sense that Kate and Kris didn't know whether they could trust me. Classic, huh?"

"Hey Johnson, what did ya do with all that stuff?"

"The girls and I wrapped most of it up and gave it away for Christmas presents."

Jake laughed like he was going to squirt milk out of his nose.

Alden queried, "Dude, did they ever figure it out, I mean that it wasn't your stuff?"

"Oh yeah. About two years later."

"And what about her friends?"

"Jesus. Who knows? I'm tellin ya boys, the mind-set is a strange and fragile thing. Reality is this thin membrane, about the thickness of a fly's wing. All it takes is the slightest shift, bump, disturbance, look, word, or action, and one's perception is diametrically adjusted. I worked fifteen years to earn the trust of those girls, and in the opening of a black bag that I didn't know existed, I was judged, soiled and condemned. That's why parenting is so tough. You never know what is coming. You never know all the pieces. You just fumble and bumble and hope you re coming off as human. I swear to God I went to the dance that night feeling good about myself, about my life, about my relationship with my kids. I thought I was making progress. Hmmm.

Of course, we laugh about it now. But all those things take a toll. That's why kids never feel comfortable with their parents. There's always weirdness whether it's real or not."

Act Three

Paradise
in
Portable-7

TRUTH #157

Don't flatter yourself. You are not here to cure world hunger. You are here to cure your own.

-From the **Book of Truths** by Langdon Towne

THE SURRENDER

After Lopsang's death in '96, I gave up. It wasn't easy. To surrender all control was my greatest defeat. Over the course of a ten year downward spiral, I'd lost the love of my life, my kids, my job, my Les Paul (when our house was broken into) my home, and my climbing gear (after my car was broken into and all my stuff stolen by members of a local heroin ring). So I packed my Ford Festiva and moved to Kent to be closer to my teenage kids. They didn't ask me to. They thought that life was built on an 'every other weekend' visitation plan. They thought that time with dad should always be measured on a tit for tat basis. It wasn't their fault. It was all they knew. And I knew that I would go to bed every night knowing there was absolutely nothing I could do about their mom and step-dad's need to control the warmth of the sun.

So I gave up and moved to Kent anyway. I put my name on the school district's sub-list. I got called the first day of school, but blew it off to go climbing with Jeannie Probala. Of course, I felt guilty for bailing on the money, but the trip was magic, and since Jeannie would wind up losing her leg later that year, I'm glad I took a chance to seize the moment. And how much of life is like that, beating yourself up for choices you make, and then admiring your handy work from the perspective of life's unveiling?

I got called to sub at Kent Meridian the following Monday and quickly found a niche telling stories of sweet absurdity to high school students starving for an adult who was real. I told them I had surrendered, that I was a loser in search of truth. They loved that one. I told them I had learned something about life after Lopsang's death, that you can never count on anything, that best laid plans are just best laid ideas and the universe cares little for best laid ideas. I explained that pitting one's dreams on another human being or focusing one's sights on a pinnacle or goal as a sole means of fulfillment is like playing a distracting form of Russian roulette. And eventually you get to eat the bullet. And a bullet in the head is not good. They laughed at that one.

I would often mention that the only way to get happy was to make sure everybody else was happy, which takes so much energy that you rarely have time to care if you are happy or not. And God knows, you better hope you don't get the time. For time on your hands is dangerous. They understood that one.

If time permitted, and because I always made the time, it did, I would go on to say that I'd discovered that there was something I could do that no one else on the planet seemed capable of doing. I could spot people's talents, gifts, and sources of genius and compliment that individual for the aforementioned quality. So I did. And I did it often. Becoming a human being was that simple. And they believed in me for that one.

-*From the **Shipwreck** Journals*

PARADISE IN PORTABLE-7

Is this not the true joy in life… of being used for a purpose recognized by yourself as a mighty one instead of a feverish, selfish, little clod of ailments and grievances complaining that the world will not devote itself to making me happy.   *-George Bernard Shaw*

∧∧∧∧∧∧∧∧∧∧∧∧∧∧∧∧∧∧∧∧∧

[February 1998: Portable 7, Kent Meridian High School]

One Friday, the principal of KM approaches me and says he wants to create a classroom where kids will feel a sense of belonging, a place where they can be listened to. He thinks I am the man for this and wants to know if I want the job. I do a quick *Deniro* and ask if he's talking to me. He explains that many of these kids have never known success and will often choose failure because it's all they know or feel comfortable with, that many of them come from dysfunctional, addictive families, that most of them are depressed and ill-equipped for dealing with getting a job, getting along with others, or forming healthy relationships. I don't tell him it all sounds pretty normal to me.

The first week of my new career takes place in a tiny office from where I begin to mastermind my 'Life Skills' class. Being an ex-mountain guide, I am used to stomping uphill, kicking butt, topping out, and putting up with the pain of heinous descents. I am not schooled in the process of filing forms and following politically correct procedures. My purpose in life is now clear. I'm here to save kids. I've never felt so compelled in my life and am way too busy to be tuned into adults around me who have that disease people get when they've held a job too long, where they become proud of their little box and get pissed when someone tries to touch, move, or change their box. Blind to this, I start my political undoing on the third day. The administration has given me the green light to do whatever I must to get the '4-F' kids under my wing. New to the building, I do not know that the counseling department is in a cold-war with the administrators and moves I am making in that first week will wind up having my program scrapped three years later when new leadership is hired to clean up KM's image and raise standardized test scores. Oblivious, I forge on. 'Whatever it takes' is my philosophy. And it works. In four days I have fifty kids staring back at me during three different periods. Some know me, but others are wondering why they've been pulled from the business class they were failing so well just the day before.

On the fifth day I get my first introduction to Chris, a prototypical poster child for the program I have been chosen to create. Chris is an angry black male dressed head to toe in blue. He struts in to the room with sagging pants, a bandana on his head and a chip on his shoulder so large it's hard to walk next to him. He hates me the second he sees me. He thinks I'm a white-dude motivational speaker. Chris is used to getting kicked out of classes and schools. He walks in the computer lab, 'dapping' with his bros and talking out loud about how a "nigga" can't function in a room this nappy. He sits down next to a kid named Damon and loosens up the room with a greeting he learned in 4th grade: 'fuck y'all mothafuckas.' Damon looks at me. I don't flutter an eyelid. I pick up some quotes I've found to explain my philosophy of life. I use words from Thoreau, MLK, Emerson, and Jefferson. It's college level thinking from which these young minds could grab a toe hold and climb a step or two up the ridge of wisdom. While Damon and Chris roll their eyes, a black girl informs me coldly that Thomas Jefferson owned slaves.

I do not have study sheets to hand out or a textbook to follow; the 90 minute classes mean that I will be entertaining and educating these kids with whatever inspiration and knowledge I can pull out of my soul and book of truths. They are not used to my style. They are used to worksheets, drill, practice, and sleep. I do not want them sleeping during my speech, but I'm glad Chris finally nods off at the 60 minute mark. He puts his head down and the room, though still nappy, instantly grows more pleasant.

What I don't know about Chris is that he attends school to play basketball. He doesn't look like a basketball player to me until I go watch the JV boys play Auburn after school. A lot of my kids are there. I am amazed by Chris's speed on the floor. Not used to working with black kids, I have never been around this kind of athleticism. Running on legs with ankles no bigger than my wrists, Chris glides down the floor and elevates towards the rim like he's full of helium. He has talent. Speed and hops. He's worth keeping around.

By that first Friday, it becomes apparent that we are going to outgrow the cramped quarters of the computer lab. I ask the administration what space is available for my growing list of students and am told the only room is a decrepit portable out behind the gym. It used to be a classroom but it's now home to extra desks, chairs, outdated two-year-old computers, and textbooks. I go out to take a look. Upon entering I notice a sour smell and the fact that the carpet clashes with the dark, imitation-wood paneling. There are iron bars on the two windows and the floor creaks as I walk around the piles of technological junk. There is a sink in the corner that isn't hooked up to plumbing. The phone has been ripped off the wall and is hanging by the wires. It is the worst classroom I have ever seen. It's perfect.

I ask the administration how long it will be before the room can be cleaned up and they tell me the custodial staff will have to be notified. It could take weeks. I make a point to introduce myself immediately to the custodial staff and to make it clear I am on the same rope team as them. I know that without their support I will be sitting in that computer lab for the rest of the month. I also know the custodians feel overworked and do not want to clean out that portable. So I talk to Bev, the head custodian. I talk to Ron, the day-shift clean-up guy. I let them know I'm out here to help these kids.

Portable- 7 opens for use the following Tuesday.

THE BOX

In the wake of recent developments in Colorado, it is apparent that education has a greater responsibility than ever before in finding a way to reach troubled teens. It is the goal of the Life Skills Class at Kent Meridian to identify "at risk" kids and help them gain a sense of balance at school. Many of our kids come to KM carrying the negative burden of parental apathy, neglect, abuse, divorce, drugs and alcohol use. Many are dealing with emotional starvation, wondering how to fill a heart that is running on empty. It is our job to provide hope for these kids.

-From a course outline I submitted to the Kent School Board in May '98

∧∧∧∧∧∧∧∧∧∧∧∧∧∧∧∧∧∧∧

The box of public education demands that you surrender something: like your creativity, your instincts, your ability to walk away from or give the finger to rules that make no sense. The box of public education demands that you sit in meetings and sing camp-fire songs you learned in 2nd grade, songs you wouldn't be caught dead singing in 3rd grade.

All the catch phrases say public education is about helping young minds: teaching them to think and gain independence. But reality is something else. The box of public education teaches the power of conformity. The box is, was, and always will be about being politically correct.

Fear is making a comeback in the box. Fear of the parents, fear of one's standardized test scores looking poorly in the newspapers, fear of saying something inappropriate that might offend the extreme moral right, fear of saying something racially incorrect that could be misconstrued by an angry faction of the minority race. For your own protection, and to prevent expensive court dates, public education would prefer that you attend classes and refer to manuals on correct procedures for dealing with race, disruption, and motivationally challenged young persons.

Of course, no where in these neatly formatted pages does it talk of a disruptive teenager's addiction to weed, of his latest fight with the alcoholic step-dad, of his need for money but inability to find work, of his break-up with the girl-friend who was the one thing that he thought he could count on, of the fact that she is pregnant and neither are sure who the father is, that this child broke down and cried in front of you when you shut the door, that he begged you to help him get off weed, that he wants to be forgiven, to be loved, and that there is no one out there capable of loving him, not even for an hour. I didn't find that information in any of the manuals and spread sheets I perused. In the box, these people don't exist.

But in the classroom these kids do exist. And they walk the halls, heads down, eyes staring off for something they'll never find. They hate their day, hate their life, and hate themselves for not having the balls to just stick a thumb out and run away. These kids have no business being in public education. They screw it up. They don't want to come to school. They know that everything they are learning has nothing to do with being a successful adult. They don't care about standardized testing. They know it is all just smoke and bullshit. They are lowering test scores and are a blight in any administrator's eye. These kids need to be out of the school system and out on the street where they belong. They need to find jobs selling drugs and ripping off cars to ensure job security for prison guards and the contractors rapidly building more correctional facilities.

In the biz we call these kids 'at risk.' You may think that means you are *at risk* being near them. But after hanging with these kids and being their mentor, I know 'at risk' means these kids are 'at risk' of pulling out a gun and putting it in their mouth. They think no one cares. They think there is no one there to save them. They think that if they pull the trigger the world will be better off. They've heard the educational speeches. They know the test scores will go up if they are gone. And this is the sad part. They're right. These kids are smart. They know they don't belong in the box.

∧∧∧∧∧∧∧∧∧∧∧∧∧∧∧∧∧∧∧

TRUTH # 77

You must hear the voice of death before you can know the meaning of life. This, of course, is a back-asswards approach to living. You are expected to have courage, but you cannot have courage without giving up your black and white thinking. You are expected to rise above the muck, but one cannot rise without giving up pettiness and fear. Remember, if you choose not to walk to the edge and look down, do not blame yourself. Please know if you did look down, all you would be able to see is every truth you ever needed.

-From **The Book of Truths** by Langdon Towne

THE GHETTO KIDS

***Waste not.** If a large man with a black hood were to walk up to you, crack you up side the head, stuff a foot in your ball sack and stick the barrel of a gun in your mouth, you might take a moment to reflect upon every second you ever gave away wishing you were somewhere else. You might wish to make amends with anyone you ever damaged or abandoned. And as his finger squeezed off the last two millimeters between this world and that other thing, you might finally understand the reality of love: too little too late.*

*-From the **Book of Truths** by Langdon Towne*

∧∧∧∧∧∧∧∧∧∧

I live in the 'ghetto' part of Kent. On a clear day, it smells like LA. It has the same kind of sprawling, no rhyme or reason feel. I grew up back when Kent was a tiny town surrounded by a zillion acres of rolling farmland from which one could gaze at Mt. Rainier. Kids played in 10 acre fields. There were no ghetto complexes. No police roaring up and drawing aim on violent tenants in filthy stairwells, gun to gun, temple to temple, blow to blow over a twenty sack. Now, kids with basketballs on their hips stand around watching violence where we used to run up and play "kick the can."

Sex is the topic in the ghetto. It is bumping from cars at the stoplight. It is pumping through the headphones of girls and boys walking to the bus stop. Sex is the great equalizer. It is of love. And love is of God. And God is good. Sex is good too: in a parking lot, against a wall, on your neighbor's bed, anyplace you can sit on, lean against, lay on, dream on. It's a sure-fire rush that costs nothing more than the lies you have to come up with to get it and go. Little girls walk the malls with bellies out to here. Fellas who aren't shaving more than a couple of chin whiskers, brag about being the poppa of a kid. They talk about going to the mall to buy her little Nikes. "I'm spoilin that little girl rotten," they profess with self-effacing pride. Spoiling that little girl rotten with money they got selling weed to the junior high kids at McDonalds.

I run the sidewalked hills at night, exhaust fumes clinging to my sweat. A couple of five acre corner lots with white farm houses remind me of how beautiful it used to be. I spot the little sign announcing a "Public Hearing." Small type reads: Zoned: family commercial. The ultimate developer ticket. Soon, bulldozers and greed will throw up another crowded apartment complex. Pave paradise and put up a Wal-Mart.

The ghetto kids grow up adult children. They have had to stare in awed confusion at the destruction wrought by their child parents. They've had to pick up the pieces, find the glue, swallow the glass and not complain as it shreds its way down, out and through. There is a familiar lack of brightness in their eyes, the crushed hope, the glaze of denial, the numbness of TV distraction, the exhaustion of treading piranha filled waters since the day they were born.

I don't like the ghetto of Kent, but I love its kids. Love their talent, love their game, love their fight, love their willingness to be real.

ANGEL

Angel comes to me a product of nightmares from four years ago when I had him as a 7th grader. I was subbing that year and Angel had been one of the faces I'd never forgotten. He was an evil little Hispanic demon seed. He would smirk in my face, cuss when he wanted, and beg me to send him out of the room so he could leave school and do the things he really wanted to do. This kid was juvie bound, with no force in the universe strong enough to change that course. I don't normally hate kids, but Angel gave me a reason to start.

So Angel walks in P-7 and smiles at me. It isn't a cruel smile, but a genuine smile. He remembers me and he knows I remember him for something else. We get to talking and he lets me know that he is walking a tightrope right now, trying to choose between good and evil. I tell him to come to school each day and I will help him. So he does. And we talk. His story is a simple one. He has left home and is living with his brother. His brother takes care of him, keeps a roof over his head and food in the fridge. His brother has also offered him part-time work. This work involves spending a couple of hours each day standing on street corners in Auburn, selling crack to all the fiends in that predominantly white community. His brother offers good wages. Angel can make around $400 an hour. He can buy a lot of clothes and a nice ride for that. His brother drives a Lexus SUV with gold rims as proof. His brother wears more gold jewelry than an NBA all-star.

Angel's choices aren't as simple as his story. He has decided to not sell for his brother. Something in his soul has clicked and he knows that what his brother is doing is wrong. Instead he has been looking for work, and has found a job at *Jack in the Box* that pays $5.75 an hour with discounts on food. He has to wear a uniform. He has to work late hours. He will earn less in a month, than one hour on the corner.

I listen to Angel and tell him I am so proud of him- that he is doing the right thing-- that good things will happen to him as a result of him choosing to do good. He looks in my eyes and believes me.

Meanwhile, KM has developed an image problem. Word is out, with many teachers backing it, that the KM administration is not tough enough on its tough kids. Teachers are frightened that the 'at risk' kids are in control. Too many black kids roam the halls during class. Too many thugs hang around the campus after school. The McDonalds across the street is a haven for drug deals, as are the bathrooms of the school, the parking lots, the hallways and the classrooms. Kids deal and kids do. So do their parents. The kids' role models play in the NBA, and according to the kids, they use too.

Angel leaves my room fully inspired. He is so inspired that he doesn't see the thug come up behind him in the lunch line and push his back. Angel crashes into a girl and turns around to see what just went on. A black kid with a doo-rag, an attitude, and his posse behind him, starts dishing him abuse. Angel tries to walk away but the second shove sets him off and he takes a swing.

The security guard races over and sees the punch. There is no blood, but there is Angel's well-documented past. Angel is the "thug" they have been looking for to make an example of. Angel doesn't have parents to defend, support, or re-enroll him. Angel isn't a color that will wind up on the front page. Angel won't litigate or retaliate. He is marched down to the office and given a one way ticket to the streets. He is not allowed back on campus. He is not allowed back in the Kent School District. He is a non-Angel now.

FIAD

When I first walked up and introduced myself to Fiad Abdillahi at the junior high league championships, I had no idea what I had just done to that kid's life or mine. I had no clue that the next three years would be dedicated to helping the Africans on our team. I couldn't have possibly foreseen sitting around my apartment with Fiad, Asiki, and Ayanle, eating spaghetti and listening to them talk in excited voices about life and love and war and everything else a boy can think about when he feels safe enough to talk. I did not know that I would be the surrogate father for all of them. That I would get their teeth fixed, buy them running shoes, feed them, help them with their homework, get them up and drive them to practice, drive them home and make sure their hearts were in good enough shape to run like the wind.

*-From the **Shipwreck** Journals*

^^^^^^^^^^^^^^^^

Fiad Abdillahi arrived in Seattle unable to speak English and was placed in Seattle public schools where he quickly learned the rules of a different jungle. Once proud of his barefoot speed and agility on the dirt soccer fields back home, he watched in bewilderment as kids dribbled and shot a ball with their hands. Fiad approached these black children hoping to find comfort. The kids stared at him in his K-Mart pants and shoes and opened fire with

262

ridicule.

Fiad went home that night and cried himself to sleep. This became the routine of the year. He learned to hate black kids. He didn't trust white kids. He didn't understand the new language--couldn't read or write. His teacher was as overwhelmed as the kids staring back at him. How exactly was one supposed teach English to a room filled with faces from a dozen different countries?

After two years of trying to learn the ways of America, Fiad decided his situation was hopeless. After getting cut from the basketball team and told to return his uniform and shoes, he came home from school, walked out to the high rise apartment balcony and stepped up on the railing. His uncle happened to come home early from work, raced out and grabbed the kid who was screaming for mercy from a God he knew had abandoned a million children just like him.

In desperation, the uncle contacted a local youth organization and found a track club for the boy. Fiad attended practice and soon demonstrated his gift to the coaches. The coach was a good man, took a liking to the boy and saved him. As Fiad's confidence grew, so did his wardrobe. Little by little he acquired the black-American look, though he didn't look black-American. Fiad was unique. But kids his age don't want to feel unique. Kids want to belong.

∧∧∧∧∧∧∧∧∧∧∧∧∧∧∧∧∧∧∧∧∧∧∧∧

Once a quiet, shy, Muslim kid; Fiad isn't quiet and shy anymore. He is on the top-ten list for troubled students at his junior high. Fiad has rage. This rage can only be controlled through sports. He plays every sport, every season, every day, despite being small and having just learned the American form of football and basketball.

The rough, size dependent American sports are already taking a toll on his slight body. He rolls his socks down, just like his NBA heroes, and reveals swollen, damaged ankles. Fiad needs to see a doctor. He needs a cast and months of rest. Instead he turns out for the next sport, then goes home to the playground and plays until it is time for bed. He cannot stop. He is addicted to the motion. For to stop is to think about his father, and his country, and his mother, and all the people he will never see again.

His family moves to the federally funded projects of Kent and he runs track for Sequoia Junior High. He doesn't train because it hurts to run. He keeps in shape by playing basketball on the playground at night. As a 7th grader running on an ankle that looks like a rotten potoato, he races a ninth grade Somali boy in the mile. Fiad takes off on the last lap and leaves the older African with 200 meters to go. His time of 4:30 shocks the coaches.

Fiad is one of the fastest junior high distance runners in the nation. He is also one of the most lonely. He has made just two real friends since arriving in America: his legs and his anger. These trusted friends have now turned on him. His ankles are swollen and his fists are bruised. Because of the daily fights, he has become an "at risk" problem for administrators. Fiad is in their offices far too often and his grades reflect the missed class time. He is allowed to participate in sports because the coaches like his talent. (The 2.0 grade requirement that will be appointed as district policy has not yet descended to keep troubled kids like Fiad off the playing field.) He walks home from track and heads to the playground to play basketball. After dark, he walks into the door of an apartment filled with screaming kids and Muslim women wrapped in colorful shawls watching *Simpsons* reruns on TV.

Many of my kids in Portable-7 claim to have been at the junior high track meet the day Fiad ran his 4:30 mile. They also tell me that Fiad won't make it a month in high school if he doesn't get my class. The kids know that the messages of tolerance and kindness that I am teaching will help Fiad gain some control.

I show up and introduce myself to the young African at the Junior High Track Championship, letting him know that I will be able to keep him out of trouble, keep him in school, and keep him running towards a dream. The look in his eyes is powerful--regal. Lopsang had the same kind of eyes: soft, moist, with an inferno raging just behind the surface.

The next day a kid in P-7 who knows the streets and spent time in juvie before showing up in my room tells me: "Fiad is always in trouble. And that's why he needs your class, Johnson. He's your kind of kid."

LOUIS DAVIS

If I had met Louis Davis in an alley the year before I moved to Kent, I would have been scared. Louis had that stare. That look that said he didn't care anymore. He was too black and too thick and wore his hair in braids before braids were the fashion.

Louis walks in P-7 looking like he hates me, hates this school, hates the clothes clinging to his skin. He hands me transfer paper work that smells like weed, which I Frisbee to my desk prompting an eyebrow lift from him. I tell him to grab a seat because I'm in the middle of my favorite sermon: *Maslow's Hierarchy of Needs*. I tell Louis it's his lucky moment because he's walked in to hear the only thing he needs to know about achievement, belonging and self-esteem. He nods like he gets the joke and takes a seat.

I go to the board and start scratching out a large pyramid, talking as I draw lines. I tell the kids that Maslow was smart, that he came up with facts about achievement that made sense no matter which side of the street you lived on. I look at the kids to see if anyone is watching and all the kids are scratching down pyramids. Louis is watching me from inside his black sweatshirt hood. So I began my speech on Maslow's Heirarchy 101:

"At the bottom of the pyramid is basic survival. Water, food, and sleep. If you were living in a war torn region, this is all you would be after. You have to have this or you'll die. As soon as you have the basic needs covered, you need a safe, secure place to live. It's called security. How many of you in this room have that?"

I run through the why's and how's of reaching the pinnacle of self-actualization, the place where a human being realizes their full potential as a feeling, thinking, loving vehicle of the universe.

"There is a calling in your soul to help your fellow man. It is a driving force. Stronger than evil. Stronger than pleasure. Stronger than power. It is what we are meant to be."

A hand shoots up. "Are you there, Johnson?"

"Hmmm. I have been. I can look you in the eye and say that. But, right now I am trying to climb my way back up. I have been through such an ordeal lately over my need to be loved that I have fallen back down."

Carmen, a latino siren who was sent to KM on a social promotion, meaning she didn't pass 9th grade but was too old to be kept around the other kids another year, speaks up from the quiet. "You know what we think, Mister J. You're the kindest person we know."

I smiled in gratitude and replied: "That's only because I've failed more than any person you know."

Roberto, a tall, light-skin hispanic with a permanent frown offers up from the back row: "Yeah, Mister. If it weren't for you, none of us in here would give a damn about school."

"And you know what I think... I went looking for a soul-mate and wound up stuck in Portable-7 with you guys."

"We love you, Johnson." Carmen is one of several kids who makes sure I hear that everyday.

The kids start to move. Class is over. I walk to my desk to get Louis's paper work. He moves towards me like a dark cloud and stares in my eyes.

"You're different," he says quietly. "You're tapped into something."

"Thanks. I don't know. It comes and it goes. I feel like I'm struggling right now. Every time I gain a toe hold on some clarity, the storms roll in."

"No. I can see it. You mind if I come back here next period? I got shit banging in my head that needs to get out."

"Then write it down. That's what I do. Write or cry. Or both."

"Yeah."

"It's all we can do sometimes. Louis, I've walked a long way to here. And sometimes I feel like I've learned nothing. And then other times some kid like you walks through the door and I feel like I've reached that point I dreamed of as a child."

"You got a pen I can use next period?"

I handed him my last one.

"I will be back. You'll get your pen."

Next day first period I'm arguing with Chauncey Santos about the merits of staying up 'til three AM to watch teen role model Jerry Springer. The door opens and in walks Louis with my pen and a poem he wrote. He has a look in his eye that says he wants to talk. So we talk. He says he's sick of his ways, sick of smoking weed and hanging out idle. He knows his momentum has been stopped and spun downward; that he is in a hole that goodness doesn't crawl out of.

Louis has desperation in his eyes. He wants to change but knows he must swim an ocean to get to a side of himself that would meet his dreams. We sit down in desks, eye to eye, and hash out a path to reality. He tells me he stayed up late and wrote two raps; that he hasn't written anything in a long time, and that the raps are rusty. He opens up a pocket on his long black coat and pulls out two sheets. Neither are titled.

I'm in a silent phaze, drained to the core,
My own kinds violent ways, the pain of war
It's like we strive for a strong race,
But we try in the wrong ways.
We're ruthless and with our sins we call each other brother,
But the truth is we can't win cause we're killin each other...

I put the paper down and stare at Louis. He smiles knowing he has made a connection. I smile back. This young man is gold. He is a voice. But can his shoulders carry the mission he has spoken of? So I ask him.

"You up to this, Louis? Can you be the one to lead the way for these kids?"

"Shit....I can't even get off weed myself."

"But you know what's right. You can feel it."

"And I know what's wrong and I keep doing it."

Louis has the disease. Its called depression and it is insidious. It breathes, walks, eats and sleeps with these kids. They think they are insane. But they're not. Life would be way easier if they were. I read the next rap. This one is darker than the first, but not dark enough to pull Louis out of his descent.

I remember them niggaz clownin, cause my clothes was bummy
I was mad but everybody knows it was funny
It was sad cause every child that has to grow without money
At one point in his life is getting clownt by a dummy...

Louis comes to my class for most of the day. He listens to my speeches. He reads the book of positive quotations. He talks of the court dates and issues he is facing. I have no idea how to help him. But we talk. Man to young man. After a week he disappears. I see him occasionally at the bus stop waiting....

CHASE

Chase is a break dancer and a royal pain in the ass. He is the mutt of the litter, tolerated by the breakers only because the breakers tolerate everybody. Chase is white, rude, and loud. He sulks, pouts, argues for no reason, and craps in his own mess-kit every hour of every day. I tolerate him because that is my job-- to tolerate and teach *Life Skills101* to kids like Chase.

Chase is using drugs. We all know it. I give him the speeches and he just waits for me to finish. He tolerates me because the other breakers would kill him if he talked back to me. It's a circle that works, but even this circle doesn't roll without lumps and bumps making it lurch to and fro.

I tell Chase that he has to start making it to his other classes or he won't be allowed to break-dance with his crew after school. So he goes to his classes. That afternoon I receive several notes from teachers who have had Chase re-enter their world. They don't like it. They are angry with me for keeping him around. They think there is a world out there that should absorb Chase and make him go away like a bad smell unleashed in a room.

But Chase doesn't want to go away. He wants to break-dance. He wants to belong. Chase doesn't want to suck. He wants to feel important. So he practices break-dancing more than the other kids... and he still sucks.

Marco, a mix kid, shows up and busts into wind-mills without a warm-up. Chase looks on and then tries to find a move that he can call his own. At last he manages to balance on his hand and kick his legs up like a scissor.

Unlike the other guys, he can't hold the move for more than a second. But, he *is* able to send it. I figure that if a person is quick with a camera, Chase will look like he's got game. I wish I had a camera.

During class I tell Chase to quit talking and to write poetry or stories like the other kids. He gets pissed off and goes out on the porch. I go out there and he tells me to f... off. I ask him what motivated that little tirade and he starts to cry. He says he has nothing left, that he knows he's a joke. He's not living at home anymore. He's got nowhere to go. He's been living at Chauncey's house, sleeping on his bedroom floor at night, crawling through the window to come and go because Chauncey's mom doesn't like him and doesn't want him there. The boys bring him food or he wouldn't eat.

It gets quiet. The rain is louder than us. He starts fiddling in his pocket and pulls out a sheet of paper. It is an assignment I asked him to write. I take it from him and read it as streams of water cascade off the porch of P-7.

I CALL YOU ON THE PHONE AND YOU ARE NEVER HOME,
OR SO THEY SAY

I WRITE YOU LETTERS HOPING TO KNOW YOU BETTER,
YET I GET NO RESPONSE

I READ YOU MY DEEP POEMS, YET I AM STILL ALONE,
WAITING

I GIVE YOU MY LOVE, THEN IT FLYS THROUGH THE AIR
LIKE A SOLITARY DOVE...

After reading Chase's poem I think of changing the name of my class to **LOVE 101**. That would surely fly well with the district. I realize that love, or the lack of it, is the pulse beat in P-7. Kids are trying to find it at any cost. So am I. The pain of these kids makes me look inward. I realize I too am an addict, addicted to wanting to be loved and adored. It has been the demon and the angel from which I've fled and run to for the last ten years. The moth and the light bulb. And the cost has been enormous.

THEA THAN

Thea Than is a Cambodian kid who shows up every day with a tight scowl on his face. Thea and I get to talking and he lets me know that he is sickened by his small stature. Thea is only five foot one and looks even smaller in a classroom filled with basketball players. He hates his body and hates the God that cursed him with it. I try to explain to him that maybe God is a rock climber, because if Thea were a rock climber, he'd have the perfect body. He doesn't know anything about climbing and shakes his head at my attempts to cheer him up.

Thea is alone at KM. I never see him with friends. There are very few Cambodians here and the ones that walk the halls seem to be misfits. Thea doesn't want to be a misfit. He wants to belong. He wants to join the football team. But he knows he'd get killed. Thea writes a paper about love. He turns it in with no hint of emotion.

Love?
I think love is a disease, contagious and deadly. It distracts you from reality, offering a haven for the weak-minded, a safe house that is non-existent. Love, an illusional satisfaction that soon wears away in time. It makes one foolish and we hastily assume that a gap is filled, a gap made by our own desires. We bond with a woman, say we're in love and feel content. All my life I've never met anyone "in love" and truly happy. It's like a drug that wears off. The more you take it, the faster the body, spiritual body, becomes immune to it.

Thea Than
Period 3

AFRICAN PRIDE

[FALL 2000: CROSS COUNTRY SEASON, KENT MERIDIAN HIGH SCHOOL]

It isn't every day that you get to stand next to greatness. For two years I was coach to three of the finest athletes I will ever know. They were the truth. They taught me how to love again, how to laugh again, and how to give every thing you have to what you believe in again. Do or Die.

The first time Somalian, Ayanle Ismail, ran for Coach Erickson and me, we took him up past North Bend and let him loose on the railroad grade at Exit 38. He had never run anything longer than a soccer field in his life. I loaned him a pair of Cross-Country spikes and off he went. We figured he'd jog an easy five. Eight miles later he came sprinting in, barely breaking a sweat. The other top runners on our team were a half-mile back, gasping to keep him in sight. Roger Erickson, who'd been coaching for 33 years, turned to me and shook his head in amazement, "Man, can this guy run!"

Just over two weeks later, Ayanle entered his first organized three mile race. Running erratically, after a wickedly fast opening 600 meters, he pulled away from state medalist Dylan Bailey at the 2.5 mile mark. Crossing the finish line with a hundred meter lead, he collapsed in a heap and began heaving. It would be his trademark for the season.

∧∧∧∧∧∧∧∧∧∧∧∧∧∧∧∧∧∧∧

This summer, a senior cross-country runner from a neighboring high school approaches me and starts asking questions about the Africans of KM.

"What do they do? What is their secret? I want to run like those guys."

"You want to know what makes Fiad, Ayanle, and Asiki fast?"

"Yeah, man. Why do they run better than everybody else? What do they eat? What kind of mileage do they run?"

"They're African... the real deal. They run fast. It's that simple."

"But, there's got to be something they do?"

"No. These guys train about a quarter of what everybody else is doing. They're awesome. If they trained like you, Chris Lukezic, or Micah Rolfe, it wouldn't be fair."

My young friend looks bummed. It isn't what he wanted to hear, but it is the truth. Diet? Mileage? Forget it. For two years I have watched our young Africans run and I'm still amazed. Granted our guys are particularly good athletes, adept at soccer, basketball and any other sport requiring speed, endurance and agility. But what separates their talent from the other runners is the ease at which they get in shape and the speeds they can run with so little base mileage work.

Fiad Abdillahi was sent to a rival 'all-white' high school his sophomore year and had to wait a month before racial tensions got ugly enough that he was allowed to transfer to KM. He showed up three weeks before the sub-district meet. Better late than never. Unwilling to compete for the other school, Fiad had trained for cross-country races by playing pick up basketball games on the asphalt lot outside his apartment complex. He limped on an ankle that looked like he'd stuffed a tennis ball where the joint was supposed to be. To keep his metabolism finely tuned he sucked down Dr. Peppers and cheeseburgers. Three weeks after joining our team, Fiad finished second at the sub-district meet, getting passed just ten meters from the finish by a white phenom from Auburn named Chris Lukezik. Three weeks of training and he was able to show up and demolish over a 160 top 4A high school runners. All this on a minimum of mileage. His secret? Fiad is fast, African, and tough as hell.

Fiad runs from the ghosts of his past. He has told me that he considers it a miracle that he is here, that after he lost his father and moved here with no parents to escape the wars raging in Somalia, he had no reason to live. That somehow he would wind up here, running for us, is something out of a storybook. But no fairy tale story. He deals with trying to stay above a sense of despair and emptiness that loss and displacement has torn through him. Fiad's life is a daily drama, his intense soul burning through the haze and gloom of the projects of Kent.

Coach Erickson, who's been in the business of producing state champions for thirty three years, has seen the best come and go. He tells me he has never seen anything like Fiad; that the young African could run a 4:00 flat mile if he trained. Fiad is well aware of this. He knows all about Jim Ryan's 3:55 mile set back in '64. He knows he could go after it. He also knows he has to survive another bewildering day in an overcrowded Springwood apartment.

^^^^^^^^^^^^^^^^^^^^^^^^^

The kid from the other school stood there thinking. I could read what was going on. "God, I wish I could have some of what they got," he said.

I looked at him and said. "NO, my friend. You don't want their life. You wouldn't want to go through what they have had to do to survive."

These kids are fast because for much of their childhood they were running for their lives. They now run with the pain of lost parents, shattered homes and countries, crushed dreams, and the alienation of being third world transplants dropped in ghetto apartment complexes, surrounded by wealth and the trimmings of our material society. They have to use medical coupons and consequently only go to the doctor if something gets broken or torn off. They get in fights in their hoods, protecting their bit of ghetto turf. There is no parent making sure they eat a balanced diet. There are no vitamins. No medicine. No ibuprofen in the cabinet. There is nothing in the way of support. The adults they live with do not understand why they run. "Get a job!" they scream. Their fathers are dead or missing. They carry grief in their hearts, on their faces, in every thing they say and do. They react with emotions that have lived on a steady diet of pain and suffering. They will give you the shirt off their back and then beat a friend's butt for turning the channel on a boom box. Volatile, erratic, charged and ready to die for a cause; I love these guys.

^^^^^^^^^^^^^^^^^^^^^^^^

Asiki Ayume of Sudan comes to me after a race and complains of being hit with the flu and having to hold it together during the race. One of his teammates gets on him about his finishing third and Asiki gets wound up and wants to "beat his ass!" but he has to race to the bathroom first. When he comes out he is holding back tears. He says that no one understands what he is going through, of how hard the transition has been moving here from Africa, and then bouncing from apartment to apartment between aunts, uncles, and sisters. That instead of getting a job to buy food and clothes, he is running for us, has no money and has to wait until he gets to school to get his free breakfast and lunch. After practice he goes straight to the library to do his homework (Asiki is a 3.8 student) and then heads home, no parents, no support, a black kid from Sudan in the very strange land of Kent. He says his body is always hurting under the strain. He says he worries about his future all the time. He is a senior and there is no one to help him with direction or his college plans. He drops his head as the tears fall against his dark skin.

Asiki talks of living on one meal a day while interned in a refugee camp; of his sister having to stand in all day lines under the equatorial sun to receive her once a month allotment of corn meal and beans, that the sacks of food were always full of insects and rot, how there was never enough food to last the month. He tells me starvation was a daily spectre his family had to stare down. He has never been to a dentist. He has never learned to trust adults. A true survivor, he has never learned to ask anyone but his God for help.

Coach Erickson considers Asiki a favorite to win the state 800 meter title this year. He is capable of exceptional times at anything from 400-10,000 meters. Unlike the two slightly built Somalians, Asiki's muscles bulge on his piston-like legs. His body exudes power, speed, and agility. We have no idea how fast he can go. He doesn't know either. He is a rare, raw untapped talent, running with the hope of bringing some meaning to his life.

^^^^^^^^^^^^^^^^^^^^^^

Sudan and Somalia are two of the most dangerous and ravaged countries on earth. Fiad, Ayanle, and Asiki, all arriving in this country at different times, remain unspoiled, proud, passionate, and competitive. All three boys feel very fortunate to be here. All three could have easily been killed when they were children. All three are fiercely proud of their heritage and want to return someday to help their countries.

The boys spend many nights hanging out at my apartment after practice, eating spaghetti, watching TV and sharing stories of their lives 'back in the day.' Ayanle tells of his mother's escaping through machine gun fire, fleeing her home towing her kids, a tea set (which would be shot out of her hands) and nothing else. Fiad talks of being bound and gagged by a rebel soldier who then propped an AK-47 on a tree limb and fired bullets between Fiad's legs. Asiki, who hasn't talked much all season, finally feels safe enough to spill his heart. He recounts playing in a field with his best friends and being called home for dinner by his mom. As he ran home a land mine exploded amongst the kids, killing some and maiming all of them. He tells of falling in a pit hidden in the tall grass and sitting there with the skeletal remains of a soldier, of his friends pulling him out and then taking the soldier's AK-47, ammo, knife and belt, and how with absolute delight, they went back in the pit and took the soldier's bones and made drumsticks out of them. "We all became savages. Children are the best soldiers! They don't give a fuck about anything!"

On another night Ayanle comes over to work on a paper and shares a story of being sent to a military camp in Kenya and living there without his parents or siblings for two years. He explains how the most horrible thing he ever witnessed was a friend being hit by a speeding truck as she stepped out from the military vehicle taking them home from school. He described her body exploding on impact, an image of horror he would have to sleep with night after night-- no one there to talk to him, hold him or assure him life would be OK.

Later in the season, Fiad comes by to get help on homework and starts telling me about a nightmare that has been waking him up. His voice is hoarse as tears begin to form. He says there is a woman's face he can't get out of his soul:

"There was a young woman in my village who was accused of being a whore," he spews with eyes growing wild. "The village people dug a pit and threw her in. A pile of stones was placed at its edge and each person from the village was given the opportunity to throw a rock at her. One by one the rocks were tossed at the screaming girl. And as she lay dying, I picked up a rock and tossed it in the pit!"

^^^^^^^^^^^^^^^^^^^^^^^^

The 2000 season is nearly half over and both Fiad and Ayanle have spent the entire month of September battling health problems, much of which stem from serious issues with their teeth. Having never had dental care as children, and then living under the stigma of coupon kids here in America, their teeth have been sorely neglected, and they are paying. Ayanle is hurting all the time, constantly fatigued and running poorly. He is so discouraged he wants to quit, but won't because he doesn't want to let Erickson down. Both boys look exhausted all the time, no spark in their step, the joy of running something they can't remember.

Fiad comes to my class on a Friday ready to pass out after having been unable to sleep for two nights due to intense pain in his teeth. By the grace of God, I call a local dentist, Josh Cowart who ran for Coach Erickson in high school, and he stays late to work for free on Fiad's mouth after school, doing an on the spot root canal and three fillings. Unbelievable! Cowart has no idea that he has just saved our season. The next week Ayanle comes down with similar symptoms and Cowart takes care of him as well. For both boys, it is the first time they have awoken without tooth pain in over a year. It is the first time they have ever been on an antibiotic. It is the first time their muscles haven't hurt due to the infections they have been battling. It is a miracle of kindness. Within a few days, both boys are transformed.

^^^^^^^^^^^^

The KM cross country team gathers in a huddle before the start of their last regular meet, an undefeated season on the line. For the first time, all the boys are healthy, in shape, and ready to make some noise. Ayanle starts a chant that turns into a war cry, all the boys arms wrapped around each other's shoulder, bouncing, then leaping into the October air. They go 1,2,3,4,5 against two quality teams. Our white stud, Micah Rolfe dominates, but close behind is Fiad, Ayanle, Asiki, our Kenyan, Mike Ogwel, and a blonde, pony-tailed, white-African named Alden Crag. The KM Cheetah has been let out of the cage and has its sights on the big prize: the 4A-state title in Pasco. If they can remain healthy, they have a shot at something a West Side school hasn't done in over ten years. They know they are the dark hope, the underdog hope. It's do or die. African Pride.

THE MASK

A young man wandered through the mountains and valleys in search of the Dalai Lama. He was searching for truth, for a reason to be. He wanted the Dalai Lama to teach him about faith, religion, and spiritual purity. For the young man, like many his age, had lost his faith, his trust, his belief that anything he did mattered. He was lost.

His lonely travels led him through many exhausting trials. Heartache and disappointment were his companion for he never met the enlightened one. And he returned home more disallusioned than ever. He had learned nothing but how to suffer.

And then one night, while making tea in his tiny apartment, he paused to read a quote on a nearly empty box of Sleepy Time Tea. This is what the quote on the box said:

"My religion is very simple- my religion is kindness."

-The Dalai Lama

*-From the **Book of Truths** by Langdon Towne*

∧∧∧∧∧∧∧∧∧∧∧∧∧∧∧

We talk about sports in P-7. When I used to work at a climbing store we talked about climbing. When in Rome… The football players talk about where they'd like to play college ball. The ballers talk about where they'd like to play hoop.

The girls in P-7 don't talk about sports. They talk about issues. Boyfriends lead the list. Control freak moms are second. Step-parents from hell are third. The girls and I talk more about these issues than the boys talk about basketball. However, the girls don't think so and complain out loud that all I like are jocks. I find that funny because the boys think all I talk about is 'issues.' I remind myself of something Lincoln once wrote about trying to please everybody.

I hear a lot of things about me during the day. From the kids I hear that the teachers think I can only relate to thugs and drop outs. This makes me laugh. Especially when Kate comes by my room after school to drop off her violin before heading off to do charity work. Kate is involved in every community service club at school. She helps out everyone and anyone who needs a hand. She packs around her 3.97 grade point with unassuming quiet. On Wednesday nights she goes to my bedroom and practices her violin alone. Kate is trying her hardest to make sense of a world that mocks those with a heart. Kate is all heart. She cries when she sees a hurt bird. She cries when we watch movies. She belly laughs with her friends. And she is changing the world by

274

being here. Her light is too bright to ignore.

Like many bright kids, Kate is bored to death in school. I know this, even though she never complains to me or anyone about the fact that only two of her classes are interesting. Despite her love of art, she cannot take an art class. There are only two art classes offered and she'd have to drop calculus or orchestra. Kate passes the time writing short stories about life, love and relationships that will eventually earn her a scholarship to Whitman College. But, she doesn't know that now. She just knows that each day is a descent into the abyss of educational mediocrity. She knows that in every room, brilliant kids sit in front of 'dumbed-down' worksheets passed out by burnt-out teachers tired of fighting parents, administrators, and a system hell-bent on recreating a cookie cutter. She knows that test scores drive the system, a system that is driving the joy out of learning. She knows that few of her teachers still have the courage, wit and humor to engage with their students, defy the trends, and elevate minds starving for truth and challenge.

Most of the teachers at KM don't know Kate is my child. Some teachers tell my students that they don't think I'm making a difference. Most think I can only relate to thugs. On Wednesday's I tell these stories to my daughters, as I have no one else in Kent to share my world with. My kids do not think I am a joke. They think I am their dad, rich in character, troubled in spirit…they have seen me through the deserts and valleys, and now they see me working with kids that no one else wants.

During lunch I am sitting in P-7 discussing the NCAA tournament with Ayanle, Fiad, Micah and some black kids who like to hang out in my room. The door bursts open and in walks Kate with a mask on her face. It is the theatrical mask of grief worn by Greek actors. The mask has a gaping down-turned mouth and black slits for eyes that bleed tears. Kate crosses the room and hurls her body into my arms. The mask becomes her skin and real tears wet my shirt. The boys stare on as she pours forth between gasps how her boyfriend broke up with her at lunch. I sit down and hold her in my arms as her world dissolves through the chair, the floor and straight to a hell reserved for broken hearts.

The boys wait to begin talking to each other. They are respectful of Kate's pain. They all know the valleys of the heart. They have studied that soft turf below the ground. Ayanle comes over and pets Kate's shoulder. He doesn't have to say anything. I hold her for the rest of the period, wondering how divine is a life where a man as lonely as I have been gets a chance: a once in a lifetime chance, to actually be there when his child truly needs a dad. I smile in gratitude as I kiss her head. I look up to see ten pair of brown eyes staring at us in wonder. They have never seen this before, a dad there to hold his bleeding child.

THE ENABLER

For three years I devote my life and every waking moment to helping the kids of KM. 'Father Teresa' of Kent they call me. Where there is a need, a hurt, or a want; I try to be there. I coach sports— assist at games—put on talent shows that features thirty diverse acts—buy kids shoes, clothes, and books—find them scholarships, jobs—anything to make a difference.

The highlight of my teaching career comes when I walk on stage at the talent show I've arranged, produced, and directed and am given an ovation by a standing-room-only crowd made up of every race, creed, and color from the melting pot that is urban America. I return the honor by giving a speech about talent, music, love and brotherhood that would have made Martin Luther King proud. The show opens with my daughter Kris, members of the orchestra, and a band I've put together, playing Bittersweet Symphony by the Verve. As the song builds, a large black kid comes out and starts to rap over the top of us. His words are about love and doing the right thing. It is awesome and sets the tone for an evening of soaring performances by the wounded birds of KM. After the show I bear-hug my daughter and all the kids in the show. It is pure love for all, and to all a good night. That night, before I go to sleep, I give thanks for this amazing blessing. I know that all the twisted trails have led me here. At last I have some of what John Lennon said he'd give everything he had just to get a little of: peace of mind. As I drift off, I know that I've finally reached my potential as a human being.

At the end of the year, our assistant principal tracks me down and pays me the ultimate compliment: "Johnson, I don't know what you are doing out in that portable...but keep doing it. You are leading this team; we are following."

She is so impressed with the changes in the kids I work with that she asks me to speak at a principals' convention in Spokane. The district flies me and several other teachers over to talk about programs that are making a difference for kids. There is only one small glitch in the ointment. The assistant principal has just found out that she didn't get the head principal position at our school. She was voted down by a district seeking strong, new leadership. Our school's test scores are low and the district wants shiny results...or else. Something in my stomach, that mountain guide thing that can smell shit coming from a mile away, goes off like a warning bell. "Oh god. Not again."

-From the **Shipwreck** Journals

^^^^^^^^^^^^^^^^

[May 2000: Track Season]

Tuesday afternoon. Ayanle and Fiad bounce into my classroom to get money. It makes me smile because the latest word being thrown around by teachers in the loop is that I enable the kids. The boys are supposed to be riding up to Snoqualmie Pass with me to get Fiad a quality distance run in the mountains before the State Championship Track meet on Friday. Fiad has qualified for both the one and two mile. They inform me that I don't need to take them. Ayanle will drive. They just need money for gas. I am secretly relieved to have a night off from taxi service and hand Ayanle $10 for gas and burgers. As they run out the door I say to myself that I can't believe how well things are going.

The boys race off and drive all the way to the asphalt basketball court of the Springwood Federal Housing Project two miles away.

I head down to practice feeling good about myself. Running around the track, doing vicious 400 meter intervals is a kid from a rival school, Dylan Bailey. I smile and offer encouragement knowing that Fiad is up getting his lungs blown out in the pure mountain air.

Meanwhile, Ayanle dishes a pass to Fiad and then watches in horror as the potential state medalist gets clobbered to the asphalt. Fiad gets up angry anda loud verbal fight erupts.

The game eventually goes on with Fiad getting constantly stepped on and cheap shotted until Ayanle can't take it and has to leave.

I go to bed that night feeling good about life and my role in it. Fiad has finally gone the distance, done all he had to do to make his statement at state. He will medal. I sleep in peace.

Next morning I arrive at work and notice Ayanle avoiding me. I go up to him and ask him how the run at the pass went and he lets me know they didn't make it to the pass; they ran at the Soos Creek Trail instead.

"Oh... Did Fiad get a decent run in?"

"For reals. Johnson, you know, Fiad. His dedication is weak. I say, 'Fiad, you need the mountain run.' But he already has other plans and doesn't want to drive that far. So we run at Soos Creek."

"How far did you guys run?"

"I'll tell you straight up man, Fiad hates running. But we did three miles. I'm not lying, the boy is lucky he has so much talent."

It isn't what I want to hear, but at least Fiad got in a run.

Later that day one of the kids in my class mentions that he saw Fiad nearly get mawled playing basketball the night before. I quickly inform him that wasn't possible, since Fiad had gone running with Ayanle after school.

"Ayanle was there too."

"What?!"

I find Ayanle and he painfully admits that Fiad talked him into playing in the ghetto-league basketball tournament and that he is sorry because Fiad almost got killed. This is about the 10th incident where I have been made to look like an idiot during the season and something inside me snaps. It is clear that all the good I am doing for Fiad is not helping him gain a sense of responsibility.

So, on the eve of the state track meet, I decide to finally quit enabling Fiad. In the morning he is to be at school at 8:45. The van will leave at 9:00 for the State Star Track in Tacoma. I call his home and leave a message on his recorder informing him that he has to find a ride to school and that if he needs that ride to be me he was to call me or I won't be there to pick him up.

At 11:00 I go to bed. There has been no call. I awake at 4:00 and lie there thinking about the possibility that Fiad will be left sleeping in his apartment on the day of the state mile. Oh well. Maybe it's time he smelled the coffee.

At 8:05 I think about what a raced-face Coach Erickson will say when I show up without Fiad.

I call his apartment to see if he's found a ride. There is no answer. I go in to brush my teeth one last time and stand before a moral dilemma. Tough love would say to let the kid suffer the consequences of his actions. Enabling would have me going over there and getting him out of bed... reminding him to throw in his trainers, spikes, some water and a lunch. I battle back and forth.

Should I prove to him a valuable life long lesson that might make him a more responsible adult ten or fifteen years from now? Or should I at least drive by Springwood? Back and forth I go. I pound my fists down on the counter. And then my head clicks to Fiad's face and that crowded apartment. I grab my keys, get in my car and race off.

Fiad answers the door in his towel. He has just woken up thirty seconds ago. He has nothing ready for the day. I wait in my car deciding to save all lectures for another time. As soon as he is out the door, I take him to the store, buy him a coffee, (like me he needs his morning cup) some water and food for what will be the biggest day of his life. We are at the school by 8:55. I get scolded by Erickson for not being there at 8:45. I don't care. I've done my part. The enabler has delivered the talent. Now the talent better run.

THE 'STAR TRACK' MILE

The Washington State 4A Track and Field Championship is considered one of the premier high school track events in the USA. The Lincoln Bowl stadium is packed and the performances by the finest athletes in the state are spectacular. For the coaches, there is a tension at state that feels like you've downed too much coffee. Your mind races back to the workouts, the injuries, the incidents, the moments that led you here. Did you do all you could to get your kid another tenth, a hundredth, that will determine a medal and a moment on the award podium of state?

The day of state crushes these kids down. The fully prepared athletes deal with the tension. They are loose. They know they are ready. Other kids are balancing on a tight rope, knowing that if every molecule of their being is aligned at the moment the gun goes off, they have a chance at a medal. They know they will not win state. But they can win a top-eight medal.

Woe to the kids in the distance races. When the gun goes off, they have minutes, not seconds, to suffer the consequences of their preparation. In the case of the two mile, sixteen kids must negotiate eight laps of pain that can only be compared to running up a *down* escalator with elbows being thrown and spikes at your knees.

The two miler hears his breathing, and the pounding, and the voices of doubt. And then the surges begin. Usually there are three breaks in a race. These shifts to another gear separate the champions from the others. Three take off and the pack attempts to hang. One runner stays with the third man, then slips back, one step, then two, then... no man's land. He is alone. Food for the hounds. Now it is two races. The pack of three racing for the gold, the rest racing for a top eight medal. Every step something changes, every meter there is the building of pressure. You've taught these kids to relax while in pain. They relax through their breathing and movement.

And we coaches sit in the stands holding our breath and looking at our watches, no where to go, muttering "C'mon, c'mon! Stay with him. Breathe. C'mon" while our guts screw inside out. The final sprint resembles a 4 by 400 relay finish... runners full out (after eight laps at a 4:35 pace) fighting for position and a chance to stand as high as they can on the star track podium.

Fiad sits alone in the stands all day trying to figure out where he is. There are thousands of athletes and even more fans and everyone looks faster then they sounded in the newspaper. The mile isn't run until 8:00 PM.

Warming up for the distance events is an art form. Athletes must take the time to loosen, stretch and rev up an engine that has been sitting in a deep freeze of tension all day. Sips of water, a shoe lace adjustment, stretching out a small knot in a calf that didn't hurt yesterday, getting rhythm into arms with veins filled with lead and acid. The kids with good training and coaching have a well drilled routine and follow it, second by second, until they walk to the starting line.

7:15. Fiad is down warming up and looks like he belongs at state. He is the only black kid running the mile. Brandon Fuller, the other black distance runner in the meet has opted to save his legs for tomorrow night's two mile. Fiad knows he is most likely the only sophomore Somali kid running for a track medal in the world.

The mile is all about tactics, endurance and closing speed. This mile is no different. The boys take off running a slow first lap, trying not to be the fool who plays the rabbit. A break away takes place at the 600 meter mark, but the entire pack goes with it. Twice Fiad fights off elbows to keep his place inside, using his basketball agility to keep from being tossed into the infield. The second break away comes at the 1000 mark and twelve of the sixteen boys take off chasing the rabbit. The next lap and a half are a blur of quickening pace, with kids using every ounce of a year's training to push their tendons faster than they've ever run.

Three boys bust out in the last 200, leaving nine to fight for 4th through 8th. Fiad is in 6th until the last forty meters, when boys with more kick get on their toes and push past him, grabbing the last spot on the award stand. Fiad is 9th, too stunned to notice he won't be on the podium.

In the stands I know the truth. Fiad has been injured most of the season, and sick and disheartened during all of it. He has only been training for one month. Coach Erickson brought him along easy, got him ready to place at league. "Stay alive," is how he put it.

At districts, Fiad stunned us all by easily qualifying in the mile, and then running with the west side's top gun for six laps in the two mile before blowing his tank empty and stumbling over the last fifty meters to 4th place.

The week of state he had the best Monday practice we had ever seen-clipping off 400's like a cheetah. Erickson was grinning and yelling at me to "Look at that! Have you ever seen anything like that?!"

I hadn't. And a little voice inside my head, the one that Erickson doesn't hear, said, "And you probably won't see it again."

Down on the Star Track infield, Fiad now realizes he finished 9th and his head drops. Erickson finds me in the stands. He is shouting Fiad's time: 4:19!! It is eleven seconds faster than the previous week. Erickson doesn't care about the medal, he cares about improvement and that time is gold.

Fiad is quiet on the drive home. He nods when we praise him for setting a KM sophomore record. He is thinking of tomorrow's two mile. Quietly, he tells me that he wanted that medal to show his aunt and brother and cousins and all the people living in his apartment who don't know what he is doing with his life. There is a long silence before he says he wanted to give that medal to his mom back in Somalia. He lets me know he hasn't seen her in three years.

THE TWO MILE

So you find your little boat and paddle up your stream, knowing that this channel may be the one. And you fling your entire being into the cause, risking it all for this, your latest, most significant journey. But the river eventually runs out, and the same rapids that turned you back when you were young, reappear to steal your thunder.

-From the Shipwreck Journals

^^^^^^^^^^^^^^

Saturday at state. Finals and fear. Fiad sits by himself, listening to music the entire day. He talks to no one. He disappears into that place distance athletes know about. That quiet chamber of anticipated pain. Thirty minutes before the race, Fiad finds me in the stands and asks me if I have any food. I look at him in confusion. I prepared sandwiches and bought Power Bars for him. They were in a bag at his feet all day.

"Fiad, you race in thirty minutes. You can't eat now."

He looks at me, shuts off the desperation and goes down for his warm up. Chants of EAST SIDE...EAST SIDE... fill the stands on the west side of the stadium. Eastern Washington runners have dominated 4A distance running for years. (Fiad tells me later that their arrogance was pissing him off.) The west side, especially our league, features a stable of young studs who are ready to make a statement of their own.

I don't want to be near Erickson for the two mile as he will want to take lap times and I am too nervous to read a watch. Ticking through my head are the hours spent running Fiad around, buying shoes, trips to the doctor, the dentist, getting him out of bed, and out of trouble, fighting every step of the way, all for this, for a chance to watch a miracle.

The gun goes off and I sit down next to Matt Rowe, a college coach who ran for Erickson. Fiad gets right behind the West Side's top gun, Fuller, who tucks in behind Kiter, the state champion from Spokane Falls. Everyone knows the plan. Kiter will set a pace that will grind the field to pulp.

The pace is fast, faster than last week's district meet. I am thinking of the practice Fiad missed, that extra bit of lung power he could have taken from the mountain run. Fiad isn't thinking about that. He is trying to keep on the inside lane and grab on to Fuller's tail. The break comes early and four go with it. Fiad is in third. The pace is so fast that 30 meters separates 4th and 5th. The laps click off. Rowe is calm and gives me positive updates on the race Fiad is running. "Perfect!" he says, lap after agonizing lap.

Kiter moves out again and the pack of four chases after him. Fiad looks relaxed as he goes by on lap six, his breaking point of last week.

Matt asks in an excited voice, "How much did this kid train?"

"Not enough. Twenty miles a week, max. And that was just at the end of the season."

"Well I know the Spokane kids are doing eighty a week."

I explain to Matt how just four weeks ago I was in the team room with Fiad as he sat and sobbed, sick with the flu, sick of life, telling me he couldn't run anymore, that his ankle hurt too much, that he was ruining his ankle.

"Unbelievable!"

I can't talk anymore. My legs are bouncing in place. I keep mouthing, "C'mon, c'mon..." hoping that the Power Bar Fiad never touched doesn't suddenly empty his tank.

With 600 meters to go Kiter breaks again, with Fuller on his heels and the kid from Kelso trying to maintain contact. He and Fiad drop two lengths back, and then another two. I see it-- just a glance-- but I know the look. Fiad's tank just hit E and he has a lap and a half of Star Track left.

Fiad comes by us at the 500 mark. He is alone in 4th-- too alone-- no man's land. The kid from Kelso is running his guts out, keeping his eyes on Fuller's yellow Lincoln High's yellow jersey. Fiad is looking at the great empty... he is seeing Africa, and nothing, and Kent, and nothing. His legs are moving in wet cement. 5th place is fifty meters behind him and closing. These kids look ragged, fighting for air, clawing away with all they have to catch the only target they see: Fiad's black frame inside a racing jersey of blue and red.

Kiter and Fuller take off on the last 400 and a year's worth of mileage and intervals kicks in to trumpet the premiere moment of their lives. The stands below me are bouncing with black kids in yellow who are here to see their inner city hero fulfill his dream. Kiter pumps down the back 100 trying to bury Fuller's will. These are the best athletes in the state, side by side. They come out of the turn with Fuller moving to Kiter's right...and as he sweeps past, he turns his head slightly and looks straight at his fans with an eye that says, "Watch this white boy." He kicks into a gear that Kiter has never felt, sending his fans into a frenzy.

Fiad is running with the anchors pulling him down. With 300 to go he is passed by the 1st frantic runner. He is in 5th and the boy three places behind him, Dylan Bailey, the Kentwood kid who was down making himself puke on Tuesday while Fiad was off playing basketball, is fifty meters back. The boys round the turn and eyes are wide, faces pulled back in pain, arms flailing though they know not to break form. 'There is no tomorrow.' All the cliches are finally true: 'Great success is proceeded by great preparation.' Four boys hurl themselves at Fiad down the last 100 meters. They run from view in a mix of bodies. I see Fiad's jersey in the darkness. He is one step behind Dylan Bailey.

"Oh my GOD!! Not again!" My thoughts begin to spin out of control. Erickson runs up, his grin lifting his glasses off his face. He has Fiad at a 9:19! The greatest two mile ever run by a sophomore or junior at KM.

Erickson is looking at the bright side of everything as Fiad collapses on the infield, his hands over his eyes. He is sobbing. This time he knows his place. There will be no medal. Erickson lets me know that 9:19 would have placed Fiad 5th last year.

Ayanle finds us. Like me he is already looking at the other side of things. As soon as Erickson is out of ear shot he gets close and tells me, "God damn Fiad. No medal at state cuz of stupid basketball."

After the medal ceremony I find Fiad hanging with the other young talent from the west side. The two white kids are wide-eyed and ecstatic. Chris Lukezic, from Auburn, (who would later go on to be state champion and earn a full ride to Georgetown University) can't believe Fiad's race. He tells us: "Just wait til next year. Fiad, Dylan and me are going one, two, three!"

I look at Fiad, who looks at me and says: "I wanted that medal for my mom."

He walks off shoulder to shoulder with the jubilant boys for his moment in the spot-light. I alone know the story going through his head as he smiles and receives congratulations from teammates, coaches, media, and fans.

I walk alone up the stadium steps heading for the van and a shiver goes up my shoulder, the one that always signals a moment of truth. I turn and look at Fiad and the Lincoln Bowl Star Track.

"There will be no next year, Fiad. I hope you enjoyed this moment."

SHIRLEY KAIRU

TRUTH #11:

For every up there is a down. *For every kind, generous, giving, loving soul, capable of great healing, nurturing, warmth and love, there is a cruel, stingy, selfish, unfeeling, evil asshole, capable of brutality and the crushing of hearts and hope. It must be so. The laws of the universe are set and cannot change for something as trivial as human need and folly.*

*-From **The Book of Truths** by Langdon Towne*

∧∧∧∧∧∧∧∧∧∧∧∧∧∧∧∧∧∧∧∧∧∧

I like reading World War II history, which is why I don't like our new principal and the 'iron fisted' way he runs our teachers' meetings. He dictates in a strong controlled voice where our school is going and how it will get there. Then he pauses and asks us if there is anyone who doesn't agree. Of course, most of the teachers in the room disagree vehemently but our leader knows these are educated sheep not village idiots.

Knowing somebody better say something before our school is turned into a brave new correctional facility, I raise my hand and point out that I think the proposed fear-based policies go against everything I believe in as a parent, educator, and human being.

Despite the ensuing stare-down, I know I am doing the right thing. I know that to control with fear and punishment will destroy creativity and higher learning. I know that catering to testing rather than connecting with these kids will lead to drop outs and educational apathy. I also know that I just signed a black ball being rolled out the door.

A friend who used to work for huge corporations once told me that one of the ways to get rid of trouble makers was to give that trouble despicable, overwhelming tasks which cannot be completed, thereby proving the employee incompetent and unwilling to toe the company line.

Shortly after speaking up at the meeting, I am cordially invited by a smiling *Captain Queeg* to attend a meeting where he'd like to chat about ideas for next semester. Ever the optimist, I meet with Ann, a co-worker and come up with a proposal where she and I team teach English and social skills to the "at risk" population. I am so excited about her ideas I invite her along to participate.

Upon entering the war room, the door is shut behind us and we are asked point blank by a red faced *Queeg* what Ann is doing here. As he rubs his shiny head with his palms, he mumbles something about wanting to know why he wasn't included in the loop. I want to tell him it's because everyone is terrified of him, but decide to hold my tongue. Instead, I carefully explain my reasoning to the administrative team as Ann tucks away her three page proposal and shrinks into her seat. I'm presented a new deal that smells like paranoia. When I mention this fact, I'm told Portable-7 and my "Life Skills" program will not exist next semester. In crisp, tight, corporate speak, I am informed of the exact requirements of our leader's highly successful credit retrieval computer based program. The students are going to have to jump through enough hoops that they will eventually trip and be officially removed from the district's legal responsiblity.

Asked if I have any special requests, I work up enough courage to suggest that the new program be housed in the computer lab upstairs. Unlike the sweatbox mini-lab downstairs, it is spacious, next to the English department, and has many windows for ventilation and sanity. I am acknowledged for my astute thinking and released.

On the first day of the 2nd semester, I am sent to the downstairs sweatbox and told not to enable the "at risk" kids by listening to them. I am told to create an atmosphere that makes them dislike my class so they are encouraged to accumulate more than three absences, guaranteeing their termination as stated in the contract they signed. They will not be allowed to step foot outside the computer lab except for one bathroom break. At the end of their two and one half hour day I am ordered to escort them to the doors of the building.

During that first week the kids tell me they feel like in-mates. I tell them that is exactly what we are. They laugh. Now bonded, the kids keep coming back to sit with me in the stifling bin. They work hard on Nova-Net computer-based curriculum and write papers at home. I create data to ensure the kids putting up with this abuse will receive credit.

The nit picking emails that greet me each morning remind me of every error I am making in record keeping, following mandates, and preparing curriculum. When I bring this up to several of the old party who had driven out the previous, benevolent leadership, they laugh at my sniffling and say they appreciate the quiet halls and willingness of the new boss to toss out kids who mouth off.

Later on that year, our surprised staff learns that all written forms of communication regarding the school must be cleared through *Captain Queeg*. They also discover that *Captain Queeg* cannot be reached during the school day and all correspondence with the leadership is to be done via e-mail. Not exactly a personal touch. And for human oriented educators used to having a strong say in what they are doing, losing all control of said voice creates a bewildering Catch-22. Those with enough backbone to question or complain are shown where the door is. Soon the rule of the building is to talk about *Queeg* or any criticisms of building policy in hushed voices. Soon, faces drop and eyes become glazed in teachers who were coloring the school with hope the year before. Soon, teachers who spent countless hours in meetings, planning out the gardens that were to be purchased and cared for with promises of a brave new educational order, rationalize their frustrations by mentioning again how the halls are much quieter than last year.

The 4th quarter begins with me and eighteen kids shoved in the sweaty computer lab. We are under constant surveillance. A student reading a newspaper article related to a history lesson on the Nova-Net has the paper snatched out of his hand by one of *Captain Queeg's* hench-men. The sight makes me sick.

I have the kids read inspirational quotations to help both of us get through the day. I ask them to write papers in response, which we print and post on the walls outside our room. In the morning, many of the papers are missing from the wall. This keeps going on for the rest of the year. The kids write the truth and the building leadership takes it away

Shirley Kairu is a brilliant transfer student from Kenya who arrives mid-semester without official transcripts and gets stuck in my computer lab. She speaks five languages, was educated in the finest schools and doesn't belong in this box. Shirley grows weary of staring at the canned programs of Nova-Net. I suggest to her several books but we have to be careful that *Captain Queeg* doesn't see her reading a novel instead of staring at the computer screen.

Eventually, I get fed up with watching kids like Shirley lose their spark. I hand her books and quotes and have her write comments and essays on the computer. Shirley loves the quotes and writes volumes each day. Her writing is flawless, which doesn't surprise me. What does is the fact that this young female from Africa writes from a heart that matches my own, thought for thought, beat for beat.

Happiness comes more from loving than being loved... To love, and to be hurt often, and to love again- this is the brave and happy life.

-J.E. Buchrose

Loving comes from a very brave person who is willing to take the risk of opening up his feelings and exposing his heart at someone else's disposal. It is similar to trusting someone with your life because suffering from a broken heart is the closest thing that I have ever come to death. Allowing yourself to love is a great risk, but it is a risk worth taking. Love, is an emotion that many feel empty without, yet many refuse to open up and let love lead the way. They have all sorts of excuses for the emptiness. They do not realize that no amount of wealth can fill this emptiness. Love is the reason that we afford an inner smile, internal peace and happiness. The worst thing about love is that it comes with no guarantees. It brings a lot of pain with it at times. But the most brave are not those who love, but those who have experienced the pains and joys of loving, yet take that risk again.

-Shirley Kairu

JAKE BURLEY

TRUTH #138:

Becoming human is like walking on stage, being handed a violin, and told to play a little Vivaldi concerto. And that's the good news. The bad news is your audience happens to be a packed house of 8th graders who've been tossing down Super-Sized Cokes all afternoon and haven't gone pee since their morning shower.

*-From **The Book of Truths** by Langdon Towne*

^^^^^^^^^^^^^^^

[AUGUST 2001: THE CITY OF ROCKS]

"Hey, Johnson!" Jake Burley picked up a rock climbing camming device and squeezed the trigger over and over and over. I tried to ignore the incessant squeak.

"Hey, Johnson, why is this like the tightest thing ever? Watch." He pulled the trigger again. I bit my lip. "Hey, Johnz, how come your kids don't live with you?"

"Hmmm. That's a long story. Basically, they don't want to. They spent too many years getting used to their other house. Now they don't know what normal even looks like."

"Are you saying you're normal?" Alden Crag was reading *The Shipwreck Journals.*

"Uh huh. Exactly. Anyway…"

We pulled into the Ranger Station in Almo. Afternoon temperatures at the City were about 105. The region was having a record heat wave. To beat the heat, we headed for the Almo General Store every afternoon for beverages to sip in the shade of the massive willow trees out front of the Ranger Station.

We lay on the tables, stripped to shorts, writing, reading and napping until the sun began to dip and climbing was once again an option. As the boys read stories, I dumped my climbing rack on the table and organized it for the evening's round of classics.

I went into the Ranger Station to inquire if a certain Pat and Boyd still owned the restaurant/general store in NAF. Everyone in the building knew their name. Pat and Boyd had sold the store and retired, but still came out to NAF and their trailer home on the weekends. I wrote their phone number down and started thinking back to the night Eric and I took that wrong turn and wound up walking in for burgers. Boyd's reunion and the tale of Okinawa had been the defining moment of that road trip. It was that defining point where you walk through a door and realize you are not in control of your direction home. I walked out of the station with Boyd's number and sat down at my journal. Jake was lying on his back, sleeping with his eyes slightly open. It was one of the weirdest things I'd ever seen. He was staring right at me and drooling at the same time. Suddenly a black cat with a trail of green snot bubbling out of its nose jumped up on the table and started rubbing up against his side. Jake started to pet the cat. He rubbed on the spot right above its tail and then turned to me and said: "Hey, Johnson. If you pet cats right here, they get horny."

"Uh huh." I kept writing.

"Hey, Johnson?" Jake got up and started stretching out.

I turned to Alden, "I think 'Hey Johnson' is Jake's mantra."

"Hey, Johnson, what's a mantra?" Jake caught his reflection in the Ranger Station window and began flexing his biceps and making his pecs jump and twitch.

I told Jake it was a chant one emits over and over to gain the courage to arise each day with creaking joints and convince oneself that one's prostate isn't enlarging, that the mole on one's back isn't turning black and that the hole in one's heart isn't going to weld itself permanently open.

"Kinda like REDRUM, REDRUM, REDRUM, huh, Johns?"

"Sure, Jake. Only a little more fluffy than that."

I went on to explain how the use of positive mantras had helped me accept my single-parenting plight, how I'd learned to use despair to fuel my obsessions, how through all the muck and mire I'd never missed a Wednesday visit or one of my weekends with my kids, how though we were dirt poor, we were ghetto smart and knew how to stretch a quarter, how we went for lots of walks because walks are free. I told them that my mantra for helping the girls went: "Whatever it takes."

"Johnson, how did your kids ever turn out normal?"

I had to think about it. "Hmmm. Road trips and hanging out with climbers."

"Kind of like this?"

"No. Way more fun than this."

The air went silent. "You're just kidding, right, Johnson?"

Jake Burley-- *'I go to bed late and get up early'*-- had come a long way since his sophomore year when he earned the honor of being the most annoying kid on our state bound cross country team. At the state 4A XC championship, he was the converted hurdler who ate two pounds of deep fried onion rings and spent the eve of the race sprinting to the jon to dehydrate. Jake didn't sleep that night as he showed off his awesome speed and talents to any girl who might be wandering the hall after 3:00 am on the eve of the biggest race of their lives. The following day, a worn out Jake ran a steady three-mile race to save something for his .1 mile kick. When that kick finally happened he was in 151st place. He wound up passing the kid with the torn achilles for 150th.

His junior year was a different story. Despite not running on our awesome, African-dominated, cross country team, Jake got himself in shape and wound up the 4A state track champion in the 300 hurdles. To win, he had defeated his older brother Tyson, as well as six other seniors in the field.

Before that race, Jake, who called himself 'The White Panther: Yo, check it out... I'm a white kid with black speed" had only beaten Tyson in two races. That happened to be two more than anybody else in the state as Tyson was kicking some serious butt on his way to earning league and district titles. The two races (out of twenty) that Jake won, were classic products of hormonal imbalance. During the first victory, he was still flying high from the effects of dumping the prettiest girl in the school earlier in the day. The 'White Panther' ditched his brother at the 5th hurdle and would have popped over the stadium fence if the thing had been painted white. On the second victory, he was pissed off from having a rival beat him in the 110's. So incensed was Jake, that he out-leaned Tyson at the tape, a before unthinkable act, because Jake was not about beating his brother in the 300's. 2nd to Tyson at State was the plan. The Brothers Burley: One-Two.

The day of state, Jake was having a typically disturbed day. After running poorly in the 110 hurdle finals, his mood descended to theatrical absurdity as he sought out blame for his faltering performance. With the 300 hurdle finals slated for later, we all went off to lunch, and it was my job to try and light a fire under the sulking 'White Panther.' Tyson and I tried the usually effective ploy of creating an enemy with, "Hey Jake, that guy from Shadle Park said you were garbage!"

"Huh?"

"For reals. We were walking behind him and he was spouting off *big* time"

Jake didn't say anything, but about five minutes later he asked, "Hey, Johnson, what did he say?"

"Oh...just that you were nothing, and how he was just cruising in the prelims." (More silence.)

When we got back to the stadium, I figured my little pep talk had been the ticket to get Jake his medal. Fifteen minutes later, as I walked down the rapidly filling stands, I realized I was wrong. Jake's dad came roaring up to me, ringing his hands, and pulling his baseball cap off his head.

"Johnson, you better get down there. Jake's doing his thing....oh jeez, oh my."

I hopped down the steps to where 'The White Panther' was lying in the burning sun, moaning about his thigh. He had been complaining about dead leg all day, but that was normal. I took one look at him and said, "Jake, get up and get down to the infield and warm up."

I was still counting on the fabricated bit about the Shadle Park kid popping off being the spark to light Jake's fire, but my conscience began to squeak and then creak and then scratch like nails down a chalk-board which made me walk over to the Burley brothers and watch them warm up for the first time since the first practice of the season. I never watched them warm up because they didn't need me. Other than keeping Jake's head in check, they never needed me. Especially here. I sat down at the end of the bleachers trying to decide if I should open my mouth or just wait for things to fall. The noise in my head wouldn't stop so I hollered to Tyson, and told him to get Jake for me. He sprinted over to the slumping Panther, who then limped over to me, hobbling heavily on his very dead leg.

He finally made it to the fence where I stood searching for the right words. We were out of time. I looked at him, then took a breath.

"Jake, you run in about five minutes. I want you to get over there and do some build ups and ..." My voice changed tone, "....look at me. Jake. When this thing is over, I want you in this place."

As I said place, I held up one finger. "Number *one* Jake."

I almost couldn't believe I said it, but I did. And in that moment, I meant it. He was fast enough. He could beat anybody in the state; he just needed permission to beat his brother.

I turned to my right, like a swimmer taking a breath, and spotted a girl from a rival team that I knew Jake thought was pretty. I called her over and said, "Hey, Tahoma, tell Jake something to make him run fast."

Jake looked up at her walking over to us and the transformation in his manner was laughable. The surly, doubting, troubled track star had rearranged into a smiling, self-confident, suave young dude with a gleam in his eye. She said a couple of nothings, giggled a couple of times and then the two of us walked away as Jake sprinted back to his brother.

"Don't laugh," I told her, "but you probably just got Jake a Gold Medal."

The race was awesome. Jake warmed up behind his starting blocks by busting a C-walk as his name was announced. By contrast, his usually loose brother looked tense. The stadium was packed and the nervous energy emanating from the hundreds of premier athletes was thick enough to chew.

The gun went off and the boys blew out of the blocks with Jake gliding over the hurdles in brilliant form. By the third hurdle, I knew he had a top medal. Tyson came out of the turn after a slight stutter step, but set himself up perfectly for the gold, as he was dead even with Jake and two other athletes approaching the final 100 meters. No one had out-kicked Tyson all year. His Gold and Jake's Silver were in the bag. "ONE-TWO-ONE-TWO!" Tyson and Jake hand in hand on the podium!

With seventy meters to go, Jake was still in front of Tyson, and with fifty to go, there was just Jake! The rest of the horses were fighting for 2nd. Tyson pounded his way to 3rd as the younger Burley crossed the line in front of him, arms raised in triumphant disbelief. He had done it! He had WON STATE!!

I could see Jake soaring with each step, his eyes turning to the heavens, his hands reaching out and then coming down on to his head in utter amazement that he could be the one. Five steps of glory. Five seconds of joy. Five seconds to relish the fruit of dreaming and planning and pushing his entire being for this one chance to shine. And then he turned slightly to his right and his elated, victorious eyes caught the sight of his warrior brother, who he loved far more than hurdling, slumping over, grabbing his head, his face falling with crushing disappointment, his body crumbling under the weight of unthinkable defeat. Five seconds. Jake's face fell, his legs collapsed, and he went down on both knees. He buried his head in his hands that cried out to God: "How could I?!!"

The medal ceremony was a strange pose for the newly crowned champion who didn't smile on the podium and then avoided reporters as he walked straight to the end of the track and sat there. I sprinted through the stands and ran down the stairs and called him over. And that 6' 2" stud, walked up, buried his face on my shoulder and wept like the child he was at that moment.

"God, Johnson, I stole it from him. I stole it from him" was all Jake could leak out between gasps for breath.

I walked him up and out of the stadium, letting him wretch, bawl, and throw up, until enough of the pain had worked its way out to allow him to walk back in and answer the questions about how it felt to be a champion. Friends and media gathered around him as he squared up his shoulders, and a changed Jake, so different from the boy I'd taken to lunch, did what he had to do to get through his moment with dignity.

I continued past the crowd, head down, bee-lining for Tyson, who was still sitting, frozen in place, where his brother had left him. I ambled carefully down the steps, weighted with the words about to pour from my heart, knowing it was finally time to be what my parents had always said I could be.

And then I paused at the railing and watched the boy and waited for him to look up and allow me the chance to finally be his "coach."

Finale

It's A Wonderful Life

*"My life has been
Extraordinary
Blessed and Cursed at Once!"*

Muzzle- *The Smashing Pumpkins
From: "Sing alongs for a Shipwreck"*

The Tunnel

The adult experience is spent in little tunnels that you crawl into, thereby providing focus and purpose and quality to your life. Of course the obvious result from out here is that this same tunnel also blocks the view. Absorbed with the sounds your own heart-beat reverberating from the walls, you march on, certain your cause is a just cause. You grind away and finally arrive at the end of the tunnel and upon emerging the sense of disorientation is immense. You are not certain where you are. You are not certain what you have done. You are not certain that anything you did really mattered. For you see that you have missed a huge piece of life, while pre-occupied with self. And grief is immediate and swift. One must let go at this point...which is precisely what the tunnel prevented. The tunnel was happiness itself. The end of the tunnel is despair. The moral being that freedom is despair in the adult heart...for no direction is the fear of every sailor, climber, adventurer, seeker, pilgrim, father, mother, and son. Only the child can live with no direction and be content. And it is this child-like state that one must return to in order to preserve our true self.

*-From **The Shipwreck** Journals*

THE PEARLY GATES

TRUTH #23

Fear prevents miracles. Please remember that if you are terrified to buy a house, simply go out and buy two houses. Now buying one house will seem easy.

-*From The **Book of Truths** by Langdon Towne*

∧∧∧∧∧∧∧∧∧∧∧∧∧∧∧

[August 2001: Inspiration High Camp, North Cascades]

"Dude, you awake?" The tent was completely black. I could hear a voice coming out of the hole. It was Langdon's voice, ready to rattle at dark thirty AM. "Listen, I just thought of how your movie should start. You awake?"

I tried to talk. "Hmmm… What movie? Can't this wait?"

"No, it can't wait."

"Jesus, Towne. The sun will come up tomorrow...or so I have read."

"This will only take a minute. You know if I don't say it, I'll lose it. It'll be gone. I need to tell you so you'll remember it in the morning."

"Yeah. So you can sleep and I can lie awake all night."

"Exactly... So, here it is. Are you ready?" Deep silence filled the tent. Finally, Langdon exhaled. "OK….It's simple. I mean we talk and dream about women, about these trivial hurts and petty fucking disasters. But, in the end there's only one thing that really matters."

(Silence) I was awake now. "That's it? That's how the movie starts?"

"No... here it is. You and me lying in a tent... all you can see is your eyes. And after a long silence I ask you the question every human being needs to answer when he gets to those *Pearly Gates.*"

Towne took in a breath and let it out slowly: *"Did you live your life?* And that's it. The next scene is the start of a road trip."

There's a game we used to play as kids where we'd take a deck of cards and make buildings out of them. All it took was a breath to knock the structure down. And even knowing that we'd always lose our creation to a wayward sigh or elbow, we'd build and build...absolutely content in the process.

"Well...what do you think?"

I lay waiting for the last card to fall. When it finally touched down, I picked it up and turned it over. My eyes blinked while fumbling through all the reasons, whys, should haves, and what if's. Finally, in a voice barely audible to my heart, I answered: "No... I was frozen when my kids were little and needed me and now they're grown and I'm ready to love them and they're gone. I have to try and somehow....(I gulped for air in the silence) No...."

Whereupon, Langdon began to chuckle.

"OK... Thanks, Towne. I'm glad you asked. Jesus..."

"No, no... I got it." (more laughter) "And, and ... you got it. Dude, you aren't done. In fact you're just getting started."

He put his hand over his mouth and took in a deep breath, then let out a large sigh. "Listen, you're right. You've been afraid your whole life. Afraid to go out there and be what you swore you would be. Afraid to turn over the controls and deal with what greatness brings: pain and doubt and betrayal and confusion and questioning. There is nothing easy about going after your dreams. Better to stay under the clouds where you won't get burned by the sun. And now your kids are grown and you're ready to live and love and laugh and go for the glory and you know your life is way past half over. And it sucks to think you wasted so much time. So you lay there wondering if it's worth it. And only you know the answer to that one."

"Thanks... I feel so much better now." I shook my head knowing sleep would not be an option tonight. Towne was right, of course. I knew I'd walked a million lonely miles to get to this ridge, and when I looked over the other side, I saw that I was only half way home. And I knew there was no going back, but how was I supposed to drum up the strength to go forward?

I took in another deep breath trying to clear my lungs of the smoke and ashes of the bridges I'd burned. I turned and stared in the darkness at the smiling face of Langdon Towne.

"So, what are you going to say, Towne... if you ever get up to those Pearly Gates?"

"I've thought about it a lot actually... played the whole thing out in my head a thousand times."

"And?"

"And I know exactly what I'm going to say. Something like: 'Where to now, St. Peter, if it's true I'm in your hands? I may not be a Christian, but I've done all one man can."

"I hope your God is an *Elton John* fan."

"Yeah. He is. But, just the old school stuff."

"Thank you, Jesus."

"So... I get on my knees and say to this holy, bearded figure in white: 'St. Peter, here's the truth! I've loved and learned and triumphed and failed and been on my knees a thousand times! I've searched the deserts, the mountains, and the valleys of my heart for answers. And life has never made any sense. So please! Tell me now! Was it supposed to be that fucked up?'"

I rolled my eyes and muttered: "Great... we'll be lucky if we're not struck dead by lightning tonight."

"No, no, no. And here's the best part. St. Peter looks at me with these fatherly eyes and gets this big grin. Then, in a voice that you only get to hear once, says:

"Blessed are you, my son. For thou hath truly lived! Enter the Pearly Gates! Enter and rejoice! Behold the gathering place of true believers!

I DIE WITH YOU MY BROTHER

"But as we embark on a new century of adventuring in the East, it is the image of the Sherpa as corrupt mercenary--Bhuddism chucked aside, loyalty to Sherpa culture just deep enough to guarantee a sizable tip from the client."

- ROCK AND ICE: APRIL 2000.

"By the time Jon Krakauer described the terrible events of 1996 in 'Into Thin Air,' the process seemed complete. Plenty of readers saw Lopsang Jangbu, Scott Fischer's sirdar on his ill-fated expedition, as an example of how the gentle people of the Khumbu had become ambitious and westernized. Lopsang seemed to want material success and fame, not a peaceful life in the mountains."

- ROCK AND ICE: JUNE 99

"The Sherpas represent more than a third (about 60) of the mountain's victims."

-ROCK AND ICE: JUNE 99

[FEBRUARY 2000: JOSHUA TREE NATIONAL PARK]

February vacation at Joshua-Tree National Park. I'm with Kate and Krissy, reading a stack of climbing magazines in our tent as we wait out a rainstorm. I read an article about what it takes to be a mountain guide and am struck with the thought, " My god, I used to do this. This was me." Then I open up another rag and they're talking about Sherpas and they happen to mention Lopsang Jangbu as an example of the corruption of the Sherpa. 'Oh my god! It won't go away.'

For the most part I've blocked out the years '93-97. They were spent busting my ass to make a nickel, risking everything I had to make sure a client got his summit. They were lost in the haze of poverty, exhaustion and an on again/off again addiction to my ex-wife. I've tried to let go of Lopsang and those years of climbing and falling. I run around distracting myself in any way I can. Sex (or actually thoughts of sex) climbing, rock music, getting busy, helping others, feeling important about my work. Nothing works. For all I have to do is open a climbing magazine or overhear a conversation at some climbing area where the word 'Sherpa' comes up and behold, everyone has an opinion on what happened on May 10th, 1996.

I also had an opinion. I wanted to send out the truth about Lopsang shortly after his death, but there was so much hoopla going on that I wanted no part of that circus. I continued to write rebuttals to the criticisms of him, but wound up keeping them to myself in fear that I would come off as a Gold-digger. As the losses mounted, I lost my fight. I lost my confidence. Without Scott Fischer, Rob Hall, or Lospang around, who would have believed me anyway? I tucked the file away and went climbing.

Backpacker Magazine called me that year. They wanted me to do a piece about what makes the Sherpa so strong. I couldn't write it. How do you explain to readers how a kid who'd been beaten his whole life, found the strength to summit Everest on his first attempt, ferrying loads and climbing in gear that none of us would consider adequate for hiking up our local crag? Backpacker wanted diet tips, packing tips and training habits. Right. I told the editor that Lopsang trained by going dancing all night. He had a frameless pack made by an obscure company in Norway that he liked because it was bright yellow and fit all his gear. He ate whatever he could. He had no insurance, no benefits, no help from anyone. He was alone with his desire to be the best, and he died with the world thinking he was something else.

∧∧∧∧∧∧∧∧∧∧∧∧∧∧∧∧∧∧∧∧∧∧∧∧

I'd never gotten used to the surreal phone calls in the middle of the night from Lopsang's widow in Kathmandu. His son needed money for school. She needed money to survive. 'Namaste. Could I help them please?'

I would ask her if she'd tried one of the wealthy expedition leaders who Lopsang had worked for. She'd tell me they did not return her calls. She had no one else to turn to. There would be a huge pause... then 'hellos,' with echo delay... with my head pounding, and my heart breaking. How could I explain to Choki, who didn't understand English, that I was just two steps from the gutter myself? And how could I explain to myself that I was choosing to turn my back on Lopsang's family? So I'd tell her she could come stay with me in America. And then what?

After four years I thought I had put this one to rest. Of course, I know better: that which we do not confront comes back over and over to remind us of our vulnerabilities and weaknesses.

Now, I know that to look in the mirror I have to clear Lopsang's name.

So when I get home from the trip, I open the file again:

After the May 10th Everest tragedy, I began to learn the truth about Himalayan Climbing Expeditions. As far as I could ascertain, climbing Everest the guided way was all about bottled oxygen, elitism, racism, selfishness, and a willingness to let 'little brown men' take the risks, do the work, lead the way, and take the heat when things went wrong and people died. With the advent of the $65 Grand club, Mt. Everest was suddenly one more thing for the 'upper class' to stand on.

"Hey, step right up, drop your $65,000 bullet in the chamber, and pull that trigger. Feeling lucky? Well, why not? All you gotta do is "scuba dive" up behind the Sherpas, let them do every last thing possible for ya, and with a bit of luck there'll only be a couple deaths."

"What?"

"Oh, don't worry. It won't be you. Are you kidding? The Sherpa will be out front catching the heat. You'll be cruising behind, looking out for #1. It's the Gilded Highway! Carry nothing, drink the tea the Sherpa bring ya, slap on that mask, screw up your tank, and follow those fixed lines to the top of the world. You can do that, eh?"

Living in our insulated western world, it used to be easy to ignore the staggering number of Sherpa killed on Himalayan climbing expeditions; buried beneath ice falls, avalanches, or littered on the flanks of Everest. I used to read the Himalayan stories and see a printed line saying, "...and four Sherpa died when a block of ice collapsed as they were preparing to fix rope....." and as if driving by a fatal traffic accident, my head would look for a second and then flip to the next line. But, now those crushed vehicles have become recognizable. The body lying in the shattered glass is someone I loved and the accident represents a river of sorrow.

My friend Lopsang Jangbu was slandered, tainted, and portrayed erroneously by an author who did not know him. In a typical Western tabloid style, the printed word erradicated a lifetime of heroic achivement, reducing his love for life to a stereotype that is no more than a reflection of the greedy soul of western man. The depths of Outside magazine's error, the basity of the allegations, and the pain of the inevitable consequences of those allegations-- which certainly led to Lopsang's death-- leave me quaking in awe at the insanity of western conceipt and arrogance.

Lopsang spoke eight languages in an attempt to be able to communicate with the flood of trekkers and climbers coming into his village. To escape working as a cook and laborer in his village hotel, he, like many young Sherpa, strived to make a living carrying loads and fixing camps for expeditions. Lopsang came from a family where eight out of nine uncles had reached the summit of Everest. Only his father had never topped out, having been to 8,800 meters before turning back to rescue a sick team member.

Pride, loyalty, honor, and a competitive spirit were what fueled Lopsang's quest to set a record for ascents of Everest without the aid of oxygen. Not greed. By twenty three he already had four summits under his belt, with plans to make the top three times a year for three more years, thereby setting a new record...

I file the unfinished piece knowing I will complete it and send it to off later.

(Please forgive me Lopsang for taking so long to publish this. I have never forgotten you or your light. Namaste.)

JEANNIE PROBOLA

There is no estimating the wit and wisdom concealed and latent in our fellow mortals until made manifest by profound experiences; for it is through suffering that dogs as well as saints are developed and made perfect.

- JOHN MUIR

The first time I laid eyes on Jeannie Probola I fell in love with her. She walked in to HMR and promptly erupted a thunder clap in that extra-special place solely reserved for wonder and Kleenex. I tried not to babble as I told her where to find the cans of white gas fuel for her backpacking stove. My young Mormon friend, Dear David, looked at me with an all-knowing smile. I tried to wipe the boyish grin off my stupid face. I couldn't.

Five years later I got a call from Jeannie one late summer day. She was wrapping up her latest climbing road trip. She had invited me to go with her, but I declined. A little of Jeannie I could handle. But all of Jeannie for two months straight? Alone? Every night? So, she asked a young buck to join her quest for the perfect hand jam crack. Now, on this summer's eve, her voice sounded relaxed. In a non-chalant, 'hey and by the way'manner, she began to tell me how she'd just had her lower leg cut off by a large boulder which her young climbing friend had accidentally dislodged, how she had managed to save her own life by holding down the pressure point on her pelvis thereby preventing bleeding to death in mere minutes, how doctors and help arrived to move the rock and whip her off to Salt Lake City, how she had made the decision-- despite the doctors advice to the contrary-- to save her foot, have it surgically reattached, and then the eight inches of bone that was currently missing between her knee and ankle re-grown in one of those metal cages that looks like something out of a John Carpenter movie. I kept swallowing as she rambled on as if she was talking about a blob of ice cream that had fallen off its cone and landed on her favorite climbing shorts.

Weeks later she arrived at Harbor View Hospital in Seattle. Her pretty little eyes of blue lay sunken in dark circles of pain and morphine. Her body was being used as a grafting tree from which pieces of skin, tissue, tendon, and muscle were being removed to create a new lower leg. She began to cry and asked me, "Why?" She wanted to know what she had done to deserve this. There was nothing to explain it. There was nothing to say. Jeannie was the kindest, sweetest, most generous person I knew. She was a dream, a wonder. She was perfection. Not anymore.

I tried to make her laugh, tried to look on the bright side. I asked her how long until she could walk again. The doctor had told her two years to never. He said there was an outstanding chance that the bone would not attach, that something would go wrong, and that she would go through this pain for nothing. A prosthetic was the only sensible choice. Hack off the leg, sew it up

298

and slap a modern miracle on where flesh used to be. She wasn't buying it. She'd take her chances. All I could think was, "God, god, god, what a cruel f...ing world."

Jeannie's situation taught me something about myself. I am a shitty friend. Oh, I'm great when things are going well. But get your leg chopped off or catch a cold, and see if I come to see you. I found it harder and harder to visit her as every time I walked into the hospital my little bubble promptly burst, leaving me gasping in the stench of iodine, bloody bandages, and approaching decay. I couldn't handle the reality of Harborview. People don't get admitted for cosmetic mole removal. The rooms are occupied by gunshots, car wrecks, plane crash victims, sleeping pill overdoses, and missing body parts of one form or another. Despite the gorgeous nurses, the halls and rooms were a romp of ghouls on parade. I thought of spending a day at Harborview, riding the elevator with a cam-corder and filming whoever was waiting as the door opened. No acting or make-up would have been necessary. It would have been 'le misery' at it's most sorrowful best. With just the right music, the short would have been worthy of a nod from David Lynch. Fortunately, I didn't own a cam-corder.

[FEBRUARY 2002: JOSHUA TREE]

Jeannie is leading a 10C gear route at Joshua Tree, with me shivering in fear as the sunset erupts in purples and pinks. She is making moves up there that will surely reinjure my sore shoulder when I have to second the climb. She yells belay off and whips up the rope and then me. I grunt and cuss my way through one tough ass move after another. I keep screaming through clenched teeth, "Oh my God- Jeannie- oh my God!"

The next day, as we are walking to another classic crack she mentions with an off-hand shrug that she climbed Mt. Olympus in a day the previous summer. I do one of those- clean your ears out- come agains. She says in a voice that sounds like she's asking you to pass the dental floss. "Oh yeah, it wasn't bad. We left the car at midnight and were back in just under 24 hours."

I mutter obscenities to divinity.

Mt. Olympus, the crowning jewel of Washington State's Olympic Range, features an eighteen mile approach hike before you reach the mountain proper. It has to be another five miles or so to the top, plus you start at sea-level and finish at nearly 9,000 feet. In a day? On a foot that doesn't bend normally? On a leg that was fabricated from parts of her ass, back, and shoulder muscles? I turn to stare at this miracle next to me and realize my sore shoulder doesn't hurt anymore.

I was with Jeannie the day she started climbing again. We went over to the Feathers at Vantage and climbed routes up to 5.10. She still had her metal bone-stretching cage on her leg and I'm sure the doctor would have ordered himself a bypass if he'd seen what the two of us were up to. The cage had about twenty pins that were buried in the flesh of her shin and calf. They were there to keep the bone growing where it was supposed to. The flesh on her leg was constantly tearing as the bone grew like a tree branch in the spring. She managed to only bang her cage on the rock a couple of times.

In the tough guy business of climbing and coaching, you hear all the stories. You see guys and gals who rate tough. You listen to tales of practices from hell, games from the edge, boot-camp marches, sticking a landing with a broken ankle, mountain ridges of doom and suffering, all night vigils of rescue and heroism: all tough, all measures of character and grit. And then there's Jeannie.

So, how do you measure tough? Tough is that little blonde girl I wheeled down a side-walk in her wheel chair four months into her recovery. Her hands trembled the whole time, as the terror of her leg possibly shattering by a wayward jar gave her anxiety attacks. She had already insisted on taking herself off morphine and was dealing with the pain of missing those eight inches of bone, as well as the hazy relief that the drug had provided. Nevertheless, she made me take her to the playground and wheel her under a bar. And I helped pick her bony little body up so she could hang from it. She tried with everything she had to lift herself just a few inches towards the sky. And she couldn't do it. You should have seen her face. The fear, the blank slap of reality pasting her cheeks white. She slumped down, shaking her head in disbelief at how bad it really was. And then she made me lift her again. And I was crying inside for all she'd lost- seemingly forever. And she grabbed that bar again, as if it was her last act on earth. And she pulled with a grimace on her face that only a true champion could ever know. And she moved… not much, but goddammit she moved… and I shook for her as those tiny arms trembled in effort. There was no finish line visible on any horizon. There was no summit out there with a sign of hope. It was just Jeannie and pain and a belief inside that if she didn't quit.

I rarely went to see her after that day. It was too '*hard*' for me. It's funny how fast time goes by when you run off distracting and playing and pretending you're important. But how slow does time creep when waiting in bed for a tree limb to grow and produce those first few buds of spring?

It only seemed like weeks had gone by when Jeannie called to invite me to her CAST-OFF party. She had done it! She had grown a new leg-bone and the cage was coming off. I asked her how long it had been. The forgiving tone of her answer told me only she could ever know the true measure of those seconds.

I know tough. Her name is Jeannie Probola.

THE ORPHAN

TRUTH #16

Men cannot fill the hole of emptiness with the connection of the umbilical **cord.** *Men lose their connections. Men cannot produce life. Men cannot produce milk. Men cannot mother. Men get to be Lone Rangers, Lone Rangers who wish they had a boob in their mouth. And because they don't have the breast, and have no way to fill that want for the breast, they must turn to a God for sustenance, a God who will let them down and abandon them in their moment of need. Please know it cannot be helped. Just remember, the road to manliness runs through a valley of tears.*

-From the **Book of Truths** *by Langdon Towne*

∧∧∧∧∧∧∧∧∧∧∧∧∧

[May 2001: East Hill Apartments, Kent]

Asiki read aloud the words of *Truth # 16*, then put *The Book* down on my kitchen counter. "Man, what the hell is this fool talking about?"

I stirred away at spaghetti noodles as they boiled in the pan. "He's using breasts as a metaphor... for unfulfilled want and need; you know, a boob in your mouth makes you feel whole."

Asiki stood in my kitchen, black as a tire, a war child-refugee from Sudan, looking at me with eyes I understood, the moist, red eyes of despair. He wasn't impressed so far with *The Book of Truths.*

I watched his powerful frame slump against the wall covered with pictures of my kids and felt the emptiness sweep towards me like a wave of cold air. His eyes began to water up and I knew the taste of those tears, knew without a doubt that he too was my child.

"You feel alone, huh?"

He nodded as he wept.

"Orphans, man." I said softly. "We're all a bunch of orphans."

He broke down and sobbed. He cried for all the frustations and fears that had piled on his solid shoulders since the day he walked out of an African refugee camp and wound up in an apartment in Kent. In war torn southern Sudan, he had learned to fight, learned to drop at the sound of machine gun fire, learned to duck, but not flinch, learned to sleep despite the nightmares of seeing death, learned to hate those who had committed these acts, learned the emptiness of a belly that cried for nourishment, learned the patience of waiting to capture doves to fend off starvation, learned how to suffer.

Asiki went in to the living room, grabbed a microphone and began to flow. I drained the spaghetti, then went over to my guitar, turned on the drum machine and started playing "*I Wait For You*" to the beat. Dinner could wait.

He spit prose of his days as a young boy in Africa, of living in camps, of disease and starvation taking its daily toll, of his sister getting captured and tortured by soldiers, of her losing the child she was carrying in the process, of stepping out of a house one morning with the guts and brains of dead soldiers blown all over the bullet ridden walls, of packing an AK-47 to soccer practice, of knowing how to use a gun as a child, of needing to know how to kill, of fighting everyday to stay alive. And now he was fighting in Kent. Fighting with his sister, fighting with his teammates, fighting with his God. He was frightened of his future, frightened that he would just curl up and not move anymore, that he would give up and become useless.

Earlier in the day, Asiki had confessed that he was running slow because he hadn't eaten all week. He couldn't take the chaos anymore. I told him to come over after practice; that he could stay as long as he needed, that I had an extra room as my kids were only here on Wednesdays and every other weekend, that he could eat, and study, and listen to music. He would be safe. He could rest. He could heal.

We stopped playing the song, sat down and stared at the floor. "I'm lost, man. I'm fuckin' lost."

"We're all lost, Asiki. I don't feel connected to anyone. I see more of you and Ayanle than my own kids. I'm alone when I go to bed and even more alone when I wake up. I fill my days to the breaking point. Weeks are a blur that turn into months. I just give all I've got til there's nothing left....then I give some more. It's what we have to do, Asiki. We're here to help others. But, it doesn't cure the loneliness. Nothing cures that."

"Except death, man. Sometimes, I think dark thoughts. Like giving up."

"I know, I know. You have to feel that... but then you get up again."

"Like who would give a fuck if I live or die?"

"Well… you know the answer to that. You can't give up. Not you, Asiki. This world needs your light. You can never give up."

"Yeah. Better an orphan than dead." Asiki got up, put on a beat and started flowing with a rage that pummeled the room like fists on a punching bag.

Asiki knew what death looked like, had seen his first fresh corpse at age five. I had seen my first live-death the previous fall. It had been enough to change me. The sight of that first dead face was a revelation, a turning point, a pivotal moment of truth. In fact, it was so powerful that I didn't figure it out until two years later when after wandering, grieving and climbing through a record heat wave at *The City of Rocks*, I found myself running up a mountain ridge with the sky going black under the weight of one of those classic ten-miles-high thunder heads. And as lightning pounded the hillside and thunder kicked at my chest I was suddenly overwhelmed with calm. I no longer feared death. I no longer feared life. I raised my arms up at God and began screaming "AHHHH!!!!!!!!!" And as the power filled my being, I finally understood the meaning of Zen:

"Be thou, now, a rock, against which the waves of life rush in vain!"

302

IF YOU LOVE SOMEONE...

*In one's lifetime, if one is willing to take the risk, one may achieve a profound affinity with another human being. When it happens, it will feel as if the other person's soul is wrapped inside yours. You will be able to feel and hear their heart as you would your own. It is awesome and terrifying. Your power to hurt or heal this human being will become evident as words tossed from your mouth are absorbed like a kiss or a punch, and weather created by your actions sets the temperature of the air. And here's the kicker: of all the things in life that you **cannot** control, you **can** control your mouth and actions.*

*-From the **Book of Truths** by Langdon Towne*

∧∧∧∧∧∧∧∧∧∧∧

[August 2001: Inspiration High Camp]

Langdon picked up his *Wild Things* pack and turned it upsidedown, dumping out the contents in search of another package of GU.

"I love the way you organize," I said with a chuckle.

"It's great isn't it? A product of perfectionist parents. I can't even match my own socks." We both laughed. I looked down and noticed he wasn't kidding.

"So, what are you going to do about Lyla, I mean Angelina Armoni?"

Towne took in a breath as a smile formed on the corners of his mouth.

"Hmmm. Maybe I'll call her Margo."

"Jesus, make up your mind. Well, are you going to talk to her again?"

"Nope. I can't. I have to let her figure it out. I have to suck it up and do the only thing left to do, something I read on a Hallmark Card about thirty years ago."

"What's that?"

"If you love someone set them free, and if they come back to you..."

"*...set them free.* Whoa! That's pretty cliché coming from you."

"Like anything to do with love isn't cliché?"

Langdon sat down on a rock, scratching his head and pulling out his hair to let it blow away in the light, warm breeze. He started to laugh.

"Ya know the truth, don't you?"

"What's that?"

"That card should have read: ...And if they come back to you, write a fucking book about it because you are one rare and very lucky SOB."

We both laughed at the merit of this truth.

"So Towne. What keeps you awake at night? What haunts you the most?"

"You mean besides the obvious big hitters: losing a child, war, disease and the entire death process?"

"Yeah. While you're still able and vibrant."

He took a long breath and let it lift his shoulders. "Probably sitting alone in your mess and hearing a beautiful song on the radio and realizing that you could have done that. That if you hadn't been chasing your own tail and beating your fists into your own head, you could have poured your energy into something immortal: a book, a song, a piece of work that could have touched every human out there."

"But, you have written stuff. You have recorded songs."

"Oh, my God! Do you see the masses flipping through the pages of my soul? I've done so little with my talent!"

"You sound like nothing is good enough."

"Good enough is waking with purpose and using all you have with all you've got. I haven't done that. I've sat in my shit, stupefied by love's amputations. Once you lose at love, nothing can fill the need to be recognized. That is the truth."

"But there will be other chances."

"I don't believe that. It's like saying there are other planets we can head to after we destroy this one. It's a bunch of crap!" Towne picked up a rock and hucked it at a tree, missing by a foot.

"I don't mean to be the devil's advocate here, but I just read where they've proven that there isn't any one individual who is *the one*, that there are many women out there that we could be compatible with and fall in love with."

"What the...?! Who are *they*? What genius came up with that formula? The greatest minds have been trying to understand the power of love since man could record thought and some cat writing a doctoral thesis decides there is a theorem for love? Jesus, that's like reading one of those step by step sex manuals to make love. Talk about manipulation!"

"Well, the article talked about how chemicals are released when you see a certain type of female and..."

"Fuck that! Of course there are chemicals. But then they open their mouth. Or pick at their hair weird. Or introduce you to their mother. Chemicals! I know the truth! I've been truly comfortable around one person. One! She was my garden, my Mozart: able to make sense of the notes playing in my head. I could rest around her, could breathe all the way down into my toes, could hear the truth pouring forth as clear as the water flowing over white granite in a mountain stream. I felt purified. She was religion. She was from God."

"You're talking about Angelina, right?"

"Yeah."

"Ya know, I still think it's lame you won't tell me her real name."

"You wouldn't think it lame if her husband showed up after reading your book and cut my balls off."

"But I'm not writing a book."

"But you might. Ya know what I'm sayin?"

I did.

THE EMBRACE

TRUTH #20

Faith is a belief in a turning point. And that turning point is hope. Just remember you must find the bottom to know which way is up.

*-From **The Book of Truths** by Langdon Towne*

^^^^^^^^^^^^^^^^

My oldest daughter, Kate, was deeply in love and had waited five months to see the lad, who had moved with his family to Alaska, turning their romance intensely long-distance. Now he was here, waiting in Kent, to catch a bus that would take him across Washington State.

Having been in love with Ann for a year, I knew full well the length of seconds, minutes, hours, days, and months. I had seen time stop as I waited in a parking lot for Ann to show up; had seen hours become minutes as she and I walked and talked and caught up on life. Kate had endured the five months, but it was those last seven hours that had her losing her mind. His bus would leave Seattle at five and not arrive in Walla Walla until midnight. She did not know how she would keep from coming unscrewed.

Their meeting day turned out to be the day after I had my encounter with Ann's husband and I was bleeding from every pore. I kept waiting for a phone call from her, telling me that he had kicked her out and she was moving in with us. I had no idea what might be coming next. I sat still trying to bring something out of the murk and I thought of my kid, and her plight, and how brutal that wait was going to be. Suddenly, another thought came in. Why couldn't I run her boyfriend to her? The drive was only four and half-hours. If we left early enough, I could have him there as soon as she got home from work.

I told my idea to Krissy and we called Travis and asked him to come over. I ran my idea by him with the suggestion that maybe he could refund his bus ticket.

"I haven't gotten around to getting the bus ticket, yet."

"Then, do you want me to take you down?"

He thought the idea was brilliant, but he'd also made commitments to his grandfather. I suggested that we run our plan of action by granddad and see if his heart still carried memories of the importance of love. Grandfather, of course, agreed to cut the visit short a couple of hours. Departure time was set for 1:30 sharp. At 1:00 the phone rang. It was Ann. She was sobbing and spoke in a tiny, frightened voice. She was calling to tell me she could never see me again; that her husband had come apart and that she had to try and save the marriage at any cost. She wanted to meet me tomorrow to say goodbye forever.

I said all the right things to her and hung up the phone like a gong, knowing full well that any chance of love for me was over. I looked up, swallowed, and Travis pulled up for his ride to bountiful.

He and I blew out of Kent and in a blinding three and a half-hours were screeching up the road to Kate's farm with:"Today is the Greatest," on ten. Travis, white as a sheet, hovered next to me in the sweet sickness of acute anticipation.

I parked the car where we couldn't be seen and ran behind some bushes allowing Travis to walk up out of the blue. He knocked on the front door, but she wasn't in the house. We walked to her shed. She wasn't there either. We walked the length of the farm grounds to the tent she stayed in by a river. We were both shaking.

And there, walking slowly through the woods, I caught a glimpse of my beautiful child, dressed in her prettiest skirt and loveliest necklace, her hair brushed and a cord-less phone in her hand. (We had told her Travis would call at 5:30 and to be there to get his call). Her face was purity, and innocence. Her head was tilted in a melancholy stare, as one does when waiting in faith for love to come, knowing full well that fate might have other plans, that nothing can be taken for granted, that hope is hard to hold on to when it is standing before us, everything else stripped away.

Travis walked up, bathed in the evening light as Kate lifted her head and glanced in his direction. Her face went blank. She could not comprehend what she was seeing. Her hands fell to her side, the phone landing in the grass. Travis walked the last few steps and gently embraced my daughter. Kate's arms came up around his neck and their heads leaned into each other.

All the poems, sonnets, and prose ever written could not do justice to the beauty of that moment. As I kneeled to the ground, I saw the image of life and love in all their glory. I couldn't escape the irony of my presence here, me embodying the darkness of love lost, my heart breaking apart as my child filled hers to bursting with joy unbounded. I wept, overwhelmed by the miracle before me.

After several speechless minutes, I hugged her, wished her happy birthday, decided I wasn't needed here, and began the four and a half hour drive back home. As I left Walla Walla, with the Smashing Pumpkin's "Muzzle" roaring on my tape deck, the sky toward the west filled with smoke and I ended up driving through a raging brush fire.

"Where are the fire trucks?" I no more than got the words out when truck after truck came roaring up.

"I'll bet they shut this highway down."

The highway behind me was shut down for the rest of the night. Travis would have never made it to Walla Walla that evening and Kate would have waited in vain at the bus stop as seconds became hours and hours became days and her heart became more brittle with every single beat.

THE SOUL MATE

Alone with your thoughts, you sift back through the rings of your life, as exposed and raw as freshly cut tree trunks in a forest. All the events that ever happened to you are there, waiting to be processed. But, to analyze one, you must analyze all. So you keep chopping away, choking on the splinters and dust as you ruin the beauty of the woods. Soon you want to stop. You want to go home. You want to put the trees back up like they were before, make things right again and walk away. But that won't be happening. There is no home anymore. You are lost in that forest of fallen trees. The rings are everywhere and you must process them one by one until you unmask the lies of decades, centuries, and millenniums; back to the exodus, and the crusades, and the plague, and all the wars that were waged in the name of God, and love, and greed.

And you understand all this, but no one understands you. Even your mother cannot understand you, just as you will never understand your own children, even though you will think you do, just as your mother thinks she understands you...and so it goes, same as it ever was and always will be until the day you finally find a friend to laugh with, a friend who can lead you out of the forest and let you see your life from the ridiculous perspective that it is, was, and always will be.

*-From **The Shipwreck** Journals*

^^^^^^^^^^^^^^^^^^^^^

KENT, WA: August 2001

It's a beautiful day and I don't have enough guts left to pick up the phone and call Tim about a belay. I'm frozen in fear and have no clue what to do.

That is not true. I know what to do. I need to go climbing. It is all I know when there is nothing left. It's taught me how to put one foot forward when your heart, will, and spirit have given up; that you can self-generate, that you can go up no matter what love has done to your heart, that you can turn on the light from within, that by risking, you live, that everything else is a waiting room for death.

I glance at a Latok 33 carabiner sitting next to my toothbrush and think of all the times I've felt like shit on climbs. And there were a lot. Then I think of what love hath wrought. How many hours, days and months have I wept in agony over lost love? It's like comparing a stroll to the grocery store with a march across the arctic.

My feet are going numb so I get up and stare out the window at the upper half of Mt. Rainier. A few months ago, I could see the whole mountain. Now a row of "affordable" vacant condos block most of the view. Down in the parking lot I see a tenant I've never met, opening the door of his car from his wheelchair. I watch as he spends nearly five minutes getting himself into the car. Thank you, God for small favors and blessings. Thus awakened, I take a minute to write a final letter to Ann:

Dear Ann

Please know that if this were my last day on earth, I would want to talk to you, and see you, and tell you some things: My whole life I have struggled up and down a long twisted road to my heart. Because of this path, my heart is true and knows real beauty, goodness, and love. I doubt many things, but I do not doubt the sincerity of my heart. I doubt the intentions of most people, but I do not doubt you. I found you innocent and kind, and honest with me. When I told you I loved you, I meant it. It was as real and as powerful as the air filling my lungs right now. Loving you was the easiest thing I have ever done. It was a gift, a reminder of the power of light. It was meant to awaken you, to enlighten you, to bless you, to give you life. If you perceive me as a curse, your pain as a curse, the changes and questions you are dealing with as a curse, then I am sorry, and yes you must put your clothes back on and pretend that you did not see the truth. But I remain naked. I am too old, and can no longer pretend that I am greater than life. Life controls me, not the other way around. I am humbled, blessed, and thankful for each second that I get to live. It is all precious. All of it. I stumbled into a river ten years ago. It has led me here. It swept me by you. I touched you as I went by. It was beautiful and a moment I will never forget. I will always remember you like a favorite place on this earth where I rested and felt perfect, absolutely perfect, for a day. Nothing can compare to that, and I suppose, nothing should. I have only been perfect once in my life, and it was with you. That was your gift to me. And mine to you.

^^^^^^^^^^^^^^^^^^^^^^^^

Later that afternoon, Towne and I walked slowly down a trail in North Bend. Neither of us were in a hurry to get anywhere.

Langdon looked at me after reading the letter to Ann. "She was the one?"

"Yep. God, I miss her more than air."

"Nice."

"Ya know, this morning I stood at the window wondering where I was supposed to find the strength to go on."

"It's pathetic isn't it? How quickly we can feel powerless and weak."

"Makes you wonder sometimes. Like that scene in *It's a Wonderful Life* where Jimmy Stewart is on the bridge wishing he'd never been born."

"Yeah, except there's no angel. And Zu Zu's petals fell out of your pocket a long, long, time ago." Towne went quiet as he nodded his head.

308

I broke the silence. "I want to write a book about loneliness: on feeling lost, disconnected, abandoned, unable to find a home."

"And how about a chapter on finally finding your soul-mate. And she matches your emptiness, your madness, your ability to generate light step for step. Except for one minor detail." Langdon was all smiles again.

"And you can never see her or talk to her again. Yeah, that would be perfect."

"Perfectly fucked."

We were laughing, but it's no joke feeling alienated, isolated, and alone; it's a disease, a product of alcoholism and addiction and cruelty and war, all linking back and back to the beginning of man. And you cannot change what happened. And you cannot change what will. All you can do is fight your every waking minute trying to change what is; and you can't even do that.

I looked at Langdon and then looked at the sky and realized the universe had suddenly tilted. The power began to roll up out of me and in that change of heart beats it became clear why Ann had been drawn to me.

"She fell in love with me, Towne! Me!! She adored me. She wanted me! She thought I was perfect! Jesus! She was beautiful, extraordinary, and she loved me! And now she's in hell and I'm stuck here in purgatory! Christ!!"

Towne pushed his tongue into his cheek then opened his jaw once before pursing his lips in thought. He started to speak and then caught himself with a light chuckle. Finally he took a deep breath and exhaled with a long slow whistle before offering his reply. This is what he said:

"Life ain't fair, dude. **Truth # 1.**"

I looked away unable to keep from smiling. Towne always did that to me. We walked to the edge of a creek and sat on some boulders to sip water and finish what was left of our snacks. Sitting in the silence, I grabbed my pen and began writing as if the next breath depended on the pressure of that .5 mm Pilot P-700 crossing the little green page.

Alone with your thoughts, you sift back through the rings of your life, as exposed and raw as freshly cut tree trunks in a forest...

After slowly reading the page aloud, I put down the steno-pad, looked at Langdon, and began to cry.

"I think I'm crazy, Towne."

"No, you're just lonely. You feel no connection. You feel you've lost that one and only soul mate. And that's not crazy. That's the human condition. And here's the kicker..."

"What?"

"You know what you just said about being lost? Well, dude, you're right. You don't have *a* soul-mate. **You have a billion soul mates.**"

IT'S A WONDERFUL LIFE

TRUTH #103

Modern man has learned nothing to save himself. *The Scientific Man has studied DNA, quasars, galaxies, and the molecules of Mars and yet knows less about the human spirit then a peasant before the invention of the wheel.*

*-From **The Book of Truths** by Langdon Towne*

∧∧∧∧∧∧∧∧∧∧∧∧∧∧∧∧∧∧∧

[AUGUST 2001: THE CITY OF ROCKS]

"Hey, Johnson. Watch out for the lightning!" Jake yelled through the rain and thunder as I punched my way up the hill.

The boys and I had decided to go on one last lung busting mountain run before I took them to the bus station in Burley. Black thunder clouds billowed above our heads as the track stars raced each other to the summit and down. The sky was bursting with energy. Exposed and vulnerable, with flashes smashing about, I felt close to the power and wanted more. I began to scream and throw my fists at the air as I ran. I was coming back. I could feel the life kick in me. Bounding up the road, I was filled with an energy that I was afraid might have been lost. I reached the top of the mountain and watched the miracle of lightning crashing through the black sky. Right then, I knew I would get through this.

As I bolted from the summit and sprinted back down to meet the boys, my foot hit a rock and my ankle rolled sharply, with little blue sparks flashing before my eyes. And it was at that precise moment, as thoughts of ripped ligaments dashed in and out of my skull that I finally grasped the full meaning of the dead Lady Del Campo's message:

And you cried
And you complained of your pain and misfortune
And then you saw the truth
And that position of complete helplessness
Her ashen face, with its gaping mouth and blank eyes
Her palms upraised as if beseeching God to lift the block of ice
And now you cried in silence and questioned this God
His choices, and the whole point of existence
And you cried as you stared at her crushed legs and the certainty of death
And your soul erupted in the next breath
And you dropped to your knees in thanks
To this God and every misfortune you had ever known

For the truth was now clear:
Take nothing for granted
Assume nothing
Abuse nothing
Waste not
Hurt no one
Do not create turmoil in your heart
Lest you steal from this day
This gift
This most precious of all gems
Where every moment, no matter how empty or foul,
Is still a walk up the grand staircase
Compared to the last hopeless breath of the Lady Del Campo.

THE CURSE

The quest for divine love will lead you to despair. And it is despair that will lead you to the truth. And it is the truth that will lead you back to divine love. And so goes the circle.

-*From **The Book of Truths** by Langdon Towne*

∧∧∧∧∧∧∧∧∧∧∧∧∧∧∧∧

[AUGUST 2001: CAMPSITE 34, THE CITY OF ROCKS]

Kristan turned the pages of the *Shipwreck Journals* slowly. "I know how you feel," she said.

And I knew she knew. And when I looked at the eyes of a young mother behind me in the grocery line of any town, anywhere, I knew she knew. And whenever I looked in the eyes of the beautiful kids I taught and coached in any school anywhere, I knew they all knew. We were the ones who were never good enough, who felt unloved and unwanted. We were the people with gifts and talents and emptiness. We all had the curse: freaks.

"And that's how it is, Kristan. The world looks on that outer façade of beauty, applauding the gifts-- gifts you have never used to their potential-- gifts which have taunted you from their lofty perch--gifts which you've only fully embraced when loved. And you've only felt love when you couldn't have it. So you walk away and the door slams shut, and you stand in the shower until the water goes cold, knowing you will always be alone."

"So many people feel that way," Kristan spoke softly. "Why don't you write a book about loneliness and alienation? That could be your gift."

"Hmmm. I don't think that's going to be happening."

"Why not?"

"Have you seen my sock drawer?"

Kristan got the joke. "But, look at your life. Look how you've attracted people you could help, and who could help you. The way I see it is you are sitting here like an instrument of God."

"Oh, C'mon! Be careful with that stuff, there might be lightning in those clouds."

"It's true! You doubt and yet you have faith. Otherwise you wouldn't be here. Your faith has allowed you to take huge risks, to push yourself."

"Hmmm. I don't know... it feels pretty desperate most of the time. Maybe the answer is to just remain ignorant. Those people seem a lot more happy."

"They do, don't they?"

"Or, maybe, happiness is just buying into whatever myths you can swallow, like those placebo pills doctors give their patients to make them think they are well. And maybe that's all faith really is. Swallow this!"

"There you go again! You know, earlier today, when I was stuck on that difficult section of the climb, you said: Keep going, there's a great hold on the other side of the crux. When I still couldn't do it, you told me: Just face it and power through it. Step up and reach, you'll get it. What a message of hope you were giving. What a lesson for life!"

"Hmmm. I suppose that is a form of faith."

"Yes. That's the key. And that's the beauty of where you are. You haven't given up. You've take your bruises; you've gotten discouraged, but you keep getting up... and deep down, no matter what happens, you love your life."

"True."

"Through it all, you've become more complete. You no longer have a need to impress, to overextend yourself, to prove anything. You just climb and love and teach because it has become beautiful to you. And it is that beauty, shining from you, that attracted Ann."

I was stunned by her words and wanted to kiss her. "Honestly, I think my life has been about getting a handle on my phobia and fear, of overcoming the pull of that voice inside that told me I was a mistake."

"That makes perfect sense. Because you have fear, you must climb. Fear prevents miracles and you have way much to do to be trapped in that cage anymore. Climbing helps you love and love is the cure."

"Damn, I have to write this stuff down."

Kristan grinned, "I already did."

"So where do I start the book. How do I begin?"

And she said, "You can begin it here with me, sitting in Campsite 34, sifting through the wreckage of a shipwreck, writing about how you came to be a loving man despite life's attempts to crush it out of you."

"But isn't that everyone's story?"

"And isn't that why you must tell it?

"Ya know, Kristan. You're right. Love *is* the cure. It's like a warm pool of water where you can let go of fear and that feeling of being a misfit. I know for me all of my actions were suddenly sharper and exceptional. I was always *on*, never had to think or form thoughts. Nothing was forced. Everything was easy. And I wanted to hold that love.... wanted it inside of me."

"And that is why romantic love is so addictive and so disappointing. It's such a powerful short-cut to feeling happy and normal."

"Yeah, and as soon as you discover it's the cure for your disease, you also learn you can't have it."

Kristan laughed. "Do you think that a romantic love can last."

"I believe it. Passion can last if two people are well matched and stay affectionate. But loving and passion are different. The key to loving is learning to communicate about everything, sharing all your fears and concerns, sharing the weight of this life. It's making sure each person feels safe and cared for. It's being able to be that wonderful, vibrant person you were when you fell in love. Once you have all that... well, that's it, the dishes are done."

"That's beautiful."

"And that is why I'm sitting here, lost in Idaho, wondering how I'll ever get home."

Kristan reached over and picked up my manuscripts lying on the picnic table and smiled: "I know what you can do to find your way home."

I gave her a look like she was about to offer me sexual favors. "What?"

"Write that BOOK!" And a small bell inside my heart went: "Gong!"

There's one scene in Rocky II, that makes sitting through the film worth it. It is where Rocky hangs out at Adrian's hospital bed for about two weeks, waiting for her to come to. And if you've ever been in love, and known what it feels like to possibly lose that connection, you know his pain. I remember sitting in the theater, with my ass hurting, wishing like hell the movie would hurry up... when Adrian finally moved, and Rocky laid his massive hand in hers, and she asked him to lean over, and she looked in his eyes and said, "There's something I want you to do for me."

And of course he said: "Absolutely. Anything." And he meant it. For it is in desperation that we can make those kind of promises.

And he leaned in closer and she had just enough strength left to say one word: "Win."

And that bell went off.

And Rocky started doing one-armed push-ups and I started bawling.

And I kept crying while Rocky ran up those stairs again.

And I cried while he chased the chicken again.

And it didn't matter that he looked stupid doing it, because somebody believed in him.

And I wondered right then and there if anyone would ever do that for me.

One friend who believes in us is all we need. *- Langdon Towne*

THE BLESSING

TRUTH # 192:

The sweetest fruit is at the end of the limb. Please know that unless you are willing to fail, you will never taste it. Do not be discouraged if you have given up climbing the tree. It is not your fault. You are human; you are weak, therefore you have chosen to be safe and sane. You have learned that if you take risks, you will lose. You have learned that the easily picked "sort of sweet" fruit is pretty darn good. Just remember- that to remain safe at the foot of the tree, you must live like a hamster and dress like a sheep.

-From the Book of Truths by Langdon Towne

^^^^^^^^^^^^^^^^^^^^^^^^^^^

"So you've been to the bottom. You've stood alone on the ridge. What's the meaning to it all? What's the secret, Langdon?"

Towne took a last dried bing cherry out of a sandwich bag and plopped it in his mouth. He paused for a second and then spoke between bites. "To help others. That's it. End of list. Nothing else will make you happy."

"Of course, you are taking into consideration the fact that every single human being we serve is selfish, greedy, and liable to not give back."

"Serve anyway. It's all you can do."

"Hmmm..."

"You serve yourself first. You have to. We're all greedy bastards too, ya know. We all gotta meet our own pathetic needs. And then once you're lubed up enough to roll, you go out and do what you can."

"Ya know, that is exactly what Boyd said the night Eric and I happened to show up at his Okinawa Invasion reunion."

"Yep. Three days pinned down in a landing craft, in tropical heat, with Jap aircraft bombing the living shit out of ya would clear out the bullshit a bit. Our man Boyd got tapped into the truth."

^^^^^^^^^^^^^^^^^

[AUGUST 2001: THE CITY OF ROCKS]

For three straight days Kristan and I jotted down notes, sorted, reflected, and processed the churning wake of my *Shipwreck Journals*. Her excitement about my artistic abilities had lit a flame, giving me energy and an outlet for unloading the weight of my latest tragedy. Protected by the safety net of our platonic blanket I had told her everything, confessed my every sin. And she

314

liked me anyway. There was something remarkably rich about a friendship with a woman who I hadn't, wasn't and would not be having sex with. There was no pressure, no expectations, no highs and lows. Our talks were open, honest, and bare bone sincere. I could lie next to her and sleep, my concerns filtering elsewhere. And they did.

On the third night, my last thought before falling asleep was one of thanks for how peaceful I felt compared to just a few days before. With my mind buzzing over thoughts of finally writing *the book*, I rolled over and smiled to the heavens. I thought about knocking on wood, but the closest thing around was a tree up by the picnic table and the idea of tapping my own head seemed ludicrous.

And that was that. I awoke in the middle of the night from a nightmare. Ann was drowning and I could not get to her, could not find a way to save her, and the reality of the symbolism left me shaking as I crawled my way up the tick list of realities waiting for me back home:

No job.

No lover.

No ex-wife #2 to think about getting back together with.

Ann's husband wanted me dead.

The book project Kristan had me excited about, would have to be written. And writing took inspiration. And how was that going to happen?

So, after ten days of healing the gray mist returned, filling my eyes, coating my skin, and clinging to my hair like the smell of car exhaust after a walk around the block in Kent. Once again love was somewhere under a heel and the dust swirling across the desert floor was the remains of my heart. And with that simple shift of thought I was back to the reality from which I had started, except instead of driving away from Kent at the end of my rope: no hope, no peace, no rest, and guilty as sin, I would be driving toward Kent. The circle had come complete. Nothing in the rear view mirror had changed.

I wanted to tell the world how sorry I was for falling in love with the wife of another, but I knew the world could care less. On any given corner of any given block in any given city in any given state, even Utah, there were greater sins being committed every second of every day. My wretchedness was not even a blip on the radar screen of evil. Maybe the universe could care less about my sins.

But I cared. I sat like a pariah, unworthy of the light.

Yet, I knew the light would keep coming. And my breath would keep filling my lungs. I had found that out when I came down off that ridge with my *Confession*, broken and unable to look anyone in the eye, and the kids who knew me, showed up and looked in my eyes anyway. They didn't care about my darkness. All they could see was something I thought had gone out inside of me.

I picked up my pad and wrote a letter to my daughters as the sunrise began to glow pink.

Dear Girls,

The truth rolls out of me, thunders off the mountain wall. I see my part in everything I have done to alter your life: to cloud, to brighten, to enrich, to steal, and I exult and weep at all I have done, as your father, your provider, your leader, your coach.

As a parent I spent more time raising myself than you. I was so inadequate for the job, so insecure and trumped up on pride and ego, searching for a way out of mediocrity, out of fog and jealousy and a desire to leave all that I was not.

I walked in paradise thinking myself a prisoner. I walked out to a dark, cruel world, where I would find me, stamped on the faces and souls of every human I met. Come one, come all! I was no longer immune or blind to the eyes and hearts of every creature, wretched or brilliant, heaved upon my shore. And I bled for them all, died a million times for all I had failed to see. Finally empty and useless, devoid of anything that resembled me, I at last learned the truth and the meaning of my heart. I held still and prayed for words. And all that came to me, all I could say was:

"Love."

It is the only reason you are here. It is all you must do. I love you and praise God for the miracles that you are.

Your Dad

∧∧∧∧∧∧∧∧∧∧∧∧∧∧∧∧

I closed my eyes and thought of Zoë and decided to write her a letter. It was through our endless skirmishes that we had both learned to *forgive*. Could she ever be happy without me in her heart? I had been her wall, her detour sign, her shield of resistance which always reminded her which way she wanted to be heading: 'The other way.' After all the years of losing, I had thought she would wind up hating me and the day she ever met me.

I started the letter, wanting to tell her how sorry I was for all the harm I'd brought her life. But the pen stopped on the page as I thought of the sweet words she had said to me on our last walk, just before she had left to get married to the man she wasn't sure she was in love with. Zoë had gone away with a girl friend and the two of them reminisced, much as men do, about their top ten favorite moments of her life. When the counting was complete, I was in every one of them. She kissed me and thanked me for all the memories. How strange it felt to be finally acknowledged for something I thought had gone totally unappreciated. How beautiful, sad, and strange.

I let the pen write a truth that captured the complexity of my love for all that was beautiful in life. Here is what it said:

The Truth

If one lives long enough, everything turns around. Your curse becomes a blessing and your blessing becomes a curse. If only you live that long.

∧∧∧∧∧∧∧∧∧∧∧∧∧∧∧∧∧

I turned the page and wrote a brief note to the universe and the light of love.

Please God. Please take care of Ann. Please help her children and her husband. Please embrace her heart and guide her to the right places as you have done with me. I have questioned everything for so long, have wondered about every turn in the road. And always I stumble, again and again, stumble and fall into you.

∧∧∧∧∧∧∧∧∧∧∧∧∧∧∧∧∧∧∧∧∧

I crawled out of my tent, made some coffee, rounded up my climbing gear, and painted an attitude on my face. I felt myself trying to catch my breath and flooded with an intense yearning. I wanted to run, but I was already as far away as I could get. I began to straighten up my stuff knowing that busy was good and that if I made enough noise, Kristan would surely wake up.

She did, but was slow to rise... and by the sounds of her weak good morning, I sensed she too felt the weight of her impending fork in the road. We both knew that somehow she would have to find the words to let those two gentle-Mormon callers know they were about to duke it out for the honor to make out with her. And deep inside of Kristan's heart, burned a sad, sad question: *What if neither of these guys was what she really wanted? What if a year or two from now, she had to go through all this turmoil again? Wonder if every move she was about to make would be done in the name of futility?*

We walked down to the Inner City and attempted to climb, but I could barely get off the ground. We decided it was too hot, too late, and time to close this chapter.

Of course, I had no clue of what to do or where to go. I still had four days left before Krissy was due at my place. Without her there, I couldn't fathom heading back to Kent any earlier than I had to. I racked my head on where to go. The Tetons? The Sawtooths? I chose to head for the Sawtooths simply because they were on the way back to Washington.

I waved goodbye to Kristan, Campsite 34 and drove away. Nothing out there sounded remotely interesting. Nothing sounded remotely kind. The great emptiness had returned in force. I started crying as I drove toward Sun Valley. All the hard-earned healing, reading, hoping, talking, and writing of the last ten days evaporated into a cloud of brutal self-doubt. I could not believe how quickly confidence was tossed; how I could go from feeling connected-- to abandoned.

And then I thought of my daughters and how much I wanted to comfort them and how my attempts were always in vain as they'd learned not to need me; how they'd learned to think of me as a weekend father. But I was better than that. I wanted to talk with Kate and look at her face. But she would be busy, a million things better to do than sit with her dad.

I made it to a rest stop north of Twin Falls, Idaho and had another overpowering urge to call Kate. I stared at the pay phone, but couldn't remember where I'd put her number. I kept reminding myself that she was doing her thing and didn't really like her dad popping in at any given time. I kept thinking about how annoyed she might be.

"What the hell is wrong with me?"

And the voice came quietly out of my head: "You are homesick."

"For what? I *am* home. This is it. Christ! This is all I've got!"

"For love," came the voice. "You want to love. And you need to *be* loved. You need someone to hold."

I immediately thought of my child, of how much I wanted to look at her, and be with her, and tell her how important she was to me. I also knew that she didn't need me anymore. But the more I shoved it away, the more the feeling grabbed hold. I needed to be needed. I started sobbing as I drove off to wander alone in the Sawtooth Mountains.

I made it another ten miles to Bellevue and pulled over for gas, catching my stricken face in the window. *The unwanted.* I decided to call Tim in Seattle, hoping I could catch him at work. Talking in wincing gasps I said I wasn't sure what to do. He let me know that the weather was perfect and that he'd love to go mountain climbing with me if I came home. It was a beacon, and I told him I would be home either tomorrow night or early the next day, depending on how much solitude I could handle in the Sawtooths.

I headed for Sun Valley, still thinking of Kate. In the town of Hailey, I saw a *Federal Express Truck* gassing up at a *Chevron* station, and whipped over to ask the driver how much farther it was to Boise via Stanley Basin versus turning around and going back the way I'd come. "Two hours. Oh, and there is a fire burning up in the Sawtooths. It's pretty smoky."

I jumped in my car, turned around and punched it for Walla Walla. It was 3:00 pm and I finally had found a mission. My body snapped to and resonated with a sharp focus. I calculated miles/hour/stops and figured if I hauled complete ass, I could be at Kate's farm by 8:30. With a bit of luck, she might even be home. If not, I would crash at her place, and at least be able to see her in the morning before she went to work.

I ripped to Boise doing speeds of up to 105. I gassed up once, considered calling Kate again, but blew off the thought of searching for her number amongst the heap and chaos of my car. Topped off, I blitzed on, every light turning green, every lane opening up, every car in front moving over, allowing me to fly on my way, stereo on 10, blowing past one speed trap after another.

Five hours and twenty minutes after leaving Hailey, Idaho, with the sun dipping on the golden horizon of endless wheat fields, I pulled up to the Walla Walla farm where Kate was working for the summer. Out came the owner, Bob. He greeted me warmly, then speaking as tactfully as he could said:

"Well, I don't know how to put this any different, but Kate had a very serious biking accident this morning. She hit a building with her head and it split her open pretty good. She wasn't wearing a helmet and is very, very lucky she wasn't killed. Now, I want you to know she's going to be OK. I'm sorry I had to greet you with this. I don't want you to worry. We spent the day in the hospital and got her checked out thoroughly. She has a fractured skull and a bruise on her brain that is going to require some looking after. It is very serious. But, the doctor seemed to think she'd be OK after a week or so of rest. He said the preliminary prognosis looked good and that she would probably recover. But, uh yeah... she needs to go back in tomorrow for more tests."

My mouth answered without a thought: "I can do that. I will stay here tonight if you don't mind."

"That would be great. She's pretty banged up, but it could have been a lot worse."

So, there it was. Early that morning, as Kate lay in a pool of blood, begging for bystanders to come to her aid, I had nervously stirred a cup of coffee, wondering why clarity had just fallen off my shoulders.

Kate came out of the house, a phone to her ear, talking to her Travis in Alaska. She handed me the phone and put her arms around me, burying her face in my shirt.

I gently said goodbye to Travis and then looked at my child. She showed me her wound-- the Frankenstein suture running from behind her ear to the base of her neck-- just an inch any other way and the hug would have been far different.

"How in the hell did you hit there?" I asked, pointing behind her ear.

"I have no idea, Dad. The doctor said that if I would have hit my head anyplace else, either my face would have been crushed or I'd be in a wheelchair or worse."

My car door was still beeping so I walked Kate over to it and noticed the piece of paper with her phone number hanging out of the door tray.

Kate started talking as if all her thoughts had been dammed up for a month and the blow to her head had released the pressure. As I stood there letting her ramble in hyper-speed, it suddenly occurred to me that every turn, every twist, every questioned choice in my life had led me to this exact spot, to this exact moment, so that I might be here to hold my daughter when she needed me most. All the doubting that there was no meaning, that I had lost my way, that I had no direction to my life, vanished in that breath. It was the crowning moment of a lifetime of crowning moments. There was no where else I would rather be. All I wanted was to be here holding my child.

That night Kate let me wash her hair for the first time since she was a little girl, and we still took baths together. We flopped on Bob's couch and watched *Little Big Man* and then she went to bed. I set my sleeping pad on Bob's living room floor with another strange 'slice of world' humming in my ears. I felt overwhelmed with serenity and gave thanks for the twisted, winding, miserable paths that had humbled me and made me weak enough to listen to my guts and turn that car around. I had never felt more blessed.

My hand was lying on Bob's bare wood floor and I thought about knocking on it to protect the moment, but then laughed knowing I could finally let that silly superstition go. Before I rolled over and went to sleep, I had one last thought:

'Love is everything.'

The next morning I awoke to a new sensation. I had no fear. I was home. I was in no hurry to be anywhere, or do anything. There was no where else I wanted to be, and how grand did that simplicity feel?

We drove down to the medical center and giggled through the necessary medical hoops to have her released. We were laughing and conversing with the receptionist until Kate went in to be examined by the neurologist. She was given a green light to live. "75% chance she won't have an aneurysm and die," the good doctor said. We liked the odds and danced merrily out the door. Love was with me for another grand moment. My daughter was not dead. That was enough. I was happy.

We talked about my trip to *The City,* about Kristan and how she had liked the *Shipwreck Journals* , the *Confessions* and even the bawdy *Book of Truths*.

"Does she know, Dad?"

"Know?"

"About Langdon Towne. Does she know the truth about *The Book of Truths*?"

"Uh…" I started to chuckle.

"Dad, you told her, right?"

"Hmmm. I came close a couple of times… But I decided to wait."

"So, you didn't tell her there is no Langdon Towne? That you are Towne…I mean, his voice. That Langdon Towne was just a name you took from *Northwest Passage*!"

I started laughing. "Nope. I couldn't do it. God knows, I told her everything else. Don't worry. I'll tell her. I'm just waiting for the right moment. It's like I didn't want her accepting all of Towne's truths just because it was me who wrote them."

"Oh my God, Dad... that rocks!"

It was a day of celebration, so we decided to drive to her favorite record store and blow a wad of cash on late 60's vinyl.

Kate screamed as we jumped in the car: "And guess what, dad? It's half-off-everything in the store day!"

Of course it was! It all fit! It was all meant to be! I roared down Isaac Avenue. Kate looked beautiful, her face illuminated by the sunlight filtering through the dirty windows. I couldn't quit smiling and kept looking at her, shaking my head in amazement that I had wound up in Walla Walla.

"This feels perfect, hon. I can't believe how life can turn so quickly."

"Yep. It's unpredictable. And beautiful."

I turned and looked at my child again and for a moment I saw her from the eyes of the man I had always dreamed of being. For a moment I was complete, and loving, and generous. And a speech I'd written to her a thousand times formed in my head and began to pour forth with me thinking that maybe, just maybe, this time I'd get it right. Maybe this time I'd be able to finally give away all the love I'd always had at the ready for my children.

"Kate, before you were born, I had no idea what love was, or what it felt like. I was just guessing all the time."

"You've told me that before, dad."

"I know, but... but, let me say this."

"OK."

"The moment you were born I felt that arrow hit my heart. It was love at first sight. And I knew right then, as I held you in my arms and stared at your scrunched up, purple little face, that it would be forever."

Kate began singing, "Would you believe in a love at first sight?"

"Yep. It happens all the time. You were proof, hon. Proof that love was real. And my God, it was hard to lose you after the divorce and watch you grow through the little bits and pieces of time. There were so many things I wanted to give you, so much of me that you never got to see because I was always struggling and unhappy."

"It's been hard, dad. I feel like I had to parent you a lot of the time. I had to be so strong as a kid."

Her words were the truth and their innocence cut deep. I looked at her. "I am so sorry, Kate. Please forgive me."

"I do, dad. I have." We pulled up to a red light. Kate grabbed a 'Best of Melanie' tape and punched it into the deck. *Candles in the Rain* began to play... *Lay it down, lay it down...*

"So much of what you are: your writing, your emotions, your sensitivity, the way you talk, your choices of music, are the parts of me I like and wanted you to have." I looked at her and smiled.

"I get by with a little help from my friends."

"Hey! Do you remember last Christmas, when you came home from Whitman and brought your violin and asked me to play with you?"

"That was so awesome!"

"It was such a change. I mean you had never wanted to do that before. We sat on the carpet and Travis and Krissy were our audience and I played this melancholy piece on my acoustic which told a bit about how my heart was doing. I mean I hadn't seen Ann in two months and was still missing her in every breath."

"I know that feeling." And she did. Kate had only been able to see her Travis twice over the course of the year.

"You stared straight ahead and began to play these notes that I swear to God were coming from my very soul. It was such an agonizing lead and it flowed and swirled and washed the room with uncertainty and hopelessness. It tore through me and lifted me into your hands; and your fingers were mine; and it was me playing... and you knew it. You made sure the carpet and ceiling were covered with the agony of a true love lost. You were so incredible! You were born with that, Kate. All the disasters and disappointments could not take that blessing away from you. You had the gift!"

I looked over to see if any of what I had said was registering through her first-born-child filters. She just smiled like a young girl is supposed to smile when her heart is filling up.

"Ya know, dad. Everything is going to be all right."

"And guess what, hon?"

"What?"

"It's been more than five minutes."

"Five minutes?"

"Yeah. Five minutes of happiness and..."

"No cannons. No kim chee!"

"Yep. Hey. Lean over here so I can knock on..." I swung my hand to the right and caught myself about to knock on her stitches. "Oops. I better find some other wood, huh?"

She chuckled.

"Ya know, Kate, I think you bashing your head in finally broke the curse!"

"Well, dad, there ya go. It's all good. Life is finally..."

And then, out of the corner of my eye, I saw the squirrel. It was large and bushy and bounding like a hound across the manicured lawn, heading straight for the sidewalk, then the avenue, then the front of our car, whereupon Kate my vegetarian animal lover, also saw the fur ball. And before I could form a positive reply to her warm appraisal of life's gratuities, our mouths dropped open as the whirl of gray dashed head long for Isaacs Avenue and our rapidly approaching car wheels. So rapid was the squirrel's advance that my right foot instinctively hit the brakes before I could check my rear view mirror for semi-trucks and armored vehicles. Kate turned to me wide eyed as I turned to her, our mouths trying to form words through the slow-motion sound of tires squealing and our chests pressing against seat belts as our voices erupted from the safe corners of hearts that just moments ago felt so warm...

"WATCH OUT FOR THE SQUIRREL!!!"

We both screamed as the car came screeching to a smoking stop. We looked out hoping to see fur dashing away. Nothing. 'First there is a squirrel, then there is no squirrel....'

Kate looked at me and started laughing. "Oh my God, Dad! There's your ending! You and me sitting here staring at each other, going:

"What the ....!!?"

THE END

Author's Note: I was just kidding about the names and dates being changed to protect the innocent. There are no innocents in here. It's all true. Rock on.

The Underture

*Peters, Prague
and
Thirteen Lucky Pennies*

**First there is a Langdon
Then there is no Langdon
Then there is...**

*Sung to Donavon's:"First There is a Mountain."
From: "Sing-alongs for a Shipwreck"*

Why We Tremble

Bewildered is he who must open arms tortured by love's famine
Forgotten are age, wisdom, or distinction
For when we unveil ourselves to love's humbling touch
We are once again a child
All that is and was beats inside our heart
The heart we have filled and broken from earliest memory

We have loved, tried to love
Been carried by love and crushed by love
It is all the same: now, then, tomorrow and forever
It is the one constant thread through all that is human
Love brings light
The absence of love brings darkness

Of which were you blessed?
On whose hands were you held on high?
On what wings did you learn to fly from despair?
Is it not the same truth for all of us?
And is that not why we tremble
At the sight of the beloved?

*-From the **Shipwreck** Journals*

'ALL THE LONELY PEOPLE...'

I'm standing in the shower thinking: 'Why God?' And an answer comes out of nowhere: "The book is about loneliness, that desperate need for a connection." And suddenly I'm humming: "All the lonely people..."

When I was a kid I didn't want to be a writer. I wanted to be a Beatle. In 1963 I was riding in my Uncle Bill's Fastback Mustang when "I Saw Her Standing There" came on the radio. It was love at first chorus.' Three years later I bought the 45' single, Eleanor Rigby, Paul McCartney's haunting ode to loneliness. I'm fairly certain the Beatles didn't intend that tune to be understood by an eleven year old. But, I got it. Even then, I was already lost. And decades later, as a single dad whose youngest daughter owned every one of their albums, I still secretly wished I could have known what it felt like to be a Beatle. The closest I ever came was a month where my book was in the hands of teenagers at the high schools I was subbing. Kids were raving about the candid truths and the stories dedicated to my daughters. Many told me it was the first book they had ever read cover to cover. Others let me know they normally hated reading, but couldn't put my book down. Some told me it had changed their lives, had helped them deal with their relationships or their parents or themselves. It felt powerful to be so validated. That was my 'Ed Sullivan' moment right there.

I'm not into nostalgia, but I do like looking backwards. It's a lot more predictable than looking ahead and often a lot kinder than where you are right now. When it comes to remembering the '60's and *The Beatles*, I remember Paul singing *Yesterday* on *Ed Sullivan* and John in bed with Yoko asking the world to give peace a chance. It seems romantic now that Lennon's words of hope and love were being sung at a time when America was being bludgeoned by Viet Nam, assassinations, race riots and Watergate.

Like so many kids from the "my generation" era, I learned the truth a bit too young. In the space of time it took to go from 4th to 10th grade, we lost JFK, MLK, RFK, Jimi Hendrix, Jim Morrison, Malcolm X, Mama Cass, the *Beatles* disbanded, Vietnam erupted, and any belief that the adults in charge could be trusted abandoned us like an H-bomb mushroom cloud fading into a tropical sunset. I remember sitting in Mr. Hamby's creative writing class comparing military draft numbers with my friends. Plans were being devised to escape America. None of us wanted to die for a lie. As we wrote our tales of fiction for Hamby, *Black Sabbath's: 'War Pigs'* played on his turn table:

> *"Generals gathered in their masses*
> *Just like witches at black masses.*

Between riots, protests, drugs, Tin Soldiers, the Iron Curtain and a billion

Chinese militants, most of us sophomores weren't waging bets we'd live to see twenty-five.

August 2003: Prague, Czech Republic

Sitting here writing an epilogue to 'CZ' in post-communist Prague, where people are free to say whatever they want about anything they want, it's difficult to imagine an America where John Lennon would have to apologize for anything he ever said and even harder trying to picture the US government going through such great lengths in its attempt to deport the greatest artist of the 20th century. At a time when there is no Berlin wall, no Soviet threat, and you can drive across most borders in Europe with no hassle, it seems odd to recollect an America where kids burned *Beatles* records after Lennon muttered an off-hand nothing to an off-duty reporter about Jesus. The comment that shocked the world was simply a poignant observation by the ever sardonic Beatle on the sad state of the youth of the 60's; where something as silly as a "pop" band from Liverpool could be more popular to kids than Jesus Christ. I remember that America quite well. I remember the newspaper headlines too. Lennon's words were splashed in ink reminiscent of Pearl Harbor: **"BEATLES BIGGER THAN JESUS!!"**

And of course if you had a brain in your head you knew what John really meant. But no one seemed to have a brain in their head. The media and former adoring fans just wanted to have an excuse to turn on their hero. And so America turned on the fab four. The bible belt burned their records on bonfires that would have made the KKK envious. Stations throughout the country that professed freedom of speech, banned the Beatles from their airwaves. And the kids on my school bus in Kent lifted up their legs when we crossed the railroad tracks because if you didn't lift your feet it meant you liked *The Beatles*, and if you liked the *The Beatles* it meant you didn't like Jesus or America. And some little-blonde-puritan-princess at the front of the bus would announce this fact at every railroad crossing, then turn around to see who wasn't lifting their feet. As far as I could tell, I was the only sinner. I just sat there, feet down, shaking my head and humming: *"I think I'm gonna be sad, I think it's today... yeah!"*

Having survived the sixties and all the falls from grace that went with it, I have to admit the experience of going from angel to outcast in the space of a careless book sale got me thinking back... back... back... to that look on Lennon's face when he tried to explain to the dogged media just what he meant by what he didn't say about Jesus. I could see the hill and the cross etched against a darkening sky. I wanted to find my copy of the *The Ballad of John and Yoko,* but I'd let Kate take it to college. I had to laugh. All these years of being pissed off and it took a catastrophe for me to finally forgive John for marrying Yoko.

"Christ! You know it ain't easy
You know how hard it can be..."

PRISONER OF PORTABLE-6

Abuse nothing. Please know that you were brought into this world to heal others. But you cannot heal others, because to heal others, you must first heal yourself. You must somehow turn off those weapons of destruction you are using to render your soul barren and worthless. You must say goodbye to the games, the control, the manipulation, the petty needs, the chaotic patterns, the dreams of war, the insatiable avarice. When you no longer want to hurt yourself, you will learn the meaning of kindness.

*-From the **Book of Truths** by Langdon Towne*

^^^^^^^^^^^^^^^^

[September 2001: Kent, WA]

The night before the start of the 2001 school year I sit on the edge of my bed trying to process a kaleidoscope of "stranger than fiction" events that have led me here. Out of the silence a voice rolls up with an original thought: "If you ever have five minutes of happiness, get on your knees and pray." My pen starts to move as a series of rules on how to deal with love, loss, and loneliness roll out filling the pages of my shipwreck journal. This goes on through the afternoon and into the night. Finally at 1:00 A.M, I put the steno-pad down and try to sleep. I can't. I lie there thinking it will be too funny if I get called to sub on the very first day of school. That never happens. At 5:30 A.M. the phone rings. Kent Junior High needs a sub.

KJH is a 'mean streets' zone of drug abuse, alcohol damage and single parent chaos. First period I take my class to the library as our portable is being recarpeted. There is another class next to us in the same predicament. That class has a teacher named Betty who talks softly from a soft body with soft eyes. She tells her behaviorally-challenged, colorfully-diverse class about her life. She is trying to set the tone for the year, introducing herself over the din of ebonics. I overhear her say with a big smile, "I suppose you'd like to know how I met my husband?"

At which point a reply is muttered, "We don't fuckin care bitch."

In the next breath a large projectile is hurled across the room. She doesn't even flinch. She just keeps talking. This is her career. This is what she has chosen to do with her life. She does this five periods a day, 181 days a year, minus the twenty days she will take for sick leave.

I ask her later how she can stand her job and she says to me, "OH! This isn't bad. It was much worse last year."

On the third day I am in a portable straightening up the desks when a sharply dressed man bursts in the door. He looks like a poster boy for teacher of the decade: handsome-strong-and confident.

We do quick introductions and I compliment him on his fine clothes. He looks at me to make sure I'm not kidding, then quickly informs me he's more of the Thoreau type, where you don't change clothes for a job. He says he's a jeans and t-shirt guy, used to drive truck, was a mountain climber in the 70's, and got his degree last year to answer a higher calling and finally do something worthwhile with his life.

I already like him and ask him how the new *"higher calling"* is going.

He says he is on his way over to the office to submit his resignation. He wants out of his contract.

"What?"

Turns out he has Betty's class the period after her. He tells me he is being devoured. The kids are screaming and cussing and a tiny Vietnamese girl keeps shoving her hand down her pants so she can wipe ass smell on her class-mates. He says she runs the classroom.

"Jesus…what do you say to her when she does that?"

"She doesn't speak a word of English. She doesn't understand anything I'm saying. She has me by the balls."

Peters goes over to the office already counting on being a truck driver by this time next week. I decide to wait around and hear how his request to get out of his contract went.

A half hour later I see him staggering towards his VW van.

"So how did it go?"

"They won't let me out. If I break the contract, I will never work for this district or any other district in this state again."

"Damn!"

"I'm a fucking prisoner!"

"Well at least you've got a nice portable." I'm joking. His room, Portable-6 is the size of a wall boarded meat locker. It smells like a BD class should after PE with no showers and no deodorant.

"You better hit Costco for a year's supply of air freshener."

"I'm heading there now. I hope they're not out of Kleenex and Tums."

Peters grins as he gets in his van and punches in *AC/DC's Highway To Hell.*

LUCKY THIRTEEN

Lopsang's wife has e-mailed again asking for help. I return her messages with encouragement but no means to assist her financially. I feel the guilt. She sends me pictures of Lopsang on Everest. I stare at them and it hurts.

I had helped her apply for a VISA to this country, and then 9/11 happened and her VISA was rejected by a paranoid new world order. She writes again needing money to escape the country. Six years since his death and there is no peace. I am bewildered as to what I should do. My own kids need support. The students I mentor and coach need my assistance. True to form, I turn my back on her pleas and carry on. I am sorry Lopsang. I am so sorry.

-From the **Shipwreck** Journals

∧∧∧∧∧∧∧∧∧∧∧∧∧∧∧∧∧

The obsession of writing my *book of truths* consumes the entire 2001-02 school year. Knowing that I've been cracked open and hurled to the bottom, I don't question my direction, my purpose, or why I'm pushing myself to the absolute edge. I seal myself in the tunnel of artistic commitment and write until my eyes and senses fail. I have to finish the book and give it to Ann. I know this commitment to self will be my salvation, or my ruin.

Soon, providence begins to work on my behalf. Peters watches on in amazement as one door after another opens just when I need it to. Every day we walk and talk, and on every walk I find a lucky penny and put it in my pocket. Pretty soon, Peters is picking up pennies and knocking on wood.

Meanwhile, *Captain Queeg* is spreading darkness down the halls of KM. Word gets back to me that Fiad has been tossed to the ground and handcuffed by the newly appointed 'tighter' security. While it sickens me, it doesn't surprise me at all.

Peters and I try to process the paranoid post 9/11 world we have found ourselves in. Both products of the sixties, we are highly amused by the frightening similarities between 'back in the day' and now.

By late spring, with track season building towards state and late night binges of editing stealing the night, I know that I must finish 'CZ' by the end of the school year or be admitted. The last day of school becomes my deadline. After that I'm leaving on a road trip for *The City of Rocks.* Working round the clock in a manic whirl wind, I fire off the manuscript to RPI printing the day before school is out. Three days later, Kris and I drive in to Seattle to pick up a loose bound proof and then drive over to see my parents. We stop at the QFC in the 'valley of tears' to get us something to drink. In the parking lot is Ann's car! All the blood falls from my head. I tell Kris I can't go in there, so she walks in and finds Ann. The two of them come out like visions and I show Ann the book I wrote for her. I tell her I wanted to put her name in the dedication, but... She starts to cry and tells me she is so sorry for the horrible way our love affair ended. I tell her I still love her and am actually doing OK; I'm just a little exhausted. I show her the pages and she looks on in amazement. It is finally over. I drive away screaming in the car with Kris. No Ann for eleven months and she shows up in a parking lot the day I pick up *Crossing Zion!*

Two days after the books are printed, I leave for *The City.* Ready to unleash 'Towne' upon the world, I don't count on a massive avalanche of shyness taking over my voice as delusions of becoming the next best-selling 'grassroots' author quickly fade away. I am shocked how awkward I feel trying to convince someone to pay me money for something I've created.

330

When I get home from the trip, I am greeted with six large boxes of books taking up most of my bedroom. It begins to dawn on me that my obsession with Towne and the number thirteen may have led to my ruin. 427 is the number I printed because that figure was the number of books Towne chose to publish with his skimpy bank account. Towne had picked 427, because 4 + 2 + 7 = 13. Except there was no Towne, no book of truths and I had a $4,000 hole in my pocket with no job lined up for next year.

THE CREEK

There was a king who sat in his castle and wondered how his soul could be so empty. There was a wanderer who sat near a mountain and wondered how his heart could be so full.

*-From the **Book of Truths** by Langdon Towne*

"Johnson, I got the ending to my book figured out." Peters had stopped to tie a running shoe.

"The book you haven't started yet?"

"Dude, I've been busy... So I am cooking dinner last night and the ending comes to me... I'm down in the basement with a gun in my mouth, toe on the trigger, and a light comes on and tells me to change my life and put the gun down."

"That's good. I hate sad endings."

"And I stand up, raise my arms to the heavens in thanks and the gun falls to the floor, goes off and blows a hole right between my eyes."

"That's nice. So that's the ending? To which book?"

"My love story." Peters took a swig of water and marched off up the Soos Creek Trail.

"Well I'm not quite sure about my ending, but I know how my next book begins."

"Yeah. Let me guess. Something like: *she came up out of a creek.*"

Peters and I were walking fast, trying to process the latest turn in my life. Earlier that year we'd started up our own twelve step program. We called our group: Dirt Baggers Anonymous. Currently, there were only two people attending our meetings. Jeff and me. We met on trails or at my apartment or at the store, wherever it was appropriate to stand up and announce our introductory saying which went like this:

"Hello. My name is Keith. And I'm a f...ing idiot."

One of us would then go on to tell what we had done in the last day or hour to prove this fact. Usually it was something mundane, like leaving a wallet on a bank's garbage can after using the cash machine. As one of us announced his latest screw up, the other would applaud quietly the way people do at meetings where they're forced to applaud too many times for nothing much.

Peters had become an over-dedicated junior high teacher who got up at four to write lesson plans and then headed for work at five to make sure he was fully prepared for a day of special-ed. This morning he had left his neatly written plans next to the coffee pot and had to drive back home to get them.

I had lightly applauded Peters forgetting his teaching essentials. I applauded again when he spoke of the ignition switch not working on his VW van when he got back in. I applauded once more when we got back from our walk and had to push start the van to get it started. He appreciated my support and of course I appreciated changing the subject and talking about Zuzana again.

"She came up out of a creek. I still can't believe it. I mean what are the chances?"

"Let me think..."

"I was sitting on that bridge at Mt. Rainier National Park thinking I'll never find someone, that'll I'll be alone the rest of my life. The only reason I was there was because it was too hot to hike. I was exhausted... you know the year I'd been through. I just sat there knowing I was like this strange, complicated, mosaic poured out on a sidewalk..."

"And graying rapidly."

"Thank you... a thousand intricate pieces of colored glass, and who could ever match that puzzle? So I said something to the universe like: I'm going to be alone forever, and that's going to have to be OK."

"Sounds like a nice ending to me."

"I no more than got the words out and her brown hair and shoulders popped up out of that creek bank. I couldn't help but laugh. It was too classic. One of the true miracles of my life."

"That you found a soul-mate coming out of a creek?"

"Yep... and that I found the balls to say something to her in the little grocery store she stopped at on her way home."

Peters applauded to show his appreciation of miracles.

"She walked to her car, pulled out some maps and sat there. All the while I am staring at her... waiting for her to look up and see me. I had to laugh because I knew my acceptance of loneliness had lasted all of five seconds."

"I don't see you entering the monk-hood any time soon."

"So I did one of those things where you go...OK, if she drives over the bridge and turns around next to me, there is a God."

Peters applauded my obvious choice to mock the God I'd been on my knees praying to all year.

"And if she doesn't drive over the bridge?"

"She didn't. She did a U-turn and drove off. And that was the end of that."

Light, tasteful, clapping.

332

"Five minutes after the lady had gone, Kris and her boyfriend came back and we headed home. I couldn't help thinking, 'What would I have said to that woman had she stopped and stared at me? What do you say to a total stranger you are attracted to?"

"How about: Hi, my name is Keith, I'm 47 and had a vaz back when you were eight." Peters knew all the punch lines.

Zuzana and I hadn't gotten around to discussing our age difference until we were wrapped in each other's arms inside a tent on the side of Mt. Sahale. It was only our second date, and I have to admit being slightly jarred when the first words out her mouth after we first kissed were a tearful, "How is this going to end!"

And on the second night, when she announced in joy that her dream was to have lots of kids, I felt the hand of doom come up to my opened heart and seize what little joy the moment had brought me. And as she slept peacefully, I lay awake wondering how to form the words to tell those angelic eyes I could not give her a child.

Knowing I couldn't wait til morning to drop that bomb, I shook her awake and told her the truth. She sat up in horror, looked in my eyes, burst into tears, and fell sobbing onto my chest. And as I stroked her lovely brown hair, I vowed to never hurt this tender soul as long as I lived. When she was done crying, she took my face in her hands and kissed me as if I would be the love of her life.

The next day, realizing our budding romance had better come to an abrupt end, we laughed half-heartedly about coming up with a sign board for dating. Mine would have read: 47, Vaz, and a Shy Bladder.

That sign board would have been enough to keep her from ever giving me two seconds of her time. She would have seen the truth, given me a quick smile to acknowledge my candidness and then jumped in her Chrysler and bolted for the safety of a promising Czech future. She would have never known my name. She would have never held my hand. She would have never looked in my eyes and seen a hint of magic. She would have never crawled into my arms and released her pain. She would have never crawled into my soul and painted the universe a different hue. She would have never awoken to thoughts of a future, vastly altered, a million miles from the dreams she had carried since a child.

"Anyway, we drove on toward home, crawling up behind slower traffic. Several cars passed the car holding things up. When the last car went around it, there she was, the woman in the creek. I got behind her and didn't pass."

"We call that stalking where I come from."

"She drove on to the town of Greenwater where her blinker started signalling a left. My pulse began to race as I flicked my blinker on. Krissy shouted from the back seat: 'What are we doing, dad?!'

"Getting ice cream."

"We never get ice cream."

"I've changed."

The woman got out and I followed her in, my mouth turning to stone. Knowing this was my moment, I walked up to her hoping something witty would fall out of my mouth."

"Jesus…I hated pick up lines back in school."

"Oh yeah. I never learned any. Anyway…she turned around and I blurted out: 'I just saw you coming up out of the creek.' And her eyes went wide. I'd never seen eyes like that... like a Greek statue or Rembrandt painting. She looked scared. So I turned around, handed Kris a five and walked out."

"Damn. That was a bad line."

"How could I have known she was down there naked? People from the U.S. don't hop in creeks by a busy road and soap up. And I didn't see anything anyway, though I wish I had."

"Uh huh. If you had you never would have gotten a word out."

"I've thought of that…. So anyway, she walked out of the store with treats and I looked up at her and she smiled at me. Relieved, I asked her where she was from and she said, 'Prague.' I said, 'Where is that?' And she said, 'Czech Republic,' which left me looking at her with a blank expression.... 'Next to Germany....' I finally had it. So I asked her what she was doing in the U.S. She said she was a nanny and ski instructor here and a teacher back home."

"You're a teacher; she's a teacher."

"I asked her what she liked to do and she said hiking, climbing, reading and cross country skiing."

"You like to hike and climb and ski and..."

"...and I asked who she went with just as Krissy walked up and gave me a hug. Zuzana said she had no one to hike or climb with. Krissy walked over to grin at me with her boyfriend. I thought she was happy for me but she told me later they were laughing because my hair looked so bad and my shorts had holes and food stains."

"Your shorts always have holes and stains."

"I know, but you never notice stuff like that until you are standing next to a pretty woman. Zuzana told me that before she saw Krissy hug me she was thinking of making up a boyfriend so she could bail."

"Women do that."

"Yes they do. I asked her if she would like to go climbing with me sometime and she said she'd like to. I went on to tell her about 'Crossing Zion' and she said she wanted to read it. She mentioned that 'CZ' just happened to be her country's abbreviation. And with that affirmation I got a number and her name. Zuzana. I'd never asked out a woman with Z's in her name before."

"What about Zoe? Your ex-wife in your book?"

"Right. But, her name isn't Zoe. It's Ileen. You know that. Typical Ileen.

Here she is this 5'9", olive-skinned, auburn-haired, Scorpio and when I asked her to pick out a name for the book, she picks one that makes her sound short, fuzzy-haired and Jewish. Anyway, after Zuzana left, I asked Krissy how long I should wait before I called her. She thought a day. Her boyfriend said at least two. He said anything less looked like I was desperate."

"You were desperate."

"Right. Later that night, I asked some of Krissy's friends what they thought and they said that I should wait at least three days. That seemed insane to me."

"No shit."

"So I called Heather, who is forty and has been dating since she got divorced in '92, and she said that if I liked this girl to call her anytime I wanted because she was sick and tired of all this dysfunctional game playing bullshit."

"RIGHT ON!"

"I called Zuzana that night. I got one ring and a beep. I said... 'hello?' and hung up. I was so nervous. I could hear my pulse in the phone."

"Funny isn't it? Now she's the only thing that calms you down."

"I couldn't remember if I'd left my number. So I wrote everything down on a piece of paper and called her again, apologized for all the calls and gave my canned speech."

"Did she call you back?"

"No. I had to call her the next night."

"God, you are such a loser." Peters was grinning.

"My curse."

"And your blessing."

THE CHAMPION

[Kent, WA: December 2003]

Asiki calls from his sister's apartment and says he'll be over in a couple of minutes. He shows up dressed in new Robin's egg blue Fubu sweats with matching sneakers, his hair in corn rows and his face glowing with pride that he's earned.

Asiki finished 2nd in the 4A State 800 and graduated from Kent Meridian with a 3.75. He doesn't drink, doesn't smoke weed, helps everyone he knows, and is considered one of the finest human beings Erickson, a three decade legend in coaching, has ever met. He is home for the holidays and wants to see coach and me. He tells me about college, of the friends he's made, of playing soccer for the first time since he lived in Africa.

He asks me how things are going. I tell him I'm subbing high school, coaching cross-country, selling 'Crossing Zion,' and still dating the Czech woman I met up at Mt. Rainier. I tell him Kris is surviving her last year of high school and has been accepted by the top four colleges in Washington state. He asks about the KM talent show and I explain I'm not doing it this year because I don't want to deal with *Captain Queeg*.

At the mention of KM's dictator, Asiki's smile turns. He starts talking about his visit with Erickson earlier in the day, how he showed up at the campus and *Captain Queeg* was in the parking lot monitoring security, how he'd approached the principal with a handshake and a smile, introduced himself as Asiki, one of Erickson's runners, and said he'd come by to visit his former coach. *Captain Queeg* grinned and told him to check in at the office to get a visitor's pass. And as he walked across the parking lot to the main door, *Queeg* radioed the front desk and informed them they were not to issue a pass to the person about to enter the building. Dawn, the secretary, stood before Asiki in disbelief. She knew him, knew me, loved us all. She told Asiki the truth: that *Captain Queeg* wouldn't allow him a pass.

Asiki now rises before me in rage. He shouts how he wants to write the local paper and call the news media, that he wants this paranoid tyrant and the district that protects him exposed. He tells me he wants to help me write a book about what's going on in high schools, wants someone to tell the truth.

So that night I start writing about the 'teenage wasteland' that is secondary public education. I too have rage. I write seventy pages in three days…the words flow from me like water off a duck. It is a writer's wet-dream.

GONNA CRUCIFY ME

I'm having a nightmare. The phone is ringing and I pick it up. It is my daughter Kris, one of the people on this planet I trust with everything I have, telling me that they are coming after me. I ask her why and she says, 'Crossing Zion.'

I wake up and head off to sub. In every class kids are coming up wanting a copy of my book. Zuzana told me the day before not to sell the book at school anymore. But, I can't say no to these kids. Those who have a copy come to me and thank me for writing the truth. Many tell me it is the first book they have ever read cover to cover. A lovely girl I've never seen before, buys a copy. I sign the book with a nice passage on the power of kindness.

The next day I am on the phone with the school district's lady in black. She is in possession of the girl's copy of 'Crossing Zion.' She tells me that the district is putting me under investigation. Two weeks later I'm terminated.

My termination letter cites as evidence that Towne's 'Book of Truths' was banned from public schools and that he was called a devil in several countries. The fact that I made all that stuff up is a bit of comic irony that I decide the 'higher ups' wouldn't find amusing.

The district files a letter to the Superintendent of Public Instruction in Olympia in an attempt to have me banned from public education. A month later the agent from Olympia comes to my apartment to interrogate me. We wind up talking about my daughters, the team of African refugees I coached, and the four week road trip Zuzana and I are going on in May. I pause to offer her tea, which she declines because she is on the clock. So I offer her a copy of 'Crossing Zion' which she accepts as a gift for her son who couldn't put down: 'Into Thin Air.'

^^^^^^^^^^^^^^^^^^^^

I wake up early and turn on my computer like a bad habit. There is an e-mail from Chris Lukezic, last year's 4-A state champion in the mile, and runner up by a hair in the two. He is finally responding to the copy of CZ I sent him last fall. During the five years I coached cross-country and track at Kent Meridian, Chris was one of the most gifted kids I had the pleasure of getting to know. An amazing talent, Chris had been born with a shiny silver-spoon and legs to match. I didn't coach Chris. He ran for Auburn High. I coached kids at KM who ran in Asics I picked up from Thrift Stores.

Johnson,
The book is amazing my friend. I don't think I have ever been more moved and touched by a book than the one you wrote, and I mean that with all honesty. I think I have learned more about my own life by reading about yours. That part near the end about Fiad and all our Africano bros in Kent really made me think. Why the hell did I get the shot at doing this and Fiad didn't? What makes me so special? I have taken for granted for so long the life I was born into- the parents always there for me at every meet, the nice house, getting anything and everything I have ever desired. Reading that part of the book couldn't have come at a better time in my life. I'm on spring break and still here at school (Georgetown University) alone and hanging out, but trying to think about life and what the hell I'm doing with it and what it's all about, trying to fill that empty void that has been here since I arrived. Trying to get my mind clear of the rich kids concerned only with becoming rich. I realized that I'm f...ing lucky and I've probably never been more humbled by that than anything I've ever experienced. It brought tears to my eyes reading that, man. It really made me think for the first time in my life how ungrateful one can be when he has and gets everything he can possibly desire and has never experienced anything else. This book has taught me more about life than I will probably ever get out of attending classes at Georgetown. I just wanted you to know how much reading this book meant and I'm sure I could go on all night, but I'll quit for now and leave the rest to myself to figure out.
Chris

I cry the whole time I read the letter. I cry for the beauty of it all, for the ridiculous way life turns on you, for the kids who will never get a chance at greatness, for the miracles that almost are, for the blessings we hold and never appreciate, for the force of love that keeps one connected to greatness.

Chris has no idea how perfect his timing is. I didn't need these words in the fall. I need them now… for my will isn't a force, it is a leaf at the end of a long limb….and I am holding on as the winds of change blow.

I close the internet, open a word document and start to write another chapter: one for the Africans I coached and befriended, for the advantaged kids at Georgetown who need to understand the laws of scarcity, for the mom's of those single kids I taught who find a way to feed and clothe their kids with God knows what for support, for the black kids who taught me how not to be a honky, to all the unwanted kids I happened to shed a light of truth on, and to those two kids I failed because I was too busy falling into my own holes.

PRAGUE INTERNATIONAL AIRPORT

All the riches and opportunities of kings mean nothing when a heart is missing that one most noble and essential thing.

*-From the **Book of Truths** by Langdon Towne*

∧∧∧∧∧∧∧∧∧∧∧∧∧∧∧∧∧∧

[August 1st, 2003: Prague, CZ]

The door blinks open. Strangers with bleary eyes walk away from one world into another. She sits on a bench waiting for me. I am still over Prague. I am in the airplane bathroom, trying to control my stomach by breathing down to my toes.

"Do you have any tums?" I ask the stewardess.

I have been deep breathing since we flew over the Czech border. It's been two months since I saw her and so much has gone wrong. The stewardess gives me a palms up and I am left to get through the next forty-five minutes practicing lamaze technigues I learned in birthing classes. I am not sure she will be at the airport. I am not sure she wants to see me or deal with this. I am not sure she will touch me. Silence over the distance has let the demons out.

Zuzana sits on a bench watching the door open and close, open and close. Bewildered faces try to adjust to natural light. Most are towing massive suitcases on rollers. The door closes. Zuzana has no idea how to meet the challenge being asked of her heart. She is in love with someone unable to give her the one thing she has wanted her whole life: a family. She is in love with someone twenty years older, someone who she told on the second date that she could not love because he wasn't Czech, wasn't her age, and didn't have live ammo in his gun. But she fell in love anyway. The four week road trip did it. The hotsprings at Bridgeport, making love as the sun set over the snow covered Sierras. That was a first for both of us, and the final touch of paint that washed memories of a former lover completely out of her heart. Now her heart cried for something she could not understand.

The door opens again and fears rise up out of her belly. Nothing could ever work. The door closes and love washes up like a foamy wave... She has never gotten love letters like this. Never been loved like this. Never trembled like this.

I am standing at the baggage claim, waiting as a hundred other passengers get their bags and walk away. I have one of my bags. But not the other. I have learned the definition of a second. Every tick of the clock has aged my soul. There are no veins in my arms. No blood in my face. I am the walking dead. I can only hope she will hug me when she sees me.

The bag falls out...the last one. I grab it and limp out the hall. The pathway goes left or right. I choose left. I always choose left. I walk out of the blinking door and stand in the light. There are faces and bodies and no Zuzana. I look from one group to another.... and nothing.

I walk slowly with my bags to a wall trying *not to* picture her *not* coming to the airport. I stand for a minute, wondering what to do... where to go. And then I see her. On the bench, studying the other door-- the right door.

She sees me and walks towards me. Her face looks different, with deep lines etched in her forehead. She looks tiny and fragile. I wrap my arms around her head and shoulders and speak softly as tears fall on her sweater:

"Hi... hi, Zuzana. Oh my God, I love you. I love you, Zuzana... hi."

THE LAST TRUTH

No man is useless who lightens the burdens of another

Author's Note: Fall of 2004. In August I was at Alden Crag's working on a cover for another book abuot a Cambodian Man who survived two and a half years in the killing fields. As I stepped out of my car, a silver 2003 Mustang pulled up at the stop sign. I looked at the driver and noticed he was hispanic. I studied his features for a second and realized the young man looked like Angel. The kid looked at me, smiled, and rolled his window down. It was Angel! He jumped out and we embraced each other. I looked in his eyes and asked him what had happened after he got kicked out five years ago. My worst fears were true. He had never gone back to school, sold for his brother, got involved in gang violence, had fathered a child, and was in fear for his life every waking moment. I asked him what he could do and his words were chilling. "There's no way out, Johnson." We exchanged email addresses and then he walked back to his Mustang to answer a beeper call. I mustered up my strength and offered him the only words I could think of. "Don't give up, Angel. Don't give up."

Acknowledgements

With the deepest gratitude I give humble thanks to:

Mom and Dad for the usual stuff that every artistic kid needs, to Angelina Armoni for giving me the juice to write around the clock, to Ileen O'Leary for the number 13, to every *Phobic* out there thinking you're a freak, to Langdon Towne for showing up with his *Book of Truths* after my heart had broken, to Kristan for looking in my eyes after reading *The Loser* and telling me: "This stuff is Gold!," to my daughter Kate for telling me at page 85 to "Just go for it, Dad...tell it all," to Jeff Peters for coaching me and telling me he believed in me (over and over and over) to my younger daughter Kris for being mature enough to allow her father to go blindly off, chasing his latest obsession, to Tim for climbing with me and being my friend since '72, to Asiki, Ayanle, and Fiad who taught me the true color of Africa, to Jeannie Probala for saving her foot, to the Junior High kids I taught during the year '911' who, with charmingly special behavior, allowed me to be insane enough to write a book during their school year, to John and Jake for that road trip that brought me back from the dead, to Jami for straightening up my apartment and saying thank you after reading '*The Phobic*', to all the amazing students, athletes, musicians, friends, lovers, and soul-mates I've met over the last twelve years, to every God I've ever prayed to for allowing me to finally become a human being, to Zuzana for sharing her beauty, to the kids of Ellensburg and Yakima who restored my faith in humanity, to the kids at AC Davis for their brilliance and laughter, to every kind soul and kindred out there who talked with me and reminded me that I was not alone on this journey, and finally to all of you who've ever taken a risk and loved, cuz' that's the key right there. If you can love, the dishes are done.

Apologies:
To all the children I have ever been unkind to, please do better than I did. To the wives and friends I failed, please forgive me. I did not know me then.

A Final Note: As to the current whereabouts of *Langdon Towne,* who I now refer to as: *The Sage of Hearts,* last I heard, he was seen standing at the edge of a cliff like the *Road Warrior,* the sunset painting his face, the wind making his breaker crack like a muffled AK-47. And speaking of the *Road Warrior,* there was something about Mel Gibson standing there at the end, alone, bloodied and broken that helped me form a *truth* of my own: *Never, ever, confuse movies with real life. Movies have a summit and an ending. Real life is an endless-mountain-sea.*

FYI: For more information about KM Johnson, CZ, or other projects, please go to: crossingzion.com. Contact Keith Mark at crossingzion@hotmail.com